A Book of

PHARMACEUTICAL ENGINEERING

For

B. Pharmacy Semester - II Students

Dr. Anant R. Paradkar

Ex. Professor of Pharmaceutics,
Bharati Vidyapeeth University,
Poona College of Pharmacy,
Erandwane, Pune 38.

NIRALI PRAKASHAN
ADVANCEMENT OF KNOWLEDGE

N1706

PHARMACEUTICAL ENGINEERING **ISBN 978-93-5164-958-8**

First Edition : January 2016

© : Author

Published By :

NIRALI PRAKASHAN

Abhyudaya Pragati, 1312, Shivaji Nagar
Off J.M. Road, PUNE – 411005
Tel - (020) 25512336/37/39, Fax - (020) 25511379
Email : niralipune@pragationline.com

✦ DISTRIBUTION CENTRES

PUNE

Nirali Prakashan : 119, Budhwar Peth, Jogeshwari Mandir Lane, Pune 411002, Maharashtra
Tel : (020) 2445 2044, 66022708, Fax : (020) 2445 1538
Email : bookorder@pragationline.com, niralilocal@pragationline.com

Nirali Prakashan : S. No. 28/27, Dhyari, Near Pari Company, Pune 411041
Tel : (020) 24690204 Fax : (020) 24690316
Email : dhyari@pragationline.com, bookorder@pragationline.com

MUMBAI

Nirali Prakashan : 385, S.V.P. Road, Rasdhara Co-op. Hsg. Society Ltd.,
Girgaum, Mumbai 400004, Maharashtra
Tel : (022) 2385 6339 / 2386 9976, Fax : (022) 2386 9976
Email : niralimumbai@pragationline.com

✦ DISTRIBUTION BRANCHES

JALGAON

Nirali Prakashan : 34, V. V. Golani Market, Navi Peth, Jalgaon 425001,
Maharashtra, Tel : (0257) 222 0395, Mob : 94234 91860

KOLHAPUR

Nirali Prakashan : New Mahadvar Road, Kedar Plaza, 1st Floor Opp. IDBI Bank
Kolhapur 416 012, Maharashtra. Mob : 9850046155

NAGPUR

Pratibha Book Distributors : Above Maratha Mandir, Shop No. 3, First Floor,
Rani Jhanshi Square, Sitabuldi, Nagpur 440012, Maharashtra
Tel : (0712) 254 7129

DELHI

Nirali Prakashan : 4593/21, Basement, Aggarwal Lane 15, Ansari Road, Daryaganj
Near Times of India Building, New Delhi 110002
Mob : 08505972553

BENGALURU

Pragati Book House : House No. 1, Sanjeevappa Lane, Avenue Road Cross,
Opp. Rice Church, Bengaluru – 560002.
Tel : (080) 64513344, 64513355,Mob : 9880582331, 9845021552
Email:bharatsavla@yahoo.com

CHENNAI

Pragati Books : 9/1, Montieth Road, Behind Taas Mahal, Egmore,
Chennai 600008 Tamil Nadu, Tel : (044) 6518 3535,
Mob : 94440 01782 / 98450 21552 / 98805 82331,
Email : bharatsavla@yahoo.com

niralipune@pragationline.com | www.pragationline.com

Also find us on ⨍ www.facebook.com/niralibooks

Preface of First Edition

Fast development in the pharmaceutical processing field is possible due to collaborative efforts of pharmaceutical technologist and chemical engineers. The basic purpose of studying "pharmaceutical engineering" is to develop the approach of application of mainly chemical engineering to the field of bulk drug manufacturing and pharmaceutical processing. The text covers all important unit operations with specific applications to the pharmacy. More emphasis has been given on principles, mechanisms and theories of different operations. Mathematical treatment is included wherever necessary so as to clarify the concepts.

This book is a sincere attempt to simplify the concepts of pharmaceutical engineering with more practical orientation. The topics are selected so as to cover pharmaceutical engineering curriculum of most of the Universities. Your suggestions regarding coverage of topics, typographical mistakes are most welcome.

I am grateful to Dr. S.S. Kadam, Principal Poona College of Pharmacy for encouragement provided by him during completion of this book. I extend my special thanks to Mr. S.G. Bidkar and Miss Meera Honrao for their valuable suggestions. I wish to thank Mr. Sagar Padhye, for assistance in preparation of manuscript and Mr. A.R. Ketkar for cover design.

I appreciate, the co-operation and interest taken by Mr. Dineshbhai Furia and Mr. Jignesh Furia of Nirali Prakashan.

Last, but not the least, I thank all the faculty members of Poona College of Pharmacy, Pune and Nagpur College of Pharmacy, Nagpur for their co-operation, encouragement and timely suggestions.

A. R. Paradkar

■■■

Syllabus

■■■

Contents

■■■

CHAPTER

Introduction

1.1 Pharmaceutical Engineering

Industrial processing of drugs and pharmaceuticals has gained significant importance in recent years. This has increased the interest in the engineering aspects of pharmacy. The objective of studying pharmaceutical engineering is to understand the engineering principles involved in the processing of drugs and pharmaceuticals. The pharmaceutical technologist may not have to design the process equipment in detail but he should understand how the equipment operates. With an understanding of basic principles of process engineering, he will be able to develop the new pharmaceutical processes and modify existing ones. The pharmaceutical technologist must also be able to make himself clearly understood by design engineers and by the suppliers of the equipment he uses.

Only a thorough understanding of basic sciences applied to the pharmaceutical industry can prepare the pharmaceutical technologist with ability to tackle the complex problems of pharmaceutical industry today. In pharmaceutical engineering, we mainly study chemical engineering with special relevance to pharmacy.

1.2 Unit Operations

Processing in the drugs and pharmaceuticals or any other industry involves complex physical processes. The various physical processes of importance can be analysed by breaking into a small number of basic operations, which are called 'unit operations'. The unit operation considers only the physical changes that take place during processing. Application of concept of unit operations simplifies the study of pharmaceutical engineering. Instead of studying each process separately, the basic principles of unit operations can be applied in all processes where it is involved. Some important unit operations are fluid flow, heat transfer, evaporation, crystallization, distillation, mixing, size reduction, filtration etc. In many cases, the same general principles apply to many unit operations. For example, drying, evaporation and distillation all involve simultaneous heat transfer and mass transfer.

1.3 Stoichiometry

The word "*stoichiometry*" was invented by **Jeremias Richter** in 1792. It is a combination of Greek words that mean finding the proportions of magnitude between materials that cannot be further divided. Thus, stoichiometry is the study of material balances, energy balances and the chemical laws combining weights as applied to industrial processes.

1.3.1 Material Balance

"Material balance" is a mathematical treatment given to the data of a process or unit operation on the basis of law of conservation of mass. The law of conservation of mass states that *mass cannot be created nor destroyed*. Thus in a processing plant, the total mass entering the plant must be equal to the total mass of material leaving the plant, less any material accumulated. If there is no accumulation, then the simple rule holds that "what goes in must come out". Unit operations can be treated on the same basis.

For example, if an aqueous extract of crude drug is concentrated by evaporation, then by application of law of conservation of mass,

Mass of extract entering evaporator per hr. = Mass of water evaporated per hr. + Mass of concentrated extract obtained per hr.

This is overall material balance for the evaporation process.

Similarly, the law of conservation of mass applies to each component in the entering material. For example in the concentration of extract, we can apply law of conservation to one of the components of the stream, suppose water then we can say,

Mass of water entering evaporator per hr = Mass of water evaporated per hr. + Mass of water in concentrated extract per hr.

Some component in the system is such that it comes into the process in just one stream and leaves unchanged only in one stream. Such component or material is called a 'tie substance'. Presence of tie substance in the process simplifies the stoichiometric calculations.

1.3.2 Energy Balance

"Energy balance" is a mathematical treatment on the basis of law of conservation of energy. The law of conservation of energy states that *energy cannot be created nor destroyed*. The total energy in the materials entering the system, plus total energy added to system, must equal the total energy leaving the system. This is a more complex concept than the conservation of mass, because energy can take various forms such as kinetic energy, potential energy, heat energy, electrical energy etc. During operation, some of these forms of energy can be converted from one to another. For example, mechanical energy of fluid can be converted into heat energy through friction. Mechanical energy of the fan is converted into kinetic energy of fluid. But the total sum of all these forms of energy are conserved.

Broadly speaking, there are two primary classifications of energy, potential energy and kinetic energy. Potential energy refers to the energy of a body or a substance has, because of its position relative to another material or because of its components. This can be further broken down into internal and external potential energy; for example, a wooden piece has a certain external potential energy when placed at a fixed distance from the earth's surface because of its ability to fall and strike the earth with a momentum dependent on its mass and speed. The wooden piece has internal potential energy because of its ability to give off heat when burned. Kinetic energy refers to the energy due to motion.

The flow of heat from one body to another may be considered as energy in transition. When heat flows from hot to a cold body, the internal energy of the colder body is increased and that of the hot body has decreased. Work is also another form of transition energy. This may be defined as the energy transferred by the action of a mechanical force moving under restraint through a tangible distance. Work cannot be stored as such, but the capability to do work can be stored as potential energy or kinetic energy. For exmaple, work has to be done for compressing the fluid, this fluid has capability to do the same when released from compressed state (i.e. allowed to expand). This is known as *pressure energy of fluid*.

The most common and important form of energy is heat energy. In operations such as drying, evaporation, humidification, distillation conservation of heat energy has to be considered and enthalpy i.e. total heat balance has to be developed. Heat is absorbed or evolved by some reactions in pharmaceutical processing but usually the quantities are small as compared to other forms of energy entering the processes, such as sensible heat and latent heat. Latent heat is the heat required to change, at constant temperature, the physical state of materials from solid to liquid, liquid to gas or solid to gas. Sensible heat is that heat which when added or subtracted from the material changes its temperature and thus can be sensed. Sensible heat is obtained by multiplying the specific heat with mass of the material.

As energy balances are complex, it is advisable to determine first those factors which are significant in the overall energy balance. The simplified heat balance can be developed by neglecting insignificant factors.

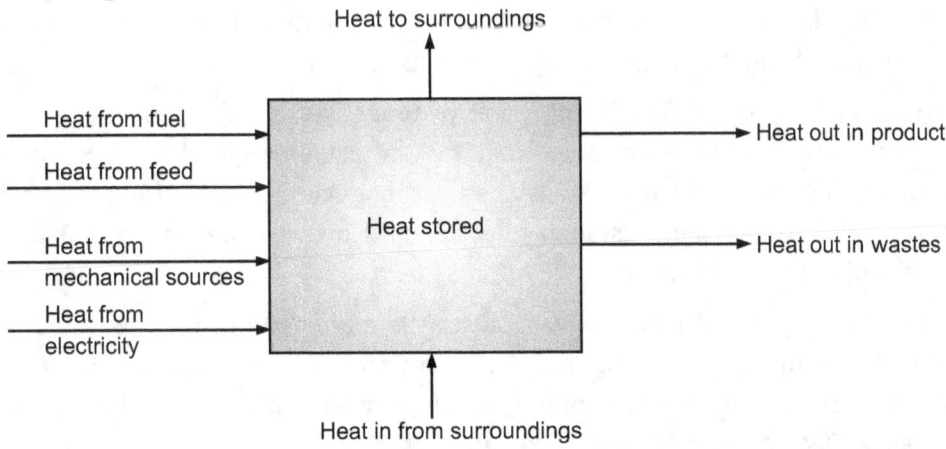

Fig. 1.1: Energy Balance with respect to heat energy only

Thus, in nutshell, from these laws of conservation of mass and energy, a balance sheet for materials and for energy can be drawn at all times for unit operation. These are called material balances and energy balances.

1.3.3 Laws of Combining Weights

The chemical laws of combining weights are to be considered when chemical changes occur during the process e.g. synthesis of drug. The relationship between the mass of reactants and products involved in the chemical reaction can be obtained by considering the equation for chemical reaction and the molecular weights of the materials involved. By going through the reaction and the conversions of materials at molar levels, the relationship between mass of reactant and product may be easily drawn. While applying the principles of stoichiometry to gases, the relationships among mass of material, temperature, pressure and volume are very important. Various gas laws are, considered such as perfect gas law i.e. PV = nRT, Dalton's law etc. As the operations associated with gases and chemical changes are not very common in pharmaceutical processing these are not considered here in details.

1.4 Dimensions and Units

The fundamental dimensions of any mechanical or physical quantity are conventionally expressed in terms of a set of three primary quantities, mass, length and time. Mass is denoted by [M], length is denoted by [L] and time is denoted by [T]. The square brackets in each case imply the dimension. For example, since area possesses both length and breadth, the dimensions are [L^2], and typical units are square inches and square cm. Similarly, dimensions of volume are [L^3], and typical units are cubic inches and cubic cm. Dimension is a descriptive word, a unit is a definite standard or measure of dimension. A unit is defined as a particular amount of the quantity to be measured. For example, milimeter, centimeter, inches, foot are different units indicating different but definite lengths, while the dimension common to all these units is length. Some basic units used are as follows:

The second (sec.) is the fundamental unit of time. The primary standard of length in United States is United States prototype meter 27, a platinum - irridium (90% platinum – 10% irridium) line standard having X - shaped section. One yard is 0.9144 metre and one foot is 1/3 yard. As per metric system, the standard meter is defined as 1,650, 763.73 wavelengths of the orange - red line of krypton 86.

Mass is the property of matter which causes the matter to resist acceleration. Mass is independent of earth's gravity. Weight is dependent on both earth's gravity and mass. One kilogram is, by international agreement the prototype mass of platinum - irridium located in Sevres, France. One pound is 0.45359237 kilogram.

All physical equations must be dimensionally consistent. This means that both sides of the equation must reduce to the same dimensions. Dimensions can be handled algebraically and therefore, they can be divided, multiplied or cancelled. As equations are dimensionally consistent, dimensions of unknown quantities can sometimes be calculated. Dimensions and units are given in Table 1.1. The conversion of units are given in Appendix – I.

Table 1.1: Dimensional Analysis of Various Quantities and Variables

Quantity	Symbol	M – L – T	Typical Units
Area	A	L^2	m^2
Volume	υ	L^3	m^3
Velocity	V	LT^{-1}	m/sec.
Acceleration	a or g	LT^{-2}	m/sec^2
Angular velocity, in radians	ω (omega)	T^{-1}	sec^{-1}
Mass	m	M	$kg\ sec^2/m$
Mass density	D or ρ (rho)	ML^{-3}	$kg\ sec^2/m^4$
Weight	W	MLT^{-2}	kg
Force	F	MLT^{-2}	kg
Weight density or specific weight	w	$ML^{-2}T^{-2}$	kg/m^3
Discharge	Q	L^3T^{-1}	m^3/sec
Weight rate of flow	G	MLT^{-3}	kg/sec
Intensity of pressure or stress	p or σ (sigma)	$ML^{-1}T^{-2}$	kg/m^2
Modulus of elasticity	E	$ML^{-1}T^{-2}$	kg/m^2
Absolute or dynamic viscosity	μ (mu)	$ML^{-1}T^{-1}$	$kg/sec/m^2$
Kinematic viscosity	ν (nu)	L^2T^{-1}	$m^2/sec.$
Power	P	ML^2T^{-2}	m - kg/sec.
Torque	T	ML^2T^{-2}	m - kg
Shear stress	τ (tau)	$ML^{-1}T^{-2}$	kg/m^2
Surface tension	σ (sigma)	MT^{-2}	kg/m

1.5 Dimensional Analysis

Dimensional analysis is a scientific technique based on the principle of dimensional homogenity. It is useful to determine the relationship among the physical variables in certain types of processes. Dimensional analysis is very useful in determining dimensionless ratios, and relationship of variables in terms of dimensionless ratios.

Some simple dimensionless numbers or ratios are specific gravity, trignometric functions such as sine, cosine, etc. Table 1.2 shows some dimensionless numbers commonly used in pharmaceutical engineering operations to compare or correlate some mechanisms.

Table 1.2: Dimensionless Numbers

Sr. No.	Name	Formula	Mechanism Ratio
1.	Reynolds Number	$\dfrac{Du\rho}{\eta}$	$\dfrac{\text{Inertial force}}{\text{Viscous force}}$
2.	Froude Number	$\dfrac{N^2D}{g}$	$\dfrac{\text{Inertial force}}{\text{Gravitational force}}$
3.	Nusselt Number	$\dfrac{h_cD}{k}$	$\dfrac{\text{Temperature gradient at a boundary}}{\text{Temperature gradient across the fluid to boundary}}$
4.	Prandtl Number	$\dfrac{C_p\eta}{k}$	$\dfrac{\text{Molecular diffusivity of momentum}}{\text{Molecular diffusivity to heat}}$

In the above table:

D = Diameter (length parameter)

u = Velocity of fluid

ρ = Density of fluid

η = Viscosity of fluid

C_p = Heat capacity

h_c = Convection heat transfer coefficient

N = Rotational speed in r.p.m.

g = Gravitational acceleration and

k = A constant.

Buckingham postulated that "the number of dimensionless groups involved in a mathematical representation of a physical process is equal to the number of physical variables involved, minus the number of fundamental dimensions used to express them." Thus, dimensionless analysis carried out to get the relationships.

But there are some exceptions to Buckingham's rule. Therefore, dimensional analysis is carried out by algbraic method. The results obtained by dimensional analysis can be used as guidelines to establish relationship among variables, but it should be confirmed only by experimental tests. Dimensional analysis is also very useful in checking equations, investigating validity of formulae and checking units. The study of dimensions and dimensional analysis will often help in making a description of physical phenomena easier and more convenient.

The algebraic method of dimensional analysis to generate equations is illustrated below:

For example, the discharge (Q) of a liquid, in volume per unit time, through a horizontal capillary tube is thought to depend upon the pressure drop per unit length ($\Delta P/L$), the diameter (D), and the dynamic viscosity (η); then in this case we can say:

$$Q = f\left(\frac{\Delta P}{L} \, D \, \eta\right)$$

or $$Q = k\left(\frac{\Delta P}{L}\right)^a (D)^b (\eta)^c$$

The dimensions are as follows:

$$Q = \frac{\text{Volume}}{\text{time}} = [L]^3 \, [T]^{-1}$$

$$\Delta P = \text{Pressure drop} = [M] \, [L]^{-1} \, [T]^{-2}$$

$$\eta = \text{Viscosity}$$

$$= [M] \, [L]^{-1} \, [T]^{-1}$$

For L and D dimension is $[L]$.

Dimensional equation becomes:

$$[L]^3 \, [T]^{-1} = \left([M] \, [L]^{-2} \, [T]^{-2}\right)^a [L]^b \left([M] \, [L]^{-1} \, [T]^{-1}\right)^c$$

a, b and c are exponents for three variables.

Equating the respective power for time, mass and length

Time [T] $-1 = -2\,a - c$

Mass [M] $0 = a + c$

Length [L] $3 = -2\,a + b - c$

By solving simultaneously the above equations, we get a = 1, b = 4 and c = – 1. By substituting values of exponent, the equation becomes

$$Q = k\frac{\Delta P}{L}\frac{D^4}{\eta}$$

From experimentation it was found

$$k = \frac{1}{128} \quad \text{then equation becomes,}$$

$$Q = \frac{\Delta P \, D^4}{128 \, \eta \, L}$$

Questions

1. Explain laws of combining weights.
2. Define the following:
   (a) Material balance
   (b) Energy balance
   (c) Unit operations
3. Write note on pharmaceutical engineering.
4. Describe dimensional analysis.

■■■

CHAPTER

Mass Transfer

2.1 Introduction

Mass transfer is the complex phenomenon occurring frequently in almost all unit operations. Extraction, humidification are the operations involving transfer of solute and water molecules respectively. Evaporation, drying and distillation are the operations which involve simultaneous heat transfer and mass transfer.

Mass transfer can occur through different mechanisms such as, molecular diffusion, convection or bulk flow, and turbulent mixing. To understand the various mechanisms, molecular diffusion is discussed in details for gases and liquids, followed by turbulent mixing in single phase, and various theories for interfacial mass transfer.

2.2 Molecular Diffusion

2.2.1 Molecular Diffusion in Gases

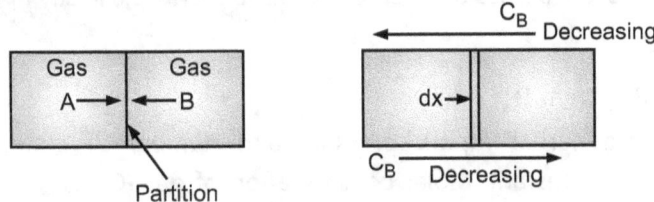

Fig. 2.1: Molecular diffusion of gases A and B

Molecular diffusion is the main mechanism of mass transfer in fluids under stagnant condition or moving in laminar flow. Consider that, two gases A and B are present in two chambers (Fig. 2.1). The partition forming two chambers is removed, then molecules of A will move towards B and B towards region of A. If we check concentration of A with distance towards chamber B or B towards A, the variation in concentration of the component with distance in the system is known as *concentration gradient*. The movement of molecules of A or B is taking place due to concentration gradient, is called *molecular diffusion*. Fick's law states *that the rate of diffusion (N_A) is proportional to concentration gradient $\frac{dC_A}{dX}$ existing across the direction of movement of A.*

(2.1)

The Fick's law may be written as:

$$N_A \, \alpha - \frac{dC_A}{dX} \quad \text{(negative sign, as concentration decreases with distance)}$$

$$\therefore \qquad\qquad N_A = -D_{AB} \frac{dC_A}{dX} \qquad\qquad\qquad \text{... (2.1)}$$

For molecules of gas B moving from chamber B to A, we can write

$$N_B = -D_{BA} \frac{dC_B}{dX} \qquad\qquad\qquad \text{... (2.2)}$$

where, D_{AB} and D_{BA} denote diffusivity of A in B and B in A respectively expressed as cm^2/sec. N_A and N_B are rates of diffusion of A and B respectively, expressed as gm. moles/cm^2/ sec.

The two important conditions which may occur in gaseous mass transfer are:

(a) Equimolecular Counter Diffusion:

Consider, over a small element dX in the system, if molecular diffusion is the only mechanism of mass transfer then,

$$N_A = -N_B \qquad\qquad\qquad \text{... (2.3)}$$

i.e. rates of diffusion of A and B are equal and opposite. Consider, dP_A and dP_B are changes in partial pressures of A and B over the element dX. As we have assumed that there is no bulk flow, i.e. total pressure across the element is same then we can say $\frac{dP_A}{dX}$ is equal to $\frac{dP_B}{dX}$.

For an ideal gas,

$$P_A V = n_A RT$$

where, P_A and n_A are partial vapour pressure and number of moles in volume V at temperature T. R is gas constant. Molar concentration of gas (C_A) is n_A divided by volume, therefore,

$$P_A = C_A RT$$

$$\therefore \qquad\qquad C_A = \frac{P_A}{RT} \qquad\qquad\qquad \text{... (2.4)}$$

Substituting in equation 2.1, we get,

$$N_A = -\frac{D_{AB}}{RT} \frac{dP_A}{dX} \qquad\qquad\qquad \text{... (2.5)}$$

Similarly, for gas B,

$$N_B = -\frac{D_{BA}}{RT} \frac{dP_B}{dX} \qquad\qquad\qquad \text{... (2.6)}$$

But for equimolecular counter diffusion $N_A = -N_B$, therefore,

$$N_A = \frac{D_{AB}}{RT} \frac{dP_A}{dX} = -\frac{D_{BA}}{RT} \frac{dP_B}{dX} \qquad\qquad \text{... (2.7)}$$

Therefore, $D_{BA} = D_{BA} = D$. The equation for equimolecular counter diffusion for A can be obtained as,

$$N_A = \frac{D}{RT} \int_{X_1}^{X_2} \frac{d\,P_A}{dX}$$

$$N_A = \frac{D}{RT} \frac{P_{A_2} - P_{A_1}}{X_2 - X_1} \qquad \qquad ...(2.8)$$

where, P_{A_1} and P_{A_2} are partial pressures of A at distances X_1 and X_2. Similar equation can be written for counter diffusion of B.

(b) Diffusion Through a Stationary, Non-diffusing Gas:

In case of movement of molecules from liquid surface or film on drying solids, occurs to a non-diffusing gas (atmospheric gas). Suppose, molecule A is moving from surface to atmosphere due to gradient in partial pressure $\frac{dP_A}{dx}$, but as B is not moving towards the surface, the bulk flow (convective transfer) must be taking place away from surface in such cases. Therefore, rate of mass transfer of A takes place by molecular diffusion and bulk flow.

2.2.2 Molecular Diffusion in Liquids

According to Fick's law, for diffusion in liquids we can write,

$$N_A = -D \frac{dC_A}{dX} \qquad \qquad ...(2.9)$$

Similarly, for equimolal counter diffusion it will be:

$$N_A = -D \frac{C_{A_2} - C_{A_1}}{X_2 - X_1} \qquad \qquad ...(2.10)$$

where, C_{A_1} and C_{A_2} are concentration of A at points X_1 and X_2 respectively. The diffusivities of liquids are much less than diffusivities of gases (nearly by a factor of 10^4). For example: diffusivity of gaseous ethanol in air is 0.119 cm²/sec, whereas diffusivity of liquid ethanol in water is 1×10^{-5} cm²/sec.

The molecular diffusion of liquids across a stagnant liquid is complex and not used frequently, therefore is not considered here.

2.3 Mass Transfer in Turbulent and Laminar Flow

Single phase mass transfer in turbulent and laminar flow is explained by boundary layer or film theory.

When fluid flows, there is formation of a boundary layer adjacent to the surface over which it flows. Now we will consider two regions, boundary layer and bulk. If bulk of fluid is flowing in laminar fashion, then rate of mass transfer in such fluid is given by molecular diffusion equation discussed above.

If fluid bulk shows turbulent flow, then rate of mass transfer is dependent on transfer rate across the boundary layer. The boundary layer consists of three sub-layers viz. laminar sub-layer adjacent to surface, buffer or transient sub-layer and turbulent region towards the bulk of fluid. In the turbulent region, the macroscopic packets of fluid or eddies move under inertial forces causing mass transfer. The rate of mass transfer is high and concentration gradient is low. In the buffer layer combination of eddy diffusion and molecular diffusion is responsible for mass transfer. Molecular diffusion is the only mechanism of mass transfer in the laminar sub-layer. In this region, concentration gradient is high and rate of mass transfer is low. Thickness of laminar sub-layer decreases with increase in the turbulence in the fluid. The rate of mass transfer in this case of boundary layer and bulk in turbulent flow, is dependent on the resistance given by the boundary layer. The rate of mass transfer can be estimated by considering a film which offers the resistance equivalent to the three sub-layers of boundary layer.

Consider a gas flows over a surface and equimolar counter diffusion occurs. A moves away from surface and B towards the surface (Fig. 2.2).

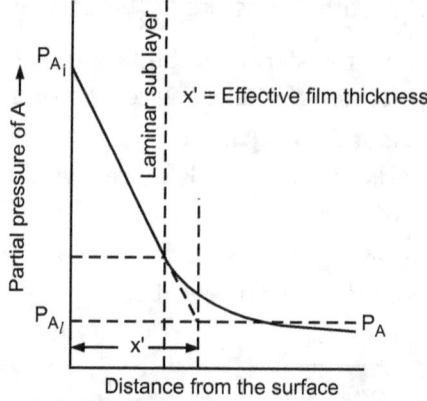

Fig. 2.2: Boundary layer – Mass Transfer

Let P_{A_i} be the partial pressure of A at the surface which decreases sharply to P_{A_l} at the end of laminar sub-layer of thickness X. P_{A_b} is the partial pressure of A at the edge of boundary layer. It can be seen that partial pressure decrease in the laminar sub-layer is very fast and is very slow after that. It is because molecular diffusion is the only mechanism in the laminar sub-layer. If we consider molecular diffusion as the only mechanism further also then partial pressure P_{A_b} would have reached at distance X' only, instead of boundary layer edge. Therefore, we can say a film of thickness X' gives resistance equivalent to the boundary layer. The concentration gradient can now be written as $\dfrac{P_{A_i} - P_{A_b}}{X'}$. Then according to Fick's law for diffusion,

$$N_A = \frac{D}{RT} \frac{P_{A_i} - P_{A_b}}{X'}$$

... (2.11)

X' is not known, therefore a constant k_g known as mass transfer coefficient is introduced which is diffusivity per unit length. Now equation becomes,

$$N_A = \frac{k_g}{RT} \left(P_{A_i} - P_{A_b}\right) \qquad \text{... (2.12)}$$

Mass transfer coefficient k_g is expressed by unit cm/sec. We know $C_A = \frac{P_A}{RT}$,

$$\therefore \qquad N_A = k_g \left(C_{A_i} - C_{A_b}\right) \qquad \text{... (2.13)}$$

where, C_{A_i} and C_{A_b} are concentrations of A on either side of the film. Similar equation can be written for liquid also with mass transfer coefficient k_l.

The mass transfer coefficient is dependent on diffusivity of the molecule and thickness of laminar sub-layer.

Dimensional analysis of mass transfer analogus to heat transfer, correlates it to dependence on Reynolds number (Re) and Schmidt number (Sc).

$$\frac{kd}{D} = \text{Constant} \times (Re)^q \, (S_E)^r \qquad \text{... (2.14)}$$

where, k and D are mass transfer coefficient and diffusivity of molecule respectively, d is a dimension related to geometry of the system. Schmidt number is analogus to Prandtl number in heat transfer, it is ratio of molecular diffusivity of momentum to molecular diffusivity given by $\frac{\eta}{\rho D}$.

2.4 Interphase Mass Transfer

We have discussed single phase mass transfer, but frequently we have to deal with two phase mass transfer e.g. distillation, liquid-liquid extraction. The phenomenon of mass transfer across interface of two phases was studied by many workers and various models or theories have been proposed to explain it. The important theories are discussed below:

2.4.1 Two Film Theory

This theory has been developed by Nernst, Lewis and Whitman. The theory postulates that two non-turbulent fictitious films are present on either side of the interface between the phases. The mass transfer across these films occurs purely by molecular diffusion. Interface does not offer any resistance to mass transfer, therefore, total resistance for mass transfer is summation of resistances of two films.

Consider that solute A is transferred from gas phase to the liquid. This will involve diffusional transfer of A across the two films adjacent to the interface (Fig. 2.3).

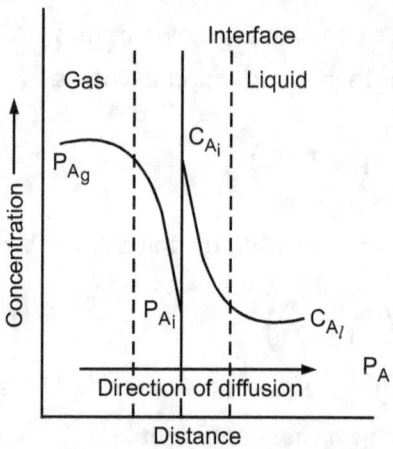

Fig. 2.3: Interfacial mass transfer

Let, P_{A_g} = Partial pressure of A in bulk of gas

P_{A_i} = Partial pressure of A in gas at the interface

C_{A_i} = Concentration of A in liquid at interface

C_{a_l} = Concentration of A in the bulk of liquid.

k_g and k_l are mass transfer coefficients of individual films of gas and liquid respectively.

But it is difficult to know P_{A_i} and C_{A_i}. Hence, concept of overall mass transfer coefficient is used. Consider,

P_{A_e} = The gas phase partial pressure of A which is in equilibrium with concentration of A in bulk of liquid (C_{A_l}) and,

C_{A_e} = Concentration of A in the liquid phase which is in equilibrium with partial pressure of A bulk of gas $\left(P_{b_{A_g}}\right)$

K_G and K_L are overall mass transfer coefficients. Then applying Fick's law,

$$N_A = K_G \left(P_{A_g} - P_{A_e}\right) \qquad \text{... (2.15)}$$

or $$N_A = K_L \left(C_{A_e} - C_{A_l}\right) \qquad \text{... (2.16)}$$

The equilibrium between two phases is expressed by the following equation,

$$P_A = H C_A + b \qquad \text{... (2.17)}$$

where, H and b are constants.

By considering individual film transfer equations (2.12) and (2.13) and overall mass transfer equations (2.15) and (2.16) and equilibrium equation (2.17), following relationship can be developed between overall and individual phase mass transfer coefficients.

$$\frac{1}{K_G} = \frac{1}{k_g} + \frac{H}{k_l} \qquad\qquad \text{... (2.18)}$$

$$\frac{1}{K_L} = \frac{1}{HK_G} = \frac{1}{Hk_g} + \frac{1}{k_l} \qquad\qquad \text{... (2.19)}$$

If H is very large i.e. A is less soluble in the liquid, then $K_G \approx \dfrac{k_l}{H}$ and process becomes liquid phase controlled.

If H is very low i.e. A is highly soluble in the liquid, then $K_G \approx k_g$ and process is gas phase controlled.

According to this theory, mass transfer is directly proportional to molecular diffusivity of solute in the phase into which it is going and inversely proportional to thickness of films.

2.4.2 Penetration Theory

Higbie proposed penetration theory to explain mass transfer considering unsteady-state at interface. According to this theory, fluid eddies travel from bulk to interface by convection, and remain there for a equal but limited period of time. When the eddy is at interface, the solute moves into it by molecular diffusion and gets penetrated into the bulk when eddy moves to the bulk. The theory suggests that rate of mass transfer is proportional to square root of molecular diffusivity and inversely proportional to the exposure time of eddy at interface.

2.4.3 Surface Renewal Theory

Danckwert contradicted the assumption by Higbie, that each eddy gets equal exposure period at the interface and proposed surface renewal theory. According to this theory, the turbulence in the bulk phase is extended to the interface i.e. there is continuous renewal of interface by fresh eddies, which have composition that of the bulk. The turbulent eddies remain at the interface for time varying from zero to infinity, and then taken back into the bulk phase by convection currents. Thus at any instant, the interface consists of eddies having different ages. According to this Danckwert's theory, also rate of mass transfer is proportional to square root of molecular diffusivity.

Questions

1. Define mass transfer and explain molecular diffusion in gases.
2. Describe in detail mass transfer in turbulent and laminar flow.
3. Explain interphase mass transfer.

4. Write short notes on the following:

    (a) Molecular diffusion in liquids.

    (b) Two film theory.

    (c) Penetration theory.

    (d) Equimolecular counter diffusion.

■■■

CHAPTER

Drying

3.1 Introduction

Drying is a widely used unit operation in pharmaceutical industry. Proper knowledge of drying mechanisms and equipments will help to resolve the drying problems in the industry. In pharmaceutical industry, drying of granulation for tabletting, heat sensitive materials and continuous drying of powders need special attention.

The term drying refers to the removal of liquid from a solid by thermal means. It also includes removal of volatile liquids or water from another liquid or gas or a suspension. Process of evaporation involves removal of much larger quantities of liquid per hour and per unit plant than in the drying process. The product obtained from an evaporator is either concentrated solution or suspension or a wet slurry, whereas that from a dryer is substantially dry.

Significance of Drying:

Drying is an important operation in pharmaceutical industry:

(i)   It enables the product to be presented in the form, suitable for subsequent processing or marketing. For example, tablet granules are dried to the extent suitable for further compression; liquid extracts are dried to a dry form.

(ii)   Transportation costs are reduced as drying reduces weight as well as volume of the material.

(iii)   Physical and chemical stability of the product is affected in presence of moisture. Removal of moisture significantly reduces rate of chemical reactions, chances of microbial attack or enzymatic actions and thus imparts better stability to the product.

(iv)   Adoption of a suitable method of drying enables to obtain a product with desired physical properties, e.g. spray dried lactose is free flowing and compressible.

3.2 Mechanism of Drying

Drying involves heat transfer and mass transfer simultaneously. Heat transfer takes place from the heating medium to the solid; except in dielectric or high frequency electric drying, where heat is generated within the solid and flows to exterior surface. Mass transfer involves movement of the moisture to the surface of the solid and its subsequent evaporation from the surface. Movement of moisture depends on physical characteristics of the solid and moisture content. The transfer of vapours from the surface to the surrounding is affected by external conditions like temperature, humidity, air flow rate, pressure and evaporating surface exposed.

In a solid, moisture is present in two forms; bound and unbound moisture. The bound moisture in a solid exerts equilibrium vapour pressure lower than that of the pure water at the same temperature. Water retained in small capillaries in the solid, adsorbed at the solid surfaces, water of crystallisation, solution in cell or fibre walls is bound moisture. The unbound moisture exerts an equilibrium vapour pressure equal to that of pure water. Various theories have been proposed to explain the internal movement of the moisture. They are as follows:

(a)   Diffusion theory

(b)   Capillarity theory

(c)   Pressure gradient theory

(d)   Gravity flow theory

(e)   Vaporization and condensation mechanism.

Of the above mentioned theories, first two theories predominate in the drying of pharmaceutical substances.

Diffusion theory suggests two ways of moisture movement:

(i)   Water diffuses through the solid to the surface and then diffuses into the air surrounding the solid.

(ii)   Evaporation of water occurs at an intermediate zone much below the solid surface and then vapours diffuse through the solid into the air.

Diffusion theory assumes that the effect of capillarity, gravitational and frictional forces is too small and the rate of flow of water to the surface is proportional to the moisture gradient. But the diffusivity decreases with decreasing moisture content and temperature and increases with pressure. Due to this limitation, the theory can not predict drying rate and moisture gradient over a range. Hence, capillarity theory was put forward.

Capillarity theory applies to the air drying of porous granular solids. A porous material contains a complicated network of interconnected pores and channels which are not circular or straight. The cross-section of these capillaries at the drying surface forms various sizes of pores. As evaporation proceeds at the surface, a miniscus is formed across each pore. Due to interfacial tension between water and solid, the miniscus formed sets the capillary force. These capillarity forces act as driving forces for the movement of water through the pores towards the surface. The curvature of the miniscus which depends on pore diameter, determines the strength of capillarity forces. Greater capillarity forces are developed in small pores as compared to larger ones. Thus small pores can pull more water than large pores and larger pores are emptied first. In this emptied pore, air enters readily and the moisture concentration near the surface can remain relatively high. But in a tightly packed wet material air replacement is not possible and normal capillary flow cannot carry the liquid to the surface. Hence, capillarity theory holds good only for free water in the bed and hygroscopic materials tend to agree with the diffusion theory. Capillary movement of the liquid takes place in the granules as well as in the spaces between the granules. As the pore diameter in the granules is considerably smaller than the surrounding capillaries, the liquid surrounding the granules is removed before the pore liquid.

3.3 Theory of Drying

Depending on the external conditions and internal mechanisms of fluid flow solids show different drying patterns. A typical drying cycle of a solid can be divided into three distinct zones.

(a)   Initial Adjustment Period

(b)   Constant Rate Period

(c)   Falling Rate Period.

These drying zones are shown in Fig. 3.1 (a) and (b).

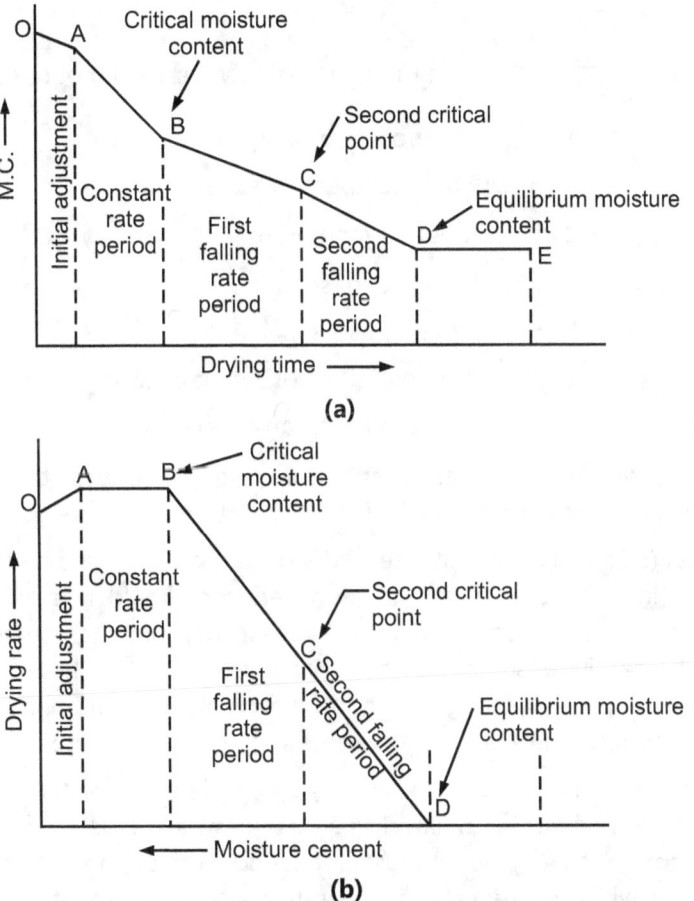

Fig. 3.1: Drying curves of solids

(a)   Initial Adjustment Period: In the Fig. 3.1 (a) and (b) it is OA which is also called as 'Heating up period'. An wetted substance when kept for drying it absorbs heat from the surrounding and vaporization of moisture takes place which cools the surface. Heat flows to the cooled surface at higher rates, leads to rise in temperature and evaporation again. This continues and then an equilibrium is reached when the heat transfer to the material just balances the heat required for the vaporization of water. If all the heat transfer is taking place by convection, the material should attain wet bulb temperature. But if there is additional heat flow by conduction and radiation, then material attains higher temperature. If the initial temperature of the material is higher than WBT, then it reduces to WBT.

(b)   Constant Rate Period: During this period there is a continuous liquid film over the surface of the solid. Evaporation from this film at WBT proceeds at a constant rate and the film is continuously replaced by moisture from inside. As long as the delivery of water from the interior to the surface is sufficient to keep the surface completely wet, the drying rate remains constant as shown by region AB. Drying rate in the constant rate period is given by:

$$\frac{dW}{d\theta} = \frac{A\, h_c\, (t_d - t_w)}{\rho\, L\, \lambda} \qquad\qquad \text{... (3.1)}$$

where, $\dfrac{dw}{d\theta}$ = Rate of drying in kg of water per kg of dry solid

A = Area exposed to drying

t_d = Dry bulb temperature

t_w = Wet bulb temperature

ρ = Bulk density of solid

L = Thickness of solid bed

λ = Latent heat of vaporization of water

h_c = Convection heat transfer coefficient.

Thus, particle size, bed height, air temperature and humidity of the air are important factors which affect the constant rate period.

From equation (3.1), it is clear that rate of drying can be increased by increase in surface area exposed e.g. in spray drying, due to atomization of liquid fine droplets are formed which expose high surface area for drying. Increase dry bulb temperature and WBT is maintained low, by continuously replacing the hot air. Convection heat transfer coefficient can be maintained high by agitating the solid and maintaining the film thickness on solid surface as low as possible. The solid bed thickness should be maintained low.

As drying proceeds, the coarse capillaries are completely depleted of water and solid fails to maintain a complete uniform film. The area over which moisture film is not present is known as 'dry spot'. Such dry spots start appearing and drying rate starts falling. The moisture content at which decrease in drying rate starts is called critical moisture content and the time as first critical point.

(c) Falling Rate Period: Due to dry spots on the surface, the area of constant mass transfer decreases and the heat transferred to the dry spots will be utilized to raise the temperature of solid to dry bulb temperature. Thus, as number of dry spots increase, heat transfer and mass transfer rates fall which is called as first falling rate period. The solid surface becomes completely free of liquid film due to emptying of fine capillaries and now movement of moisture to the surface takes place by diffusion. The time at which fine capillaries are also empty and no film is present on surface is called as 'second critical point'. After second critical point the drying rate falls further as the rate of moisture movement by diffusion is very low. At the end, the drying rate becomes zero, and moisture content of solids at this point is called Equilibrium Moisture Content (EMC). EMC may be defined as *mass of water per unit mass of dry solid when the drying limit has been attained by use of air at any given temperature and humidity.* EMC will be determined by nature of the material, temperature and humidity of air.

A crystalline or granular material holds water near to the surface and hence show easy transport to the surface, by maintaining a continuous film over the surface. Therefore, constant rate period for such substances is long. An amorphous substance holds water in the interior and cannot maintain film for long times exhibit shorter constant rate and longer falling rate periods. At equilibrium moisture content, the exerted vapour pressure of water in the solid is equal to the partial vapour pressure of water in the air. The moisture in the bound conditions, entrapped in the interiors cannot exert complete vapour pressure. Therefore, the substances with bound moisture or deeply entrapped water show higher values of EMC. Similarly, increase in humidity of air increases the EMC, whereas temperature has inverse relationship with the EMC. EMC plays an important role in residual moisture in granules for compression, gelatin capsule storage and preparation etc.

3.4 Drying Equipments

3.4.1 Tray Dryer

Tray dryer is a batch dryer where forced convection heating takes place. It consists of a small cabinet or a large compartment in which the trays containing wet materials are inserted. The trays are either loaded onto the trucks in tiers or may be inserted directly into the dryer cabinet. The heating air is circulated by means of fans which also removes the humid air from the cabinet. The trays containing the load remain in the dryer until drying is complete, after which they are withdrawn, emptied and recharged for drying the next batch.

In tray dryers, the air travels very short distance around two to three stacks of trays. The operation involves recirculation of hot drying air with partial rejection of humid air and its replacement by fresh air. Thus, recirculation type tray dryer involves, use of large volumes of recirculated air with frequent heating, together with controlled introduction of fresh air into the cabinet and controlled exhausting of humid air. Stacks of trays when placed properly may act as horizontal partitions and permit recirculation. Thus, recirculation and reheating facilitate drying at low temperatures than that possible with a single passage of heated air through a tray dryer.

The trays in a dryer are spaced in such a way that the pressure losses are low. The trays which are 1.25 to 1.5 inches deep are spaced around three inches apart. Air velocities upto 1000 ft/min. are commonly used. High air circulation ratio alongwith large quantities of fresh air are necessary in the initial stages of drying cycle so as to remove large quantities of moisture present in the material. Once solid reaches the falling rate period, the air recirculation ratio upto 90 – 95% without supply of fresh air is sufficient.

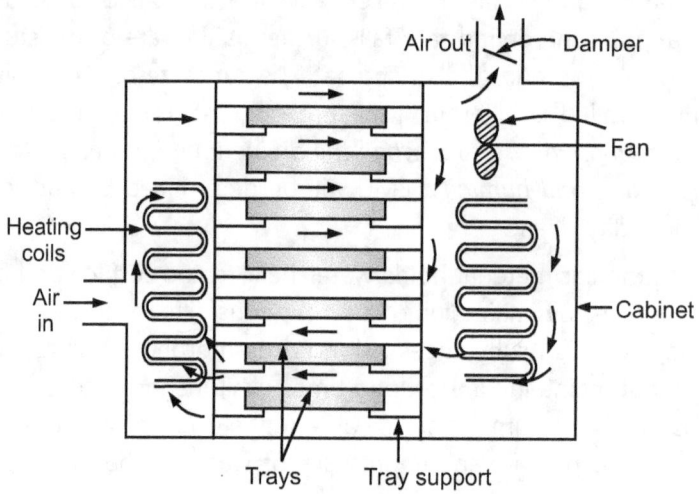

Fig. 3.2: Tray dryer

Thermal efficiency of the dryer is very low for materials which are to be dried to a very low moisture content because in such cases, the falling rate period will be lengthy requiring longer drying time.

3.4.2 Tunnel Tray Dryer

In a tunnel tray dryer, the trucks loaded with wet material at one end of the tunnel and dried product is discharged at the other end of the tunnel. The tunnel is comprised of number of units each of which is thermostatically controlled. Throughout the length of the tunnel fresh air inlets and humid exhausts are suitably spaced.

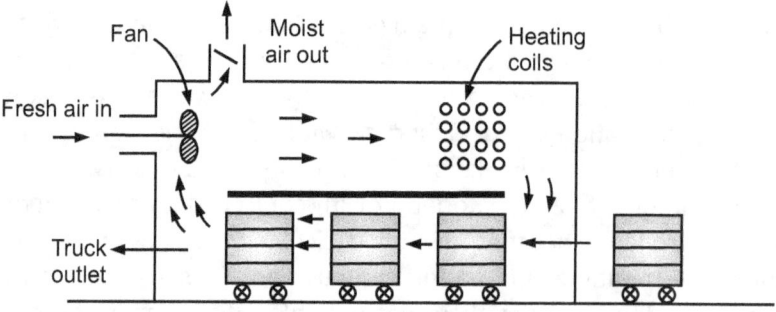

Fig. 3.3: Tunnel dryer

The movement of the air from inlet to outlet may be parallel or countercurrent in relation to the movement of the trucks. Thermal efficiency of the dryer is higher with countercurrent flow of air and the material.

3.4.3 Turbo-Tray Dryer

It is a continuous tray dryer (Fig. 3.4) in which wet material is continuously introduced onto a series of trays and is discharged continuously in a dried form. It consists of a cylindrical or hexagonal vertical housing with internal or external compartment having heating coil. In the housing several tiers of segmented trays rotate slowly at around 0.1 r.p.m. In the central area centrifugal fans are fixed on a vertical shaft. This facilitates high air flow rates over and above the trays and through the heating coil.

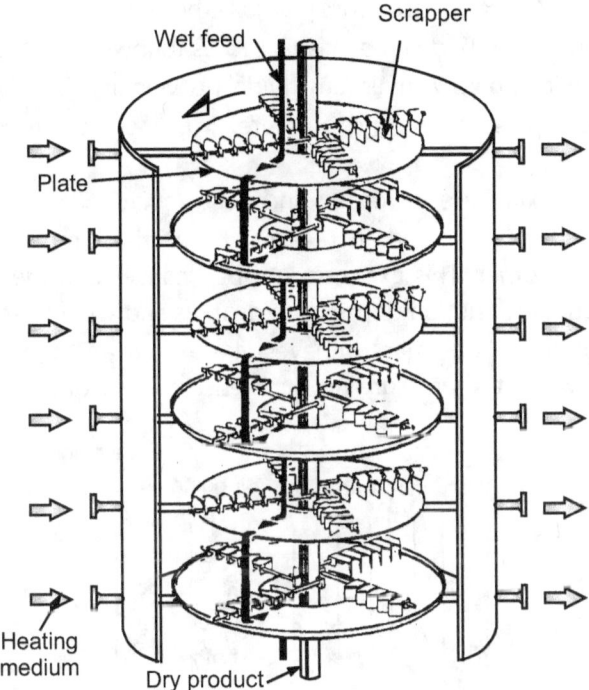

Fig. 3.4: Turbo-tray dryer

3.4.4 Fluidized Bed Dryer

Fluidized bed dryer enjoy widespread popularity for drying of pharmaceuticals and many other industrial products. It has maintained popularity due to high thermal efficiency, gas - solid contact, low capital and maintenance cost with high reliability.

In fluidized drying, the wet material on a suitable perforated plate is subjected to a stream of hot air at a certain temperature. The material is removed from the dryer when it is sufficiently dry.

Principle: Consider the solid material like tablet granulation is resting on distributor plate in a tube. Now, if a vertically rising stream of gas is introduced at the bottom, the difference in pressure across the granular bed (ΔP) is linearly proportional to the flow rate of air. As per Kozeny – Carman equation, this pressure drop across the porous bed will be:

$$\Delta P = \frac{150\ V_g \eta\ (1-\epsilon)^2\ L}{(D_p)^2\ \epsilon^3}$$

where,

V_g = Velocity of gas

η = Viscosity of gas

ϵ = Porosity

L = Bed height

D_p = Diameter of particle

ΔP = Pressure drop across the bed.

Now, the behaviour of the bed can be visualised as follows:

(i) For gas velocities below minimum fluidizing velocity (V_{mf}) i.e. $V_g < V_{mf}$; the bed behaves like a packed bed and pressure drop increases from A to B as shown in Fig. 3.5.

(ii) When gas velocities are increased and past V_{mf} i.e. $V_g > V_{mf}$ as shown by point B, the granular bed expands (L increases), the particles move apart and are able to slide past each other. This expansion of bed causes considerable increase in voids with consequent reduction of pressure drop as shown between points B and C.

Now the entire particle - gas mass behaves like a fluid and the system is called to be fluidized. Here onwards, the pressure drop increases only slightly with increase in air flow rates.

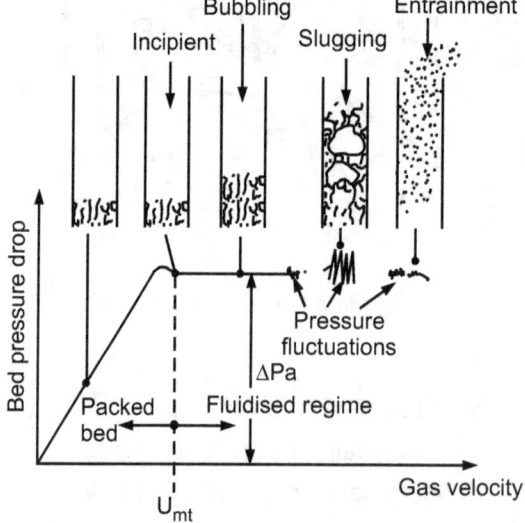

Fig. 3.5: Pressure drop - air flow rate relationship

(iii) If the velocity is further increased, the bed becomes more and more expanded and the solid content becomes more and more dilute.

Construction: Horizontal F.B.D. is used for continuous process and vertical F.B.D. is for batch process. The fluidized bed dryer whether used for continuous or batch process incorporate similar features regardless of their design. The dryer consists of:

(A) **Air Handler:** Which is a source of fluidizing air. It is also attached by a means of heating and dehumidifying air, if necessary.

(B) **Plenum:** It consists of a screen or plate to distribute the incoming air as it enters the dryer.

(C) **Product Container:** This container holds the product which is subjected to drying.

(D) **Expansion Chamber:** This chamber is situated above the product container and holds the suspended material.

(E) **Filter:** The upper part of the expansion chamber has filters. It prevents fines from escaping into the atmosphere or collecting on the blades of fan which pulls the air through the drier.

(F) **Explosion Relief Duct:** It helps to avoid the explosion which may occur due to rapid pressure build up due to organic solvents.

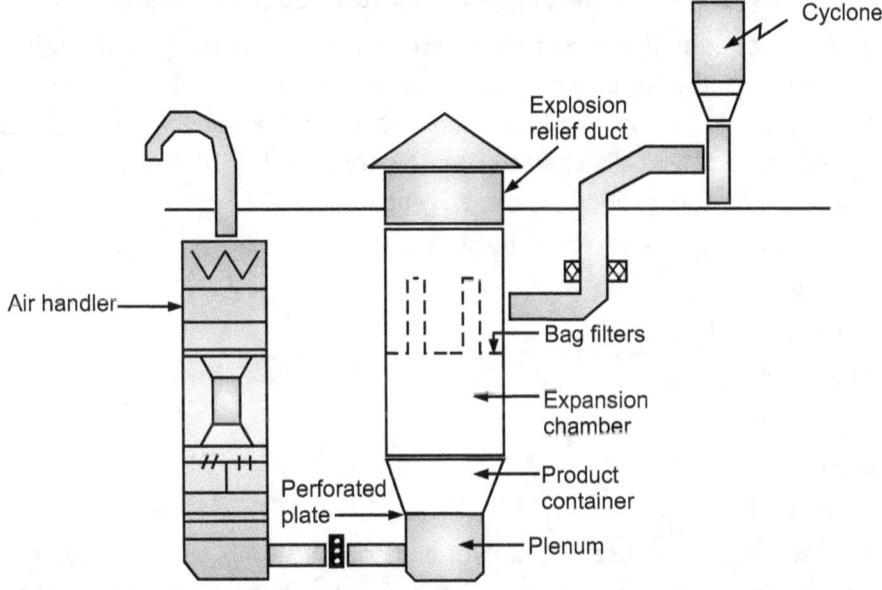

Fig. 3.6: Fluidized bed dryer

Applications:

1. Coating of Tablets:

The fluidized bed dryer can be used in coating process as well. The technique is called as Wurster technique. The design is modified slightly. It has three basic designs.

1. Top spray: It is similar to the fluid-bed granulation process.
2. Bottom spray.
3. Tangential spray.

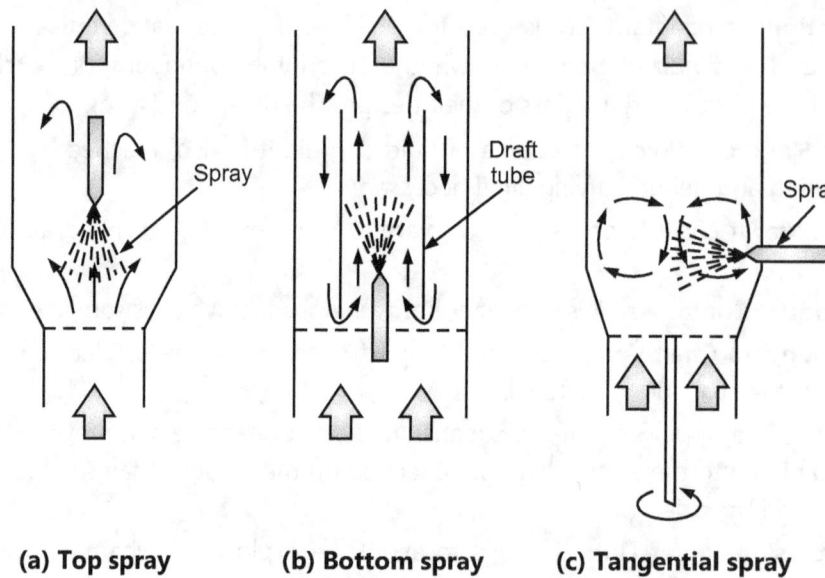

(a) Top spray   **(b) Bottom spray**   **(c) Tangential spray**

Fig. 3.7: Three basic types of fluid-bed coating processes

During normal operation, production is accelerated by fluidizing air through the inner partition that defines the spray zone. Deceleration occurs in the region of expansion chamber and the product is dropped back in the coating chamber. The product coated by the Wurster technique is typically characterized by uniform distribution of coating and high gloss. Also the process also exhibits excellent drying qualities.

The parameters which need to be controlled are:

1. Batch size
2. Fluidizing air volume
3. Inlet air temperature
4. Inlet air humidity
5. Spray rate.

2. Wet Granulation:

Fluidized Bed Dryers are used as wet granulators. Powders are agglomerated in the drying chamber and liquid binder is sprayed over it, while hot air flow simultaneously dries the agglomerates by vaporizing the liquid phase. This is advantageous due to reduction in handling and reduction in contamination by dust.

Advantages of Fluidized Bed Drying:

1. Efficient heat and mass transfer facilitate high drying rates. Heating time of thermolabile materials is minimized.
2. Individual particles of the bed get dried in the fluidized state. So, most of the drying will be at constant rate and the falling rate period is very short.

3. Temperature can be controlled uniformly.

4. A free-flowing product is obtained.

5. Since the bed is not static, free movement of individual particles eliminates the risk of soluble materials migrating.

6. Containers can be mobile, so handling is simple and labour cost is reduced.

7. Short drying time yields a high output from a small floor space.

Disadvantages:

1. Turbulence of fluidized state may produce fines due to attrition.

2. Fine particles lead to segregation, so they must be collected by bag filters.

3. Static charges may be produced due to vigorous movement of particles in hot dry air.

3.4.5 Spray Dryer

Spray drying is a one step continuous drying process which involves transformation of feed from a fluid state into a dried particulate form by spraying the feed into a hot drying medium. The feed may be either a solution, suspension or paste. The feed is atomized into a spray and contact between the spray and drying medium takes place resulting in moisture evaporation. This is continued until a dried product is obtained.

In pharmaceutical industry, spray drying is successfully used for drying of antibiotics, enzymes, vitamins, yeasts, vaccines, plasma, hormones, plasma substitute etc.

In spray drying, moisture flow through a droplet is by diffusional mechanism, supplemented by capillary flow.

Construction and Working:

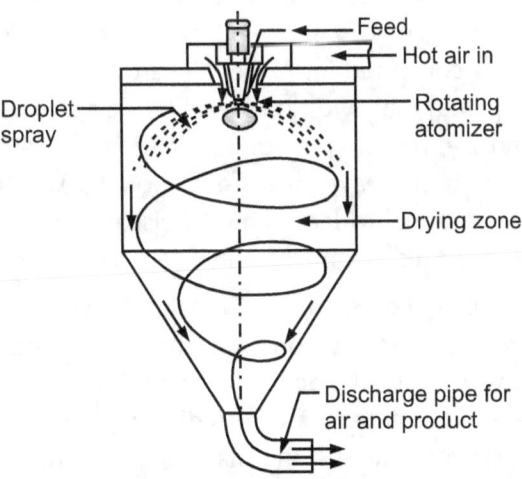

Fig. 3.8: Spray dryer

The spray drying process involves four basis stages:

(i)   Atomization of feed into a spray.

(ii) Contact of spray and air.

(iii) Evaporation from droplet.

(iv) Separation of dried product from air.

(A) Atomization of Feed into a Spray:

Atomization is carried out by an atomizer which produces from liquid bulk a spray of individual small droplets having uniform size. Small individual droplets offer high surface to mass ratio ensuring quick evaporation, short drying times and low surface temperature. Uniform droplet size ensures uniform dried product characteristics.

Atomizers are classified as follows on the basis of different energy forms applied to break up the bulk of liquid.

(a) Centrifugal Atomizers: For example: Rotary Atomizer. In rotary atomization technique, the feed liquid is centrifugally accelerated to high velocity before it is discharged into the drying chamber. The liquid is distributed centrally on the wheel disc or cup. The liquid extends over the rotating surface as a thin film. Maximum centrifugal energy is imparted to the liquid when the liquid acquires the peripheral speed of the wheel or disc before discharge. Then the liquid film disintegrates to give droplets. Centrifugal wheel atomizer is commonly used for pharmaceuticals. Slurries or pastes having either heat sensitive, thermoplastic, abrasive, corrosive or high viscous properties can be successfully atomized. Rotary atomizers are used to produce fine to medium coarse product having size 30 – 150 μm.

(b) Pressure Atomizer: For example: Centrifugal pressure nozzle. The pressure nozzle is based on the principle of conversion of pressure energy within the bulk of the liquid into kinetic energy of a thin moving liquid sheet. The feed concentrate is fed to the nozzle under pressure. Pressure energy is converted into kinetic energy, and feed issues from the nozzle orifice as a high speed film, that readily disintegrates into a spray as the film is unstable. The feed rotates within the nozzle, resulting in cone shaped spray patterns emerging from the nozzle orifice. The pressure nozzles have pressures of about 10,000 lb/in^2. Mean droplet size of the spray is directly proportional to feed rate and viscosity, and inversely proportional to pressure. Pressure nozzles are used to obtain coarse particle powders of 120 –250 μm.

(c) Pneumatic Atomizer: For example: Two fluid Nozzle atomizer. This atomizer is based on utilisation of kinetic energy of one fluid to break another fluid into droplets. It involves impact of liquid with a high velocity gas or air. The high velocity gas creates high frictional forces over the liquid surfaces leading to disintegration of liquid into droplets. The stream of gas is rotated within the nozzle and may come in contact with liquid either within the nozzle or after emerging of liquid from the orifice.

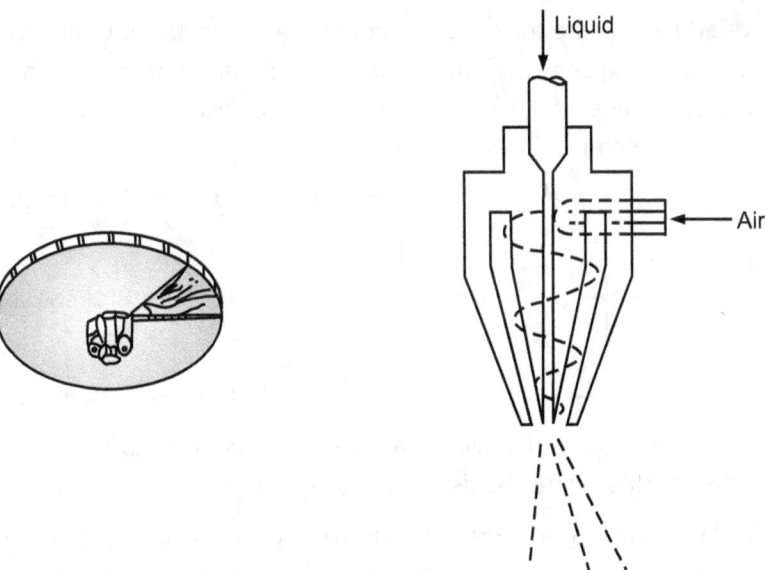

Fig. 3.9: Atomizers

It can handle high viscosity feed producing medium coarse spray with less uniformity. But for low viscosity feeds, product having low size between 15 – 20 μm and high degrees of homogeneity are obtained.

(B) Spray – Air Contact:

The spray and air can flow through the dryer in *counter-current flow* i.e. the product and air pass in the same direction. Counter-current contact is preferred for heat sensitive products, because the spray evaporation is rapid, as fresh droplets contacts with hottest air and drying air cools accordingly. Thus, drying time is short. The product is not subjected to heat degradation. Product temperature is maintained low when bulk of the evaporation takes place and droplet temperature is at wet bulb temperature. Temperature of dried product does not rise as it is in contact with comparatively cool air. Counter-current contact minimizes the bulk density of product.

In *counter-current* contact the spray and air enter at the opposite ends of the dryer. It has advantage of better heat utilisation. But the dried powder comes in contact with hottest air, and temperature of dried product is high. Thus, it is more suitable thermostable substances. This is widely used when high product temperature is required to obtain case hardening effect. Counter-current contact gives product with high bulk density.

(C) Droplet Drying:

Heat is transferred by convection from air to droplet. Vapours formed by evaporation of moisture get transported to surrounding air by convection. The moisture from the interior at the droplet migrates to the surface maintaining the surface wetness. But generally the air temperature is so high that moisture migration is incapable of maintaining the surface wetness and a dried layer is formed at the surface of the droplet.

Now, this dried layer is the main resistance for mass transfer of moisture to the surface. The rate of heat transfer exceeds the rate of mass transfer and evaporation of moisture takes place below this solid layer. Vapours set up pressure inside the droplet. The effect of pressure depends on the nature of the surface layer.

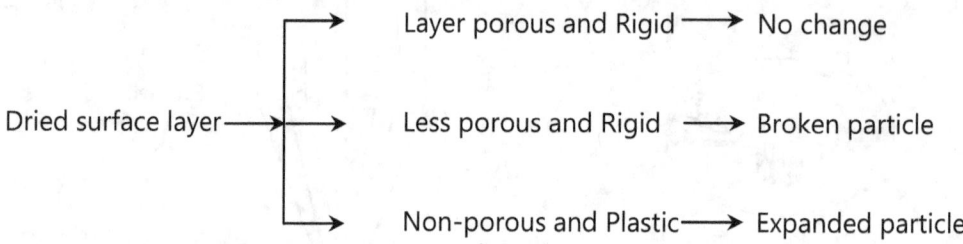

Formation of expanded and hollow particles is a main feature of spray drying. The hollow particles are formed by mechanisms mentioned below:

(a) The surface layer is semi-impervious to vapour flow. The droplet puffs out as vapours are formed in the droplet and it expands with increase in droplet temperature.

(b) In crystalline products, rate of moisture evaporation is more than the diffusion of solids back into the droplet interior. This leads to formation of air voids.

(c) Due to capillary action, liquid flows with the accompanying solids to the droplet surface, creating void at the centre of the droplet.

(D) Separation and Recovery of Dried Product:

This process recovers solids and exhausts dust free air. Majority of dried product falls to the base of the chamber where primary separation takes place. A small fraction of product passes out entrained in the air, which is recovered by a suitable separation equipment. This secondary product separation is carried out by cyclone separators, bag filters, electrostatic precipitators and wet scrubbers.

Advantages of Spray Dryers:

1. Operation is continuous, easy and adaptable to automatic control.
2. It can be used for both heat sensitive and heat resistant materials in solution, slurry, paste or melt form.
3. Flexibility in design allows drying of toxic materials, organic solvent containing feed, feed forming powders explosive with air. It can also be used for aseptic conditions.
4. Product quality remains constant all over the process when other conditions are kept constant.

Disadvantages Spray Dryers:

1. Due to it's larger size, fabrication and installation cost is very high.
2. Thermal efficiency is very poor or large amount of heat is wasted in exhaust air.

Applications of Spray Drying:

Spray drying is used successfully for drying of pharmaceutical infusions, extracts, digitalist, adrenaline, etc. Spray driers for pharmaceuticals are of three types:

(a) Standard open cycle type.

(b) Aseptic open cycle type.

(c) Closed cycle type.

First two types use atmospheric air as a drying media while the third type which is commonly used to remove organic solvent uses inert gas like nitrogen.

Blood plasma, serum, bacitracin, vitamins, penicillin, yeast, chloramphenical succinate, dextran, harmones, enzymes, etc. are dried using aseptic or closed type spray direct. In aseptic type sterile air is obtained using 'HEPA' filters.

Closed Cycle Drier: Closed cycle drier is used when: (a) Solvent system is flammable, (b) Drying of toxic substances, (c) To prevent atmospheric pollution, (d) If powder forms explosive mixture with air and (e) For complete solvent recovery.

Spray Congealing: In this process, a melt of certain substance comes in contact with a stream of air, and gets cooled to form fine solid particulate product. When a slurry of some insoluble material in a molten mass is spray congealed, the product obtained is insoluble particle coated with congealing substance. This is mainly used in chewable formulations to mask the taste or improve stability of drugs. e.g. one part of vitamins like riboflavin, pyridoxine hydrochloride, niacinamide and thiamine monohydrate is mixed with two parts of fatty acids or mono and diglycerides of fatty acids and spray congealed to get free flowing powder. The taste of vitamins is also masked. Spray congealing is also used in sustained release formulations.

Spray coating and spray encapsulation involves evaporation of solvent from solution forming a coat on the substance to be coated. For coating of liquids, an emulsion is prepared, where, the liquid to be coated is present in the internal phase and the coating material in the external phase. After spray drying, solvent from continuous phase evaporates leaving a coat over the dispersed particles. Similarly, a suspension is prepared and spray dried to the solids.

It is also used for micro-encapsulation by interfacial polymerization, where the dispersed phase contains liquid to be encapsulated and first reactant and solution of emulsifier and second reactant as continuous phase.

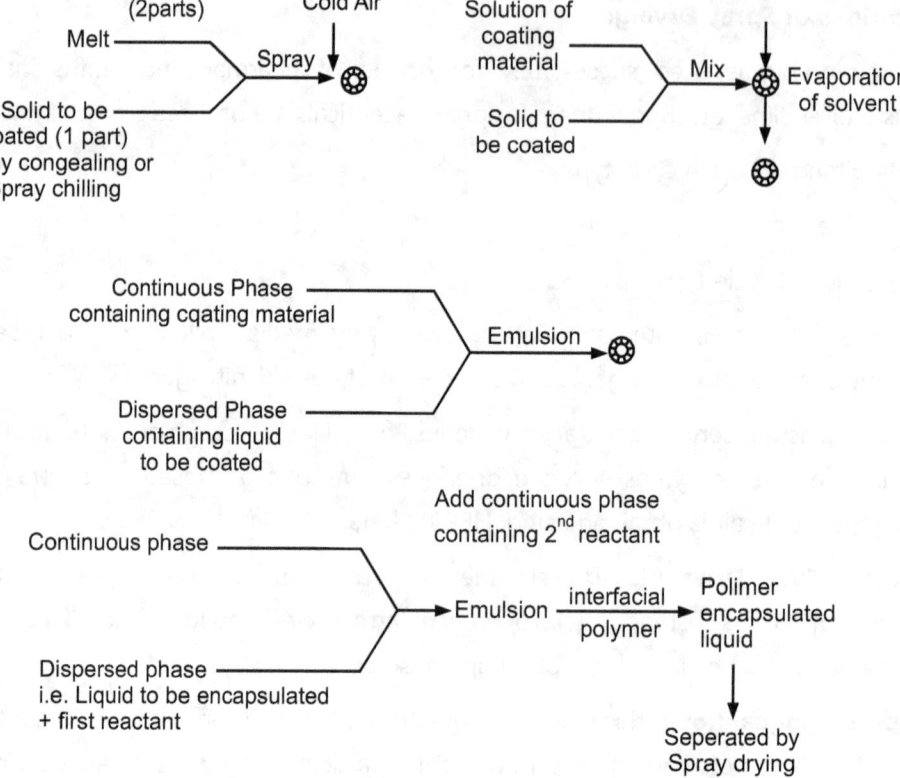

Fig. 3.10: Spray congealing and coating

3.4.6 Freeze Drying

Freeze drying is a method of drying where the liquid in the solid - liquid mixture is frozen by cooling and is subsequently caused to sublime. Generally, the liquid to be evaporated is water. It is also termed by lyophilization i.e. "made solvent loving". Freeze drying is widely used for drying of pharmaceuticals which are highly heat sensitive e.g. blood proteins, vitamins, antibiotics, human protein hydrolysates and animal vaccines, penicillin. Freeze drying consists of freezing of the material followed by sublimation of ice or frozen moisture under vacuum of 100 to 300 micron at temperature – 10°C to – 30°C. The sublimated water vapours are then condensed. For sublimation heat is supplied at a controlled rate so that sublimation of ice takes place avoiding melting of the material. As drying proceeds, ice surface recedes gradually within the body of the material, leaving behind a porous structure in the dried product through which water vapour moves to the surface. All the original constituents of the material remain frozen in their original positions. Thus, dried product usually retains its original shape and size with considerable porosity resulting in ready solubility in water. The freeze drying operation consists of:

(a)   Preparation and pretreatment.

(b)   Pre-freezing to solidify the water.

(c)   Primary drying (sublimation of ice under vacuum).

(d)   Secondary drying (removal of residual moisture under high vacuum).

(e)   Packing.

(a) Preparation and Pre-treatment: In some cases pre-treatment is given before pre-freezing e.g. protein solutions take eight to ten times longer period than pure water. Therefore in such cases, it is desirable to pre-concentrate the solution under normal vacuum tray drying unless a very highly porous product is required.

(b) Pre-freezing to Solidify the Water: The aqueous solutions packed in vials, ampoules or bottles are cooled by using cold shelves (around – 50°C), alcohol baths, (around – 50°C) or liquid nitrogen bath (– 195°C). Normal cooling rates in pre-freezing stage is around 1 to 3K/min. Thickness of the frozen material affects the rate of drying, thinner is the layer, higher is the drying rate. The thickness is usually maintained between 1/2 to 3/4 inch. During this stage cabinet is maintained at low temperature and atmospheric pressure.

The freezing rate during this stage is important to be controlled, large ice crystals are formed at low freezing rate resulting in relatively large holes on sublimation of ice. Dextrin solution when lyophilised at freezing rate between 3 to 25 K/min resulted in a product having pore size 1 to 4 micron.

(c) Primary Drying (Sublimation of ice under vacuum): Once the solution is frozen, during primary drying vacuum is applied of the value of about 0.5 m bar. The temperature is linearly increased to around 30°C. in a span of 2 hrs. and temperature is maintained constant during primary and secondary drying. As a necessary condition of sublimation temperature of subliming surface should be below its eutectic point. Thus, subliming surface is maintained around 1 to 8 K below the eutectic point. The supply of heat controls movement of ice layer inwards and it has to be controlled in such a manner so as to get highest possible water vapour pressure at ice surface without melting material. Primary drying stage removes easily removable moisture. During this stage around 98 to 99% water is removed. This is followed by secondary drying.

(d) Secondary Drying (Removal of residual moisture under high vacuum): This stage removes (sublimes) the moisture which is difficult to remove during primary drying, temperature is maintained constant at 30°C. But now vacuum is lowered to 0.07 m bar. The rate of drying is very low it takes around 10 to 20 hours.

(e) Packing: Closing of vials or bottles occurs in the drying plant after the vacuum has been broken by dry inert gas. Removal of residual moisture takes considerable time. In drying sera containing 10% of solid has shown that 80% of the total drying period is required to remove 95% of the total moisture, whereas 90% of total drying period is required to attain 1% residual moisture and remaining 10% of the drying time is required to remove next 0.5%.

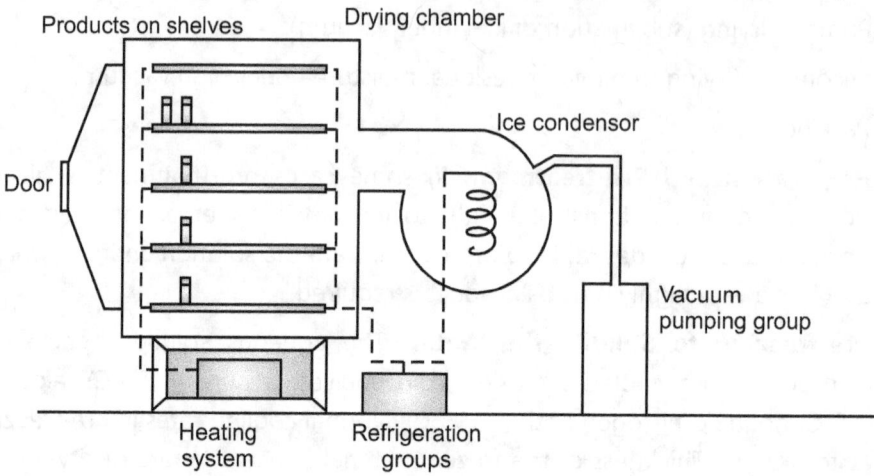

Fig. 3.11: An industrial freeze-dryer for pharmaceuticals

A freeze dryer (Fig. 3.11) consists of:

1. A drying chamber in which the trays are loaded.
2. A heat supply in the form of radiation source, heating coil.
3. Vapour condensing or adsorption system.
4. Vacuum pump or ejector.

Types of Freeze Dryers:

1. **Batch dryers:** As the name implies it deals with one fixed quantity at a time and that usually completed. The product is arranged to be static, while the whole process is performed, environment, variables being altered around it to suit.

2. **Continuous dryers:** These are large freeze dryers refers to sequence batching in the main where trays or dishes rest throughout the stages of the process, each stage being in an assigned part of the dryer where the environment is set principally by the heating temperature. Physical entery and discharge are affected by means of locks, capable of dealing with carrods or single tray.

Factors Affecting the Process Rate:

The greater the depth of the product more will be the time required for drying process. Therefore, product to be frozen by placing the container on refrigerated shelf (plug freezing) should be filled to planned limited depth. If the large volume of the solution must be processed, the surface area may be increased and the depth decreased by freezing the solution on a slant or while rotating the container at an angle in a liquid refrigerant bath such as dry ice and alcohol.

The passageway between the product surface and the condenser surface must be wide open and direct, far effective operation. Evacuation of system is necessary to reduce the impending effect that collisions with air molecules would have on passage of water molecule.

The amount of solids in the product, their particle size and thermal conductance will affect the rate of drying. Fluidized beds were more popular where vibration is used to shuffle and gently throw the material onwards. Both vertical and horizontal forms have been used. Because of short drying times, particle size distribution has to be very close. (1 – 2 or 1.5 – 2.5 mm) recycling of fines occur far more than in static dryers.

Advantages:

Freeze drying as a result of the character of the process has certain special advantages:

1. The solution is frozen such that the final dry product is a network of solid occupying the same volume as the original solution. Thus, there is no case-hardening and the product is light and porous.

2. Drying takes place at very low temperatures, so that enzyme action is inhibited and decomposition, particularly hydrolysis is minimized.

3. The porous form of the product gives ready solubility.

4. There is no concentration of the solution prior to drying, hence salts do not concentrate and denature proteins as occurs with other drying methods.

5. Under high vacuum, there is no contact with air and oxidation is minimised.

Disadvantages:

There are three main Disadvantages of freeze drying:

1. The porosity, ready solubility and complete dryness yield a very hygroscopic product. Unless dried in the final container and sealed in suitable packing, it requires special conditions.

2. The process is very slow and uses complicated plant, which is very expensive. It is not a general method of drying, therefore, is limited to certain types of valuable products that cannot be dried by any other means.

3. It is difficult (but not impossible) to adopt the method for solutions containing non-aqueous solvents.

Applications:

1. It is utilized in maintenance and preservation of microbial culture.

2. The solution of penicillin must be kept at $0 - 2°C$ and used within two-three days. If freeze dried and stored in hermetically sealed ampoules, full activity is retained for several months.

3. Fibrinogen is dissolved in sodium chloride injection and whipped into a foam, which is them clotted by addition of human thrombin. The foam is then freeze dried.

4. A solution of gelatin containing traces of formaldehyde is foamed, freeze dried, sterilised and used as a surgical dressing.

5. Freeze dried Haemoglobin formulated with sucrose to minimise inprocess degradation.

6. In general, a product is freeze dried if aqueous solution does not have any sufficient stability and if the product cannot be crystallized in bulk. Compared to spray drying, freeze drying is a low temperature process and is normally regarded as being less destructive to the product, particularly for proteins.

This technique is mainly used for drying immune serum, blood products, certain enzymes, a variety of viral and bacterial preparations, plant extracts, diagnostics as well as mammallian tissues useful in skin and bone graft surgery.

Also employed for preservation of products like several antineoplastics, vaccines, toxoids, hormones, vitamins and many food–stuffs.

3.4.7 Pneumatic or Flash Dryer

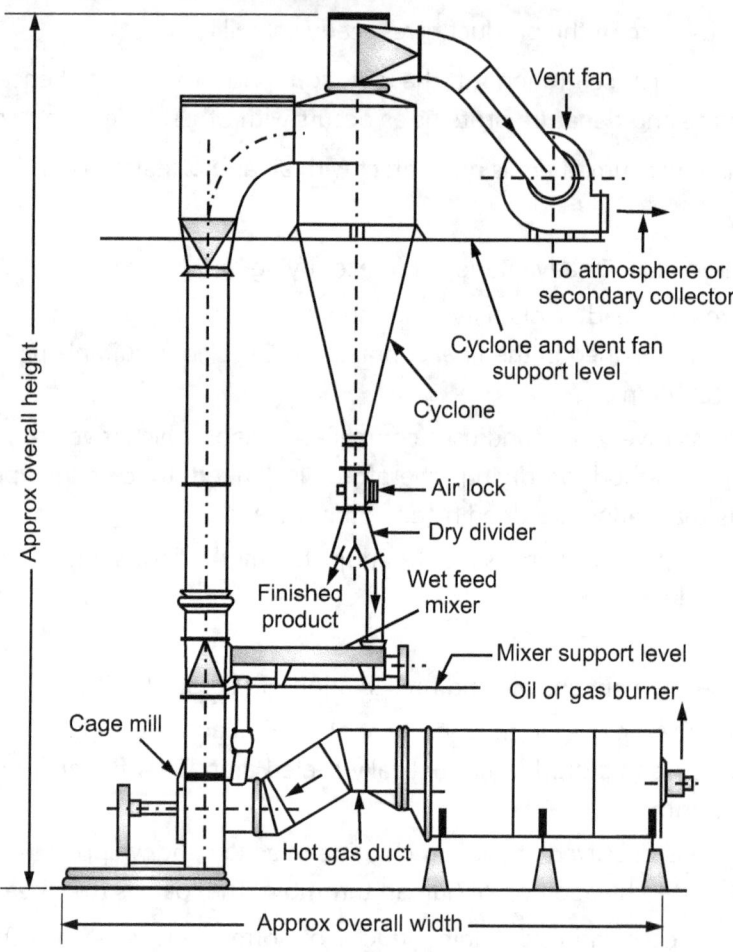

Fig. 3.12: Pneumatic dryer

Pneumatic drying process can be considered as a cross between fluidised bed dryer and the spray dryer. In pneumatic drying process, there is a continuous flow of particulate matter which is dried with warm or hot air while being transported by air stream. The free flowing medium size particles when introduced to a flow of hot air at adequate velocity become totally dispersed and entrained in such a way that it will be dried and pneumatically conveyed from the fill point to the point of delivery. The dried product is separated from air by reduction in velocity. Generally, cyclone is used for this separation purpose. It is suitable as a pneumatic conveyor also to convey the moist material from point of production to a convenient post where it can be stored or packed in its dry form.

In flash drying, gas velocity is appoximately ten times as compared to fluidised bed dryer and thereby requires large cyclones. The exit gas velocity is around 10 to 30 metres/sec. Some important points to be considered are as follows:

1. Particle Size: The maximum particle size of the material is about 1 to 2 mm because the particles larger than this are not entrained by the air and require longer drying period than that achieved by flash dryer. If the material in its initial condition is not suitable for entrainment, it may be subjected to preliminary disintegration in cage mill to disintegrate it while the drying gas is passed through the mill. Sometimes the feed is made suitable by back mixing it with the product.

2. Gas Velocity: The velocity of the air stream must be above the terminal velocity of fall of heaviest particle, so that general movement of all the particles is upwards without any fallback. The gas velocity for pneumatic handling is around 40 to 80 feet/sec. The high gas velocity may cause abrasion or dust formation. Dust formation is promoted by gas velocity, when the smaller particles are eroded from the feed particles. The ratio of weight of air to weight of material should not be less than 2 : 1. It may exceed in some cases like drying of relatively coarse material containing 2 to 3 per cent (low) moisture of elevated temperature.

The flash dryer essentially consists of:

(a)   Source of hot gas

(b)   A material feeding device

(c)   A drying column or duct with ventury section at material feed point.

(d)   Cyclone for solid air separation.

(e)   Air exhaust fan for discharging humid air.

The main drying duct is circular having well finished internal surface so as to avoid any interference to gas flow. The drying duct is around 1 metre in diameter and 10 m to 30 m in length. A ventury may be fitted at the feed point. As the heat transfer from hot gases to the material is instantaneous, material although subjected to very high gas temperature period of contact is very short.

Advantages:

Time of contact between the material to be dried and hot gas is very short only few seconds. Therefore it is suitable for drying of heat sensitive materials having good drying characteristics which helps in complete local entrainment of the material and also produces point of suction for filling without necessity of other mechanical feeding device.

Thus in a pneumatic dryer there is small particle size, high gas velocity, high temperature difference, between gas and material provides optimum drying condition with minimum drying period. During drying the material remain at weight bulb temperature of the gas and never exceeds the outlet gas temperature. For drying of materials, containing explosive or inflammable solvents earthing all parts of dryer is necessary.

Limitations:

1. It is not suitable for materials which are sticky and greasy in nature or where attrition may cause damage to the dried product.

2. For materials having high moisture content about 60% and above flash dryer is ineffective as high air velocities provide insufficient residence time so as to release all the moisture.

Drum or Roller Dryer (Film Drum Dryer):

It is a conduction dryer where heating medium generally steam is present inside a rotating cylinder. Heat is transferred by conduction to the metal surface of cylinder to the film of liquid to be dried (Fig. 3.13).

It is used for drying solutions, slurries, like liquid products and suspensions. The drum rotates at the speed of 5 – 20 revolutions per minutes. The time of contact between material and heating surface is very short around 3 to 12 sec. These dried material attains the temperature of heating surface for a very short period. Hence, film drum dryer dries material without significant thermal degradation.

Drying in film drum dryer involves transfer of heat from condensing steam within the drum through the metal of the drum to the thin film of liquid on the outer surface of the drum. The overall heat transfer rate during this drying process depends on solid content and its physical properties, film thickness, steam temperature, metal thickness and its thermal conductivity. The temperature drop through the metal drum is about 65 to 35 °F.

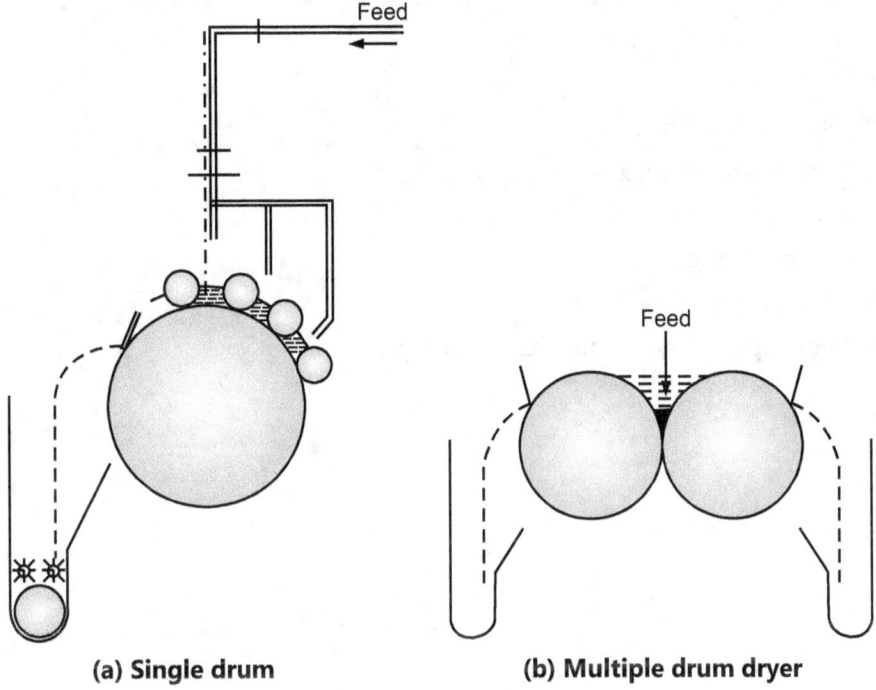

| **(a) Single drum** | **(b) Multiple drum dryer** |

Fig. 3.13: Roller Dryer

The roller dryer may be encased in a vacuum tight chamber for drying of materials which are heat sensitive, are subject to oxidation or where solvent has to be recovered.

Film drum dryers are extensively used in chemical and pharmaceutical industries yeast, pigments, meat extracts, distillery by products, antibiotics, glandular extracts, insecticides, D.D.T, calcium and barium carbonates and other organic and inorganic salts.

Disadvantage:

Maintenance cost of film drum dryer is higher than the spray dryers.

Questions

1. Explain in detail mechanism of drying.
2. Describe drying equipments.
3. Explain construction and working of spray dryer.
4. Write advantages and disadvantages of freeze dryers.
5. What is flash dryer, explain?
6. Write short notes on the following:
   (a) Significance of drying
   (b) Constant rate period
   (c) Tray dryer
   (d) Fluidized bed dryer
   (e) Centrifugal atomizers
   (f) Droplet drying
   (g) Freeze drying
   (h) Roller dryer
7. Write the applications of fluidized bed dryer.

■■■

CHAPTER

Heat Transfer

4.1 Introduction

Heat transfer is a dynamic process in which heat is transferred spontaneously from a region of higher temperature to a region of lower temperature, e.g. if heat is added to a metal vessel which contains liquid or vapour, the molecules of the metal vibrate faster. These vibrating molecules strike the fluid molecules. In this way, the heat energy is transferred to a liquid or vapour. Now, if the liquid or vapour inside a vessel is hotter than the metal of the vessel, the faster moving fluid molecules strike the metal molecules and make them vibrating faster. In this way, the heat energy is transferred from more energetic molecules to those with less energy. Therefore, substances always tend to equalize in temperature if they are in contact.

4.2 Mechanisms of Heat Transfer

Heat is transferred by three mechanisms:

(i)   Conduction

(ii)   Convection and

(iii) Radiation.

(i)   **Conduction:** When a solid is heated, the vibrational energy of the heated molecules is transferred to their neighbouring molecules by the movement of free electrons. Solid metals are good conductors, whereas, non-metals and liquids are poor conductors where conduction generally takes place by transport of individual molecules along the temperature gradient. Gases or vapours are the worst conductors of all, where conduction occurs by the random motion of the molecules. Thus, heat is diffused from hotter regions to colder ones.

(ii)   **Convection:** When a liquid or vapour is in contact with hotter metal, the fluid molecules alongside the metal get speeded up almost instantly, although, they transfer the momentum to their neighbours slowly. The layer of more active molecules expands and its density becomes less than other molecules. This hot layer rises and a cooler fluid flows in, to replace it and is in turn brought into contact with the hot surface. This movement of group of molecules continues. The movement of hot and cooler molecules in group is known as *convection*. When this movement occurs due to difference in density of molecules, it is known as *natural convection* and as the motion continues to give continuous flow of molecules in the liquid, it is known as natural convection currents. The convection currents if set with the help of an external energy supplying device as pumps or agitator then it is called as *forced convection*. Forced convection is independent of density difference in two regions.

(iii) Radiation: Radiation is the transfer of heat energy by electromagnetic waves. All bodies with a temperature above absolute zero radiate heat in the form of electromagnetic waves. The radiation emitted by any material is independent of that being emitted by other material in sight, or in contact with it. Radiation heat transfer is important to be considered mainly at very high or very low temperatures, because in other conditions, its effect is blanketed by other two mechanisms.

4.3 Heat Transfer by Conduction

Heat transfer by conduction is considered under the following categories:

(i)   Fourier's law and thermal conductivity.

(ii)   Steady state heat transfer.

(iii) Unsteady state heat transfer.

4.3.1 Fourier's Law

The rate of heat transfer depends upon the differences in temperature between the bodies, the greater the difference in temperature, the higher is the rate of heat transfer. Thus, temperature difference acts as a driving force for heat transfer. The medium through which heat transfers from one body to another offers certain resistance to the heat flow. Thus, rate of heat transfer can be written as,

$$\text{Rate of Heat Transfer} = \frac{\text{Temperature difference}}{\text{Resistance of the medium}}$$

This concept is expressed by Fourier's law which states that '*rate of heat transfer across a surface is proportional to the temperature gradient at the surface*'.

$$\frac{dQ}{d\theta} \; \alpha \; \frac{dt}{dx}$$

Thus, if A is the area normal to the heat flow then,

$$\frac{dQ}{d\theta} = -kA\frac{dt}{dx} \qquad\qquad \text{... (4.1)}$$

where, $\dfrac{dQ}{d\theta}$ = Rate of heat transfer

A = Area of cross-section of heat flow path

$\dfrac{dt}{dx}$ = Temperature gradient i.e. rate of change of temperature per unit path length.

k = Thermal conductivity of the medium.

Equation (4.1) is known as Fourier's equation. The negative sign indicates that the heat flow occurs from hot to cold region.

Thermal Conductivity: In Fourier's equation, k is a proportionality constant which indicates the resistance per unit flow path and is independent of temperature gradient. The numerical value of it depends upon the material of which the body is made and temperature. But over a small temperature range, change in k value is negligible and can be considered as constant. If temperature range is large, then k is related by equation:

$$k = a + bT \qquad \qquad \ldots (4.2)$$

where, a and b are constants.

At a given temperature, thermal conductivity is a function of bulk density of material. Thermal conductivity is expressed in units as: B.T.U./ft^2 – h – ($^\circ$F/ft); Watt / m – $^\circ$C or J m^{-1} s^{-1} $^\circ$C^{-1}.

Values of thermal conductivity for some materials are given in Table 4.1.

Table 4.1: Thermal conductivities (B.T.U. / ft^2 hr ($^\circ$F/ft)

Material	Temp °C	k	Material	Temp °C	k
Solids			**Liquids:**		
Metals:			Mercury	0	4.8
1. Silver	100	238	Ethyl ether	40	0.080
2. Copper	100	218	Water	100	0.39
3. Aluminium	100	19			
4. Iron (cast)	100	30			
5. Mild steel	100	26			
6. Stainless steel (304)	100	218	**Gases:**		
Non-Metals:			Air	100	0.018
1. Carbon (graphite)	50	80	Steam	100	0.0136
2. Glass	50	0.63	Nitrogen	100	0.018
3. Glass wool	100	0.036	Carbon dioxide	100	0.013
Ice	0	1.2	Hydrogen	100	0.124

4.3.2 Steady-State Heat Transfer

When rate of heat transfer remains constant and is unaffected by time, then it is termed as steady-state heat transfer. For such conditions, $\dfrac{dQ}{d\theta}$ in Fourier's equation is constant called as A. Thus, Fourier's equation for steady state heat transfer can be written as:

$$\frac{Q}{\theta} = q = -kA \frac{dt}{dx} \qquad \qquad \ldots (4.3)$$

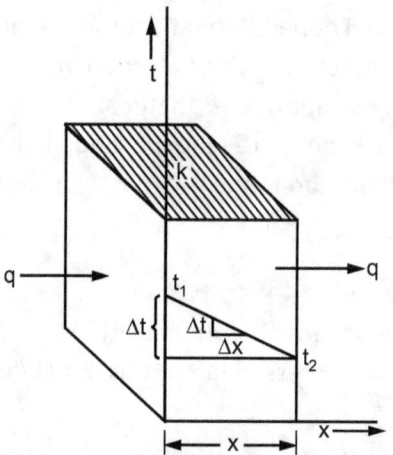

Fig. 4.1: Heat conduction through a slab

Thus, if we consider a slab of a material (Fig. 4.1) of which two faces have temperatures t_1 and t_2. If t_1 is greater, heat flows from higher temperature t_1 to other face having temperature t_2. If x is the thickness of the slab then by Fourier's equation, rate of heat transfer is given as:

$$q = kA \frac{(t_1 - t_2)}{x}$$

$$q = \left(\frac{k}{x}\right) A \, \Delta t \qquad \qquad \dots (4.4)$$

But many times, heat flows through several consecutive layers of different materials (Fig. 4.2); in such condition equation (4.4) has to be applied for every layer separately. Thus, if steady-state condition exists i.e. the same quantity of heat per unit time passes through each layer then,

$$q = A_1 \Delta t_1 \frac{k_1}{x_1} = A_2 \Delta t_2 \frac{k_2}{x_2} = A_3 \Delta t_3 \frac{k_3}{x_3}$$

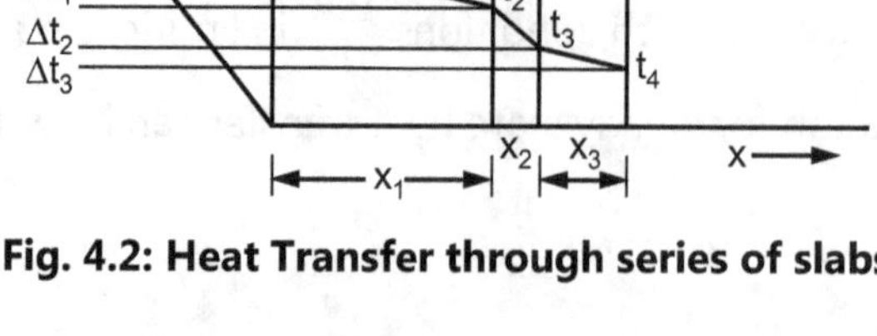

Fig. 4.2: Heat Transfer through series of slabs

If cross-sectional areas of the layers are same

i.e. $$A_1 = A_2 = A_3 = \ldots\ldots = A$$

then, $$q = A\,\Delta t_1 \frac{k_1}{x_1} = A\,\Delta t_2 \frac{k_2}{x_2}$$

$$= A\,\Delta t_3 \frac{k_3}{x_3} \ \ldots\ldots$$

$\therefore$ $$q\left(\frac{x_1}{k_1}\right) = A\,\Delta t_1$$

$$A\,\Delta t_2 = q\left(\frac{x_2}{k_2}\right)$$

and $$A\,\Delta t_3 = q\left(\frac{x_3}{k_3}\right) \ \ldots\ldots$$

$\therefore$ $$A\,\Delta t_1 + A\,\Delta t_2 + A\,\Delta t_3 + \ldots = q\left(\frac{x_1}{k_1}\right) + q\left(\frac{x_2}{k_2}\right) + q\left(\frac{x_3}{k_3}\right) + \ldots\ldots$$

Sum of the temperature gradients across each layer is equal to the difference in temperature between inside and outside surface. i.e.

$$\Delta t_1 + \Delta t_2 + \Delta t_3 + \ldots\ldots = \Delta t$$

Thermal conductivity per unit length is conductance (C). Therefore, $\frac{k_1}{x_1}$ is the conductance C_1 of first layer, if we say for all the subsequent layers then,

$$\frac{x_1}{k_1} + \frac{x_2}{k_2} + \frac{x_3}{k_3} = \frac{1}{C_1} + \frac{1}{C_2} + \frac{1}{C_3} + \ldots\ldots$$

$$= \frac{1}{U}$$

where, U is overall conductance for combined layers.

$\therefore$ $$A\,\Delta t = q\left(\frac{1}{U}\right)$$

$$q = UA\,\Delta t \qquad\qquad \ldots (4.5)$$

Equation (4.5), gives the heat flow through the combination of layers and U is called as overall heat transfer coefficient.

Heat Transfer in Pipes and Tubes:

In the heat exchangers and pharmaceutical equipments, heat transfer takes place across a pipe or tube. In such cases for tubes and pipes, area values change. Therefore, it is important to determine the value of A and thickness of pipe. If we consider a pipe having length l, with internal radius r_1 and r_2 as external radius then area ($2\pi r l$) will have to be determined as per the thickness of wall.

(i)   For thin walled pipes i.e. where, $\dfrac{r_2}{r_1} < 1.5$

then mean radius $r_m = \dfrac{r_1 + r_2}{2}$

$\therefore$ $A = 2\pi \left(\dfrac{r_1 + r_2}{2}\right) l$

By substituting value of A in equation (4.5), we get

$\therefore$ $q = k\, 2\pi \left(\dfrac{r_1 + r_2}{2}\right) l \dfrac{\Delta t}{r_2 - r_1}$ ... (4.6)

(ii)   For thick walled pipes, heat transfer area is calculated using logarithmic mean radius (r_m).

$$r_m = \dfrac{r_2 - r_1}{\ln\left(\dfrac{r_2}{r_1}\right)}$$

$\therefore$ $q = k\, 2\pi \left(\dfrac{r_2 - r_1}{\ln\left(\dfrac{r_2}{r_1}\right)}\right) l \dfrac{\Delta t}{r_2 - r_1}$

$$= \dfrac{2\pi\, k\, l\, \Delta t}{\ln\left(\dfrac{r_2}{r_1}\right)} \qquad\qquad ... (4.7)$$

SOLVED EXAMPLES

Example 4.1: Calculate the rate of heat loss for a red brick wall of length 10 m, height 5 m and thickness 0.25 m. The temperature of inner surface is 105°C and of the outer surface is 45°C. The thermal conductivity of red brick is 0.7 W/m.°C.

Solution:

$$Q = \dfrac{k\, A\, (T_1 - T_2)}{x}$$

$A = 10 \times 5 = 50\ m^2$; $k = 0.7\ W/m\ °C$, $x = 0.25\ m$

$T_1 = 105\ °C$ and $T_2 = 45\ °C$

$\therefore$ $Q = \dfrac{0.7 \times 50\ (105 - 45)}{0.25}$

        $= 8400\ W$ or $8.4\ kW$

Example 4.2: A cold store has a wall comprising of 10 cm of brick on outside, then 10 cm of concrete and then 10 cm of cork. The mean temperature within the store is maintained at − 20°C and mean temperature of the outside surface of the wall is 15°C. Calculate the rate of heat transfer through the wall and the temperature at the interface between cork and concrete. Thermal conductivities for brick, concrete and cork are 0.7, 0.75 and 0.043 W/m°C. Area of wall is 1 m².

Solution: $q = U A \Delta t$

First calculate value of U.

$$\frac{1}{U} = \frac{x_1}{k_1} + \frac{x_2}{k_2} + \frac{x_3}{k_3}$$

$$= \frac{0.1}{0.7} + \frac{0.1}{0.75} + \frac{0.1}{0.043} = 2.6$$

$$U = 0.385 \text{ W/m}^2 \text{ K}$$

$$\Delta t = 15 - (-20) = 35°C \text{ and } A = 1 \text{ m}^2$$

$$q = U A \Delta T$$

$$q = 0.385 \times 1 \times 35$$

$$= 13.475 \text{ W}$$

For cork wall; $q = k_3 \dfrac{A_3 \, \Delta t_3}{x_3}$

$$A_3 = 1 \text{ m}^2$$

$$k_3 = 0.043 \text{ W/m } °C , x_3 = 0.1 \text{ m}$$

and $q = 13.475 \text{ J}$

∴ $13.475 = \dfrac{1 \times \Delta t_3 \times 0.043}{0.1}$

∴ $\Delta t_3 = 31.34°C$

31.34°C is the difference in temperature between inner wall surface and concrete-cork interface, (inner wall temperature is − 20°C).

∴ 31.34 = (temperature of cork-concrete interface) − (− 20)

∴ Temperature of cork-concrete interface = 11.34°C.

Example 4.3: Calculate heat flow rate per unit length of cylindrical pipe with inner diameter 2 cm and outer diameter 4 cm. The outer surface temperature is 100°C and the inner surface temperature is 70°C. Thermal conductivity of the pipe material is 0.56 W/m °C.

Solution: Given: r_1 = 1 cm, r_2 = 4 cm $\therefore \dfrac{r_2}{r_1}$ = 2 as $\dfrac{r_2}{r_1}$ > 1.5 we must use logarithmic mean radius. k = 0.56 W/m°C, T_2 = 100°C; T_1 = 70°C and l = 1.

$$Q = \frac{2\pi k \, l \, \Delta t}{\ln\left(\dfrac{r_2}{r_1}\right)} = \frac{2 \times 3.14 \times 0.56 \times 1 \times 30}{\ln(2)} = -157.7 \text{ W/m}$$

This flow rate should be given negative sign to indicate the flow radially inwards.

4.3.3 Unsteady State Heat Transfer

In most of the pharmaceutical systems, temperature changes with time and heat transfer in such systems is unsteady state heat transfer. Heating and cooling of pharmaceuticals during sterilisation is a best example of unsteady heat transfer. Analysis of unsteady-state heat transfer is more complex, since an additional variable time enters into the rate equation. Unsteady state heat transfer analysis involves complicated mathematical calculations including solving Fourier's equation written in terms of partial differentials in three dimensions but it is out of reach of this book.

4.4 Radiation Heat Transfer

In radiation heat transfer, heat energy is transferred in the form of electromagnetic waves. It can occur in vacuum; and is independent of temperature and geometry of the surface emitting or absorbing it. Emission of energy will occur when an electron from a high energy orbit jumps to a lower energy orbit, and the energy released from it has all properties of electromagnetic waves. These waves upon striking a receiver, the photons travel into it until they strike an electron or nucleus that is susceptible to the energy level of the photon. This collision results in an increase in the energy of receiver. In solids due to dense nature, radiation is usually absorbed very close to the surface, whereas penetration is more in liquids and it is still higher in gases.

Any body above absolute zero temperature emits radiations. The radiation that result only due to temperature is called *thermal radiation*. A part of incident radiation is absorbed by the body, a part is reflected and a part is transmitted. The absorbed radiation is transformed into heat. The proportion of the incident energy that is absorbed, reflected and transmitted depend on the properties of the receiver and to some extent wavelength of radiation and temperature of receiver. A *black body* is one that converts all the incident radiation into heat and emits all thermal energy as radiation.

Thus, we can state,

$$\alpha + r + \tau = 1 \qquad \qquad \text{... (4.8)}$$

where, α = Absorptivity, fraction of incident radiation that is absorbed.

r = Reflectivity, fraction of incident radiation that is reflected.

τ = Transmissivity, fraction of incident radiation that is transmitted.

For most of the solids transmissivity is zero, therefore equation (4.8) reduces to

$$\alpha + r = 1$$

whereas for a black body absorptivity is unity ($\alpha = 1$).

The radiation heat transfer is based on two basic laws:

(i) Kirchoff's law and

(ii) Stefan-Boltzmann law.

4.4.1 Kirchoff 's Law

Emissive power of a body, E, is the radiant energy emitted from unit area in unit time. Kirchoff's law establishes a relationship between the emissive power of a surface to its absorptivity.

If a small body is placed inside a large evacuated enclosure with wall temperature T, the be exchanged between the body and the enclosure until equilibrium is established, i.e. enclosure wall and body will have the same temperature. Then body will emit as much energy as it absorbs. Now, if E is the emissive power of the body, α is its absorptivity and G is the rate at which the energy falls from the wall on the body; then energy balance at this equilibrium state can be written as

$$G\alpha = E$$

$$\therefore \qquad G = \frac{E}{\alpha} \qquad \qquad \text{... (4.9)}$$

Rate of energy fall G is a function of temperature T, and geometrical arrangement of both surfaces. But if the body is very small as compared to the enclosure and its effect upon the irradiation field of the enclosure is negligible. Hence, G will remain constant at temperature. This is stated by Kirchoff's law. It states that "*the ratio of emissive power to the absorptivity is same for all bodies in thermal equilibrium*". Thus, for two bodies at same temperature,

$$\frac{E_1}{\alpha_1} = \frac{E_2}{\alpha_2} \qquad \qquad \text{... (4.10)}$$

where, E_1 and E_2 = Emissive powers of two bodies

α_1 and α_2 = Absorptivities of two bodies.

For black bodies $\alpha = 1$, then according to Kirchoff's law, (where, E_b is emissive power of black body)

$$\frac{E_b}{1} = \frac{E}{\alpha}$$

$$\therefore \qquad \alpha = \frac{E}{E_b} \qquad \qquad \text{... (4.11)}$$

As black body is a perfect radiator, it is used as for comparison of emissive powers. The ratio of emissive power (E) of a surface to the emissive power (E_b) of a perfectly black body at the same temperature is known as emissivity (ε) of the surface.

$$\varepsilon = \frac{E}{E_b} \qquad \text{... (4.12)}$$

Therefore, emissivity of a body is equal to absorptivity, at thermal equilibrium.

Although, emissive power of a surface varies with the wavelength, for certain materials it is a constant fraction of the emissive power of a perfectly black body (E_b) i.e. $\frac{E}{E_b}$ is constant. Such materials which have constant emissivity are known as "*grey bodies*". Thus for grey bodies, it is not necessary that the two bodies should be at thermal equilibrium to apply Kirchoff's law.

4.4.2 Stefan – Boltzmann Law

Stefan-Boltzmann law states that "*emissive power of a black body is proportional to the fourth power of the absolute temperature (T)* ".

$$E_b = \sigma T^4 \qquad \text{... (4.13)}$$

where, σ is Stefan-Boltzmann constant, its numerical value is 5.67×10^{-8} W/m^2 – K^4.

As we know, emissive power is radiant energy, emitted from unit area in unit time. Therefore, a black body of area A and emissive power E emits energy at a rate E A. Therefore, heat emitted per unit time (Q) is written as,

$$Q = \sigma AT^4 \qquad \text{... (4.14)}$$

As we know, $\qquad \varepsilon = \dfrac{E}{E_b}$

Thus for a body which is not perfectly black,

$$Q = \varepsilon \sigma AT^4 \qquad \text{... (4.15)}$$

where $\qquad \varepsilon$ = Emissivity.

Consider a black body with surface area A at an absolute temperature T_1, exchanging radiation with another black body at temperature T_2. Then rate of heat exchange will be

$$Q = \sigma A \left(T_1^4 - T_2^4 \right) \qquad \text{... (4.16)}$$

For heat transfer between grey and black bodies:

$$Q = \sigma A \varepsilon \left(T_1^4 - T_2^4 \right) \qquad \text{... (4.17)}$$

A correction factor is generally introduced to take into account the geometry and orientation of two black bodies exchanging radiations. This factor (F) is known as *view factor*.

$$Q = \sigma A \varepsilon F \left(T_1^4 - T_2^4 \right) \qquad \text{... (4.18)}$$

Example 4.4: Calculate the heat radiated per unit area from radiator which behaves like a black body and operates at the temperature of 55°C.

Solution:
$$q = \frac{Q}{A} = \sigma T^4$$

$$= 5.67 \times 10^{-8} \, (328)^4$$

$$= 0.66 \text{ kW/m}^2$$

4.5 Convection Heat Transfer

Convection is a mode of heat transfer between a surface and fluid moving over it. It involves movement of group of molecules, which transfer energy. It is restricted to liquids and gases as movement of group of molecules is not possible with solids. There are two types of convection heat transfer:

(a)   Natural convection,

(b)   Forced convection.

(a)   **Natural Convection:** In convection heat transfer, when the movement of group of molecules occur due to change in density resulting from temperature gradient, it is known as *free* or *natural convection*. The fluid molecules in the immediate vicinity of the hot object become warmer than the bulk of the fluid causing local change of density. The warmer fluid will be replaced by the cooler fluid generating the convection currents. These currents start when body forces like gravitational, centrifugal, electrostatic etc. act on fluid in which there are density gradients. The force which induces these convection currents is called as *buoyancy force*, which is due to the presence of a density gradient within the fluid and a body force.

(b)   **Forced Convection:** When a fluid is forced past a solid body and heat is transferred between the fluid and the body, it is called *forced convection* heat transfer. In pharmaceutical industry, forced convection is involved during drying in ovens, fluidized bed dryers etc. In forced convection, fluid surrounding the surface is constantly replaced, therefore rate of heat transfer are higher than for natural convection.

Rate of heat transfer by convection is given by the equation

$$q = h_c A \, (t_1 - t_2) \qquad \qquad \dots (4.19)$$

where, h_c is convective heat transfer coefficient or surface heat transfer coefficient.

4.5.1 Dimensional Analysis

The convention heat transfer cannot be analysed by simple theoretical calculations because it involves many variables. The effects of these variables on heat transfer has to be determined, and relation between the variables is established by dimensional analysis.

In natural convection, heat transfer rates depend on variables like viscosity of fluid (η), thermal conductivity (k), density (ρ), specific heat (C_p), temperature difference between the surface and the bulk of the fluid (Δt) and the buoyancy force. Buoyancy forces depend on coefficient of thermal expansion (β), gravitational acceleration (g), convection heat transfer coefficient (h_c) and length dimensions (l or D).

Taking into consideration these variables, dimensionless numbers are selected for convection heat transfer. These dimensionless numbers are as follows:

Prandtl number: $Pr = \dfrac{C_p \eta}{k}$

Nusselt number: $Nu = \dfrac{h_c D}{k}$

Grashof number: $Gr = \dfrac{D^3 \rho^2 g \beta \, \Delta t}{\eta^2}$

These dimensionless numbers are correlated by a power equation for natural convection as:

$$(Nu) = K \, (Pr)^k \, (Gr)^m \left(\frac{L}{D}\right)^n \qquad \text{... (4.20)}$$

where, K, k, m and n are constants which vary with conditions.

For example: If the natural convection is taking place about a vertical cylinder then

$$(Nu) = 0.53 \, (Pr \, Gr)^{0.25} \qquad \text{... (4.21)}$$

and $(Nu) = 0.12 \, (Pr \, Gr)^{0.33}$ ... (4.22)

Equation (4.21) is observed when product of Prandtl and Grashof numbers has value between 10^4 and 10^9 and equation (4.22) when product is between 10^9 and 10^{12}.

In forced convection, fluid is forced past over a surface by a pump or an agitator. At low fluid velocities rates of natural convection are comparable to those of forced convection heat transfer. In natural convection, Grashof number has significant value whereas Reynold's number, a dimensionless number related to fluid dynamics is used for forced convection, heat transfer. Correlation of the dimensionless numbers is as follows:

$$(Nu) = K \, (Pr)^x \, (Re)^z$$

where, K, x and z are constants which change as per the conditions.

For example: For turbulent flow of a low velocity fluid through pipe the correlation equation becomes:

$$(Nu) = 0.023 \, (Pr)^{0.4} \, (Re)^{0.8} \qquad \text{... (4.24)}$$

where, x is 0.4 for heating and 0.3 for cooling.

The correlations of dimensionless numbers in heat transfer are given in Table 4.2.

Table 4.2: Correlations in Heat Transfer

	Correlation	Condition
Natural Convection		
1. About vertical cylinder	$(Nu) = 0.53 (Pr. Gr.)^{0.25}$	$10^4 < (Pr. Gr.) < 10^9$
	$(Nu) = 0.12 (Pr. Gr.)^{0.33}$	$10^9 < (Pr. Gr.) < 10^{12}$
2. About horizontal cylinder	$(Nu) = 0.54 (Pr. Gr.)^{0.25}$	$10^3 < (Pr. Gr.) < 10^9$
Forced Convection		
1. Heating and cooling inside tubes	$(Nu) = 4$	Laminar flow, long tubes and moderate Δt.
	$(Nu) = 0.023 (Re)^{0.8} (Pr)^{0.4}$	$(Re) > 2100$ and $(Pr) > 0.5$ (for liquids)
	$(Nu) = 0.02 (Re)^{0.8}$	For gases where (Pr) is constant at 0.75
2. Heating or cooling over plane surface	$(Nu) = 0.036 (Re)^{0.8} (Pr)^{0.33}$	$Re > 20,000$
3. Heating and cooling outside tubes	$(Nu) = 0.86 (Re)^{0.43} (Pr)^{0.3}$	$1 < (Re) < 200$
	$(Nu) = 0.23 (Re)^{0.6} (Pr)^{0.3}$	For high to moderate Re values

Example 4.5: Calculate heat transfer coefficient for a laminar fully developed fluid (k = 0.175 W/m °C) inside a 6 mm inside diameter tube, under uniform wall temperature boundary conditions and moderate temperature drop.

Solution: As flow is laminar in tube with moderate Δt, from table 4.2, we can select the equation as:

$$(Nu) = 4$$

$$\therefore \quad \frac{hD}{k} = (Nu) = 4$$

$$\therefore \quad h = \frac{4k}{D} = \frac{4 \times 0.175}{0.006}$$

$$= 116.66 \text{ W/m}^2 \text{ °C.}$$

Example 4.6: Water is flowing at 0.15 m s⁻¹ across a 7.5 cm diameter sausage at 75°C. If the bulk water temperature is 25°C, estimate the heat transfer coefficient.

Solution: As the liquid is flowing through sausage (heating and cooling outside the tube), for forced convection, fluid properties are evaluated at the mean film temperature which is the arithmetic mean temperature between the temperature of the tube wall and temperature of the bulk fluid.

Equation selected is:

$$Nu = 0.23 \, (Re)^{0.6} \, (Pr)^{0.3}$$

$$\text{Mean temperature} = \frac{(75 + 25)}{2} = 50\,°C$$

Properties of water at 50°C are as follows:

$$C_p = 4.186 \text{ kJ/kg}$$

$$k = 0.64 \text{ W/m °C}$$

$$\eta = 5.6 \times 10^{-4} \text{ Ns/m}^2$$

$$\rho = 1000 \text{ kg/m}^3.$$

$$Re = \frac{Du\rho}{\eta} = \frac{0.075 \times 0.15 \times 1000}{5.6 \times 10^{-4}} = 2 \times 10^4$$

$$(Re)^{0.6} = (2 \times 10^4)^{0.6} = 380.97$$

$$(Pr) = \frac{C_p \eta}{k} = \frac{4.186 \times 5.6 \times 10^{-4}}{0.64} = 3.66 \times 10^{-3}$$

$$\therefore \qquad (Pr)^{0.3} = (3.66 \times 10^{-3})^{0.3} = 0.1858$$

$$(Nu) = 0.23 \, (Re)^{0.6} \, (Pr)^{0.3} = 16.25 = \frac{hD}{k}$$

$$h = \frac{0.64 \times 16.25}{0.075} = 138.66 \text{ W/m}^2 \text{ °C.}$$

4.6 Overall Heat Transfer Coefficients

Overall heat transfer coefficient is obtained by summation of heat transfer coefficients for conduction, convection and radiation. Generally, radiation coefficient is combined with convective heat transfer coefficient to get overall surface transfer coefficient.

$$\therefore \qquad h_s = h_c + h_r \qquad \qquad \text{... (4.25)}$$

where, h_s is overall surface transfer coefficient, h_c and h_r are convective and radiation transfer coefficients respectively.

The overall heat transfer coefficient (U) for a solid wall with two fluid layers on either sides will be given by:

$$\frac{1}{U} = \frac{1}{\dfrac{1}{(h_s)_1} + \dfrac{x}{k} + \dfrac{1}{(h_s)_2}} \qquad \qquad \text{... (4.26)}$$

where, k is thermal conductivity of wall material and x is wall thickness, $(h_s)_1$ and $(h_s)_2$ are overall surface coefficients (film coefficient) of two fluids.

4.7 Heat Transfer Between Fluid and Solid Boundary

At fluid and solid boundary heat transfer takes place by both the mechanisms, conduction and convection as shown in Fig. 4.3. A metal wall separates the warm fluid on left side from the cold fluid on the right. The fluids are moving in turbulent motion and temperatures at different locations are shown by t_1, t_2, t_3, t_4, t_5 and t_6. As discussed in chapter (Flow of Fluids), the turbulent flow shows three zones (i) Laminar sub-layer, (ii) Buffer layer and (iii) Turbulent zone.

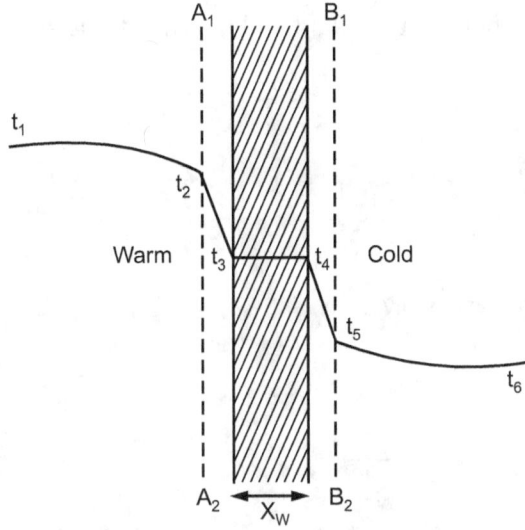

Fig. 4.3: Heat transfer between fluid and solid boundary

The laminar sub-layer on both sides are shown by A_1 A_2 and B_1 B_2. In the laminar sub-layer, the velocity gradient is maximum and the fluid mixing is almost zero, hence heat flows by conduction. But thermal conductivity of fluids is very low, therefore, due to high resistance it shows large temperature gradient of $(t_2 - t_3)$ and $(t_4 - t_5)$ on either side.

In the buffer zone, there is rapid change in velocity gradient as well as temperature gradient. In this region, conduction and convection is in combination. In the turbulent zone and bulk of the fluid, the velocity gradient is small and similarly the temperature gradient is also very small. Here turbulent mixing causes convective heat transfer.

As the thermal conductivity of metal wall is high there is no significant drop in temperature as shown by $t_3 - t_4$.

Thus, major resistance to heat flow will be from laminar sub-layer. Thickness of this layer depends on physical properties of fluid, nature of the surface and flow conditions. Higher is the thickness of the layer, higher is the resistance.

To calculate the rate of heat transfer, we have to take into consideration, resistance of layer on warm side, and cold side and resistance of metal wall. For the calculation of heat transfer through fluid film the thickness (x_1 and x_2) is taken slightly greater than the laminar sub-layer thickness because, there is some resistance to heat transfer in the buffer zone. Thus, x_1 is a thickness of a fictitious layer or film giving same resistance to heat transfer as the complex turbulent and laminar regions on warm side near the wall.

$$\therefore \qquad Q = \frac{k}{x_1} A (t_1 - t_3) \qquad \qquad \text{... (4.27)}$$

$$= h_1 A (t_1 - t_3)$$

where, k is thermal conductivity of fluid and h_1 is film transfer coefficient.

$$\therefore \qquad (t_1 - t_3) = \frac{Q}{h_1 A} \qquad \qquad \text{... (4.28)}$$

Similarly, on cold side,

$$(t_4 - t_6) = \frac{Q}{h_2 A}$$

Heat transfer through wall is given by,

$$Q = \frac{k_w}{x_w} A (t_3 - t_4) \qquad \qquad \text{... (4.29)}$$

$$\therefore \qquad t_3 - t_4 = \frac{Q}{A \dfrac{k_w}{x_w}} \qquad \qquad \text{... (4.30)}$$

Total temperature gradient ($t_1 - t_6$) can be obtained as

$$(t_1 - t_6) = \frac{Q}{A} \left(\frac{1}{h_1} + \frac{x_w}{k_w} + \frac{1}{h_2} \right)$$

$$\therefore \qquad Q = \frac{A (t_1 - t_6)}{\left(\dfrac{1}{h_1} + \dfrac{x_w}{k_w} + \dfrac{1}{h_2} \right)} \qquad \qquad \text{... (4.31)}$$

where, $\dfrac{1}{\dfrac{1}{h_1} + \dfrac{x_w}{k_w} + \dfrac{1}{h_2}}$ is called overall heat transfer coefficient U, therefore equation (4.31)

now becomes

$$Q = UA \, \Delta T \qquad \qquad \text{... (4.32)}$$

4.8 Heat Transfer to Boiling Liquids

Boiling is a convection heat transfer process which involves change in phase from liquid to vapour. Boiling may occur when a liquid is in contact with a surface maintained at temperature greater than the saturation temperature of the liquid. The boiling process depends upon the nature of the surface, thermophysical properties of the liquid and vapour bubble dynamics. We will discuss boiling process as:

(a)   Pool boiling

(b)   Boiling inside a vertical tube

(c)   Boiling with forced circulation.

4.8.1 Pool Boiling

If heat is added to a liquid from a submerged solid surface (e.g. heater), the boiling is called as 'pool boiling'. In this process, the vapour produced form bubbles which grow and subsequently detach themselves from the surface, rising to the free surface due to buoyancy effects.

The heat transfer changes with the change in temperature difference between the surface and boiling liquid (ΔT). The heat flux versus ΔT is shown in Fig. 4.4. In the initial zone (AB) when ΔT is very small, natural convection currents are observed and heat flux increases. Evaporation is taking place at this ΔT. Heat transfer coefficient (h) also increases.

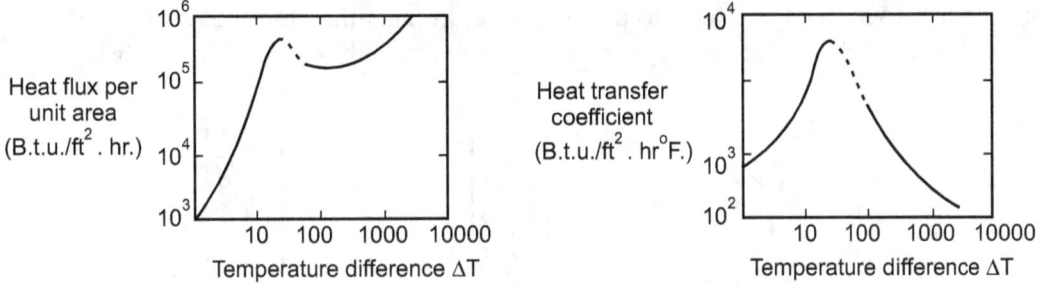

Fig. 4.4: Pool boiling

Next zone (BC) is called *nucleate boiling region*, where, ΔT is further increased. In this region, bubbles are formed continuously and rise to liquid surface resulting in rapid evaporation. At point C, heat flux is maximum, ΔT at this point is known as *critical temperature drop.*

As ΔT increases further, there is decrease in the heat flux as shown by CD, this is *film boiling* region. In this region, bubbles are formed so rapidly that they blanket the heating surface with vapour film. Now heat is transferred through this vapour film by conduction. As thermal conductivity of vapour film is very low, heat flux decreases.

After point D, we can again observe increase in heat flux as at those large values of ΔT between DE ($\Delta T = 10^3$ to 10^4), heat is lost by the surface due to radiation.

Thus from the above discussion, it is clear that heat flux and heat transfer coefficients are high in the nucleate boiling region. Therefore, the equipments involved with boiling liquids should be maintained in nucleate boiling region. Temperature of heating surface at critical temperature drop is so high that it may even cause melting of heating element, hence known as *burnout point.* Therefore, the equipment should be operated below this point.

4.8.2 Boiling Inside a Vertical Tube

This is commonly occurs in evaporators and other heat exchangers. The mechanism and hydrodynamics of boiling inside the tube is complex than in pool boiling, because the bubble growth and separation are strongly affected by the velocity of fluid.

As shown in Fig. 4.5, in a tube with low levels of liquid there are different patterns of boiling. Near the base of the tube, boiling of the liquid is suppressed by liquid column above. Heat transfer in this region takes place by natural convection. Above this height, the bubbles are formed, grow and are carried into the liquid over length of the tube, this is called as *bubbly region*. Heat transfer coefficients show significant increase in this region. As the volume occupied by the bubbles increases, the individual bubbles coalesce and form plug. This is called as *plug* or *slug flow region*. As the vapours coalesce, the escape is hindered and both liquid and vapour move upwards at an increasing speed. The vapour velocity is much higher than that of the liquid causing separation of two phases. This forms an annular film of the liquid dragged upwards by a core of high velocity vapour. This is called *annular flow*. Heat transfer coefficient remains high as long as the liquid film wets the wall. The film then thins and tend to break to give droplets then termed as *mist flow*. As the film is evaporated, dry spots appear on the tube and heat transfer coefficient drops significantly.

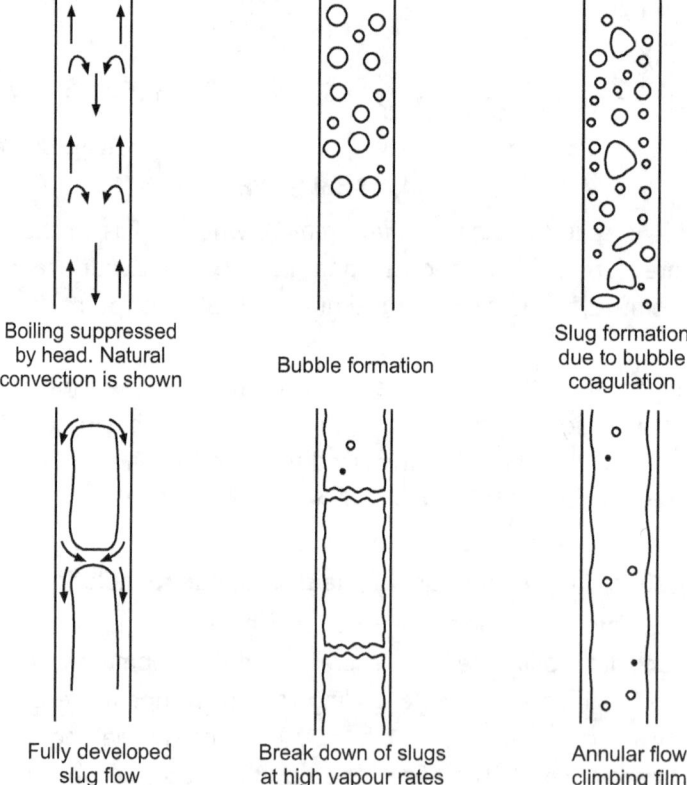

| Boiling suppressed by head. Natural convection is shown | Bubble formation | Slug formation due to bubble coagulation |

| Fully developed slug flow | Break down of slugs at high vapour rates | Annular flow climbing film |

Fig. 4.5: Boiling inside a vertical tube

4.8.3 Boiling with Forced Circulation

Boiling in an agitated vessel where the movement of fluid is caused by other than those by boiling. The heat transfer coefficients in this type of the boiling depend on the properties of liquid and the agitation used. But these coefficients are higher than that in pool boiling.

4.9 Heat Transfer from Condensing Vapours

Whenever hot vapours come in contact with a surface at a lower temperature, condensation occurs. It is the process exactly reverse that of the boiling. There are two types by which condensation may occur.

(i)   Film–wise condensation.

(ii)   Drop–wise condensation.

In *film–wise condensation*, the condensate wets the surface forming a continuous film over the entire surface. It generally occurs on clean, uncontaminated surface. The latent heat liberated during condensation is transferred through the film to the surface by condensation. Thermal gradient exists in the film and acts as a resistance to heat transfer.

In *drop–wise condensation*, the vapour condenses into small droplets of various sizes which may grow in size or coalesce with neighbouring droplets and eventually roll off the surface under the influence of gravity. During drop–wise condensation, a large portion of the area of condensing surface remain directly exposed to vapour, therefore, rates of heat transfer are around five to ten times greater than film–wise condensation. Due to these, high heat transfer rates drop–wise condensation is preferred over film–wise condensation but drop–wise condensation is very difficult to achieve and maintain for prolonged period of time. Some additives can be added to favour dropwise condensation e.g. oleic acid, but is not possible commercially. Therefore, in industrial equipments film–wise condensation occurs. The film generally shows laminar or turbulent flow. The heat transfer is naturally greater when it is in turbulent flow.

If the condensing vapour contains some non-condensable gases like air, the heat transfer coefficient is reduced significantly. Presence of few percent by volume of air in the steam reduces heat transfer by around 50%. This is due to the fact that on condensation of vapour, the non-condensable gas is left at the surface. These non-condensable gases near the surface act as a thermal resistance to the condensation process. Therefore, in heat exchange equipments like evaporators, the vent valve is provided to remove non-condensable gases.

Thus, presence of condensate and non-condensable gases near the heat transfer area decrease the rate of heat transfer. Therefore, condensate and non-condensable gases should be removed as early as possible from the heat exchanger, it is discussed in details in heat exchangers.

4.10 Heat Exchangers

Heat exchangers are the devices used for exchange of heat between two fluids that are at different temperatures. Heat exchangers are classified on the type of fluid flow arrangement and on method of heat transfer.

On the basis of fluid flow or the relative direction of the hot and cold fluids, their types are:

(i)   Parallel flow Heat Exchanger,

(ii)   Counter flow Heat Exchanger, and

(iii)   Cross flow Heat Exchanger.

In the parallel flow heat exchanger [Fig. 4.6 (a)], the fluid streams enter at one end, flow through in the same direction and leave at the other end. In counter flow type [Fig. 4.6 (b)], the fluids move in parallel but in opposite directions. In a cross-flow type, one fluid moves through the heat exchanger at right angles to the flow path of the other fluid [Fig. 4.6 (c)].

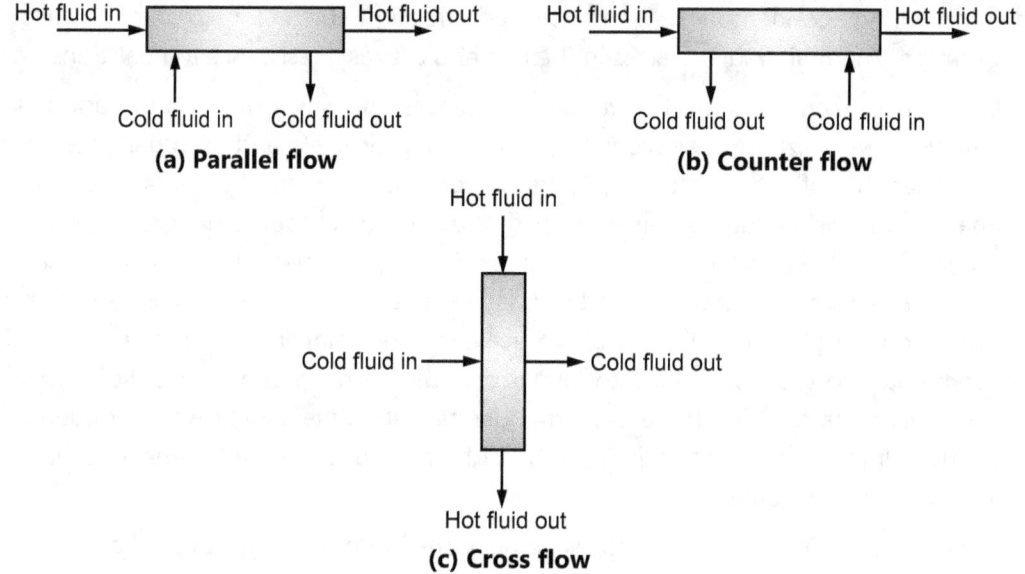

(a) Parallel flow   (b) Counter flow

(c) Cross flow

Fig. 4.6: Fluid flow arrangement in heat exchangers

4.10.1 Heat Transfer in Heat Exchangers

If flow rates and inlet and outlet temperatures are maintained same for all the three types, then heat transfer area required for these types are significantly different. A parallel flow heat exchanger requires maximum heat transfer area, a counter-flow heat exchanger requires the minimum area whereas, a cross-flow heat exchanger requires an area between two extremes. Therefore, counter flow arrangements are preferred over parallel flow type.

In the parallel flow as well as in the counter flow, the rate of heat transfer is given as:

$$Q = U A \Delta T_m$$

                                                             ... (4.33)

where, U = Overall heat transfer coefficient

A = The area of heat transfer

and ΔT_m = The mean temperature difference across the heat exchanger

Mean temperature difference is used because the temperature difference ΔT between the hot and cold fluids varies with position in the heat exchanger. Fig. 4.7 shows the change in temperature drop with distance in parallel flow and counter flow.

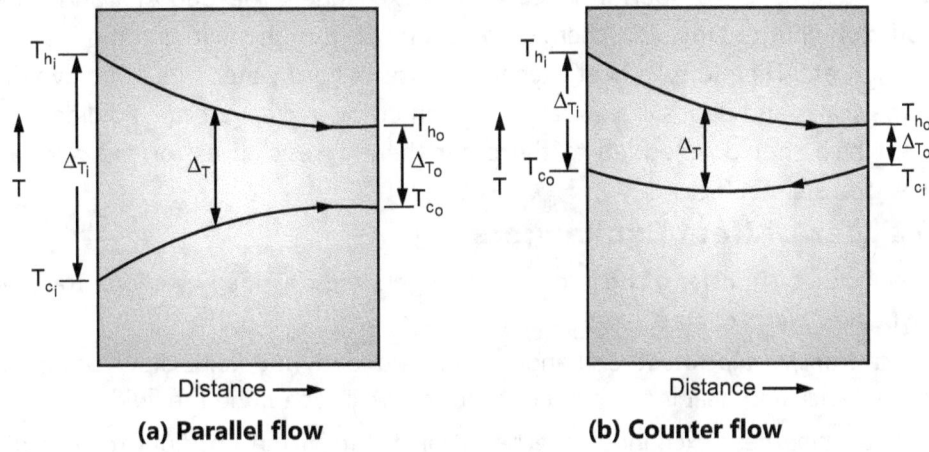

(a) Parallel flow   (b) Counter flow

Fig. 4.7: Temperature drop changes in heat exchangers

In the above Fig. 4.7.

T_{hi} = Temperature of hot fluid at inlet

T_{ho} = Temperature of hot fluid at outlet

T_{ci} = Temperature of cold fluid at inlet

T_{co} = Temperature of cold fluid at outlet

Mean temperature drop for these heat exchangers is calculated by Logarithmic Mean Temperature Difference (LMTD) method of analysis. The ΔT_m in both cases are given below:

For Parallel Flow:

$$\Delta T_m = \frac{\Delta T_i - \Delta T_o}{\ln\left(\Delta T_i / \Delta T_o\right)} \qquad \dots (4.34)$$

where, $\Delta T_i = T_{hi} - T_{ci}$

$\Delta T_{oc} = T_{ho} - T_{co}$

For Counter Flow:

$$\Delta T_m = \frac{\Delta T_i - \Delta T_o}{\ln\left(\Delta T_i / \Delta T_o\right)} \qquad \dots (4.35)$$

Although equation is same as that for parallel flow, values of ΔT_i and ΔT_o are different. For counter flow,

$$\Delta T_i = T_{hi} - T_{co}$$
$$\Delta T_o = T_{ho} - T_{ci}$$

4.10.2 Scaling

Many times, the surfaces of the heat exchanger get coated with the deposits and scales which cause decline in the performance of the exchanger. The deposits and scales are formed due to impurities in fluids, chemical reaction between the fluid and the wall material, rust formation etc. Therefore, in heat exchangers use of hard water should be avoided. The effect of the scales and deposits is usually represented by a *fouling factor*. Fouling factor is a resistance, which should be added to the other thermal resistances for the calculation of overall heat transfer coefficient.

4.10.3 Types of Heat Exchangers

On the basis of transfer of heat, heat exchangers are classified as: direct transfer type, storage type and direct contact type.

In *direct transfer type* heat exchanger, the cold and hot fluids flow simultaneously through the device and heat is transferred through a wall separating the fluids.

In *storage type* heat exchanger, the heat transfer from the hot fluid to the cold fluid occurs through a coupling medium in the form of a porous solid matrix. The hot and cold fluid, flow alternately through the matrix, the hot fluid storing heat in it and cold fluid extracting from it. It is not commonly used in pharmaceutical industry.

A *direct contact type* of heat exchanger is one in which the two fluids are not separated e.g. for heat transfer between gas and liquid, gas is bubbled through the liquid or liquid is sprayed in the gas. This type will be discussed in airconditioning chapter.

Direct transfer type heat exchangers are widely used. The two important types are:

(i)   Tubular Heat Exchangers and

(ii) Plate Heat Exchanger.

Tubular Heat Exchangers:

Tubular heat exchanger consists of circular tubes, one fluid flows inside the tube and the other on the outside. The heat transfer takes place across the wall of the tube.

Tubular heat exchangers are further classified as:

(i)   Concentric tube or double pipe

(ii) Shell and tube.

In *concentric tube heat exchanger* [Fig. 4.8 (a)], one fluid flows through the inner tube, while the other flows through the annular space between the two tubes. The heat transfer takes place across the wall of the inner tube. Simultaneous flow of two fluids occurs in the heat exchanger. There are no moving parts.

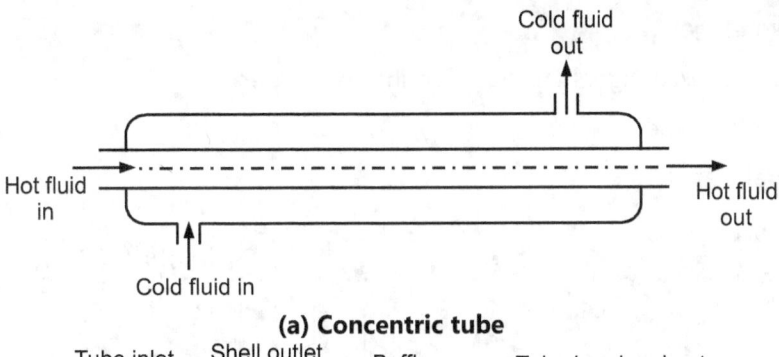

(a) Concentric tube

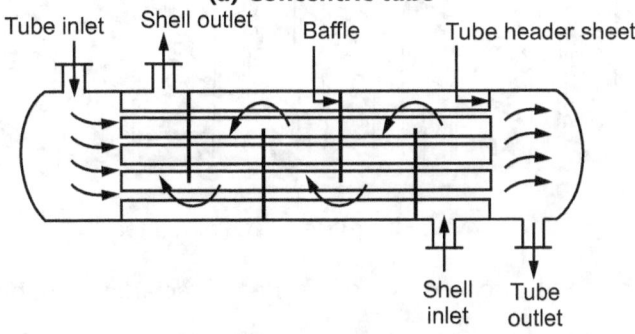

(b) Shell and Tube

Fig. 4.8: Tubular heat exchangers

A *shell and tube heat exchanger* consists of a bundle of round tubes packed together inside a cylindrical shell. One fluid flows inside the tubes, called as tube fluid and the other on the outside called shell fluid. Baffles may be provided on the shell side to prevent stagnation of the shell side fluid and promote better heat transfer.

The shell tube heat exchanger offers many advantages:

(i)   It can be designed over a wide range of capacity.

(ii)   The tubes are replaceable and can be cleaned easily.

(iii)   High heat transfer area is available per unit volume of the exchanger between 100 to 500 m²/m³.

It can be modified to Double pass arrangement as shown in Fig. 4.9.

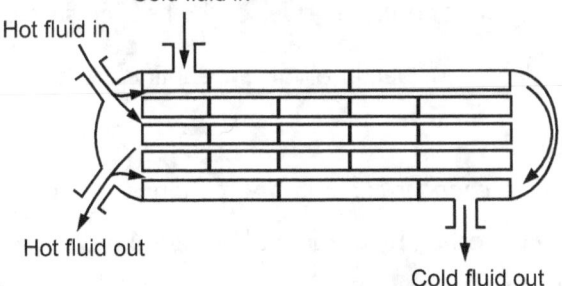

Fig. 4.9: Double pass heat exchanger

This modification increases overall effectiveness of the heat exchanger.

Plate Heat Exchangers:

The plate heat exchangers are classified into two types:

(i) Flat plate type

(ii) Spiral plate type.

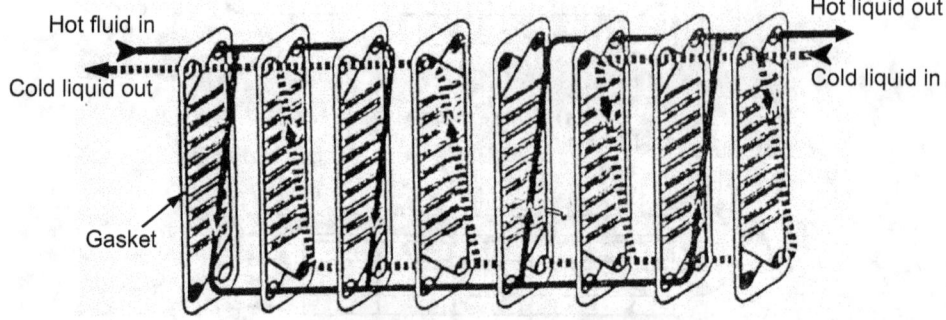

Fig. 4.10: Flat plate heat exchanger

The *flat plate heat exchanger* consists of a series of rectangular thin gauge metal plates which are clamped together to form narrow parallel plate channels. Grooves are provided along the periphery of the plates so as to adjust the gasket. Each plate has holes at the corners for the flow of fluid. The plates are arranged in parallel with each other in groups known as 'passes'. The number of plates in each pass depend upon the volumes of liquids to be handled. The flow pattern which may occur in flat plate exchanger is shown in Fig. 4.10.

Advantages of flat plate exchanger:

(i) The corrugations on the surface of the plate increases rigidity of plate, at the same time creates turbulence in fluid flow which helps in better heat transfer.

(ii) The heat transfer area per unit volume is around 100 to 200 m^2/m^3.

(iii) Mechanical cleaning of both the sides of the heating surfaces is possible.

(iv) It gives high degree of bacteriological cleanliness which is desirable in pharma-ceutical industry.

The *spiral plate heat exchanger* consists of a continuous sheet of metal formed into a double spiral, one within the other, by winding on a special type of mandrel. This spiral body is closed at both ends by covers when the unit is in operation (Fig. 4.11).

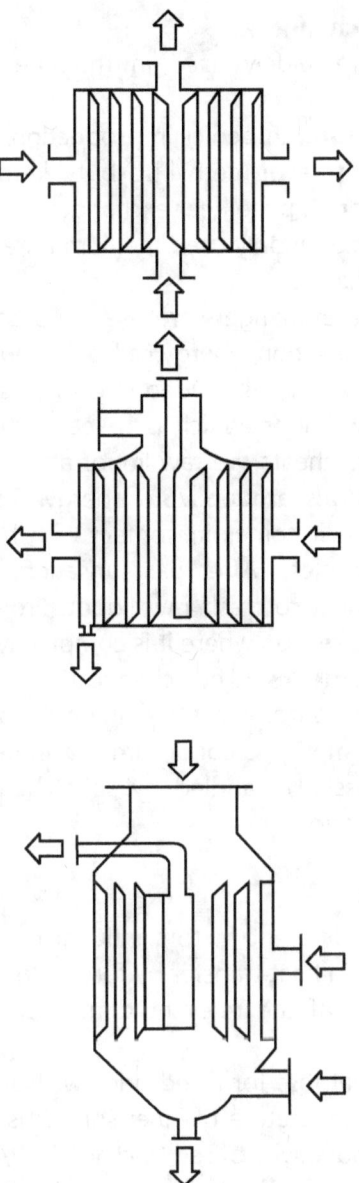

Fig. 4.11: Spiral plate heat exchanger

Advantages of Spiral Type Heat Exchanger:

(i)   It can be used for liquid-liquid as well as vapour-liquid heat transfer (flat plate is suitable only for liquid-liquid heat transfer).

(ii)   During liquid-liquid heat transfer, complete counter-current flow pattern is maintained. Thus, high heat transfer coefficients are maintained.

(iii)   The spiral can be removed for cleaning, hence we get access to both sides of the heat transfer surface.

Applications of Plate Heat Exchangers:

Plate heat exchangers are widely used in the fine chemical, pharmaceutical and cosmetic industries.

(i) **Antibiotic Manufacture:** In penicillin production, drug is extracted with solvents like amyl or butyl acetate, or methyl iso-butyl ketone. The solvent is recovered by passing the feed through plate heat exchanger.

Corn steep liquor, a commonly used medium for antibiotic production is sterilised using plate heat exchanger.

(ii) **Pasteurisation:** Plate exchangers are used in pasteurisation of gelatin liquors. In the process of pasteurisation, energy can be saved by manipulation of flow of the liquor and water. Exchanger is divided into three sections. In first section, there is contact between raw liquor (which is to be pasteurised) and a hot pasteurised liquor. This contact preheats the raw liquor and cools the pasteurised liquor to a great extent. This saves around 75% energy. The preheated liquor passes to second section where it comes in contact with hot water and remains there till pasteurisation is complete. After pasteurisation, this hot liquor passes to first section to transfer heat to fresh raw liquor. From first section this pasteurised liquor passes to third section where it is completely cooled by cold water.

(iii) **Perfumes and Cosmetics:** The chemicals used in perfume and cosmetic manufacture include benzene, acetic anhydride, acetaldehyde, glycols, isopropyl alcohols, ethyl and methyl alcohol, amyl acetate, butyl acetate etc. All these chemicals are successfully handled by spiral heat exchanger for their heating, cooling and condensation.

Questions

1. Discuss in general the different factors influencing surface coefficient and overall heat transfer coefficient in heat transfer by forced convection.
2. Explain the significance of the relevant dimensionless group in heat transfer by convection.
3. Calculate the rate of heat loss for a red brick wall of length 20 m, height 10 m and thickness 0.50 m. The temperature of inner surface is 105°C and of the outer surface is 35°C. The thermal conductivity of red brick is 0.7 W/m °C.
4. Explain radiation heat transfer in detail.
5. Discuss boiling liquids process in heat transfer.
6. Explain heat exchangers in short in heat transfer.
7. Write short notes on following:
   (a) Pool boiling
   (b) Boiling inside a vertical tube
   (c) Dimensional analysis
   (d) Stefan-Boltzmann law.

■■■

CHAPTER

Evaporation

5.1 Introduction

Evaporation is the *process of removal of the liquid by vaporization below boiling point of the system*. Though, theoretically it should be carried out below boiling point, evaporation may be carried out at boiling point, with aim to increase rate of vaporization.

Evaporation is generally adopted to obtain concentrated solutions, extracts. It may be a preliminary stage for the preparation of dry extracts.

5.2 Theory

The liquid to be evaporated is subjected to heating and rate of evaporation is dependent on rate of heat transfer from the heating medium to the liquid. Generally, heating is carried out using heating fluid and rate of heat transfer is given by,

$$Q = U A \Delta t \qquad \qquad \text{... (5.1)}$$

where, Q is rate of heat transfer, A is area across which heat transfer occurs, Δt is temperature difference between heating fluid and liquid and U is overall heat transfer coefficient.

From equation (5.1), it is clear that rate of evaporation can be increased by increase in surface area, overall heat transfer coefficient and by maintaining temperature difference high.

Surface Area: The area is maintained high by use of long tubes or coiled tubes.

Overall Heat Transfer coefficient: Overall heat transfer coefficient is a measure of resistance given by metal wall and liquid films (condensed steam film and liquid side film) present on either side of the wall. The material for wall construction should have high thermal conductivity and sufficient strength, so that wall thickness can be kept minimum. The condensed liquid on the steam side should be removed immediately, as soon as it is formed. This can be achieved by use of a suitable steam trap. The resistance on the liquid side can be minimized by maintaining the liquid turbulent or continuously moving, so that boundary layer (film) thickness is maintained low. Viscosity of the liquid should also be maintained low so as to keep the rate of evaporation high.

Temperature Difference (Δt): Difference between the steam temperature and the apparent saturation temperature of vapour leaving the evaporating mixture is called as apparent temperature difference. It is the temperature difference between the temperature of the condensing steam in the steam space and the temperature of the boiling solution of the liquid-vapour interface in the evaporator body.

Thus, boiling point of liquid is the factor which mainly controls Δt. It is important to maintain the boiling point of liquid low, which rises due to material in solution and hydrostatic head.

The boiling point rise due to material in solution is the actual surface temperature of the mixture minus the temperature of the pure solvent if it exerted the same vapour pressure as the mixture. For dilute solutions boiling point of solution may be obtained by Raoult's law. *Duhring rule* was developed for determining boiling point rise due to material in concentrated solution. Duhring rule states that *the ratio of the temperatures at which two solutions exert the same vapour pressure is constant.* Therefore, a plot of the temperature of a constant concentration solution versus the temperature of a reference substance, where the reference substance and solution exert the same pressure, results in a straight line. Pure water is generally used as the reference material (Fig. 5.1). Duhring line can be drawn by knowing two vapour pressures and temperature points required for solution to boil. Thus using Raoult's law or Duhring lines boiling point of the solution may be obtained, depending on its strength.

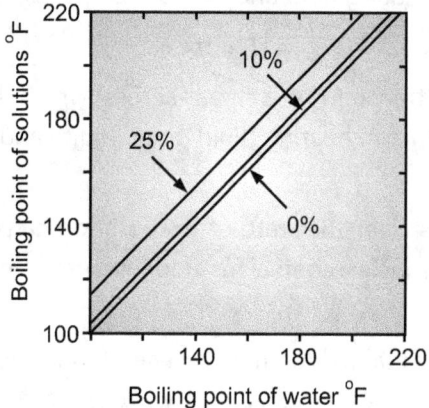

Fig. 5.1: Duhring lines of sodium chloride

In the evaporating system, the liquid which is at the bottom is subjected to the pressure of liquid column above it. Due to this, hydrostatic head boiling occurs at the bottom at higher temperature than the surface. The difference between the boiling point of the solution under pressure and solution at the evaporating surface is boiling point rise due to hydrostatic head. It can be calculated if average density and concentration of the solution is known.

Thus, hydrostatic head should be kept minimum, so as to keep high evaporation rates. Proper correction should be made for boiling point rise due to material in solution in the calculation of Δt.

Economy and Capacity of Evaporator:

Economy of an evaporator is the total mass of water vaporized in the evaporator per unit mass of steam input to the evaporator.

Capacity of an evaporator is the amount of water vaporized in the evaporator per unit time.

Different types of evaporators are as follows:

(A) Pan Evaporator

(B) Tubular Evaporators

    (a) Horizontal Tube Evaporator

    (b) Vertical Tube Evaporators

        1. Short tube (Standard) evaporator.

        2. Multiple effect evaporator

        3. Long tube evaporator.

            (i)   Climbing film evaporator

            (ii)   Falling film evaporator

            (iii)   Forced circulation evaporator

(C) Wiped Film Evaporator

(D) Centrifugal Rotary Evaporator.

5.3 Pan Evaporator

These are simple jacketed pans (Fig. 5.2). Steam is generally used as a heating medium. The pan evaporators are generally used for removal of small amount of moisture present in the extracts or semisolid ayurvedic dosage forms like avleha etc. Shallow pans are commonly used, they have capacity of around 90 – 100 litres. The agitation is manually provided to the material. The product may be removed at the end of the cycle by tilting the pan. The pans are made of copper, stainless steel, aluminium or enamelled iron. The jacket and vessel should be constructed in such a way that it should withstand the high pressure of the steam. The steam pressure is generally 40 lb/in^2 and the evaporation rates are usually 100 litres/m^2/hr.

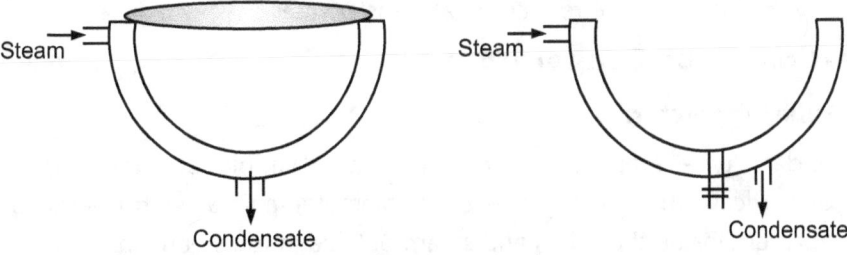

Fig. 5.2: Pan evaporator

The pans should be operated under properly ventilated conditions so that rate of evaporation can be maintained high. These evaporators are simple and low in capital cost, but they are expensive in their running costs as heat economy is poor.

5.4 Tubular Evaporators

5.4.1 Horizontal Tube Evaporator

Horizontal tube evaporator consists of four to six horizontal tubes mounted in concentric manner. The butt ends of the tubes may be connected in such a way that it forms a hairpin like structure (Fig. 5.3). It is available in two models i.e. heating medium inside and outside the tubes. The liquid enters the tube at bottom and passes upwards and steam enters the top, so as to maintain counter-current contact. Baffles may be provided so as to increase heat transfer coefficient. The tubes are made up of stainless steel. It has been used to concentrate extracts e.g. cascara extract.

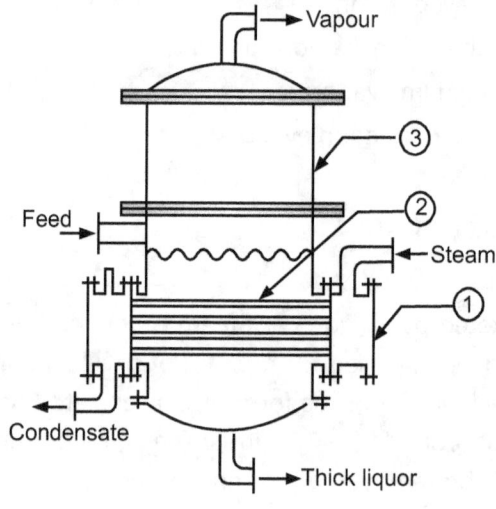

1 - Steam chest   2 - Tube   3 - Evaporator body

Fig. 5.3: Horizontal tube evaporator

Liquid circulation is poor in this type of evaporator. Fouling i.e. build up of semisolid layer on the evaporating surface reduces heat transfer rates.

5.4.2 Vertical Tube Evaporators

1. Short Tube Evaporator:

The Standard type evaporator (Fig. 5.4) is an example of short tube evaporator. It consists of vertical tubes having 5 – 8 cm diameter and a central large downcomer. The liquid is present inside the tubes and steam outside in the steam space of the calendria. The length to diameter ratio of the tubes is of the order of 15 : 1. The liquid boils inside.

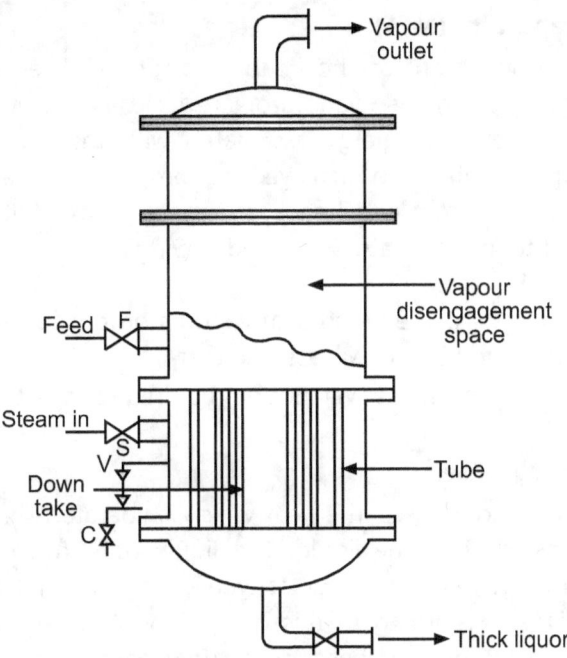

Fig. 5.4: Calendria type evaporator

There are four important controls in the evaporator:

(i)   Feed control is provided to control the feed level. The control is achieved through feed valve (F).

(ii)   A vent valve (V), is provided to remove any residual air in the steam space of the evaporator.

(iii)   Steam valve (S) is provided to control the steam input to the steam space. As soon as the steam space gets saturated with steam, the valve gets closed.

(iv)   A condensate valve (C), is provided so as to remove the condensate as soon as it is formed so as to maintain the heat transfer rates high.

The feed enters the evaporator. The tubes are submerged in the liquid where liquid is heated by steam. Boiling of liquid takes place and the vapours are separated. The liquid at the bottom is subjected to hydrostatic head of the liquid above it, hence its boiling point may not be reached. This may cause the liquid to leave the chamber without complete evaporation i.e. this liquid may "short-circuit".

As the high liquid levels are required to be maintained, hydrostatic head is a critical variable in this evaporator. Slight increase in the liquid level in the chamber, may cause significant rise in boiling point of liquid at the bottom and capacity of evaporator may decrease.

2. Multiple Effect Evaporator (MEE):

Principle: It is an arrangement of short tube evaporator to achieve economy. In this arrangement, vapours formed in the evaporator are used as the heating medium for the next evaporator. In this way, the energy associated with the vapours produced during evaporation is used many times to achieve economy. Each evaporator used in this arrangement are termed as effect and hence arrangement as Multiple Effect Evaporator (MEE). Therefore, a short tube evaporator is termed as Single Effect Evaporator (SEE).

Economy of MEE and SEE:

Economy of an evaporator is the amount of vapours produced per unit steam input. To compare economy of MEE and SEE, we will assume that

(a) Feed is at boiling point i.e. heat will not be required to raise the temperature of feed and

(b) Loss of heat is negligible.

Therefore, when steam condenses, the heat which is liberated i.e. heat of condensation will be completely transferred to the liquid. The liquid does not need heat, to raise its temperature, hence all energy is utilized for conversion of liquid into vapours i.e. as latent heat of vaporization (LHV). According to this discussion, all energy supplied if utilized as LHV, then, heat liberated during condensation of unit mass of vapours will vaporize unit mass of liquid. Therefore,

$$\text{Economy of SEE} = \frac{\text{Mass of vapours produced}}{\text{Mass of steam used}}$$

$$= \frac{1}{1} = 1 \qquad \qquad \text{... (5.2)}$$

In MEE, the unit mass of vapours produced in first effect will produce unit mass in the second effect and this continues. Therefore, if N number of effects are used, mass of vapours produced will be N kg and economy becomes

$$\text{Economy of MEE} = \frac{N \text{ kg of vapours produced}}{1 \text{ kg of steam input}} = \frac{N}{1} = N \qquad \text{... (5.3)}$$

Therefore, economy of MEE is N times SEE.

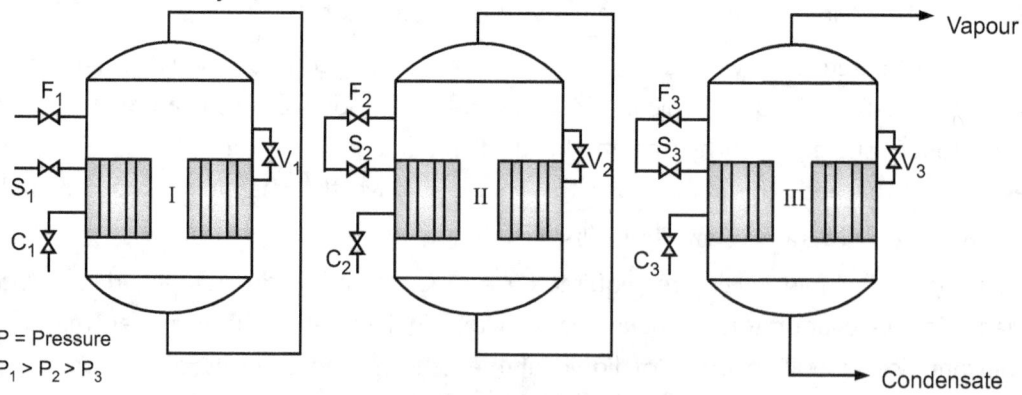

P = Pressure
$P_1 > P_2 > P_3$

Fig. 5.5: Multiple effect evaporator

Working: Consider an evaporator containing three effects (Fig. 5.5). The three effects denoted by I, II and III are connected to each other, where, F denotes feed valve, V denotes vent valve, S denotes steam valve and C denotes condensate valve. Subscripts 1, 2 and 3 correspond to the effect number I, II and III respectively.

Feed is introduced in all three effects. Steam enters the first effect and residual air is removed through vent valve V_1. The steam condenses on the outer surface of the tube; liquid inside the tube will be heated to its boiling point and vapours are formed. The vapours from effect I, pass to the steam space of the effect II. These vapours remove the residual air and vent value V_2 gets closed. Heat transfer takes place between the condensate film and liquid in II effect. Rate of heat transfer is high at initial stages, but it decreases slowly as the temperature of liquid in the tube rises causing decrease in temperature difference between vapour and liquid. As rate of heat transfer decreases, rate of utilization or condensation of vapours decreases. The rate at which vapours are utilised in effect II is less than rate at which they are produced in effect I. Therefore, the vapours get accumulated in the vapour space of effect I. Due to pressure of these accumulated vapours, boiling point of liquid in effect I is elevated.

Similar compression of vapours will occur in the effect II as they are not utilized as fast in the effect III. Due to this vapour accumulation, the temperature and pressure in three effects are different. P_1, P_2, P_3 and t_1, t_2, t_3 are pressure and temperature in effects I, II and III respectively. $P_1 > P_2 > P_3$ and $t_1 > t_2 > t_3$. The concentrate of previous effect acts as feed for next effect.

Capacity of MEE and SEE:

Capacity i.e. mass of vapours produced per unit time, is dependent on the rate of heat transfer given by UA Δt. Consider a SEE, then capacity is given by UA Δt, where U is overall heat transfer coefficient, A is area of heat transfer and Δt is difference in temperature of steam and liquid. For MEE consider that A_1, A_2 and A_3 be the areas of three effects I, II and III respectively. Δt_1, Δt_2 and Δt_3 be the temperature difference and U_1, U_2 and U_3 are overall heat transfer coefficient. Rate of heat transfer q_1, q_2 and q_3 will be given as:

In   Effect I: $q_1 = U_1 A_1 \Delta t_1$

       Effect II: $q_2 = U_2 A_2 \Delta t_2$

       Effect III: $q_3 = U_3 A_3 \Delta t_3$

Therefore, total heat transferred in three effects will be:

$$q = q_1 + q_2 + q_3$$
$$= U_1 A_1 \Delta t_1 + U_2 A_2 \Delta t_2 + U_3 A_3 \Delta t_3$$

If all effects have same area i.e. $A_1 = A_2 = A_3 = A$ and if we consider average overall heat transfer coefficient U_{av}. then,

$$q = U_{av} A (\Delta t_1 + \Delta t_2 + \Delta t_3)$$

Now if total temperature difference (i.e. temperature of steam entering the effect I and vapour leaving effect III) Δt is same as in SEE, then equation becomes,

$$q = U_{av} A \Delta t$$

same as that for SEE. According to this capacity of MEE is equal to SEE.

The capacity of MEE will be equal to SEE, when apparent temperature difference is considered. The apparent temperature difference Δt, for single effect is equal to multiple effect.

But net temperature difference (i.e. temperature difference between the temperature of condensed film in steam space and temperature of boiling liquid) ; in MEE is less than SEE. It is because the vapours are produced under pressure, and condense in the steam space of next effect at lower pressure. Hence, the temperature of condensed film is lower than that of the vapours. For example, if vapours are produced in effect I at 200°C, these condense in the steam space of effect II at 170°C where pressure is lower. Therefore the net Δt will be less than apparent Δt by 30°C. Such loss of Δt occurs in each effect in multiple effect, hence capacity of MEE is less than SEE.

Methods of Feeding: In MEE vapours always pass from first to third effect. The feed may be fed by different methods: (Fig. 5.6).

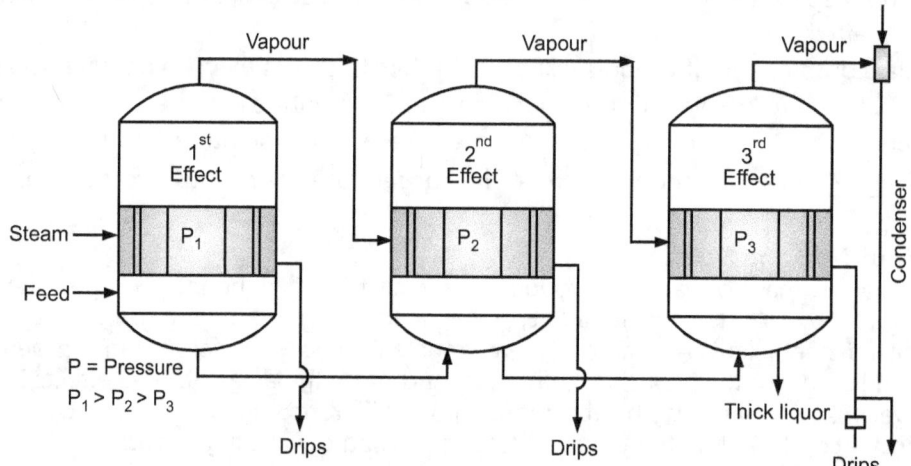

(a) Forward feed arrangement for feeding multiple effect evaporator system

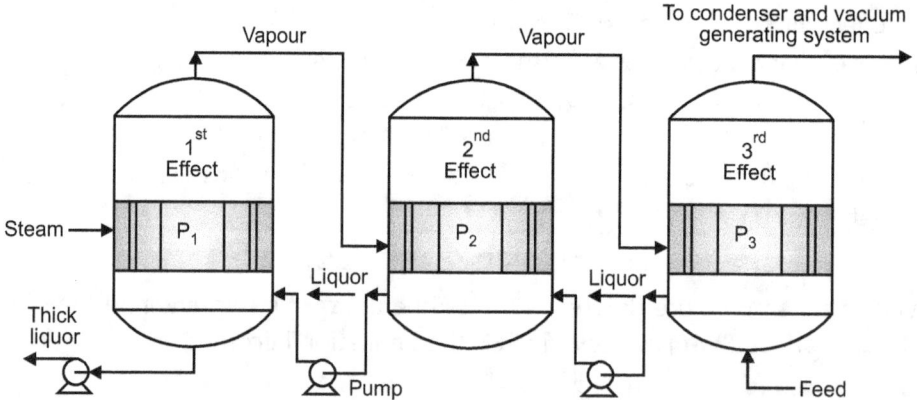

(b) Backward feed arrangement for feeding multiple effect evaporation system

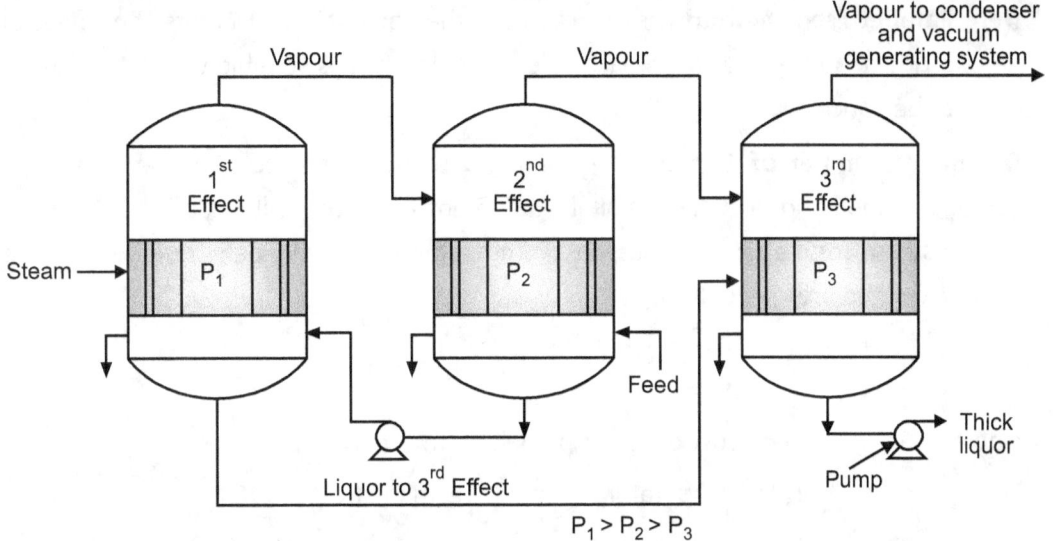

(c) Mixed feed arrangement for feeding multiple-effect evaporator system

Fig. 5.6

(i)   **Forward feed method:** In forward feed, the feed moves from effect I to II and II to III. The advantage of this method is, feed moves from high pressure to low pressure chambers, therefore, pumping is not needed. The product is obtained at lowest temperature (t_3). [Fig. 5.6 (a)].

Forward feed method is not suitable for cold feed because the steam input in the first effect is used mainly for increasing the temperature of feed and amount of vapours produced in I effect is low. The lower amount vapours in the first effect results in lower vapour production in subsequent effects and hampers economy. The method is suitable for scale forming liquid as concentrated product is subjected to low temperature.

(ii)   **Backward feed method:** In backward feed, the feed enters the last effect and moves from III $\rightarrow$ II $\rightarrow$ I. As the liquid moves from low pressure to high pressure pumping is required. The product is obtained at highest temperature (t_1) [Fig. 5.6 (b)].

It is suitable for cold feed, as the heat used for increasing the temperature in III effect, is already used for heating for N – 1 times. This will give more economy.

The method is suitable for viscous product as highly concentrated product is at highest temperature, hence lower viscosity. At lower viscosity, heat transfer and in turn capacity will be maintained high.

(iii)   **Mixed feed method:** The feed enters in the intermediate effect, moves forward and then to the initial effects i.e. Feed $\rightarrow$ II $\rightarrow$ III $\rightarrow$ I. It is advantageous as liquid moves from high pressure to low pressure II to III and then product is obtained at high temperature and low viscosity. [Fig. 5.6 (c)].

(iv) **Parallel feed method:** In this method, the separate feed enters the effect and product is taken out from each effect. The method is suitable where the feed has to be concentrated slightly.

Optimum Number of Effects: The optimized number of effects can be obtained by analyzing the operating cost and capital equipment costs of multiple effects. It involves changes in steam cost, labour charges, cost of equipment with change in number of effects. It can be calculated using equation

$$N_{opt} = \left\{ \frac{B}{C} \left[\frac{U\,(T_s - T_N)}{\lambda} \right]^m \left[(1 - f_N)\, W_o \right]^{1-m} \right\}^{1/2}$$

where,   B = Cost of steam per kilogram

T_s = Temperature of input steam in effect I

T_N = Temperature of vapours generated in N^{th} effect

λ = Latent heat of vaporization of water

W_o = Amount of water in feed solution

f_N = Fraction of water remaining in concentrate leaving N^{th} effect

C & m = Constants

3. Long Tube Evaporators:

These are the evaporators which use tall and slender tubes. The tubes having a length to diameter ratio of the order of 100 : 1, pass vertically inside the steam chest.

(i) Climbing Film Evaporators:

The long tubes with diameter of about 2.5 to 5 cm and height 6 – 7 m are used (Fig. 5.7). The feed enters at the bottom of the evaporator. Steam enters into the steam space through the inlet at the top. The height of liquid column is maintained low. In the tube, the liquid at the bottom is cold and subjected to pressure of column above it. As it moves in the upward direction temperature increases and pressure decreases. Convection occurs near bottom, as the liquid progresses upwards boiling occurs. The phases in the liquid boiling inside tube i.e. bubbly region, plug or slug flow, annular flow and mist flow are explained in chapter Heat Transfer (Fig. 4.5). The mist flow emerging at the top of the tube is then passed to the cyclone separator. The liquid concentrate and vapours are separated.

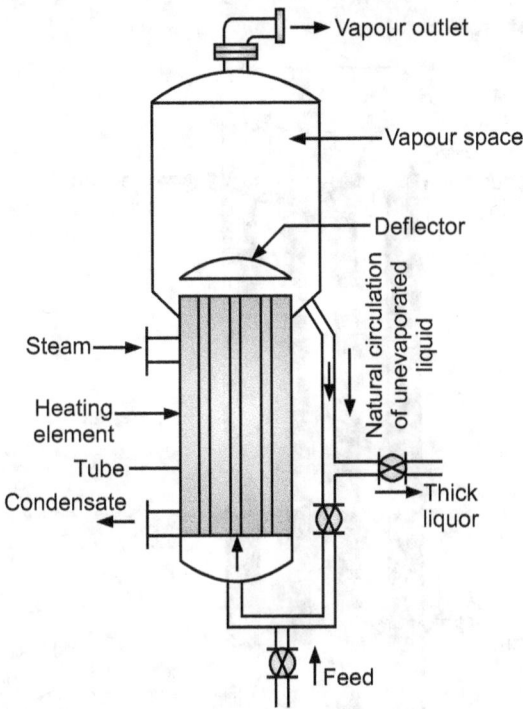

Fig. 5.7: Long tube vertical evaporator

As the film is moving in tube, high velocity vapour core propels it in the upward direction. Therefore, it is called as climbing film evaporator. The film moves at high velocity and the turbulence increases the heat transfer rates to the film. The heat transfer occurs at low temperature difference. The convection zone near the bottom where heat transfer rates are low, can be reduced by preheating the feed. The feed may be preheated using the vapours separated from the cyclone separator of the same process. This increases process economy.

Advantages:

1. High surface area is provided by the tubes causing higher heat transfer rates. Heat transfer coefficients are about five times horizontal tube evaporator.

2. Larger surface area and turbulent film keeps the residence time of the liquid very low about 5 – 10 sec. This short exposure of liquid to the high temperature make it suitable for handling of thermolabile substances, such as insulin, hormones etc.

3. It is suitable for foam forming liquids because the foam is broken when the high velocity mixture is subjected to separator action.

4. High velocity of fluid reduces scale formation and fouling inside the tubes.

Disadvantages:

1. Large head space is required.

2. It is not suitable for viscous liquids.

(ii) Falling Film Evaporator:

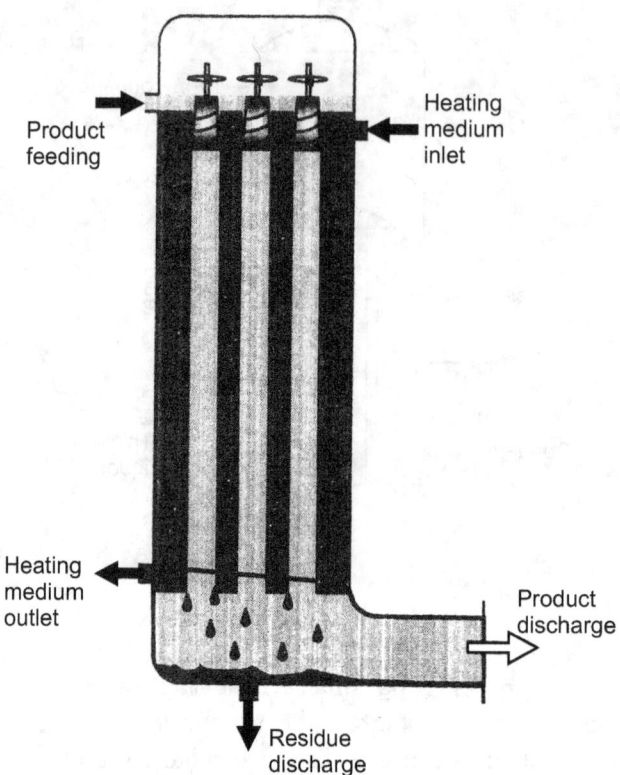

Fig. 5.8: Falling film evaporator

In falling film evaporator, the feed flows downward along the heated walls of a column (Fig. 5.8). The tube diameter is around 8 - 10 cm. These are suitable for viscous liquids, where climbing film evaporator cannot be used. The major problem with this evaporator is even distribution of the feed; therefore suitable spreading techniques may be used. Thickness of the falling film depends on properties of the solution, temperature of solution, heating medium and on their flow-rates. It can develop 'hot spots', because the laminar films created during the descent down the tube surfaces develop large temperature differences through the film. The liquid residence time is about one minute. It is suitable for separation of volatile from non-volatile materials, where the feed material is of low viscosity. There may be climbing-falling combination possible (Fig. 5.8), in which liquid moves upwards in one section and falls in the another section. Falling film evaporator is used for concentration of yeast extract, manufacture of gelatin, extracts of tea and coffee.

(iii) Forced Circulation Evaporator:

Climbing film and falling film evaporator uses natural circulation of the liquid. The low viscosity liquid flows are satisfactorily treated by natural circulation but liquids having significantly high viscosities can not be handled efficiently in the natural circulation evaporators. Therefore, long tube evaporator is modified to work under forced circulation conditions.

The forced circulation evaporator consists of two parts:

(i)   a heat exchanger and

(ii)   a vapour separation chamber.

The heat exchanger may be placed internally [Fig. 5.9 (a)] or externally [Fig. 5.9 (b)]. The liquid to be concentrated is pumped through the heat exchanger at the velocities of 2 – 6 m/s (in natural circulation it is 0.3 to1.2 m/s) where it is heated. The pressure drop and hydrostatic heat on the fluid is maintained in such a way that liquid does not boil in the tube. The superheated liquid flowing in the tubes, flashes just while entering the vapour separation chamber as static heat is reduced. The spray of liquid and vapours collide with the deflector and separation occurs. The vapours are subjected for further separation of entrained droplets if any. The concentrate is collected at the bottom.

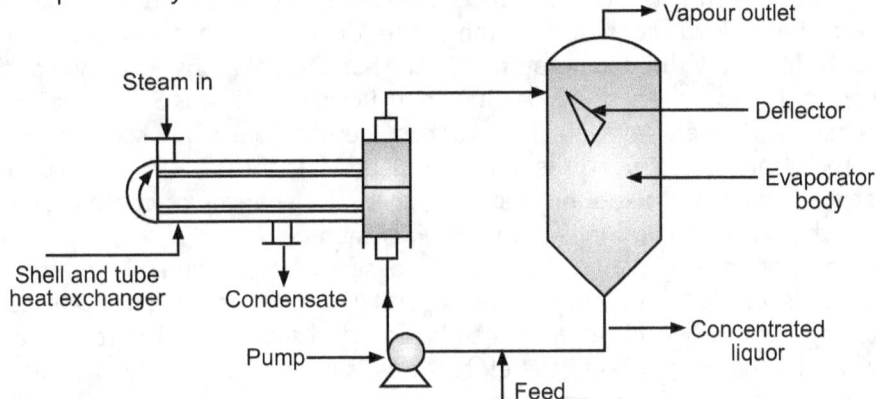

(a) Forced circulation evaporator with horizontal external heating element

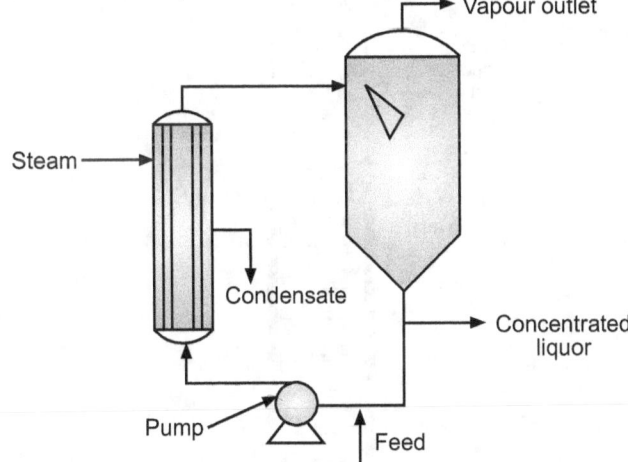

(b) Forced circulation evaporator with vertical heating element

Fig. 5.9: Forced circulation evaporator

External heating system has the following advantages over the internally heated system:

1.   Cleaning and replacement of tubes is simpler.

2.   Compact and requires less heat room.

3. Boiling of liquid can be easily suppressed just by changing the relative position of the heat exchanger, relative to the vapour space.
4. It has less chances of solids deposition.

The forced circulation evaporators are suitable for handling viscous, foam forming and thermolabile materials. The residence time of material in the evaporator is very low in the range of 1 – 3 secs. But pumping cost makes the operation expensive.

5.4.3 Wiped Film Evaporator

Wiped film evaporators (Fig. 5.10) were developed to overcome the limitations of falling film evaporator. The large temperature difference and hot spots can be reduced by use of wipers or other suitable rotary device.

As with the falling-film evaporator the feed enters onto a heated wall from the top but a fast rotating wiper element spreads it mechanically. The vapours produced flow counter currently into the upward direction into the separator. The concentrated solution is drawn off at the bottom of the evaporator. It can handle solutions with viscosities upto 3000 centipoise. The rotor speed is 200 – 500 r.p.m. Residence time is 5 – 25 sec.

The wiper blades are available in various designs such as scraper, solid wiper (Fig. 5.10). The clearance between the wall and blade is about 0.75 - 4 mm. But as there is friction between the wiper blade and the fluid, there are chances of contamination of end product with the traces of impurities from the wiper material.

Sambay evaporator (Fig. 5.10 (c)) is a special design of wiped film evaporator where the heating jacket is divided into number of separately heated segments. Due to this the temperature conditions in each segment can be adjusted separately. The rotor blades are in contact with the heating jacket, therefore, it is suitable for highly viscous materials (upto 5 pascal) and materials having tendency to form crust or coatings on the wall.

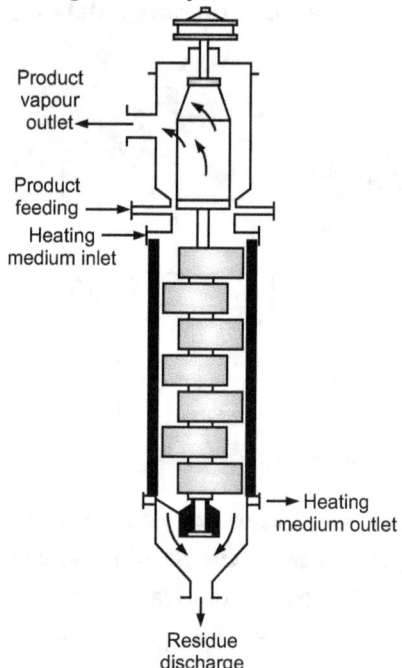

(a) The wiped-film evaporator

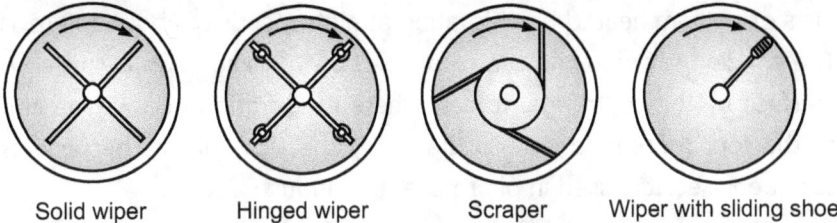

Solid wiper   Hinged wiper   Scraper   Wiper with sliding shoe

(b) Rotary wipers for thin layer vaporizers

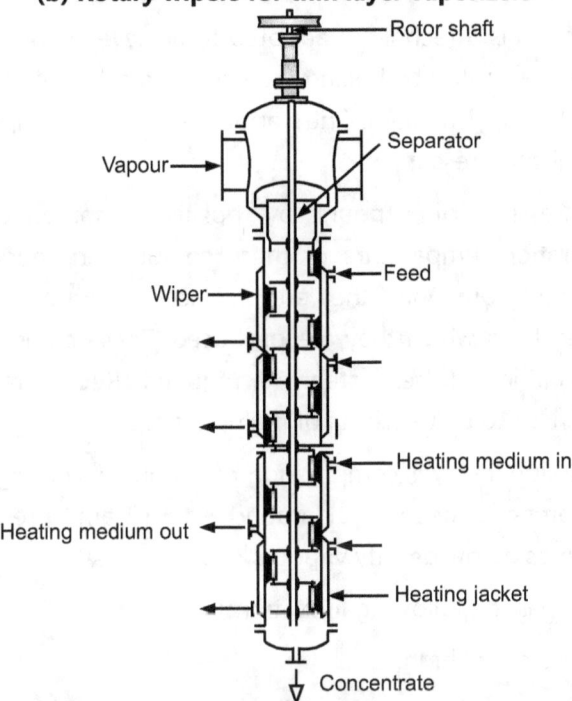

(c) Multisegmented rotary thin layer vaporizer (Sambay system)

Fig. 5.10: Wiped film evaporator

5.4.4 Centrifugal Rotory Evaporator

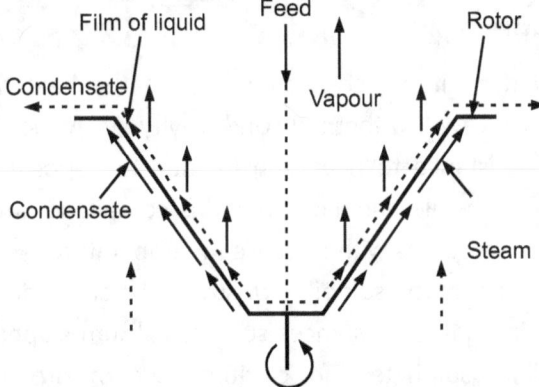

Fig. 5.11: Principle of operation of a thin layer vaporizer system

If consists of a steam heated bowl rotating at high speeds of about 400 to 1600 r.p.m. (Fig. 5.11). The solution is fed at the centre of the bowl. The solution is carried upwards on the heated surface by the centrifugal forces; where evaporation occurs. The concentrate is taken out at the top, the condensate is drawn by the side tubes. The residence time of material is about one sec. It is used in pharmaceutical industry.

5.5 Vapour Recompression

Vapour recompression is a technique adopted to achieve economy in the heat transfer processes. The vapours generated by boiling the liquid are subjected to compression so that they can be used as heating medium. The vapours can be recompressed by mechanical compressors or thermal compressors.

Mechanical compression of vapours by positive displacement or a centrifugal compressor. The saturation temperature of these compressed vapour is higher than the boiling point of the liquid from which they are produced. Therefore, these vapours may be used to heat the liquid from which they are produced. These compressed vapour may be mixed with small quantities of fresh steam if required. Recompression gives economy equivalent to that given by 10 to 15 effects of multiple effects.

Thermal recompression involves compression of vapours using high pressure steam in a jet ejector. The high pressure steam is at around 8 to 10 atm. pressure. It is suitable for handling of large volumes of low density vapours.

The recompression has the following limitations:

1. Compressor cost is very high.
2. It is useful for very low Δt operations. The cost increases with increase in Δt.
3. Cost of recompression becomes very high if liquid has very high boiling point elevation.

5.6 Scale Formation

Scales are the solid deposits which accumulate on the heat transfer surface during evaporation. The scale have very low thermal conductivity. As evaporation proceeds, there is gradual increase in the resistance to heat transfer due to deposition of scales. The scale formation problem is severe while handling solutions containing 'inverse solubility' i.e. the solutes of which solubility decreases with increase in temperature. As the liquid temperature is high near the heating surface, the solubility of such substances decreases in the localized area and scaling occurs. Inorganic substances such as calcium sulphate, calcium hydroxide, sodium carbonate, sodium sulphate and calcium salts of organic acids have scaling tendency.

The scale formation can be minimized by:

(a) Maintaining high circulation velocities so that scales does not deposit e.g. forced circulation evaporator.

(b) Manipulating the process, so that highly concentrated solution near completion of process is subjected to low temperature e.g. forward flow feeding in MEE. Periodic removal of scales should be done. The period after which operation should be stopped i.e. cycle time, so that the scales are essential to be removed can be determined by following equation:

$$\frac{1}{U^2} = a\,\theta + b$$

which shows linear increase in the resistance or reciprocal of U due to scale deposit with time (θ), a and b are constants. The operation is stopped when $\frac{1}{U}$ reaches the critical resistance value.

5.7 Evaporator Accessories

There are various devices that have to be attached with every evaporator in addition to the evaporator body. These devices are useful in many field of pharmaceutical engineering, which are as follows:

1. Condensers

2. Vacuum pump

3. Entrainment separators

4. Foam.

1. **Condensers:** If an evaporator is to operate under vacuum some devices must be used for condensing the vapours. Condenser may be classified into several groups such as:

   (a) **Surface condensers:** It is similar to tubular heater, the vapour usually outside the tube and the water inside. The heat-transfer coefficient is improved by increasing the water velocity by making them multipass. In this case the vapour is usually at a pressure below atmospheric and therefore vacuum pump must employ to remove the air. Evaporators are usually evaporating an aqueous solution hence they produce water vapour but in case of solvent other than water, practical considerations eliminate all types of contact condensers and only surface condensers can be used. If the vapour to be condensed is water vapour, the contact type of condenser is practically always used because the surface condenser is much more expensive to build

(b) Contact condensers: It consists of a vertical cylinder with shelves or baffles part way across it. In Fig. 5.12, the water rises behind the collar A, over flows the notched weir and cascades to the surfaces. Vapour is introduced near to bottom and must pass up through the cascades of water until condensed, so that finally, non-condensed gases saturated with water vapour at the temperature of the inlet cooling water leave from the top of the condenser for the vacuum pump. Fig 5.12 shows only a typical arrangement of trays and baffles, and there are many variants of this construction if such a condenser is set 34 ft or more above the hot well, it is barometric and if not elevated and water pump is attached to the bottom to remove hot water, it is a low-level condenser

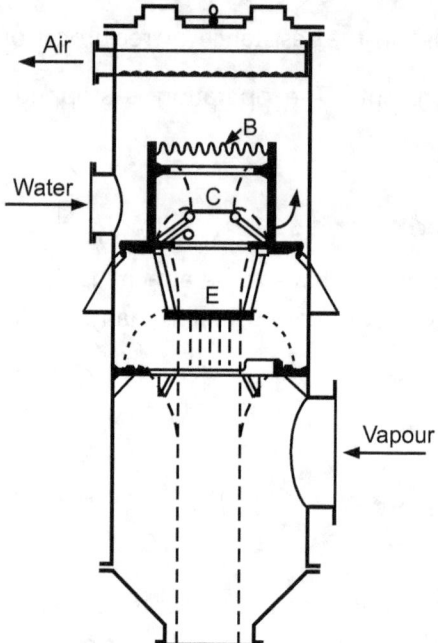

Fig. 5.12: Counter-current dry-contact condenser

The parallel-current wet condenser is shown in Fig. 5.13. Vapour to be condensed enters at the top and mixes with high-velocity jets of cold water from the nozzles. The throat below the condenser is constricted so that if sufficient water is used the velocity head at this point is high enough to reduce the static pressure to the vacuum desired, and therefore both cooling water and non-condensed gases leave together. In some cases parallel-current condensers are not operated with a constricted throat, and in such cases they must be mounted on a wet vacuum pump that removes both air and water.

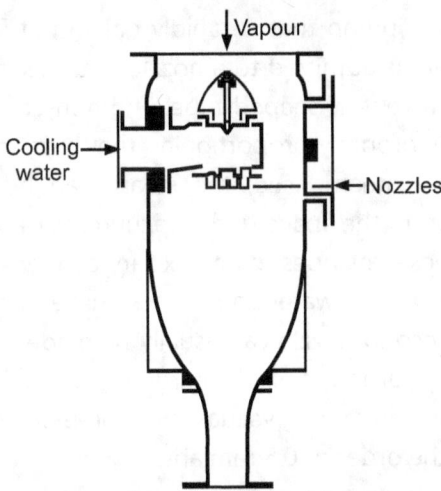

Fig. 5.13: Parallel-current wet-contact condenser

2. **Vacuum pump:** The pump used to remove hot water and non-condensed gases from a parallel-current wet condenser may be exactly similar to any ordinary reciprocating pump. The displacement is made large enough so that it will suffice for both water and air. Dry vacuum pumps used on dry counter-cement barometric condensers, or in other cases where air alone is to be removed, are constructed like ordinary air compressors except that care is taken to keep the clearances as small as possible and the valve mechanism as light as possible. Such pumps need no special description in this book.

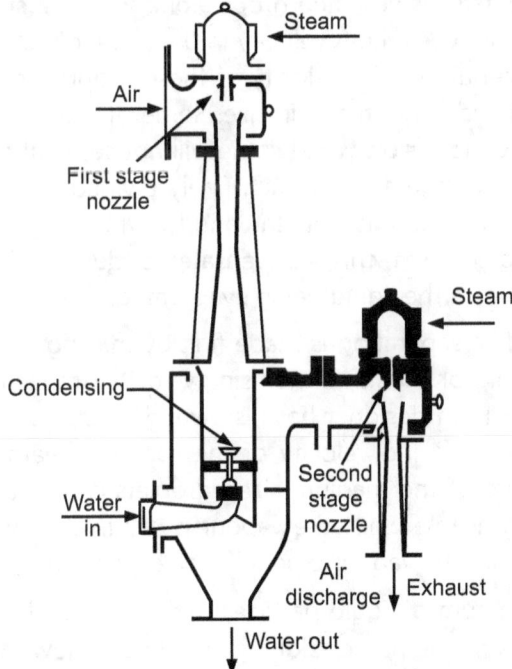

Fig. 5.14: Two-stage steam-jet ejector

One type of vacuum pump that is rapidly gaining in favor is the steam jet ejector. High-pressure steam is admitted to a nozzle. A that sends a jet of very high velocity into the throat of a venturi-shaped tube. The non-condensable gas to be removed enters as shown. By properly proportioning the throat of the venturi and the volume and velocity of the steam used, the steam can be made to entrain the non-condensed gases from the space under vacuum. For a very high vacuum the steam-air mixture from these jets goes to an auxillary condenser, where the water vapour is condensed by a jet of cold water and the residual air passes to a second nozzle . The discharge from a second nozzle can usually be made to reach atmospheric pressure and is therefore discharged at air discharge to the air. This two-stage ejector can be designed to produce quite high vacua and a three-stage ejector may be designed to produce vacua of the order of 0.5 mm abs.

Multistage ejectors are not often applied to evaporator work, but atleast the two stage are sometimes used. For a vacuum of 26 in. or over, the steam jet ejector uses less steam than a steam-driven vacuum pump and for vacua over 28.5 in. it is practically the only air-removal device possible. Another important advantage of the steam jet over reciprocating vacuum pumps is that it has no moving parts and repairs are reduced to a minimum.

3. **Entrainment separators:** When a bubble of vapour rises towards the surface of a liquid and bursts. the liquid film that forms the top of the bubble is usually projected, as it bursts, as very fine drops along with the stream of vapour. If at the same time the liquid has a high velocity in the same direction as the vapour coming from the bursting bubble, the velocity of these droplets of liquid will be increased. These drops of liquid vary greatly in size. Some of them drop back quickly into the liquid, some settle more slowly and some will not settle at all, at any vapour velocity that it is practicable to maintain. Such finely divided liquid carried along with the stream of vapour is called entrainment, and it can be the cause of (a) contamination of the condensate when this condensate is desired for other purposes and (b) serious losses from the liquid being evaporated.

A certain amount of separation is made first by making the diameter of the vapour head of the evaporator such that the rising velocity of the vapours is kept down to a reasonable figure. Each designer has his own idea as to what a reasonable figure is. Further, with a given rising velocity of the vapour stream, as the vapour space is made higher, more of the medium sized droplets can settle back into the liquid in the time that is available while the vapour is still in the evaporator. Those that are once carried out into the vapour pipe must be separated by some other method.

Due to the momentum of liquid particles, if there is sudden change in the direction of the vapour stream, the particles of liquid will not follow that change at once. It has long been customary to place battles either in the vapour space in the evaporator or in special chambers inserted in the vapour pipe in the hope that the particles of liquid would impinge on the surface of the bafle while the vapour went around it. It is the principle of all entrainment separators that if the liquid droplets can be made to impinge on a solid surface, they coalesce into a sheet and are not easily picked up again by even extremely high vapour velocities. It would also seem that if the mixture of vapour and entrained liquid were given a rotary motion, centrifugal force would tend to throw the droplets out against the side of the vessel, where they would coalesce and run down as sheels of liquid. Such an entrainment separator is shown in Fig. 5.15. The vapour is led into the entrainment separator by a tangential inlet so that it starts a whirling motion at once. The presence of a spiral vane of sheet metal emphasizes this whirling motion so that mast of the entrained Liquid is thrown out against the walk of the separator, where it runs down, to be returned to the evaporator. In the lower part of the separator the vapours turn through 180° to rise through the central vapour off take pipe, and this again projects some particles of liquid down into the bottom of the separator. Still another type or vapour separator often used in evaporators is the centrifugal separator shown in Fig. 15.16. The outlet from the evaporator body is sometimes restricted so that the vapour enters the opening A in the centre of a horizontal baffle with a relatively high velocity. Mounted above this opening is a circular cage containing spiral vanes B and closed with a cover plate on top. The vapours must escape through the spiral vanes and are thereby given a very strong whirling motion. This lends to throw out the drops of liquid against the wall C, from which they run down to be returned to the evaporator through the trap D. By means of baffles above this cage, the vapours are sent through certain other turns, and any liquid that is thrown out against the outer surface of the vapour dome runs down through trap E to he returned. Such vapour separators take up very little space in the evaporator setup, but if not carefully designed they may cause too much pressure drop.

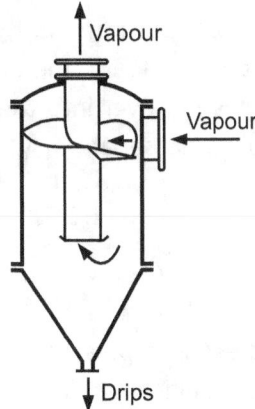

Fig. 5.15: Entrainment separator

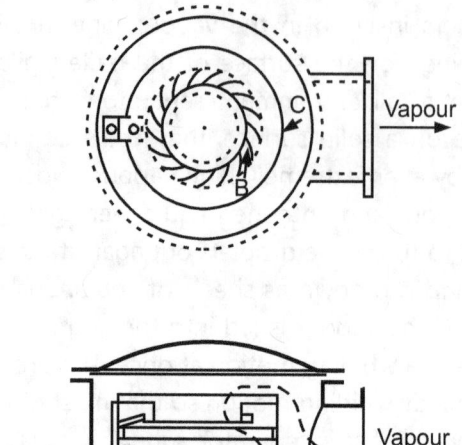

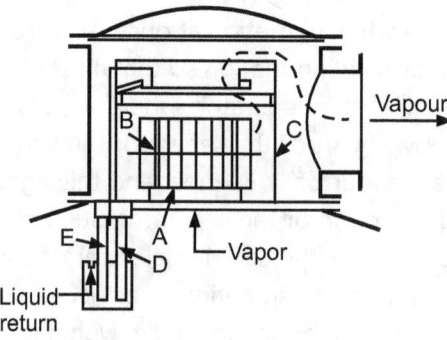

Fig. 5.16: Centrifugal separator

4. **Foam:** Entrainment separators are often called foam catchers. Foam is an entirely different phenomenon and means the formation of a stable blanket of bubbles that lies on the surface of the boiling liquid. It is familiar to everyone who has seen milk boil on the kitchen stove. The cause of it is relatively obscure, but it is known that it depends on (1) the formation at the surface of the liquid of a layer whose surface tension is different from that of the bulk of the liquid, and (2) the presence of finely divided solids or colloidal material that stabilizes the surface layer. Such factors are so intimately connected with the general nature of the liquid being handled that foam can rarely be prevented from forming by a previous treatment of the liquid. The practical methods to combat foam, therefore, amount to methods to prevent the foam from rising and passing over into the vapour pipe. If the blanket of foam ever reaches the vapour pipe, no separator will prevent its going on over into the condenser.

5.8 Removal of Condensate

Accumulation of condensate in the space for heating medium (steam) reduces heat transfer. Similarly, non-condensable gases present in the steam or entering through the leaks decrease heat transfer rate significantly. Therefore, it is necessary to remove the condensate as soon as it is formed and also the non-condensable gases like air, CO_2 and hydrogen. Steam traps are the devices used for this purpose.

5.8.1 Steam Traps

A steam trap is a simple device which opens in the presence of condensate and/or non-condensable gases and closes in the presence of steam.

The steam traps are categorised as follows:

(A)   Mechanical Traps

(B)   Thermostatic Traps

(C)   Thermodynamic Traps.

(A)   Mechanical Traps: These traps detect the presence of condensate on the basis of difference in density of steam and condensate e.g. Inverted bucket traps and float and thermostatic (F & T) traps.

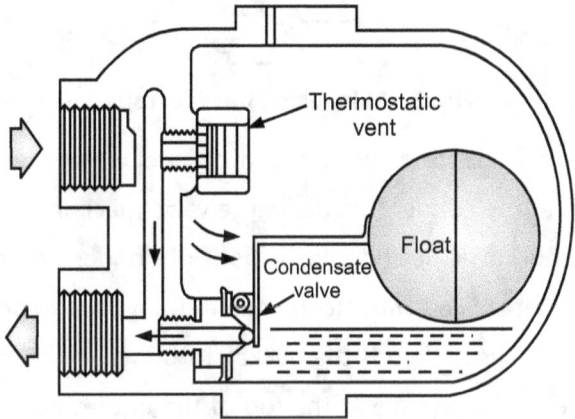

Fig. 5.17: Float and thermostatic trap

The *float and thermostatic trap* consists of a chamber, a float and a valve (Fig. 5.17).

The condensate flows into the chamber, where it raises a float. The float is directly attached to the discharge valve so that higher is the level of condensate, the more the valve opens. But the discharge valve is always submerged in condensate, so it is impossible for it to discharge non-condensable gas. Hence a thermostatically controlled valve is fitted in the vapour space above the condensate level. This valve remains closed at steam temperature and opens when the temperature in the vapour space drops below the saturation temperature of the steam. This trap discharges condensate continuously.

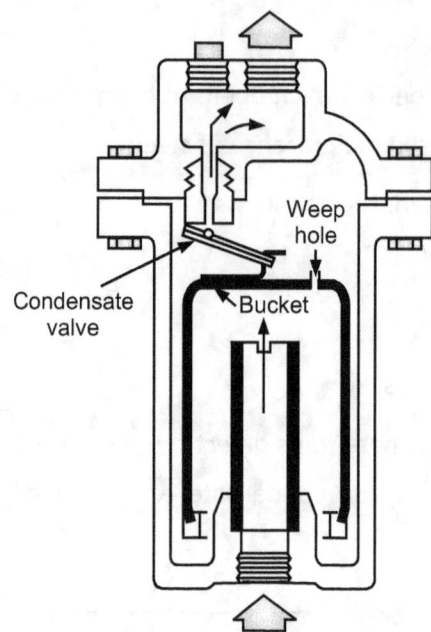

Fig. 5.18: Inverted bucket traps

Inverted bucket trap consists of an inverted cylinder or bucket open at the bottom end-connected directly to the condensate discharge valve mechanism, as shown in Fig. 5.18. The open end of the bucket is sealed with a pool of condensate at the bottom of the chamber. When the bucket is filled with steam, due to buoyancy it rises and discharge valve will get closed. When condensate floods the bucket, its buoyancy decreases and it sinks, this causes the valve to open. A weep hole at the top of the bucket provides a fixed bleed rate for removal of air and other non-condensable gases. It also provides a continuous bleed of steam trapped in the bucket. It removes condensate intermittently, one bucket at a time.

(B)   Thermostatic Traps: It operates on the principle that steam is hotter than its condensate or steam containing non-condensable gases. Thus, a thermostatic trap opens its discharge valve when temperature is lower and remains closed at high temperature.

The *balanced pressure thermostatic trap* is shown in Fig. 5.19. The trap automatically changes its opening temperature with changes in the steam pressure. The bellows is subjected to the system pressure and temperature, so the boiling point of the material in the bellows increases as the surrounding steam pressure increases. Thus, the trap is actuated by boiling liquid and the resultant expansion of a sealed liquid-filled, flexible bellows.

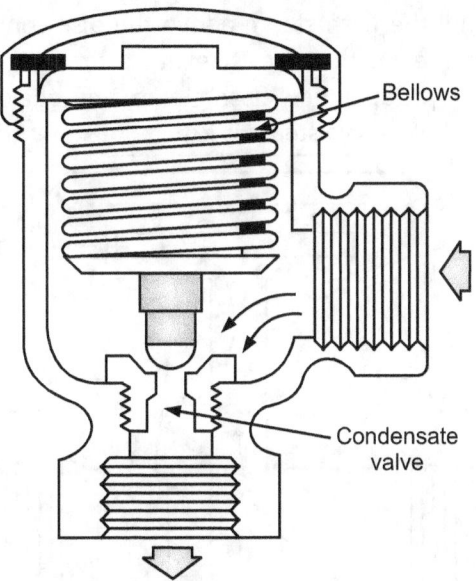

Fig. 5.19: Balanced pressure trap

Bimetallic trap consists of a bimetal plate which bends with temperature change. At the temperature of steam, bimetal plate bends and closes the discharge valve.

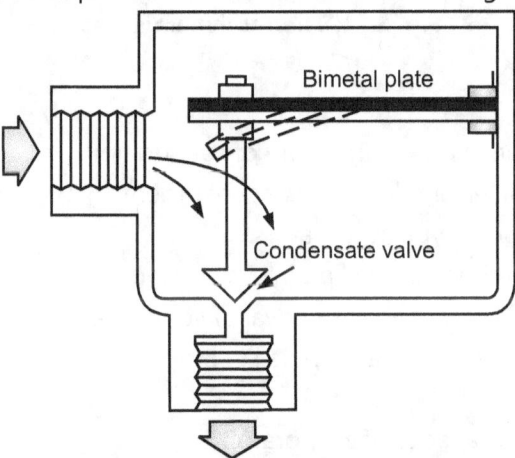

Fig. 5.20: Bimetallic trap

(C)   Thermodynamic Traps: These traps use the velocity and pressure of flash steam to open and close the discharge valve.

In a thermodynamic trap (Fig. 5.21), a flat coin-size disc lies on a flat seat and covers both inlet and discharge orifices. When cool condensate flows through the orifice, it lifts the disc, and flows over the seat to the discharge orifice. When a condensate near the steam temperature flows under the disc, this high velocity flash steam creates a low pressure area on the bottom of the disc, this low pressure between the disc and the seat, combined with a pressure increase above the disc during flow, forces the disc down onto the seat and seals the orifices. When the steam pressure exerts its upward force on the disc over inlet orifice, the disc remains closed until the flash steam above the disc condenses and loses its force. When the downward pressure on the disc is relieved, the disc lifts only long enough to discharge fresh condensate, produce new flash steam, and again force the disc back onto the seat, sealing the orifices before live steam is lost.

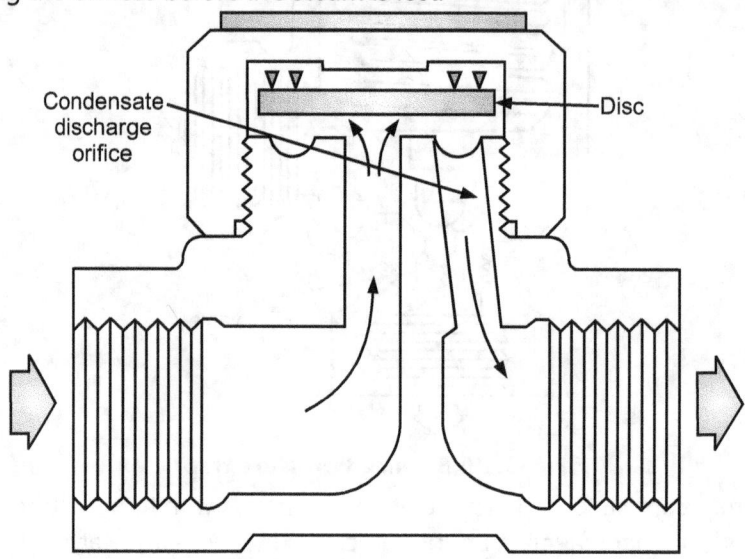

Condensate discharge orifice

Disc

Fig. 5.21: Thermodynamic trap

Questions

1. Define evaporation and explain theory of evaporation.
2. Explain factors influencing heat transfer coefficients.
3. Write in detail tubular type evaporators.
4. Explain various methods of feeding in evaporators.
5. Explain in detail devices used in removal of condensate.
6. Discuss evaporator accessories in detail in evaporation.
7. Write short notes on following:
    (a) Economy and capacity of evaporator.
    (b) Foam
    (c) Condensors
    (d) Pan evaporators
8. Explain economy and capacity of MEE and SEE.
9. Describe climbing film evaporators with diagram.
10. Explain forced circulation evaporator with diagram.
11. What is vapour recompression, explain.
12. Write short note on scale formation.

■■■

CHAPTER

Crystallization

6.1 Introduction

A crystal may be defined as a homogenous particle of solid which is formed by solidification under favourable conditions, of a chemical element or a compound, whose boundary surfaces are planes symmetrically arranged at definite angles to one another in a definite geometric form. In other words, a *crystal* is one in which the internal atomic or molecular arrangement is regular and periodic in three dimensions over intervals which are large compared with the unit of periodicity. The smallest arrangement of atoms and molecules which repeats regularly and is a true representation of crystal structure is known as 'unit cell'.

Crystal lattice is defined as a three dimensional network of imaginary lines connecting the atoms. The distance between the centre of two atoms is called as the *length of unit cell* and angle between the edges of a unit cell is called as *lattice angle*. A unit cell is shown in Fig. 6.1.

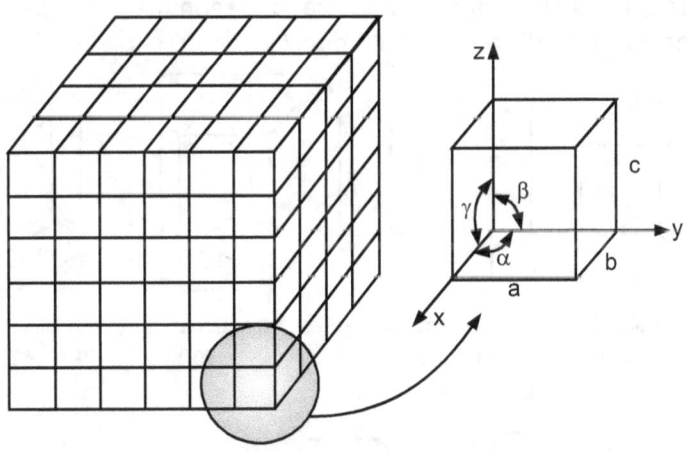

(a) Lattice structure in crystal   (b) Unit cell
Fig. 6.1: Crystal lattice and unit cell

Crystallization is a complex unit operation widely used in the industry for the production of pure solid substances. Most of the drugs are obtained in their crystalline form. Recent advances in crystallization technology have made it possible to use it as a particle design technique to change the micromeritic properties, compressibility and wettability of pharmaceutical substances. As a separation technique, crystallisation is a comparatively inexpensive process; though it involves cooling and cooling energy is costlier than heating energy. For example, in desalination of sea water, crystallization requires only $1/7^{th}$ quantity of energy as compared to distillation.

Crystallization differs from precipitation which is generally referred as fast crystallization. Precipitates are insoluble substances produced by a chemical reaction, therefore, it is an irreversible process. But the products of crystallization can be redissolved if the original conditions of temperature and solution concentrations are restored. Secondly, precipitation is initiated at very high supersaturation which results in fast nucleation and thereby large number of very fine particles may be generated. But crystallization and preci-pitation both involve supersaturation, nucleation and growth of the particles.

6.2 Crystal Form

In crystal, there is repetitive arrangement of constituent atoms in a three–dimensional network. There are only finite number of symmetrical arrangements possible for a crystal lattice, and these may be termed as crystal forms. It is described by the relationship among the crystal axes and angles between them. The various types of crystal forms are given in Table 6.1 and shown in Fig. 6.2. But in these crystal forms, the ratio between the lengths of the axes existing in a given crystal must be constant. The ability of a compound to exist in different crystal form is known as *polymorphism*. Different polymorphs have shown significant differences in their properties such as melting point, solubility rate, compressibility etc. For example, paracetamol shows two polymorphs, monoclinic and orthorhombic. The monoclinic form is stable and commercially used, is not directly compressible, whereas orthorhombic form is directly compressible.

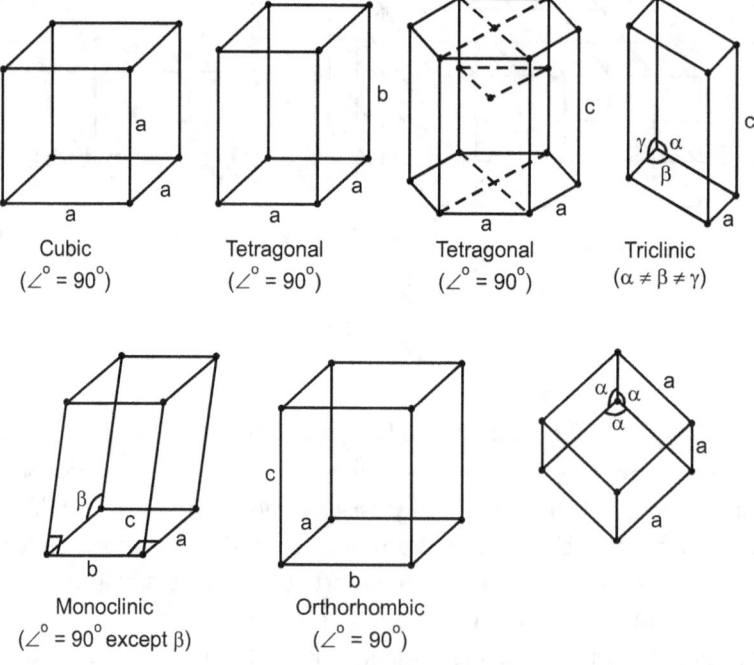

Fig. 6.2: Crystal forms

Table 6.1: Different forms of crystal

System	Description
Cubic	Three axes of identical length intersect at right angles. i.e. $a = b = c, \alpha = \beta = \gamma = 90°$
Hexagonal	Four axes lie in a horizontal plane, and they are inclined to one another at 120°. The fourth axis, c, is different in length from the others, and it is perpendicular to the plane formed by the other three. ($a = b \neq c, \alpha = \beta = 120, \gamma = 120°$)
Tetragonal	Three axes intersect at right angles. The third axis, c, is different in length with respect to a and b ($a = b \neq c, \alpha = \beta = \gamma = 90°$)
Orthorhombic	Three axes of different lengths intersect at right angles. The choice of the vertical c axis is arbitrary. ($a \neq b \neq c, \alpha = \beta = \gamma = 90°$)
Monoclinic	Three axes of unequal length intersect such that a and c lie at an oblique angle, and the b axis is perpendicular to the plane formed by the other two. $a \neq b \neq c, \alpha = \gamma = 90°, \neq \beta$.
Triclinic	Three axes of unequal length intersect at three oblique angles. $a \neq b \neq c, \alpha \neq \beta \neq \gamma \neq 90°$.

6.3 Crystal Habit

Crystal is a polyhedral solid with number of planar faces. The arrangement of these faces is termed as habit. The crystal faces are identified by Miller indices. Depending on the arrangement of faces different crystal habits are as given in table 6.2 and shown in Fig. 6.3. The crystal habit of compound may change due to changes in rate of deposition, shielding of certain faces, presence of impurities in mother liquor.

Table 6.2: Different crystal habits

Descriptor	Description
Avicular	Needle-like particle having a similar width and thickness. If the crystals are very thin, the term *fibrous* is used.
Columnar	Rod-like particle, having a width and thickness exceeding that a needle-type particle. The term *prismatic* may also be used.
Blade	Long, thin, and flat particle, which can also be referred to as being *lath-shaped*.
Plate	Flat particles of similar length and width. These may also be denoted as being *lamellar* or *micaceous*.
Tabular	Also flat particles of similar length and width, but possessing greater thickness than flakes.
Equant	Particles of similar length, width and thickness.

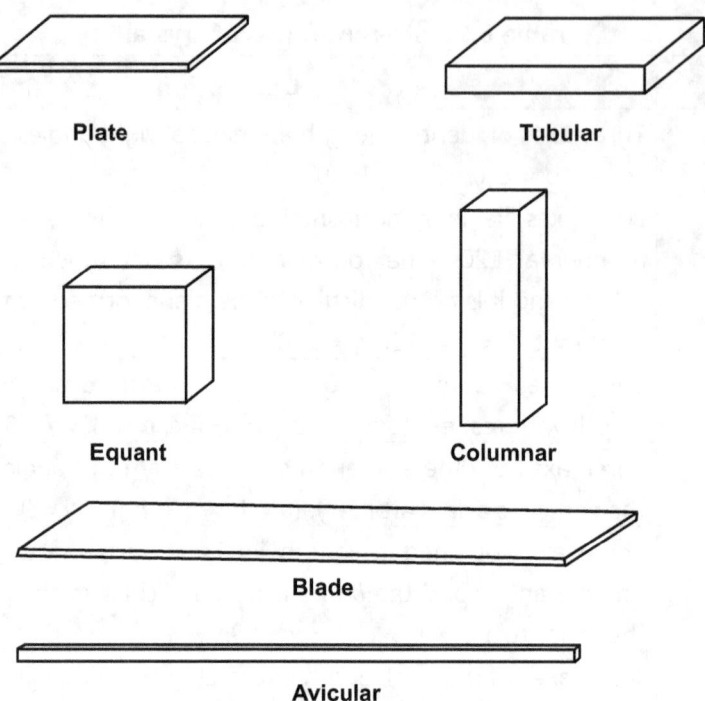

Fig. 6.3: Different crystal habits

We will discuss the crystallization phenomena as per the steps involved:

(A) Supersaturation

(B) Nucleation and

(C) Crystal growth.

6.4 Supersaturation

When a solid is brought in contact with the solvent, the attractive forces of the liquid tend to break apart the surface of the solid and disperse its ions or molecules into the liquid in the form of discrete mobile units. This process is known as *solution*. The extent to which the solute dissolves is defined as its solubility. The *solubility* is the term to denote equilibrium - limit value of solution concentration, at which point the solution becomes saturated. A saturated solution is one in which the solid is in equilibrium with its solution at a given temperature. It is a step of thermodynamic equilibrium at a specified temperature.

If we analyse the solution process on the basis of hole theory then a three steps are involved:

(i) a solute is separated into its molecules or ions

(ii) formation of hole or cavity in the solvent and

(iii) solute occupies hole in the solvent.

First two steps require input of energy and energy is released in third step. A saturated solution is one, where all cavities of the solvent are occupied by solute molecules. If the solution which is saturated is cooled or evaporated slightly then some solute molecules are thrown out of the solvent cavities as energy is reduced in first and solvent hole number reduction in the later case. Thus at this instant, the solvent holes are completely occupied by solute molecules and there are few molecules which are out of solvent hole but not out of solution. Such solution where concentration of solute is greater than the saturation concentration is known as *supersaturated solution.*

Supersaturation (S) may be expressed as:

$$S = \frac{C}{C^*}$$ ... (6.1)

where, C = Concentration of solution

C* = Equilibrium saturation concentration at given temperature.

It can also be expressed in terms of Relative Supersaturation (σ).

$$\sigma = \frac{\Delta C}{C^*} = S - 1$$ ... (6.2)

where, ΔC = Concentration driving force = $C - C^*$

6.4.1 Mier's Theory of Supersaturation

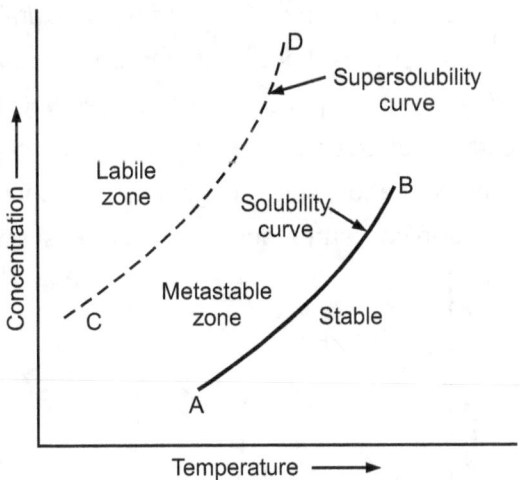

Fig. 6.4: Supersolubility curve and regions

Mier and Issac proposed a theory explaining a relationship between supersaturation and spontaneous crystallization. The theory can be explained with the help of solubility - super-solubility diagram (Fig. 6.4), where curve AB represents a typical saturation or solubility curve of an inorganic salt with normal solubility. Each point on this curve represents an equilibrium condition between a solution and solid phase. Curve CD represents a supersolubility curve, it is an imaginary region which represents temperature and concentrations at which spontaneous crystallization occurs. These two curves divide the diagram into three zones viz. stable zone, metastable zone and unstable zone.

(a) **Stable zone:** It is a well defined zone below the solubility curve where unsaturation prevails, therefore, crystallization is impossible in this zone.

(b) **Metastable zone:** It is the region between the solubility and supersolubility curve. Spontaneous nucleation occurs in this region. But crystal growth is favoured. It is a variable zone which changes as per the conditions.

(c) **Labile or Unstable zone:** It represents conditions of high relative supersaturation where only nucleation is favoured.

Mier's theory states that "*in a solution completely free from any foreign particles spontaneous nucleation occurs at supersaturation and not near the saturation concentration.*"

If a solution completely free from foreign particles represented by point E is cooled without loss of solvent, spontaneous crystallization will occur only when conditions represented by point G are reached. In some cases of very soluble substances like sodium thiosulphate further coding upto point H is necessary so as to induce crystallization. The difference between the temperature at which the solution is saturated (point F) and that at which first crystal begins to form is known as *maximum supercooling* or *maximum supersaturation concentration*. The time period which elapses between the achievement of supersaturation and appearance of crystals is referred as *induction period*. Induction period is affected by degree of supersaturation, state at agitation, presence of impurities, etc. Once crystallization occurs the solution concentration follows path as shown by GM.

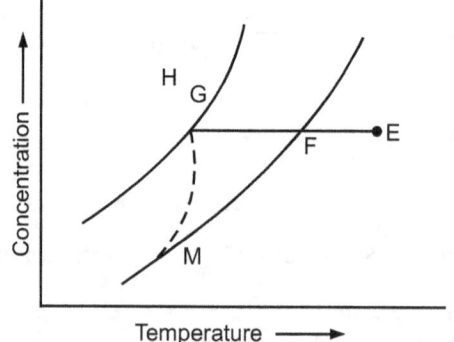

Fig. 6.5: Mier's theory of supersaturation

Mier has explained this behaviour on the basis of molecular collisions. Ions or molecules in a solution can interact to form short lived cluster which develops into embryos or sub-nuclei, many of which failed to achieve maturity. They redissolve due to their extreme unstability. When these aggregates attain the size at which cohesive lattice forces exceed the force which tend to return them into the solution, a stable or critical nucleus is formed. Statistical probability of formation of such aggregates is very low in the vicinity of solubility curve and attains significant value near the supersolubility curve.

Thus, from Mier's theory we can conclude that the crystallization must be carried out in meta stable region. A plot of rate of nucleation as a function of supersaturation (Fig. 6.6) shows that increasing supersaturation beyond the boundary of the metastable zone, rapid increase in nucleation rate takes place and large number of crystals are formed causing steep drop in supersaturation. Hence, it is difficult to attain supersaturations beyond metastable region boundary.

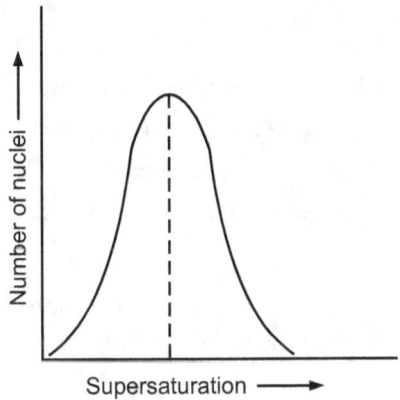

Fig. 6.6: Effect of supersaturation on nucleation

But Mier's theory has *limitations* as follows:

1. Mier has proposed the theory with the basic requirement that the solution is completely free from foreign particles. But in practice it is very difficult to occur; because many contaminants are added from the atmosphere.

2. It is reported that the large volumes of a given system nucleates spontaneously at lower degree of supersaturation than small volumes. This effect of volume has not been considered in Miers theory. This effect of volume may be attributed to greater chances of contamination as well as greater chances of collisions in larger volume.

3. Similarly, it was observed that spontaneous nucleation may occur, if the solution at lower degree of supersaturation is kept for longer period of time. This may again be attributed to higher chances of contamination and collisions with increase in time.

4. Mier has proposed that supersaturation occurs at a particular concentration. But formation of a nucleus is due to chance of collision and it cannot be specified by any particular concentration but it should be range of concentrations over which chances will be maximum. This will give the zone of supersaturation instead of a curve.

5. Miers theory is based on ideal conditions which will never exist in practice. It has not taken into consideration any external stimulus e.g. level of supersaturation which can exist and is inversely proportional to the mechanical shock or stimulus in the solution. The entire metastable zone can be made labile by producing sufficient mechanical shock.

Hence, Mier's theory is of no significant use in practice.

6.5 Nucleation

Once supersaturation is achieved, nucleation is a next essential step for crystallization to occur. Nucleation may occur spontaneously or it may be induced artificially. Nucleation is classified as primary nucleation and secondary nucleation.

Primary nucleation is the nucleation in the systems that do not contain any crystalline matter.

Secondary nucleation represents the condition where nuclei are generated in the vicinity of crystals present in a supersaturated solution.

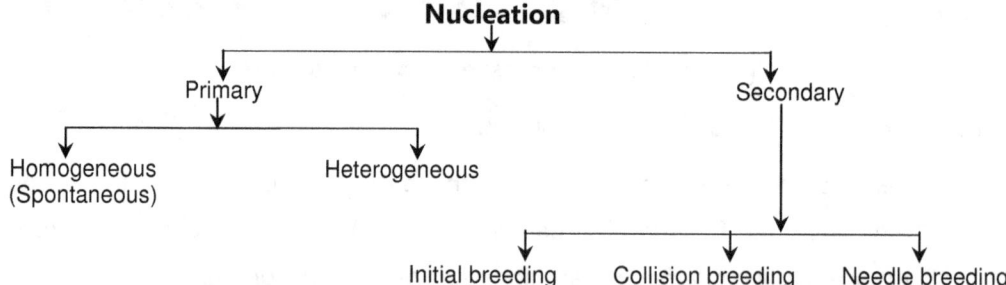

6.5.1 Primary Nucleation

This is the mode of nucleation which occurs mainly at high levels of supersaturation and is most prevalent during unseeded crystallization or precipitation. Primary nucleation is further divided into homogeneous and heterogeneous nucleation.

Homogeneous Nucleation: Formation of stable crystal nuclei within a homogeneous fluid is called homogeneous or spontaneous nucleation. During nucleation molecules / ions forming nucleus should come together, for which they have to overcome the tendency to redissolve. They also have to get orientated in a fixed lattice structure. Around 10 to 1000 such molecules are necessary to form a stable nucleus. This cannot happen by simultaneous collisions of molecules which will be a rare chance. Hence it is expected to take place by a sequence of bimolecular additions as:

$$A + A \rightleftharpoons A_2$$
$$A_2 + A \rightleftharpoons A_3$$
$$A_{n-1} + A \rightleftharpoons A_n \text{ (critical cluster)}$$

Further additions of molecules to this critical cluster results in a nucleus.

The classical theory of nucleation by Gibbs and Volmer is based on the concept of solute clustering prior to nucleation. It proposed that the cluster may grow or redissolve. Of these two processes, that process will be favoured which results in decrease in the free energy of the particle. Therefore, particles smaller than critical nucleus size dissolve, because only in this way the particles can achieve reduction in its free energy, whereas, particles larger than critical size will grow. Although energy of a fluid system is constant at constant temperature and pressure there will be fluctuations in the energy about a constant mean value. In the supersaturated region, energy level rises temporarily and nucleation will be favoured. The rate of nucleation i.e. number of nuclei formed per unit time, per unit volume is given by Arrhenius equation as follows:

$$J = A \exp(-\Delta G / kT) \qquad \qquad \text{... (6.3)}$$

where, J = Rate of nucleation

A = Activation energy

k = Boltzmann constant

ΔG = Overall excess free energy between the solid particle of solute and solute in solution

and T = Temperature in K.

The homogeneous nucleation occurs in perfectly clean systems without stirrer. Therefore, it cannot occur in stirred vessels and hence generally the nucleation in industrial vessels is of heterogeneous type.

Heterogeneous Nucleation:

True homogeneous nucleation is a very difficult event because the supercooled system unknowingly get seeded by the atmospheric dust which contain active particles or heteronuclei. The most active heteronuclei in liquid solution lie in the range of 0.1 to 1 μm. The overall free energy change associated with the formation of critical nucleus under heterogeneous condition is less than the corresponding free energy change associated with homogeneous condition. Similarly, in the presence of heteronuclei, nucleation can be induced at degrees of supercooling lower than those required for spontaneous nucleation.

6.5.2 Secondary Nucleation

Secondary nucleation involves nucleation in presence of existing crystals. The possible mechanisms of secondary nucleation involve; Initial breeding, Needle breeding and Collision breeding.

Initial breeding occurs if crystallization has been started by seeding the crystallizer. *Needle breeding* is associated with the growth of imperfect crystals and would not be expected under the regular crystal growth. *Collision breeding* involves collision of crystal, with moving parts such as stirrer, pump, impeller or crystal wall contact, under centrifugal force.

The rate of secondary nucleation is highly dependent on growth rate of parent crystals and in turn on the level of supersaturation.

6.6 Crystal Growth

As soon as stable nuclei or the nuclei above the critical size are formed in a super-saturated solution, they begin to grow. During growth of the crystal from solution the following steps are involved:

(i) Solute molecules break whatever bonds it has with the solvent.

(ii) These solute molecules migrate to the solid-liquid interface.

(iii) Adsorption and orientation of solute molecules in the crystal lattice.

This total phenomenon of crystal growth has been explained on the basis of various theories as follows.

6.6.1 Surface Energy Theory

Gibbs and Curie postulated the surface energy theory for crystal growth. It states that "*the crystal assumes that shape, which has minimum surface energy*". It suggests that the crystal faces would grow at rate proportional to their respective surface energies.

But this theory cannot explain the surface energy changes during crystal growth to influence crystal habit. The theory also failed to explain the effect of supersaturation and solution movement on the crystal growth rate.

Gibbs considered that there is a possibility that kinetic factors dominate in the initiation of crystallization and they would probably become insignificant in growth.

6.6.2 Diffusion Theory

Noyes and Whitney in 1897 proposed the theory for dissolution of solid which was applied for the reciprocal process of growth. Nernst elaborated the Noyes – Whitney theory stating that the diffusion of solute takes place through a film of saturated solution at the surface of immersed crystal. This diffusion is followed by an infinitely rapid reaction at the surface. Nernst presented the modified Noyes and Whitney equation as:

$$\frac{dx}{dt} = \frac{DS}{\delta}(C_s - C)$$

where, $\dfrac{dx}{dt}$ = Rate of crystal growth

D = Diffusion coefficient

S = Surface area of the crystal exposed

C_s = Saturation concentration

C = Concentration in the bulk phase

δ = Thickness of the laminar film through which diffusion takes place

The thickness of diffusion layer (δ) varies between 20 – 50 µm. The Noyes – Whitney – Nernst equation is applicable when the rate of growth or dissolution of different faces of the crystal is equal. This theory assumes that reaction at the surface is infinitely fast. i.e. incorporation of building units into the crystal lattice is rapid. This will be observed in cases of ionic crystals where bond energies and forces are very high, but in cases where surface reaction will be slower due to weak interaction it will be rate limiting instead of diffusion rate.

Diffusion theory is vague and cannot explain change in crystal habit due to change in supersaturation. Marc has pointed out that crystal growth differs from dissolution in many ways as follows:

(i)   It is slower than dissolution.

(ii)   Rate of growth is independent of rate of stirring if it is vigorous.

(iii)   Many substances when adsorbed, considerably reduce growth rate but do not influence the rate of solution.

6.6.3 Adsorption Theory

It was observed that when a supersaturated solution is inoculated with seed crystals, there is initially a very rapid addition of material to this base, after which normal activity is established. Considering this Marc postulated the adsorption theory and suggested that the interface of a growing crystal is better described in terms of adsorbed layer than a saturated film. It is considered that a adsorbed layer is first formed and then addition occurs to crystal lattice. Growth occurs at a measurable rate by addition to the substrate lattice from this layer, and the abstracted molecules are replaced from the surrounding solution.

6.6.4 Dislocation Theory

Kossel elaborated the process of crystal growth with crystal model as shown in Fig. 6.7. In a growing crystal, new molecules are added only at kink or repeatable step. Many positions are shown at which the building unit can be incorporated in the crystal lattice. Of these positions the one which involve maximum work of separation is the most stable site called "Kossel site" and favoured for addition of building unit. Thus the corners, edges and faces are in order the preferred building sites.

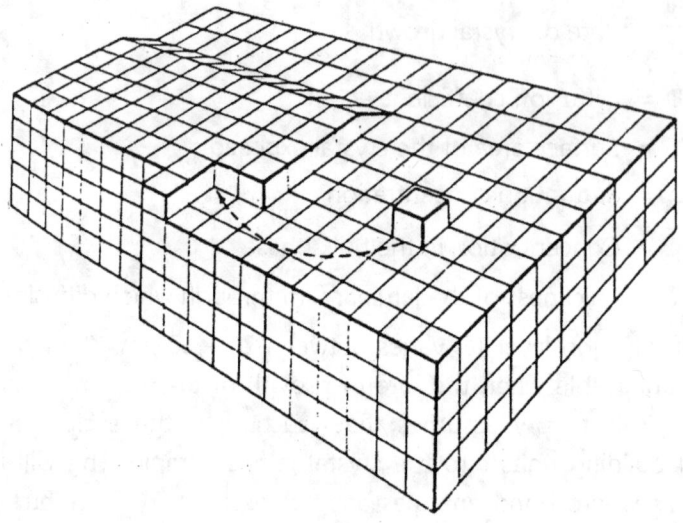

Fig. 6.7: Kossel's crystal

The path taken by soluble molecules from solution to the kink site is not certain. Deposition may either occur directly at the step via volume diffusion or solute molecules may become adsorbed on the surface and migrate to the steps by surface diffusion. Once the layer is formed it is important to have a new kink site. For generation of kink there are two possibilities:

(i) Nucleation is taking place at the surface is called *two-dimensional nucleation*.

(ii) Surface do not grow perfect and takes helical path, it is known as *screw dislocation* (Fig. 6.8).

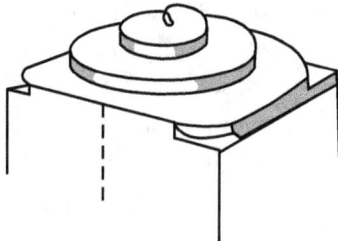

Fig. 6.8: Screw dislocation

Two-dimensional nucleation require very high supersaturations. Therefore, Frank proposed screw dislocation provides the kink site in solutions of low supersaturations. According to screw dislocation theory, the steady state growth rate is proportional to the square of concentration.

6.7 Crystallizers

The basic requirement in crystallization is achievement of supersaturation. The crystallizers are classified into the following types on the method of achieving supersaturation:

1. Supersaturation by cooling

2. Supersaturation by solvent evaporation

3. Supersaturation by adiabatic solvent evaporation

4. Supersaturation by salting out

5. Supersaturation by chemical reaction.

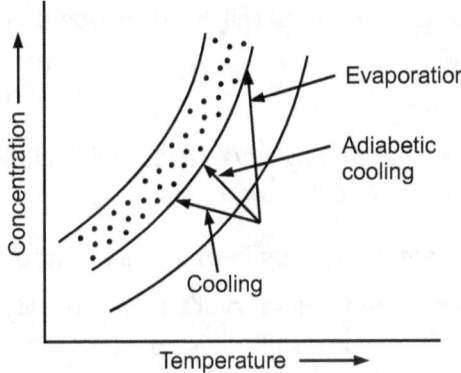

Fig. 6.9: Methods of achieving supersaturation

Fig. 6.9 shows the concentration - temperature relationships in all the methods of achieving supersaturation. Of the above mentioned methods, first three methods are commonly used.

6.7.1 Crystallization by Cooling

This method is used when the solubility of substance is strongly temperature dependent i.e. the solute has a steep solubility curve, e.g. KNO_3, urea etc. Cooling may be carried out by direct or indirect heat exchange between a hot solution of solute and a cooling medium which may be a gas like air or ammonia, or a liquid as water, brine etc.

Generally, water is used as a cooling medium. Its temperature is between 5°C in winter and 20°C in summer. The temperature achieved in the crystallizer is around 2°C higher than the water temperature. At this temperature, considerable amount of solute may remain in the solution giving low yields. Therefore, cooling should be carried out at temperature of 10°C or below.

But at low temperature the following factors should be taken into consideration:

(a)   Viscosity of solution reduces significantly at low temperature which may cause decrease in mass transfer rates and in turn crystal growth rate.

(b)   Due to increased viscosity heat transfer rates also decreases, thus heat exchange surface area has to be increased.

(c)   Mother liquor may remain adhered to the crystal surface due to high viscosity. It is not easily removed without washing; hence it may contaminate the crystals. Similarly, if washing has to be carried out the washing liquid has to be cold so as to avoid dissolution of crystals which is less effective in removal of adhered liquid.

(d)   During cooling, maximum supersaturation is attained by solution near the cooling surface and deposits of crystals will be developed. Heat transfer through such surfaces is very low.

Batch Operation:

The batch type crystallizers have many advantages and limitations as given below:

Advantages:

(i)   It uses simple equipment with very low mechanical troubles.

(ii)   Maintenance cost required is less, similarly, the quality and skill of the operator required to operate a batch crystallizer is not very high.

(iii)   It can produce large crystals.

Limitations:

(i)   Variation may occur from batch to batch in crystal size.

(ii)   It requires large head room.

(iii)   Long operation time and more manual work is required.

The crystallizers of cooling batch type are:

(i)   Tank crystallizer and

(ii)   Agitated tank crystallizer.

(i) Tank Crystallizer:

It consists of a simple rectangular tank made up of material which is resistant to any corrosive effects of the solution. Glass enamelled or stainless steel vessel of 0.5 m diameter is generally used to produce certain pharmaceutical products such as potassium bromide.

In this crystallizer, a hot saturated solution is allowed to cool naturally by contact with air or cooling medium. There is no control of nucleation or crystal growth. The product obtained is mass of interlocked crystals. The product is obtained by draining completely the mother liquor.

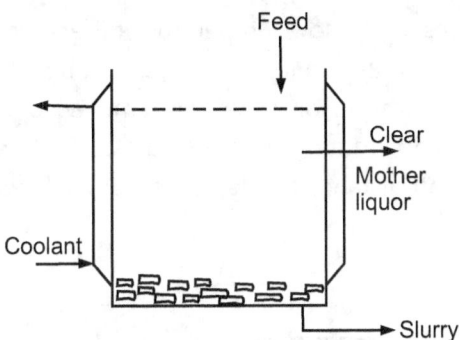

Fig. 6.10: Tank crystallizer

As the rate of cooling is very slow it requires several days to obtain the product; during which crystals reach to very large sizes as interlocked masses. These interlocked crystals masses entrap considerable quantity of mother liquor. Entrapped mother liquor may act as impurities source, but in the pharmaceutical industry where the starting solutions are very pure for the last-stage crystallization, the problem of contamination does not arise.

The product obtained by this method show wide crystal size distribution. Similarly, labour and space requirements are very high. But still it is considered as an economical method for the production of large crystals on small scale. The method is obsolete.

(ii) Agitated Tank Crystallizer:

In this crystallizer, the cooling is carried out by cooling tubes. The cooling tubes are placed internally and arranged in the form of helically wound tube or as a vertical tubular basket. A propeller type agitator is used. The tank may be open or covered.

The agitator in this crystallizer has the following functions:

(a) It carries out mixing and enhances heat transfer and helps in achievement of uniform temperature distribution.

(b) Due to agitation, thickness of the diffusion layer surrounding the crystal surface is reduced, hence rate of mass transfer and crystal growth is increased.

(c) Faster cooling due to agitation results in the formation of a large number of small crystal nuclei, which are retained in the suspension and grow to uniform size. At the same time agglomeration of crystals is prevented.

The agitator should supply adequate energy so that movement of crystals takes place in the solution. The angular velocity of the agitator should be such that the crystal suspension is well carried by the upward flowing stream.

Higher supersaturations exist near the cooling tube surface and crystals may become trapped between the turns of a helix. The crystals attached to the cooling tubes reduce heat transfer. It is recommended that the temperature difference between the tube wall and the solution should not exceed 10°C so as to prevent crystal deposition. The combination of high liquor velocities in tubes, and a low temperature difference across the heat exchanger reduces the tendency for crystal deposition. The crystal deposits over the tube surface may be removed by a mechanical scraper or it may be removed by introducing steam into the tubing for a short time. The cooling tubes may also act as a diffuser. The pitch of the helix is $1/3^{rd}$ of the tube diameter and distance of the tubes from side wall as well as bottom is not more than 3 tube diameters.

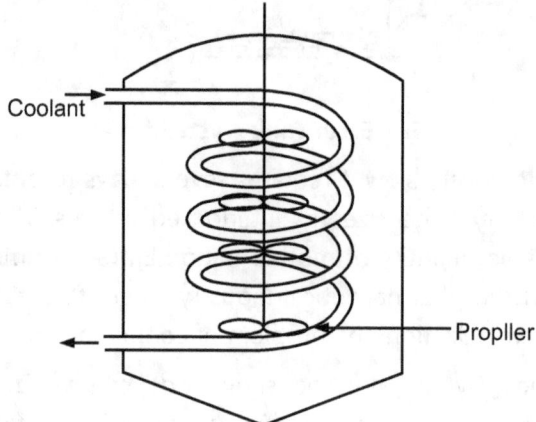

Coolant

Propller

Fig. 6.11: Agitated tank crystallizers

Swenson - Walker Crystallizer:

It is a continuous crystallizer based on supersaturation by cooling. It consists of a semicylindrical open trough about 60 cm wide and 5 m long. It is around 67.5 cm in depth. This trough has jacket from outside through which a water is circulated for cooling (Fig. 6.12). It contains relatively low-speed, long pitch spiral agitator placed horizontally as close as possible to the semicylindrical bottom. The angular velocity of the agitator is 5 – 10 r.p.m. The cooling water generally flows in the direction of the crystallizing solution, hence it is also classified as parallel flow crystallizer. Counter current contact is also possible in some cases. The jacket is divided into different sections in such a way that the cooling rates over different sections of the trough can be different.

The low speed spiral agitator functions,

(a)   to prevent accumulation of crystals on the cooling surface,

(b)   to lift the crystals and shower down through the solution to grow in free suspension,

(c)   to move the crystals mechanically towards the discharge of the cylinder.

The gap between the crystallizer wall and the agitator should be optimum. If the gap is large then there is tendency of crystal deposit formation on cooling surface. On the other hand, if the agitator blades are very close to the trough wall then it acts as a scraper and fines will be produced due to crystal attrition.

Thus, the solution enters the crystallizer, the slurry is agitated gently in the crystallizer, which provides excellent conditions for crystal growth and crystals overflow with mother liquor leaving at the discharge end.

But this crystallizer tends to produce a product with relatively wide crystal size distribution because larger particles tend to stay more at the bottom of the crystallizer near the cooling surface where supersaturation is intense, whereas smaller crystals are suspended more easily by the movement of the agitator and less exposed to the region of high supersaturation.

Heat transfer in this crystallizer is limited. The overall heat transfer coefficients which can be obtained in this crystallizer are in the range of 30 to 50 kcal/m² hr °C.

Advantages of Swenson–Walker crystallizer include less floor space, small volume in process, low labour costs and cheap cooling medium.

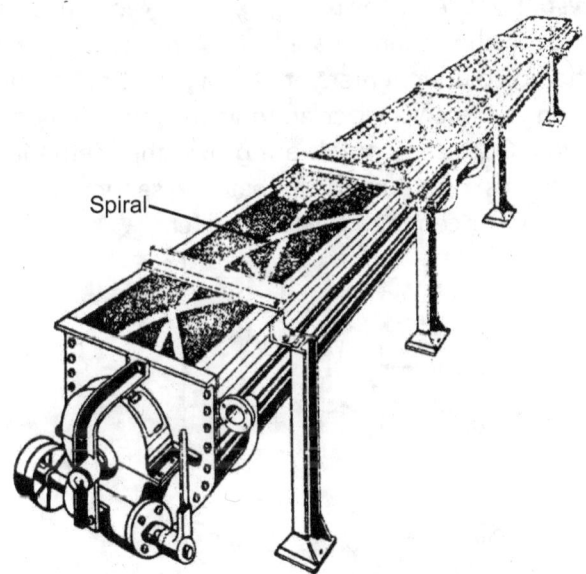

Spiral

Fig. 6.12: Swenson - Walker Crystallizer

This is used for trisodium phosphate, oxalic acid, milk sugar, naphthaline etc.

6.7.2 Crystallization by Evaporation

In this method, crystallization takes place mainly due to the removal of solvent by evaporation. It is used for those substances where there is very small change in solubility with temperature, e.g. sodium chloride, ammonium sulphate. It is also used for substances having negative effect of temperature on solubility, e.g. sodium sulphate anhydrous. Evaporators are discussed in details in chapter 11.

6.7.3 Crystallization by Adiabatic Evaporation

If a hot saturated solution is introduced into a chamber maintained at a lower pressure than that corresponding to the vapour pressure of the feed solution, part of the solvent will immediately flash off, and the liquid will be cooled to a temperature which is equivalent to the vaporising pressure. Hence, solution becomes supersaturated due to combination of evaporation of solvent and some cooling. In adiabatic crystallizer, there is no external source of heat. Sometimes, heat may be supplied externally just to flash the solution or dissolve the nuclei or crystals.

Adiabatic evaporation or vacuum crystallization has the following advantages:

(a) As heat exchange surfaces are absent it can be built in rubber lined or plastic lined steel or glass reinforced plastics.

(b) Region of greatest supersaturation is at the vapour-liquid interface, therefore, problem of crystal deposition does not arise and heat transfer remains high.

(c) Moving parts are less, therefore, maintenance of crystallizer is cheap and easy.

(a) Vacuum Crystallizer: As shown in Fig. 6.13, vacuum crystallizer consists of a conocylindrical vessel to which vacuum is applied by means of a vacuum pump. The feed which is a preconcentrated solution, enters at a convenient point and flashes into vapour. Flashing causes ebullition in the crystallizer and this natural agitation of the solution keeps the crystals in suspension. Once the crystals are grown they settle into the discharge pipe and are removed by means of a pump. In batch–wise operation, the entire slurry is discharged to the centrifugal or continuous vacuum filter.

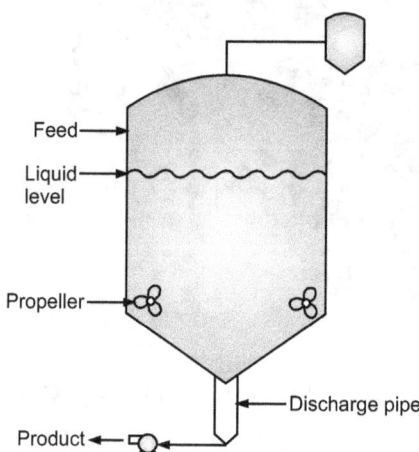

Fig. 6.13: Vacuum crystallizer

If liquid level in the crystallizer increases slightly the flashing of the liquid may not occur and the liquid may leave the crystallization chamber without flashing, this is known as 'short circuiting' of feed. So as to avoid this, propeller may be situated at the corners which will drive the liquid to the surface where the hydrostatic pressure will be less and it can flash. A sight glass is provided to check the liquid level.

As there is no mechanical stimulus or agitation provided in this crystallizer, unwanted nucleation due to attrition is minimised.

(b) Circulating Magma Crystallizer: It is a modification of vacuum crystallizer in which growing crystals are brought intentionally to the zone of the crystallizer where supersaturation is being created. The zone of generation of supersaturation is the boiling surface. The presence of growing crystals in the zone where supersaturation is created immediately utilizes this driving force, and the real super-saturation level is therefore considerably lower than other types.

Circulating magma crystallizer (Fig. 6.14) consists of a crystallizer body (A) where liquid is flashed and gets supersaturated. The crystals are deposited at the bottom. The pipe (B) contains crystals of varying sizes. From the baffles (C) situated on the lower side, a saturated stream of liquid free from crystals is taken out and pumped at the bottom up the pipe containing crystals. The upward force of the stream of saturated liquid washes the bed of crystals free of very fine crystals. This separation of particles by the liquid force is 'elutriation' and the pipe (B) is known as 'elutriation pipe or leg'. The stream of liquid carrying fine crystals carries out mixing of liquid at the bottom. The liquid containing fine crystals (magma) present near the bottom is taken out from side-pipe (D) and pumped through pump (E) to the top of crystallization chamber; during which the liquor passes through heater (F). The heater supplies small amount of energy if required, so as to increase the temperature of liquor to flashing temperature. But the negligible amount of crystals are dissolved. Thus fine crystals are available at the liquid-vapour interface where maximum supersaturation generates.

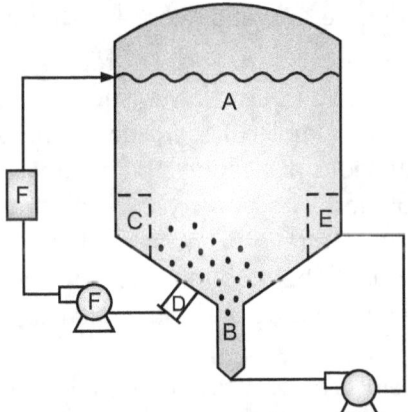

Fig. 6.14: Circulating magma crystallizer

Advantages:

1. Generation of nuclei is minimised by reduction of supersaturation by recirculation of large volumes of liquor.

2. As large seed surface is available in the zone of generation of supersaturation, the tendency of material to precipitate on the equipment surface is eliminated.

3. The time interval between generation of supersaturation and its liberation is very short due to which nucleation is reduced. This also allows operation at higher supersaturation levels.

4. It can give product from 200 – 10 mesh.

5. Suspension of solids in the zone of supersaturation leads to narrow size distribution.

Major drawback of this crystallizer is that the magma has to be pumped against high hydrostatic head.

Operating Variables in Circulating Magma Crystallizer:

In the operation of a circulating magma crystallizer, magma density and cycle time are important process variables.

Effect of Magma Density:

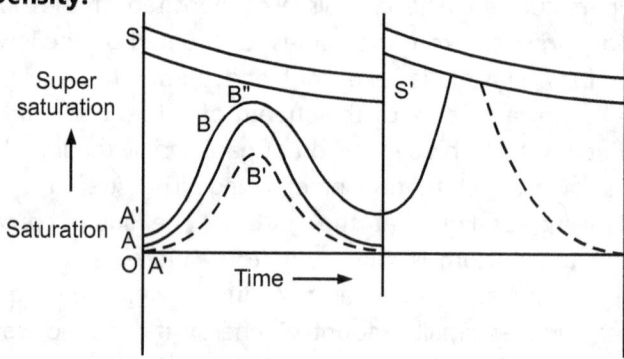

Fig. 6.15: Effect of magma density

The magma is taken out for circulation from side pipe D. Magma density is the number of particles suspended per unit volume of magma. Fig. 6.15 is a plot of saturation of solution versus time. Points on X axis denote saturation concentration below which is a unsaturation region and above is region of supersaturation. SS$'$ represent the region of spontaneous nucleation. It slants downwards because lower supersaturation is sufficient to cause nucleation as time proceeds. i.e. if molecules are given more time to colloid then lesser number may also cause spontaneous nucleation. The magma entering the flashing chamber is nothing but a saturated solution with fine crystals denoted by point A. As this solution flashes in the chamber the supersaturation is achieved upto level denoted by point B. This supersaturation is simultaneously liberated on the surface of fine crystals in magma. Supersaturation is completely liberated before solution leaves the crystallizer (as denoted by point C).

Consider that magma density is high. When solution flashes, two simultaneous processes are taking place, firstly liberation of solute molecule from solvent cavity causing supersaturation and secondly deposition of some of these molecules on the surface of magma particles.

The supersaturation achieved will be

$$\begin{pmatrix} \text{Supersaturation} \\ \text{achieved} \end{pmatrix} = \begin{pmatrix} \text{Solute molecules liberated} \\ \text{from solvent cavity} \end{pmatrix} - \begin{pmatrix} \text{Molecules deposited on} \\ \text{magma particles} \end{pmatrix}$$

Magma density is high i.e. more number of particles per volume and in turn more surface available for deposition of molecules. Therefore, due to more surface area available the second phenomenon of deposition is favoured and supersaturation achieved is reduced.

Thus, the curve A$'$B$'$C$'$ always lies below the medium magma density curve ABC.

When the magma is thin i.e. contain less number of particles per unit volume, then the surface for deposition decreases and maximum supersaturation achieved also increases. The higher degree of supersaturation thus achieved in the process cannot be liberated in the cycle time which is set $\left(A''B''C''\right)$. Therefore, the solution leaves the crystallizer in supersaturated condition C''. This continues for few cycles and degree of supersaturation continuously goes on increasing in each cycle. It becomes so high that it reaches the region of spontaneous nucleation, and large number of nuclei are generated producing fine product. Thus, a dilute magma produces fine product.

Effect of Cycle Time: One cycle in the crystallization process is the time taken by the solution from leaving the chamber and again reaching that point. It is volume of solution in the process divided by rate of circulation. As the cycle time is increased, the time available for the supersaturated solution to release the supersaturation becomes less and the solution leaves the crystallizer with higher degree of supersaturation (Fig. 6.16). Thus, degree of supersaturation of magma entering next cycles goes on increasing till it reaches spontaneous nucleation zone, producing fine product.

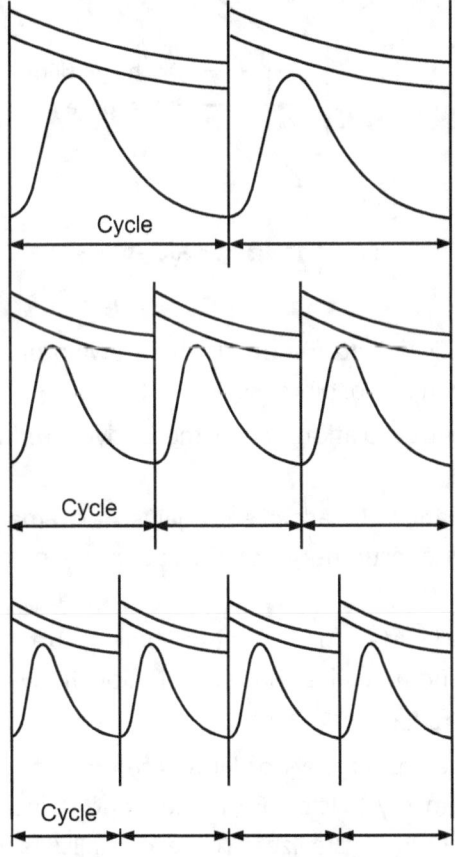

Fig. 6.16: Effect of cycle time

Draft Tube Baffle (DTB) Circulating Magma Crystallizer:

To overcome the high pumping cost encountered in circulating magma crystallizer, DTB crystallizer is designed, where a baffle tube and a propeller is introduced which carry out internal circulation under lower hydrostatic head. The propeller circulates liquid alongwith crystals from the bottom to the top of the vessel. On the outer side of the closed vessel is a settling area which maintains magma density and controls nuclei removal.

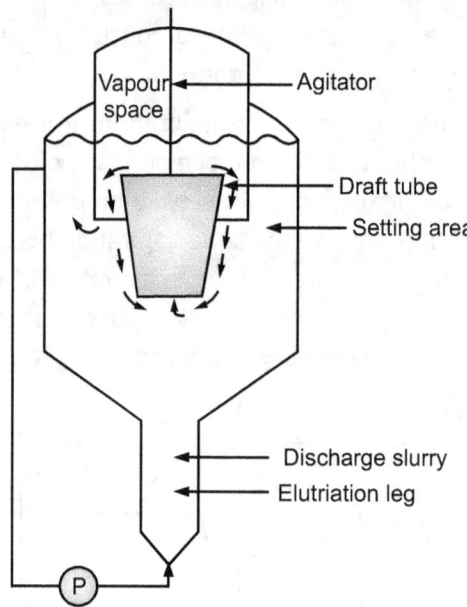

Fig. 6.17: DTB Crystallizer

Advantages:

1. It brings more effectively and frequently the growing particles to the boiling surface where supersaturation is most intense.
2. Due to large internal circulation within the body, it reduces the supersaturation at the boiling surface.
3. This internal circulation is achieved against extremely low hydrostatic heads, therefore, the power consumption for circulation is very low as compared to external circulation.
4. The appropriate seed surface present at the boiling surface allows effective liberation of supersaturation and minimizes nuclei formation. It gives uniformity of product.

Crystallizers for Large Crystals:

For some selected processes, crystals of large size are required. For this purpose some modifications of the vacuum crystallizer are carried out. It includes growth type vacuum crystallizer and Krystal or Oslo crystallizer. These crystallizers favour crystal growth and supress nucleation.

1. Growth Type Vacuum Crystallizer:

It consists of a flashing chamber (A) in which the solution is flashed. Flashing is controlled so that supersaturation is achieved but nucleation does not take place in chamber A. The supersaturated solution is transferred to chamber B where already grown crystals are present. The supersaturated solution is allowed to remain in contact with the bed of crystals; where it liberates its supersaturation on the surface of these already formed crystals. Thus, crystal growth is favoured. The overflow from chamber B containing fine nuclei and particles are passed to heater D by pump C. The feed is added before entering the heater. The heater D adds energy so that temperature of liquid raises to flashing point in vacuum and at the same time all suspended fine particles are dissolved. Thus in contrast to circulating magma crystallizer, where the heater only raises the temperature and hot magma passes to flashing chamber, in growth type the solution enters the flashing chamber. The crystal product is taken out when developed to desired size.

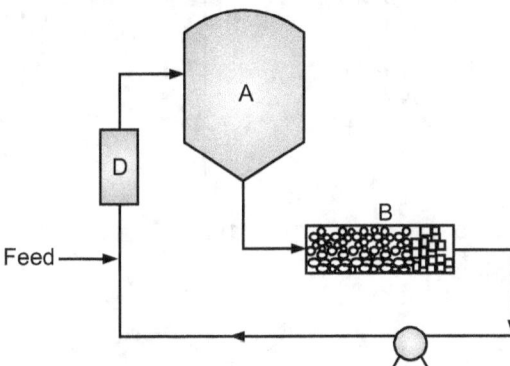

Fig. 6.18: Growth type of vacuum crystallizer

The basic limitation of this process is, it requires very long contact times between crystals and supersaturated solution. Similarly, generation of some fine crystals and again their dissolution in heater, these two exactly opposite processes are carried out continuously. Long contact times and crystallization - dissolution makes the process expensive.

The time required for/of supersaturated solution from chamber A to chamber B is an important operating variable in growth type vacuum crystallizer.

The concentration – time curve will be as shown in Fig. 6.19. The solution at just before entering the flashing chamber is denoted by point A, which indicates that solution is unsaturated. In the flashing chamber the solution flashes and gets supersaturated as indicated by point B. This solution is immediately transferred to crystal bed, during which time BC has elapsed. Point C thus indicates the concentration of solution and time at which it has come in contact with bed. On contact with crystal bed, the supersaturation is liberated on crystal bed and degree of supersaturation decreases to point D. The magma gets mixed with feed and passes through heater, where increase in temperature makes the solution unsaturated again as shown by point E, ready for flashing in next cycle. It was observed that increased fraction of undersized particles are obtained when time of transfer BC has increased. It can be explained on the basis of Mier's theory that as the time allowed increases, the lesser number of collisions may cause spontaneous nucleation. Thus, it is most important to prevent nucleation by keeping the transfer time as low as possible.

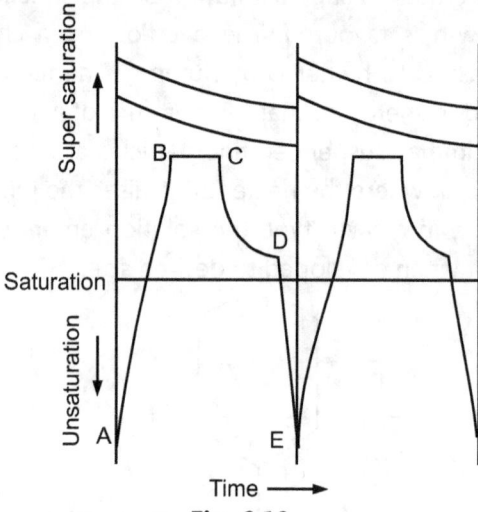

Fig. 6.19

2. Krystal or Oslo Crystallizer:

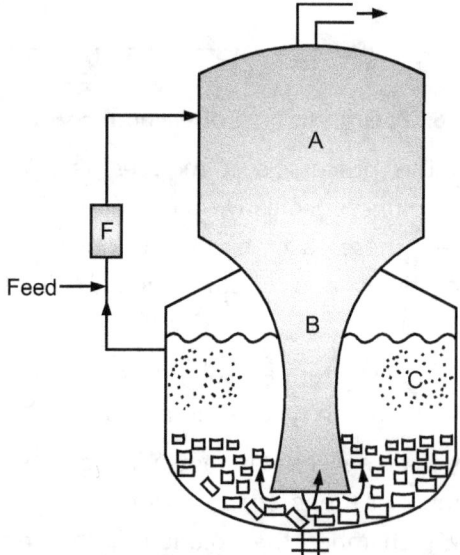

Fig. 6.20: Krystal or Oslo crystallizer

A Krystal or Oslo crystallizer consists of two different chambers. Chamber A is a flashing chamber where controlled supersaturation is achieved. The supersaturated solution under gravitational force to chamber C through pipe B. Chamber C contains a bed of already formed crystals. The solution enters the chamber C under pressure causing opening of the bed. Once the crystal bed opens it gets fractionated on the basis of size and density. The fine crystals containing supernatant is taken out from side pipe as a magma for further treatment. The feed gets added to magma and then mixture passes to heater H, where its temperature is increased sufficiently so that all the magma particles get dissolved and flashing can occur. Crystals when grown to desired size, the product is taken out from bottom.

The Krystal crystallizer offers advantages as, the time required for transfer of supersaturated solution on the crystal bed is minimised. Secondly, size separation is also achieved due to hydraulic separation in the bed. The geometry of the down pipe is such that potential energy is converted to kinetic by constriction and again to pressure energy by expansion. Thus it has low percentage of fines generation and size separation advantage.

6.8 Caking of Crystals

Caking of crystals is an undesirable effect, which generally occurs during storage. This involves formation of a saturated film on the surface of the crystals either by absorption or by migration of mother liquor incompletely removed in the separation of the crystals. This saturated solution will concentrate at the contacts of the crystals due to capillary forces and subsequently crystallize to form a solid bridge upon cooling or evaporation. The continuation of this surface recrystallization produces a hard cake or cement which creates difficulties in manipulating and handling both bulk and packaged materials. Various factors should be considered in caking of crystals.

1. **Humidity:** A crystal tends to be in continuous equilibrium with the moisture in the surrounding atmosphere, and the ratio of the vapour pressure of the moisture around the crystal to that of the saturated solution will determine whether the crystal is going to lose or absorb water. The humidity of the atmosphere in the storage space should not exceed a critical value (ϕ_k).

$$\phi_k = 100\frac{P_s}{P_o}$$

   where, P_s = Vapour pressure of the saturated solution

   P_o = Vapour pressure of pure solvent at given temperature.

2. **Contact Area:** The capability of caking of a material is directly proportional to the contact area between individual crystals. The more are the gaps between the crystals less is the chance of caking. This can be achieved with uniform crystals of as large size, preferably of shapes close to spherical. Contact area between spheres is much less than between platelets and needles of similar volume. But uniformity of particle size is also necessary.

3. **Temperature:** Temperature fluctuations are undesirable so as to prevent caking; because they cause variations in the solubility of the material. In absence of solvent also high temperature have undesirable effect, especially on low melting substances. If the product is at a temperature equal to or in excess of a quarter of the melting temperature, some surface activation of the particles occurs.

4. **Particle Size:** Particle size determines the upper limit of storage pressure. At a certain 'adhesive' pressure, fusion of the particles occurs.

$$P_a \propto \frac{1}{r}$$

Thus, caking tendency can be reduced by:

(i) Production of stable modification of the product, so that it has suitable habit, size and uniformity.

(ii) Reduction of moisture content to lowest possible level, storage under steady temperature, low stacking pressure and lower air humidities.

(iii) Powdering or impregnation of surfaces with surface active and water repellant materials e.g. $Ca_3(PO_4)_2$ on NaCl and starch on sugar and confectionaries.

Questions

1. Define crystal and crystal lattice.

2. Describe crystal form and crystal habit.

3. Write Mier's Theory of supersaturation.

4. What are the limitations of Mier's theory?

5. Discuss crystal growth in detail with different theories.

6. Explain the types of crystallizers on the base of supersaturation.

7. Explain caking of crystals.

8. Write short notes on the following:

   (a) Supersaturation

   (b) Nucleation

   (c) Secondary nucleation

   (d) Advantages and limitations of batch operation

   (e) Circulating magma crystallizer

■■■

CHAPTER

Flow of Fluids

7.1 Introduction

Fluids are the materials which deform continuously or flow as long as the shear stress is applied, but are unable to achieve an equilibrium under applied shear stress.

Many materials in the manufacture of bulk drugs and pharmaceuticals are in the form of fluids. Similarly, there is increasing tendency to handle powdered or granular materials in the form in which they behave as fluids i.e. fluidisation. Thus, concept of fluids covers liquids, gases and fluidised solids. If stress is applied uniformly over all boundaries and if fluid decreases in volume showing proportionate increase in density, it is considered as compressible. Liquids for general purpose are considered non-compressible, and gases as compressible.

The study of fluids is divided into the:

(i)   Study of fluids at rest i.e. *Fluid statics.*

(ii)   Study of fluids in motion i.e. *Fluid dynamics.*

7.2 Fluid Statics

7.2.1 Pressure

Pressure is an important property of a fluid at rest. Pressure is defined as force exerted per unit area. For a material, force exerted is equal to the product of mass and gravitational acceleration.

$$F = mg$$

For fluids, mass can be calculated from volume and density.

$$F = V \rho g$$

where, F is the force exerted, m is the mass of fluid, g is gravitational acceleration, ρ is density and V is volume of fluid.

Thus, this force exerted by the fluid due to gravity must be resisted by some supporting medium so that fluid remain in equilibrium. Lower levels of fluid must provide support for the fluid that lies above them. Fluid at any point must support the above. Thus, the fluid pressure i.e. force per unit area in a fluid is equal in all directions.

The pressure of fluid varies with depth. If we consider the fluid at depth Z below the surface and A as the area; the volume of fluid will be ZA. Therefore, force exerted will be ZA ρ g. But total force is sum of the force exerted on the surface of the liquid and force of the liquid.

$$\therefore \qquad \text{Total force} \ = \ A\,P_a + Z\,A\,\rho\,g$$

where, P_a is the pressure at the surface (atmospheric pressure).

$$\therefore \qquad \text{Total pressure} \ = \ \frac{\text{Total force}}{A}$$

$$= \ P_a + Z\,\rho\,g \qquad\qquad \text{... (7.1)}$$

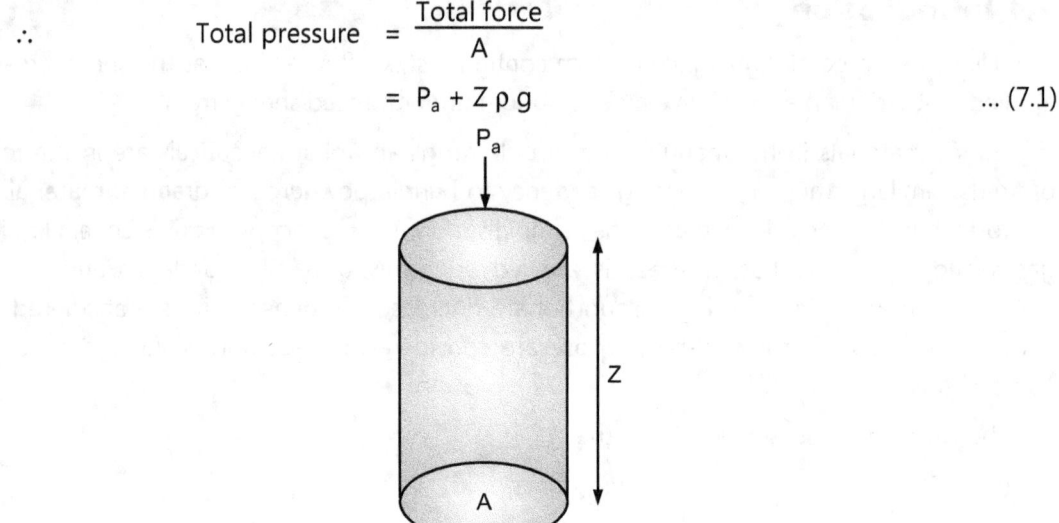

Fig. 7.1: Fluid statics

This is *absolute pressure*. But, usually pressure is given in terms of pressure above or below atmospheric pressure, i.e. considering atmospheric pressure as datum line. *This is gauge pressure*, it will be represented as

$$P \ = \ Z\,\rho\,g$$

As pressure varies with depth, the hydrostatic expression can be represented as

$$dP \ = \ -\rho\,g\,dZ$$

As liquids are incompressible, integrating the above equation within the limits P_1 and P_2 and Z_1 and Z_2 gives:

$$\int_{P_2}^{P_1} dP \ = \ -\rho\,g \int_{Z_2}^{Z_1} dZ$$

$$P_1 - P_2 \ = \ -\rho\,g\,(Z_1 - Z_2) \qquad\qquad \text{... (7.2)}$$

SOLVED EXAMPLES

Example 7.1: Calculate the greatest gauge and absolute pressure in a spherical tank of 5 m diameter filled with arachis oil of specific gravity 0.95. (density of water = 10^3 kg/m³; atmospheric pressure 1.013×10^5 N/m²).

Solution:

$$h = 5 \text{ m}$$

$$\text{Specific gravity} = 0.95$$

∴
$$\text{Density, } \rho = 0.95 \times 10^3 \text{ kg/m}^3$$

$$g = 9.8 \text{ m/s}^2$$

$$\text{Gauge pressure} = h \rho g$$

$$= 5 \times 0.95 \times 10^3 \times 9.8$$

$$= 46.55 \times 10^3 \text{ N/m}^2$$

$$\text{Absolute pressure} = \text{Gauge pressure} + \text{Atmospheric pressure}$$

$$= 0.4655 \times 10^5 + 1.013 \times 10^5$$

$$= 1.4785 \times 10^5 \text{ N/m}^2$$

The pressure of fluid is also expressed in terms of *'depth or head'* of the fluid.

Example 7.2: Calculate head of water equivalent to standard atmospheric pressure.

Formula:
$$Z = \frac{P}{\rho g}$$

Solution:
$$Z = \frac{P}{\rho g} = \frac{1.013 \times 10^5}{9.81 \times 10^3}$$

$$= 0.1033 \times 10^2 = 10.33 \text{ m}$$

7.2.2 Pressure Measurement

Pressure of a fluid may be expressed as: *Absolute pressure* which is the fluid pressure above the reference value of a perfect vacuum or the absolute zero pressure.

Gauge pressure represents the value of pressure above the reference value of atmospheric pressure. Thus, it is the difference between the absolute and local atmospheric pressure. The atmospheric pressure at sea level is 760 mm Hg or 14.7 psi or 1.013×10^5 Pa (Pascals). *Vacuum* is the amount by which atmospheric pressure exceeds the absolute pressure.

Some common pressure measuring devices include:

(A)   Manometers and

(B)   Bourdon Gauge.

(A) Manometers:

Manometer is a simple device for measurement of static pressure. There are two types of manometer discussed here:

(i)   Simple manometer

(ii) Differential manometer.

(i)   Simple Manometer:

A simple manometer consists of a U–tube containing a suitable fluid as shown in Fig. 7.2 The difference in levels (h) between the two arms is an indication of pressure difference $(P_1 - P_5)$ between two arms. The fluid to be used in manometer should have the following properties:

(a)   It should be non-corrosive and should not react with the fluid whose pressure has to be measured.

(b)   It should have low viscosity and hence quick adjustment with pressure change, and

(c)   It should have negligible surface tension and capillary effects.

Hence, water or mercury are fluids of choice in manometer.

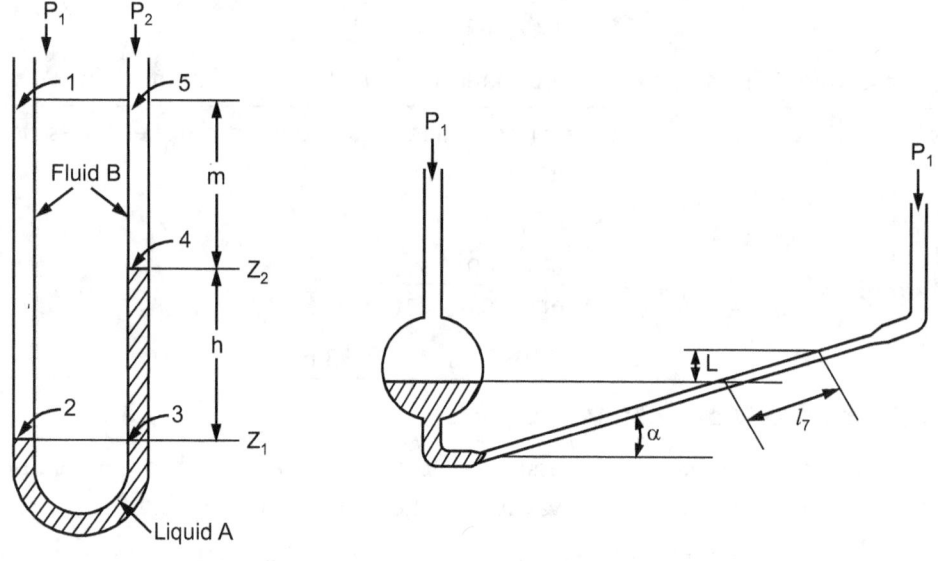

(a) U-tube manometer   (b) Inclined manometer

Fig. 7.2

The relationship between h and $P_1 - P_2$ can be established as follows: Let shaded portion contains fluid A and unshaded portion in tube contains fluid B. Let ρ_A and ρ_B are densities of fluid A and fluid B respectively, Z_1 and Z_2 are heights of liquid columns in two arms and $h = Z_2 - Z_1$. Now pressure at any point can be given by hydrostatic equation as

$$P = h \rho g \qquad \qquad \text{... (7.3)}$$

Therefore various points shown in Fig. 7.2 (a).

At point 1, P_1: Pressure is P_1

At point 2, P_2: P_1 + Pressure of fluid B column (ht . h + m) = P_1 + (h + m) ρ_B g

At point 5, P_5: Pressure is P_5

At point 4, P_4: P_5 + Pressure of fluid B (ht. m) = P_5 + m ρ_B g

At point 3, P_3: Pressure at point 4 + Pressure of column of A (ht. h)

$$= P_5 + m\,\rho_B\,g + h\,\rho_A\,g$$

But P_2 is equal to P_3

∴ $P_1 + (h + m)\,\rho_B\,g = P_5 + m\,\rho_B\,g + h\,\rho_A\,g$ ... (7.4)

∴ $P_1 + h\,\rho_B\,g + m\,\rho_B\,g = P_5 + m\,\rho_B\,g + h\,\rho_A\,g$

∴ $\Delta P = P_1 - P_5 = h\,(\rho_A - \rho_B)\,g$ ... (7.5)

If fluid B is a gas (which is a general case) then $\rho_B << \rho_A$, therefore it can be neglected. Then equation (7.5) will become

$$\Delta P = h\,\rho_A\,g \qquad\qquad\text{... (7.6)}$$

Equation show the relationship between ΔP and h is independent of height m and diameter of the U–tube; provided P_1 and P_5 are measured in the same horizontal plane. It is suitable for measurement of moderate pressure.

At very low pressures, the difference in levels in two arms will be very less and difficult to read. Therefore, for small readings, a modification of U–tube manometer, *inclined tube manometer* is used as shown in Fig. (7.2 b). The tube is inclined at some angle to the horizontal so as to magnify the linear displacement of fluid. Here, the length *l* along the inclined tube is an inclination of pressure difference ($P_1 - P_2$).

Relationship between *l* and ΔP is as follows:

The vertical length (L) of inclined leg can be obtained by inclined length (*l*) divided by the sine of angle of inclination θ (if area A_1 of one limb is significantly high as compared to A_2 for another limb).

∴ $l = \dfrac{L}{\sin\theta}$

∴ $\Delta P = P_1 - P_2$

                  $= L\,\rho\,g$

∴ $\Delta P = l\,\sin\theta\,\rho\,g$ ... (7.7)

(ii) Differential Manometer:

It is a manometer to measure small pressure differences. As shown in Fig. 7.3, the manometer contains two immiscible fluid B and C. The liquid levels in the top reservoirs remains constant due to the large chambers. The pressure will be given as:

$$\Delta P = P_1 - P_2 = h (\rho_C - \rho_B) g$$

The reading (h) will be high if fluid B and fluid C have nearly the same density.

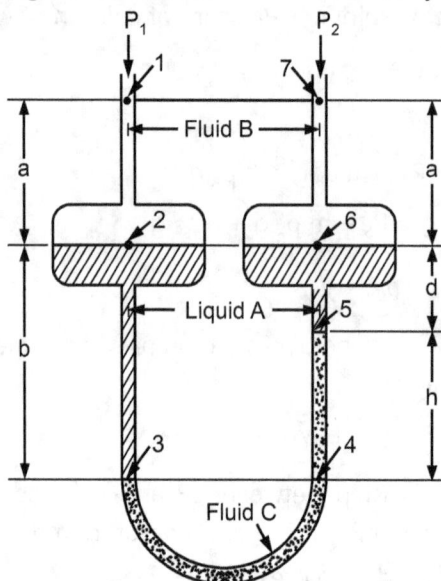

Fig. 7.3: Differential manometer

(B) Bourdon Tube Pressure Gauges:

It is a mechanical pressure - measuring element. Such mechanical elements are designed to operate under a pressure change by bending, deforming or deflecting depending upon the pressure variation. Such elements are termed as 'transducers', because they can take one form of energy from the measuring source and supply energy of a different kind to an indicating, recording or controlling system. A pressure gauge may take energy from the air compressed in the cylinder and supply enough mechanical power to move a pointer across a scale to indicate or record the pressure in the cylinder.

Eugene Bourdon invented pressure gauge in 1851. He stated that a round tubing which has flattened and a bent circular arc will tend to return to its original shape when pressure is applied inside it. A simple form of Bourdon gauge (Fig. 7.4), consists of a length of thin - walled metal tubing which has been flattened to approximately an elliptical cross-section and then rolled into a C shape. The arc of the gauge is in between $180 - 270°$. The tube has a pressure - inlet at one end and the other free end is sealed, it is called as the tip. The tube is made up of bronze, phosphur bronze, stainless steel, nickel alloys etc.

Under pressure the elliptical or flattened section tends to change its shape to a circular form. The deflection of the tip depends upon the radius of the bend, total tube length, Young's modulus of elasticity of the tube material and total tube length. Different configurations of Bourdon gauges include helical and spiral tubes apart from C - shaped.

Bourdon gauge has good sensitivity and repeatability. It is useful in the range of 10^6 to 10^8 Pascals.

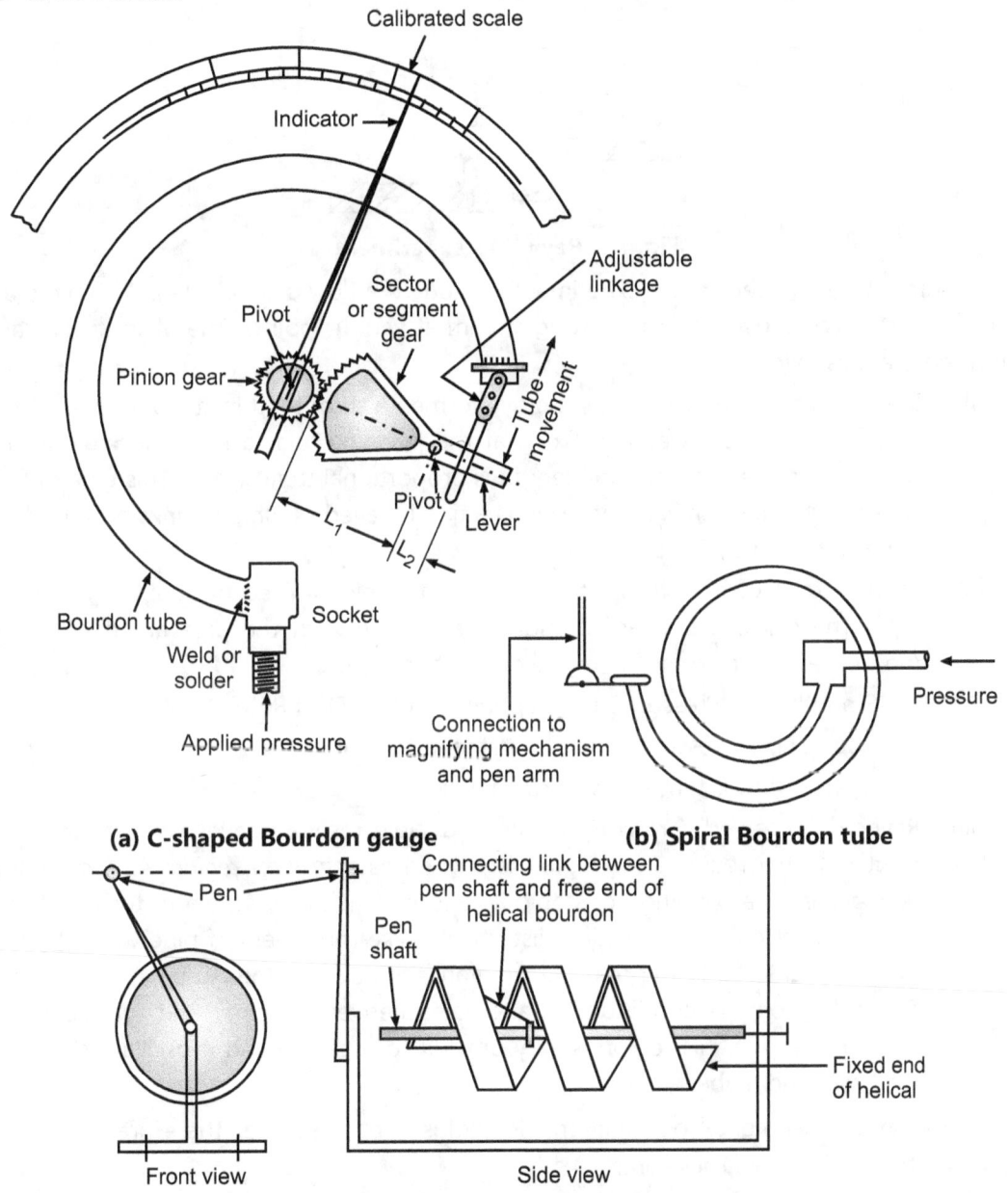

(a) C-shaped Bourdon gauge   (b) Spiral Bourdon tube

(c) A helical Bourdon tube

Fig. 7.4: Bourdon tube gauge

7.3 Fluid Dynamics

7.3.1 Mechanism of Fluid Flow

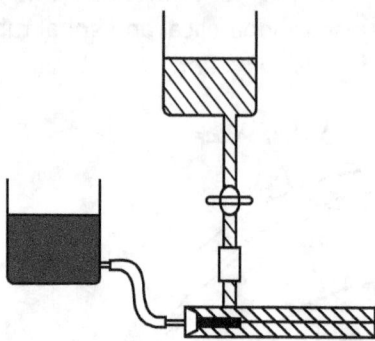

Fig. 7.5: Reynold's experiment

Osborne Reynolds performed experiment to study the flow of fluids (Fig. 7.5). In a glass tube, he introduced a dye into the flowing stream at various points. The observations and conclusions are as follows:

(i)   In the region of low flow rate, the dye formed a smooth, thin straight streak down the pipe and there was no mixing at the perpendicular axis of the pipe. In this region, pressure drop per unit length is proportional to flow rate. This type of flow where all the motion is in the axial direction is called as *laminar flow*; because fluid appears to move in layers or lamina.

(ii)   In the region of high flow rate, the dye was rapidly mixed throughout the entire pipe. The rapid, haphazard motion in all direction in the pipe along with axial motion caused rapid mixing of the dye. In this region,

For Smooth pipe: Pressure Drop per unit length α (Flow Rate)

For Rough pipe: Pressure Drop per unit length α (Flow Rate)

This type of flow is termed as *turbulent flow*.

(iii)   Reynolds observed a region of unreproducible results between the laminar and turbulent flow region. This region is termed as *transition region*. As the laminar flow occurs in a condition of stable flow form which may switch to turbulent flow due to effect of certain outside disturbance, like roughness of pipe wall, vibration of equipment etc. In the transition region, the flow is either turbulent or laminar. Depending on the conditions, it alternates between laminar and turbulent. The pressure drop in this region is very difficult to measure and it oscillates between the lower and higher values.

From these experimental observations, Reynolds concluded that there are two forces acting on the fluid in flow. These are:

(i)   Kinetic or velocity or inertial forces which tend to maintain the flow in its general direction. This force is proportional to velocity pressure ρu^2 and

(ii) Viscous forces which tend to retard the general motion of fluid and introduce eddies. These are proportional to $\dfrac{\mu u}{D}$, where, μ is viscosity of fluid and D is diameter of the pipe.

Reynolds claimed that the fluid flow changes with the change in these forces. The type of flow developed depends on the ratio of the forces, hence a dimensionless number, Reynolds number was developed.

Reynolds Number, $\quad Re = \dfrac{\text{Inertial force}}{\text{Viscous force}} = \dfrac{\rho\, u^2\, D}{u\mu}$

$\therefore \qquad\qquad\qquad \boxed{Re = \dfrac{D\, u\, \rho}{\mu}} \qquad\qquad\qquad \text{... (7.9)}$

where, $\qquad\qquad$ D = Pipe diameter

$\qquad\qquad\qquad$ u = Velocity of fluid

$\qquad\qquad\qquad$ μ = Viscosity of liquid and

$\qquad\qquad\qquad$ ρ = Density of fluid

Reynolds number can be modified for flows other than a pipe flow, by substituting the pipe diameter by a suitable length parameter.

7.3.2 Significance of Reynolds Number

(i) For fluid flow through a pipe, flow remains laminar or stream line for values of Re upto 2100; whereas flow becomes turbulent at Re values above 4000. Between the values of 2100 and 4000, the flow pattern is unstable or transition region exists.

(ii) At constant velocity fluid can change from laminar to turbulent if pipe diameter is increased. Decrease in viscosity (due to temperature change) may also show similar effects.

(iii) Higher is the Reynolds number, greater is the relative contribution of inertial forces, whereas as lower Re values viscous effects predominate the inertial effects.

(iv) Reynold's number is important in determination of heat transfer by forced convection, frictional losses in fluid flow etc.

In the most of the pharmaceutical operations, fluids are in motion. These systems are to be analysed by applying material and energy balances.

7.3.3 Material Balance

Consider fluid flowing through a pipe across two points, point 1 and point 2. Let a_1, ρ_1 and u_1 be cross-sectional area of pipe, density and velocity of fluid at point 1. Similarly, a_2, ρ_2 and u_2 denote same parameters at point 2. The material balance across the pipe between point 1 and point 2 is given as:

$$\rho_1 \, a_1 \, u_1 \;=\; \rho_2 \, a_2 \, u_2$$

Liquids are incompressible, therefore $\rho_1 = \rho_2$.

Thus, $\boxed{u_1 \, a_1 \;=\; u_2 \, a_2}$ ... (7.10)

This is known as *continuity equation* for liquids; obtained for material balance of fluid flow.

7.3.4 Energy Balance

Fluid has some intrinsic energy itself and some interchange of energy occurs with the surroundings. The intrinsic energy of fluid include:

(i)   Potential energy

(ii)   Kinetic energy and

(iii) Pressure energy or flow energy.

The *potential energy* is the capacity to do work by reason of its position relative to some centre of attraction. Thus, potential energy of a unit mass of fluid at height Z above the datum level is

$$P.E. \;=\; Zg \qquad\qquad ... (7.11)$$

Kinetic energy is the energy of the fluid due to its motion. If u is the velocity of liquid and m is mass; then

$$K.E. \;=\; \frac{1}{2} \, mu^2$$

For unit mass of fluids it becomes

$$K.E. \;=\; \frac{u^2}{2} \qquad\qquad ... (7.12)$$

Pressure energy or flow energy is energy form peculiar to the flow of fluids. Fluid exerts pressure on its surrounding. If volume of fluid is decreased, the pressure exerts a force which must be overcome while compressing the fluid. Thus, work has to be done in compressing the fluid. Similarly, work can be done by the fluid under pressure if its pressure is released. This is known as Pressure energy.

Suppose fluid is present in a cylinder having cross-sectional area A, and it moves through distance L against pressure P (Fig. 7.6). Then work done by the fluid is PAL. This work is done by AL volume of liquid having density ρ; hence by AρL quantity of liquid. Work done by unit mass of liquid is pressure energy.

$$\therefore \qquad \text{Pr.E.} \; = \; \frac{P\,A\,L}{A\,\rho\,L} \; = \; \frac{P}{\rho} \qquad\qquad \text{... (7.13)}$$

Thus, $\dfrac{P}{\rho}$ is the pressure energy or work that can be obtained by unit mass of fluid during flow.

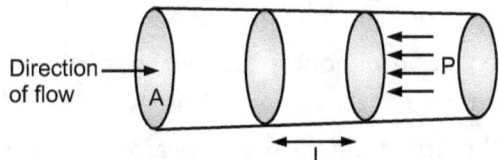

Direction of flow

A

P

L

Fig. 7.6: Pressure energy

Total intrinsic energy of the fluid is sum of potential, kinetic and pressure energy.

$\therefore \qquad$ Total energy $\; = \;$ P.E. + K.E. + Pr. E.

$$= \; Zg + \frac{u^2}{2} + \frac{P}{\rho} \qquad\qquad \text{... (7.14)}$$

Apart from this intrinsic energy fluid comes across interchange with the surroundings as

(i)   Frictional losses,

(ii)   Mechanical energy added by pumps, and

(iii)   Heat energy due to heating or cooling.

7.3.5 Bernoulli's Theorem

Application of law of conservation of energy to flow of fluids is Bernoulli's theorem. In other words, the energy balance of flow of fluids is known as Bernoulli's equation.

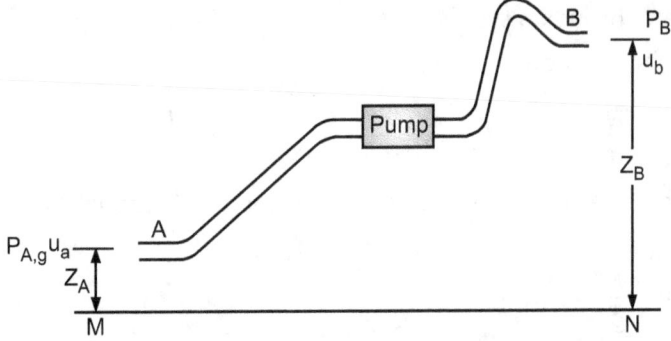

Fig. 7.7: Development of Bernoulli's theorem

If we consider a system at uniform temperature conveying liquid from point A to point B. Points A and B are at heights Z_a and Z_b from datum line. u_a and u_b are the velocities of liquid at points A and B respectively. P_A and P_B are the pressures at A and B respectively. As liquid is incompressible, there is no effect of pressure on density (ρ) of the liquid. The energy balance can be written as:

$$\text{Energy of fluid at A} = \text{Energy of fluid at B}$$

$$\left(P.E.\right)_A + \left(K.E.\right)_A + \left(Pr.E.\right)_A = \left(P.E.\right)_B + \left(K.E.\right)_B + \left(Pr.E.\right)_B$$

$$\therefore \qquad Z_a g + \frac{u_a^2}{2} + \frac{P_A}{\rho} = Z_b g + \frac{u_b^2}{2} + \frac{P_B}{\rho} \qquad \qquad \text{... (7.15)}$$

This is the Bernoulli's equation without friction where frictional losses are neglected and no addition of energy is considered.

But when fluid flows through a pipe it has to overcome the frictional resistance of the pipe wall and thus, there is loss of energy from the fluid energy resources. If we consider that F is the energy loss due to friction and W is the energy added by the pumps then Bernoulli's equation becomes:

$$Z_a g + \frac{u_a^2}{2} + \frac{P_A}{\rho} + W - F = Z_b g + \frac{u_b^2}{2} + \frac{P_B}{\rho} \qquad \qquad \text{... (7.16)}$$

This is the Bernoulli's equation for flow of fluids.

The equation can be expressed in terms of heads instead of energy as follows by dividing all the terms by g. When we get dimensions of length:

$$\boxed{Z_a + \frac{u_a^2}{2g} + \frac{P_A}{\rho g} + \frac{W}{g} - \frac{F}{g} = Z_b + \frac{u_b^2}{2g} + \frac{P_B}{\rho g}} \qquad \qquad \text{... (7.17)}$$

7.3.6 Applications of Bernoulli's Theorem

(a) Determination of Power Requirements:

Bernoulli's equation can be used to calculate the power required, if the liquid has to be driven at certain rate through a system.

As per Bernoulli's equation,

$$\frac{W}{g} = \frac{u_B^2 - u_A^2}{2g} + \frac{P_B - P_A}{g} + (Z_B - Z_A) + \frac{F}{g}$$

If the sum of changes in velocity, pressure, height and frictional losses is said to be ΔH, then,

$$\frac{W}{g} = \Delta H$$

$$\therefore \qquad W = g\,\Delta H \qquad \qquad \text{... (7.18)}$$

Thus, g ΔH is the work done on unit mass of liquid. Hence, if we want to transfer mass m of liquid in time t, then total work required to be done or power required will be

$$\boxed{Power \ = \ \frac{mg \ \Delta H}{t}}$$

To get terms of volume, i.e. if Q is the volumetric flow rate (volume flowing per unit time)

$$Q = \frac{V}{t} = \frac{m}{\rho t} \ \text{i.e. } m = Q \rho t$$

∴   Power = Q g ΔH ρ   ... (7.19)

This equation will be used to calculate power requirements.

Example 7.3: Calculate the power required to pump castor oil from a vessel at ground level to a vessel at 3 m above the ground using a glass pipe having diameter 4 cm and length 3 m. The oil has to be delivered at the rate of 12 lit./min. and frictional head for given length of pipe is 4 m.

Solution: Specific Gravity of Castor oil is 0.95.

$$\text{Frictional head for given length of pipe i.e. } \frac{F}{g} \ = \ 4 \text{ m}$$

$$\text{Density of water} \ = \ 1000 \text{ kg/m}^3$$

∴ $$\text{Density of castor oil} \ = \ 0.95 \times 1000 = 950 \text{ kg/m}^3$$

$$\text{Volumetric flow rate (Q)} \ = \ \frac{m}{\rho t}$$

$$= \ \frac{1.2 \times 0.95}{950 \times 60} \ \text{m}^3/\text{sec.} = 0.0002 \text{ m}^3/\text{sec.}$$

$$\text{Average velocity in pipe (u)} \ = \ \frac{Q}{\text{Area of pipe i.e. } \left(\frac{\pi}{4} D^2\right)}$$

$$= \ \frac{0.0002}{\frac{\pi}{4} \times (0.04)^2} \ = 0.167 \text{ m/sec.}$$

As point A is at ground potential and kinetic energy at this point is taken as zero.

$$\text{Velocity head} \ = \ \frac{\left(u_b^2 - u_a^2\right)}{2g}$$

$$= \ \frac{0.167 - 0}{2 \times 9.81} \ = 0.0085 \text{ m}$$

As point A is at zero datum level and point B is at 3 m height; potential head is 3 m.

$$\text{Power} = Q\, g\, \Delta H\, \rho$$

$$\text{Total head } \Delta H = \frac{\text{Potential}}{\text{head}} + \frac{\text{Velocity}}{\text{head}} + \frac{\text{Frictional}}{\text{head}}$$

$$= 3 + 0.0085 + 4 = 7.0085 \text{ m}$$

$$\therefore \quad \text{Power} = 0.0002 \times 9.81 \times 7.0085 \times 950 = 13.063 \text{ Ns}^{-1}$$

(b) Measurement of Flow Rates:

Bernoulli's theorem is used for the measurement of flow rate of fluids. The flowmeters are classified as:

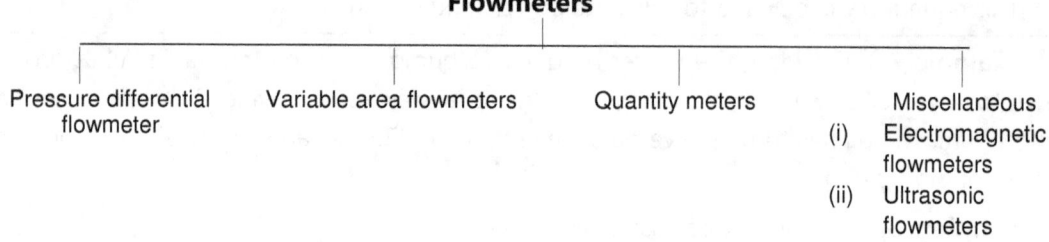

Flowmeters

Pressure differential flowmeter	Variable area flowmeters	Quantity meters	Miscellaneous
			(i) Electromagnetic flowmeters
			(ii) Ultrasonic flowmeters

(A) Pressure Differential Flowmeter:

Principle: When a fluid is passing through a pipe, it is exerting pressure in all directions. If a constriction is placed in the pipe, the fluid flows through this section more rapidly than when flowing through the rest of the pipe in order that the same quantity pass through. At the constriction, the kinetic energy of the fluid is greater and its potential energy is less so that its static pressure is less. Thus, if the pressure of the fluid at the suitable points on either side of the constriction, upstream and downstream, is measured, this differential pressure varies according to square of the rate of flow.

As shown in Fig. 7.8, the liquid is flowing through a pipe having constriction. If we consider in the pipe two points A and B,

where, a_1 and a_2 = Cross-sectional area at points A and B respectively

u_1 and u_2 = Velocity of liquid at points A and B respectively

P_1 and P_2 = Pressures at points A and B respectively.

A and B are at same level from datum line. Therefore, potential energy of fluid at both points is equal.

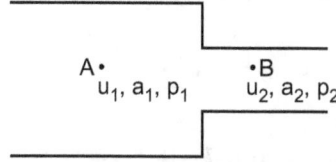

Fig. 7.8: Pressure differential

Hence, by applying Bernoulli's equation without friction we get,

$$\frac{u_1^2}{2} + \frac{P_1}{\rho} = \frac{u_2^2}{2} + \frac{P_2}{\rho}$$

$$\therefore \quad \frac{u_2^2}{2} - \frac{u_1^2}{2} = \frac{P_1 - P_2}{\rho} \qquad \text{... (7.20)}$$

From continuity equation, we know,

Volumetric flow rate $\qquad Q = u_1\, a_1 = u_2\, a_2$

$$u_1 = u_2 \frac{a_2}{a_1}$$

Substituting this value of u_1 in equation (7.20) we get;

$$\frac{u_2^2}{2} - \frac{u_2^2 \left(\frac{a_2}{a_1}\right)^2}{2} = \frac{P_1 - P_2}{\rho}$$

$$\frac{u_2^2}{2} \left(1 - \frac{a_2^2}{a_1^2}\right) = \frac{P_1 - P_2}{\rho}$$

$$u_2^2 = \frac{2\,(P_1 - P_2)}{\rho \left(1 - \frac{a_2^2}{a_1^2}\right)}$$

$$u_2 = \sqrt{\frac{2\,(P_1 - P_2)}{\rho \left(1 - \frac{a_2^2}{a_1^2}\right)}} \qquad \text{... (7.21)}$$

But $\qquad Q = u_2\, a_2$

$$Q = a_2 \sqrt{\frac{2\,(P_1 - P_2)}{\rho \left(1 - \frac{a_2^2}{a_1^2}\right)}} \qquad \text{... (7.22)}$$

But while deriving this equation we have not taken into consideration frictional losses and losses due to change in kinetic energy. Thus, a constant is introduced called as 'discharge coefficient' and now equation becomes:

$$\boxed{Q = C_D\, a_2 \sqrt{\frac{2\,(P_1 - P_2)}{\rho \left(1 - \frac{a_2^2}{a_1^2}\right)}}} \qquad \text{... (7.23)}$$

Discharge coefficient varies with type of flow and nature of constriction. C_D value lies between 0.95 to 0.99 for turbulent flow and it is still lower for laminar flow.

Various flowmeters based on pressure differential principle mainly include:

(i) Orifice meter

(ii) Venturimeter and

(iii) Pitot tube.

(i) Orifice Meter:

This is the simplest and widely used pressure differential flowmeter. It consists of a simple plate with an orifice which is fitted between adjacent flanges of the pipe. The orifice constricts the fluid. Thus when fluid passes through an orifice, its kinetic energy increases and pressure energy decreases. A manometer is connected with pressure taps, one above and one below the orifice plate.

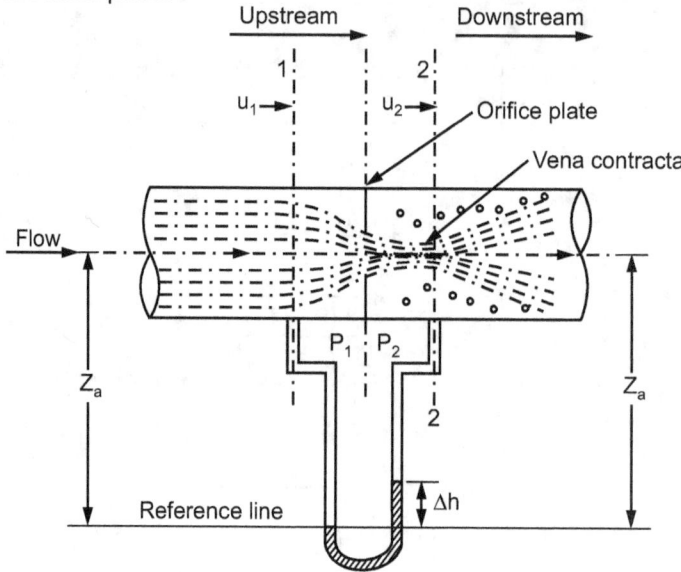

Fig. 7.9: Fluid flow through an orifice in a closed pipe

As shown in the above Fig. 7.9, the fluid passes through an orifice giving a stream having minimum cross-sectional area called as 'vena contracta'. The pressure taps are placed across points A and B (B is at vena contracta). If we apply equation (7.20), we can not determine the exact area (a_2) at point B i.e. vena contracta. We know cross-sectional area at A and at orifice but not at vena contracta, therefore, area a_2 is related to area at orifice by the following equation:

$$C_C = \frac{a_2}{a_o} \qquad \qquad ... (7.24)$$

where, a_o is cross-sectional area at an orifice and C_C is called as 'coefficient of contraction'.

Coefficient of discharge (C_D) for an orifice meter takes into consideration C_C, frictional losses and losses due to kinetic energy changes. Thus, equation (7.20) for an orifice meter becomes

$$Q = a_o \, C_D \sqrt{\frac{2 \, (P_1 - P_2)}{\rho \left(1 - \dfrac{a_o^2}{a_1^2}\right)}} \qquad \text{... (7.25)}$$

If $a_o << a_1$ i.e. orifice diameter is very less as compared to pipe diameter then $1 - \dfrac{a_o^2}{a_1^2}$ is almost equal to 1. Equation (7.25) will become,

$$Q = a_o \, C_D \sqrt{\frac{2 \, (P_1 - P_2)}{\rho}} \qquad \text{... (7.26)}$$

But $P = h \rho g$, for incompressible liquids. Therefore,

$$P_1 - P_2 = h_1 \rho g - h_2 \rho g$$

$$\Delta P = \Delta h \rho g$$

Substituting value of ΔP in equation (7.26), we get

$$Q = a_o \, C_D \sqrt{2 \, \Delta h \, g} \qquad \text{... (7.27)}$$

For an orifice meter value of C_D is around 0.6.

Generally, the plate is fitted in a pipe so that the orifice is concentric with the bore, this is changed in some conditions. When flow rate has to be measured for suspensions or dirty fluids, a plate of the eccentric type is used. The orifice is located with the lower edge coincident with the inside of the bottom of the pipe, so that solids are not obstructed in their passage.

An orifice meter plate sometimes has an additional small hole;

(i) For gas flow rate measurement, the plate is placed with the small hole below the orifice so that condensate will pass through this hole.

(ii) For liquid flow rate measurement, plate is fitted with the hole above the orifice so that gases can pass without forming the pockets.

Advantages of Orifice Meter:

(i) It is versatile and can be used for measurement of almost all gases and liquids. It is most suitable for clean gases and non-viscous liquids at moderate flow rates.

(ii) It can be used over a wide range of flow rates.

(iii) It is simple, inexpensive, and easy to install.

Most important disadvantage of an orifice meter is that, it produces permanent loss of head i.e. more resistance to flow. Therefore, it requires higher pumping cost if used for longer period. Therefore, orifice meter is not suitable for permanent installation.

(ii) Venturi Meter:

Sudden constriction of flow of fluid is a major disadvantage of orifice meter, this is overcome in a venturi meter where gradual decrease in cross-sectional area is achieved.

A venturi meter consists of two cones, an entrance cone on upstream side and a discharge cone or a diffuser on downstream side. These two cones are joined by a short length of pipe called *throat section*. The difference in pressure is measured before entering the fluid in the entrance cone and the throat section as shown in Fig. 7.10. The entrance cone gradually constricts the fluid and the diffuser carries out gradual expansion thereby reducing loss of head, reducing turbulence. Volumetric flow rate of fluid can be calculated by using equation (7.23).

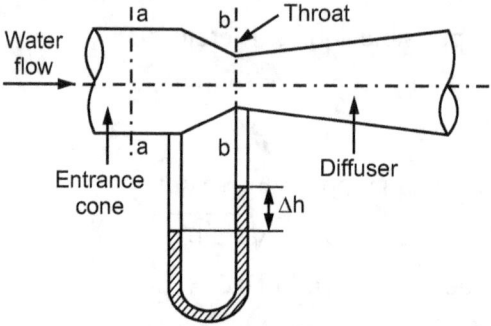

Fig. 7.10: Simple venturi meter

Main advantage of venturi meter is gradual constriction and expansion of fluid reduces the head loss considerably in a venturi meter, therefore, power loss is less with the flow meter. But it is relatively expensive and difficult to install.

(iii) Pitot Tube:

This pressure differential flow meter is also sometimes classified as insertion meter. Pitot tube is a narrow tube supported in a pipe with the head bent in such a way that the open end or impact opening directly faces the oncoming fluid. (Fig. 7.11)

In the pitot tube, B is a stagnation point where velocity of fluid becomes zero. The pressure is measured at point A (P_1) and point B (P_2). Then by using the equation (7.20), we get

$$-\frac{u_1^2}{2} = \frac{P_1 - P_2}{\rho} \qquad (\text{as } u_2 = 0)$$

$$\therefore \qquad u_1^2 = \frac{2(P_2 - P_1)}{\rho} \qquad\qquad \dots (7.28)$$

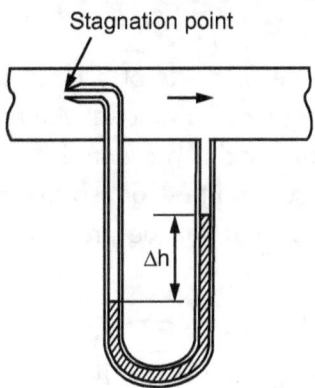

Fig. 7.11: Pitot tube

Advantages of Pitot Tube:

(i)   As tube is very small as compared to the pipe diameter, it does not produce considerable loss of head.

(ii)   It is inexpensive and easy to install.

Limitations of Pitot Tube:

1. This insertion meter determines the velocity of fluid at point. The mean velocity in the pipe can be measured by positioning the pitot tube point at different distances from the pipe wall.

2. Pitot tube cannot be used for measurement of fluids containing small solid particles as the tube opening may get clogged.

3. Pitot tube is not suitable for measurement of fluids at low velocities i.e. below 5 m/s. Accuracy of pitot tube is less than orifice and venturimeter.

4. It is not suitable for the measurement of highly fluctuating velocities, i.e. highly turbulent flows.

(B) Variable Area Flowmeters:

Principle:

In pressure differential meter, the constricted area was kept constant and the pressure differential changes with the velocity of fluid. But if the pressure differential is held constant by adjusting the orifice area then the area of an orifice at any particular instant is a measure of the rate of flow through the orifice. This is the principle of variable area meters.

Various variable area meters include:

(i)   Rotameter

(ii)   Orifice and Plug meter and

(iii)   Gate meters.

(i) Rotameter:

As shown in Fig. 7.12, rotameter consists of a long graduated vertical tube generally made up of glass having a uniform taper, arranged with the smaller section at the bottom. A float moves freely within the tube and is prevented from fouling the side of the tube by means of a series of angled slots cut into the float so that as fluid flows past the float it will be caused to spin. In some forms, float can be prevented from fouling by use of central guide rod.

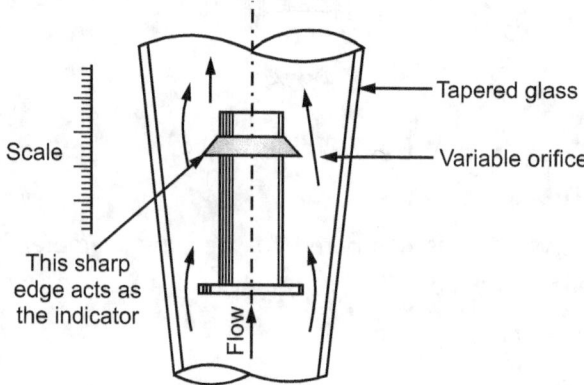

Fig. 7.12: Rotameter

When a fluid flows up the tube, it carries with it the float, as the upward force exerted by the fluid is greater than the immersed weight of the float. As the float rises, the area of annulus between the float and tube wall slowly increases, so the upward force due to the fluid velocity decreases. At a certain point all the forces acting on the float are in equilibrium, when the force due to the fluid velocity is exactly balanced by the weight of the float. Rate of flow of fluid can directly be determined by noting the reading on the scale.

Glass tube rotameters can be used for liquid flow rates from 30 ml/sec. to 5 lit/sec. and for gas flow rates from 0.2 ml/sec. to 40 lit./sec. Whereas metal tube rotameters are used for high flow rates upto 120 lit./sec.

Advantages of Rotameter:

(i) Permanent pressure loss is relatively very low.

(ii) It is highly versatile and can be used for all kinds of fluids, from heavy viscous or opaque liquids to light gases. It is useful over a wide range of flow rates and at high or low temperatures and pressures.

(iii) It is relatively simple in construction, and is inexpensive.

But errors may occur while taking the reading due to tendency of float to oscillate.

(ii) Orifice and Plug Meter:

As shown in Fig. 7.13, a tapered plug of such a form that the area of the annular space between the orifice and the plug is proportional to the lift of the plug. Therefore, the height by which the plug rises when a fluid flows past it, is a measure of the rate of flow.

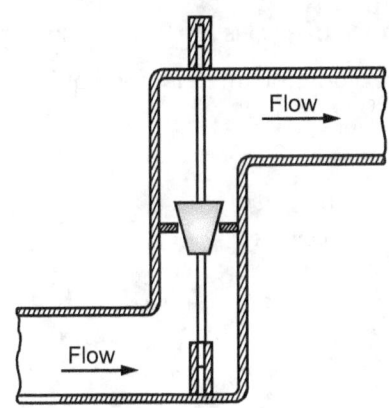

Fig. 7.13: Orifice and Plug meter

(iii) Gate Meter:

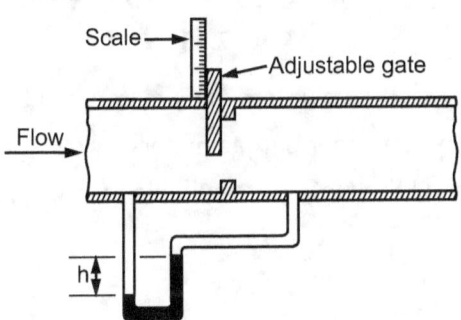

Fig. 7.14: Variable area gate meter

A gate flowmeter has gate which can be adjusted manually or automatically so that constant pressure drop can be maintained across the orifice. The position of the gate is indicated by a scale which may be calibrated in terms of flow rate.

(C) Quantity Flowmeters:

These flowmeters measure the total quantity of fluid flown in a certain time, and average flow rate is determined by dividing the quantity of fluid flown by time. These meters are divided as (i) weighing meters and (ii) volumetric meters.

In weighing meters, the liquid is weighed in weighing tanks and taking into consideration density of liquid, volumetric flow rate can be calculated.

Volumetric meters are based on the principle of positive displacement. In this type of meters, as the liquid flows through the meter, it moves a measuring element which seals off the measuring chamber into a number of compartments of definite volume. As the measuring element moves these compartments are successively filled and emptied. Thus, for one cycle of the measuring element, a known quantity of liquid passes from the inlet to the outlet of the meter. The number of cycles of the measuring element are indicated by a pointer moving over a dial. Volumetric meters for liquids are rotating lobe meter and rotating vane meter (Fig. 7.15).

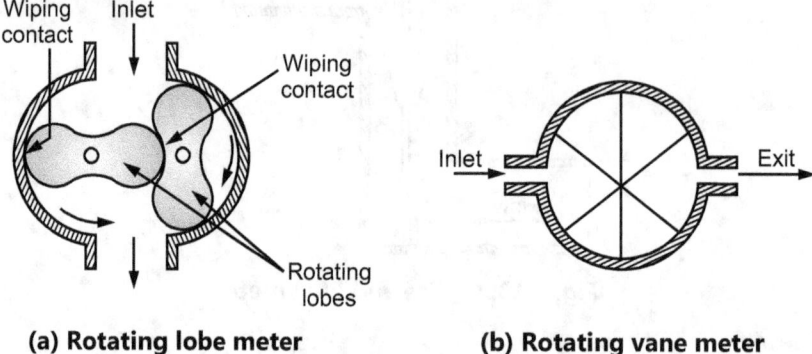

    (a) Rotating lobe meter   **(b) Rotating vane meter**

Fig. 7.15

For gas flow measurement, the volumetric flowmeters are bellows dry gas meter, water displacement gas meter and rotating lobe gas meter. Bellows gas meter is suitable for low pressure gas whereas rotating lobe meters are suitable for high gas pressure.

(D) Other Types:

(i) Electromagnetic Flowmeters:

It is based on Faraday's law of induction i.e. when an electrical conductor moves through a magnetic field in a direction at right angles both to the magnetic field and its length, an e.m.f. is generated which is given by

$$V = B\,l\,U \text{ volts} \qquad\qquad ... (7.29)$$

where B = Magnetic flux density,

                  l = Length of the conductor,

                  U = Velocity of the conductor.

Thus, if a conducting fluid is allowed to flow with velocity U along a pipe of internal diameter l and an electromagnetic system directs a magnetic field B across a section of the pipe so that it acts at right angles to the direction of motion of the fluid, an induced voltage V is produced. If the magnetic flux density is constant, the induced voltage will be proportional to the mean flow velocity.

In this flow meter (Fig. 7.16) there is no obstruction to fluid flow and no head loss. It is widely used for fluids containing suspended solids.

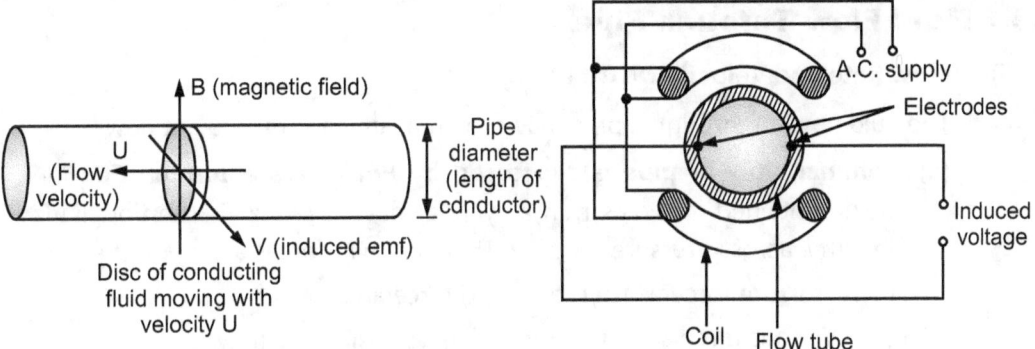

(a) Principle of the electromagnetic flowmeter   **(b) Electromagnetic flowmeter**

Fig. 7.16

(ii)   Ultrasonic Flowmeters:

These are based on the principle that a linear relationship exists between the apparent velocity of sound in flowing fluid and the velocity of the fluid. Thus, if the direction of the ultrasonic wave is not perpendicular to the flow of fluid then the component of flow velocity in the direction of the ultrasonic wave will alter the sound velocity. Its basic working is shown in Fig. 7.17.

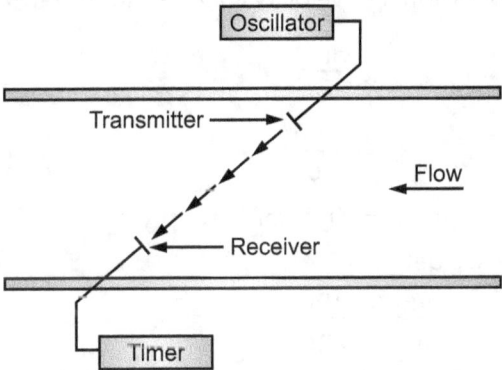

Fig. 7.17: Single path ultrasonic flowmeter

Ultrasonic flowmeters have many advantages like no head loss, good accuracy. It can be used for conducting as well as non-conducting fluid and also the slurries. But the meters are highly expensive.

(iii) Nuclear Technique:

In nuclear technique method, an radioactive tracer is injected and time taken for the passage of a tracer between two points in a pipeline is recorded using two radiation detectors and suitable recorder.

Now, we will analyse three different conditions of flow of fluids:

1. Fluid flow through pipe (as involved in transfer of solutions or gases through pipe).
2. Fluid past immersed bodies (as involved in sedimentation, suspensions, etc.).
3. Fluid flow through packed beds (as involved in filtration packed fractionating column etc.)

7.3.7 Fluid Flow Through Pipe

(i) Flow Rate and Velocity Distribution:

The fluid flowing through a pipe may exhibit a laminar or turbulent flow.

(a) **Laminar flow in pipe is expressed by *Poiseulli's equation*:** Consider the fluid contained in radius r, in a cylinder having radius R. The flow is flowing length l, across pressure drop ΔP. There are two forces acting on the fluid;

(i) Pressure force which is a driving force and

(ii) Viscous force acting on the wall is opposing the flow.

If flow is steady, pressure force is exactly balanced by the viscous force.

$$\text{Pressure force} = \Delta P \, \pi \, r^2 \qquad \qquad ...(7.30)$$

$$\text{Viscous force} = \text{Shear stress} \times \text{Area over which it acts}$$

$$= \tau \times 2 \pi r l \qquad \qquad ...(7.31)$$

But,　　　Shear stress, $\tau = \dfrac{\Delta P r}{2l}$ 　　　　　　...(7.32)

This shear stress is proportional to velocity change with distance i.e. $\dfrac{du}{dr}$ (velocity gradient).

$$\tau \propto \frac{du}{dr}$$

$$\therefore \qquad \tau = \eta \frac{du}{dr}$$

where,　　　　　　　η = Dynamic viscosity

Substituting the value, we get,

$$-\frac{du}{dr} = \frac{\Delta P r}{2\eta l}$$

As 'u' decreases with increase in r, velocity gradient is given negative sign.

$$\therefore \qquad \boxed{du = -\frac{\Delta P}{2\eta l} r \cdot dr} \qquad \qquad ...(7.33)$$

Integrating equation (7.33) between limits r to R and u to 0,

$$\int_0^u du = -\frac{\Delta P}{2\eta l} \int_R^r r \cdot dr$$

$$u = \frac{-\Delta P}{2\eta l} \left(\frac{r^2 - R^2}{2} \right)$$

$$\therefore \qquad u = \frac{\Delta P}{2\eta l} \left(\frac{R^2 - r^2}{2} \right) \qquad \qquad ...(7.34)$$

If this relation is plotted we get velocity distribution across the pipe as shown in Fig. 7.18. Thus, *velocity distribution* is parabolic when fluid is in laminar flow and maximum velocity of fluid in pipe u_{max} i.e. at centre where, r = 0, is twice the average velocity in the pipe (u_{avg}).

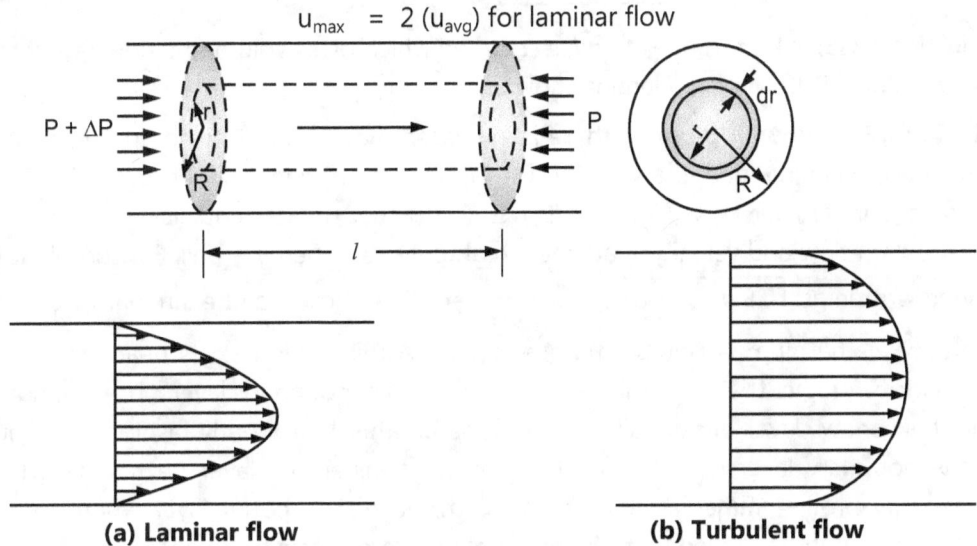

$$u_{max} = 2\,(u_{avg}) \text{ for laminar flow}$$

(a) Laminar flow   **(b) Turbulent flow**

Fig. 7.18: Velocity distribution in pipe

To determine volumetric flow rate across the tube, we will consider a small annular section of tube between r and r + dr, (Fig. 7.19), then

$$Q = u \cdot a$$
$$= u \cdot (2\pi r \cdot dr)$$

Substituting 'u' from equation (7.34)

$$Q = \frac{\Delta P}{2\eta l}\,(R^2 - r^2) \cdot \pi r \cdot dr$$

$$= \frac{\Delta P \pi}{2\eta l}\,(R^2 r - r^3) \cdot dr$$

Total volumetric flow rate can be obtained by integrating above equation between limits r = R and r = 0.

$$\therefore \qquad Q = \frac{\Delta P \pi}{2\eta l} \int_0^R (R^2 r - r^3) \cdot dr$$

$$= \frac{\Delta P \pi}{2\eta l} \left(\frac{R^2 r^2}{2} - \frac{r^4}{4} \right)_0^R$$

$$\therefore \qquad Q = \frac{\Delta P \pi R^4}{8\eta l}$$

Substituting value of π and $R = \dfrac{d}{2}$ where, d is diameter of pipe, we get

$$\boxed{Q = \dfrac{\Delta P\, d^4}{128\, \eta l}} \qquad\qquad \text{... (7.35)}$$

Equation (7.35) is known as *Poiseulli's equation* which gives volumetric flow rate through a pipe when fluid is flowing in a laminar flow.

(b) Turbulent flow in pipe: As there is increased momentum transfer in turbulent flow as compared to laminar flow the velocity distribution in turbulent flow becomes flatter than the parabolic in laminar flow (Fig. 7.18 (b)). It shows that greater equalisation of velocities occur turbulent flow and velocity gradient is high only near the pipe wall. For turbulent flow, it may be written as, $\boxed{0.8\, u_{max} = u_{avg}}$ for turbulent flow. Flow may be laminar or turbulent, the velocity at the pipe wall fluid interface is zero. A thin region exists near the pipe wall where velocity gradient is high, this region is known as 'boundary layer'. The boundary in laminar flow shows layer of fluid sliding over one another in a orderly fashion. In turbulent flow, the boundary layer shows distinct regions, a laminar sub-layer next to wall having linear velocity profile. Immediately adjacent to this layer is a buffer layer where turbulent pattern exists slightly, followed by turbulent core with large scale turbulence.

(ii) Energy Losses in Fluid Flow Through Pipe:

(a) Frictional losses:

When fluid flows over a surface there is friction between the surface and fluid. This friction is considered under two types. The friction due to the tangential force on the smooth surface oriented parallel to the direction of fluid flow is termed as 'skin friction' or *viscous drag*. When there is hindrance to fluid flow by any means (or any surface) it causes acceleration of fluid in upstream and deceleration in downstream. The friction due to this acceleration and deceleration is called as 'form friction' or *form drag*. Thus, total frictional loss in Bernoulli's equation is sum of skin friction and form friction.

The frictional losses are related to Reynolds number. It is proportional to the velocity pressure of the fluid.

Thus, frictional force per unit area of pipe wall is given by:

$$\frac{F}{A} = f\frac{\rho u^2}{2} \qquad\qquad \text{... (7.36)}$$

where,   F = Frictional force

A = Area over which friction forces act

ρ = Density of fluid and

u = Velocity of fluid

f is a coefficient called *friction factor*. Friction factor (f) is a dimensionless number, which indicates the ratio of the total loss of momentum of the fluid to the momentum loss by turbulence or eddy activity.

The energy losses due to friction are given by *Fanning equation*. If we consider a portion dL of a straight horizontal pipe with diameter D, dP is the pressure drop across length dL. (Fig. 7.19). At equilibrium, the friction drag is overcome by pressure force.

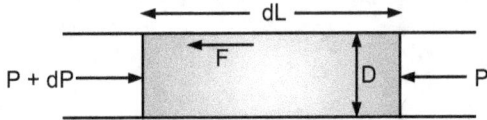

Fig. 7.19: Energy balance over a length of pipe

$\therefore$ $\quad$ Pressure force $= dP \times \dfrac{\pi D^2}{4}$ $\quad\quad$ ... (7.37)

and $\quad$ Friction force $= \dfrac{F}{A} \times$ Wall area of pipe

$$= f\dfrac{\rho u^2}{2} \times \pi D \cdot dL \quad\quad ... (7.38)$$

If we equate equations (7.37) and (7.38)

$$\dfrac{\pi D^2}{4} \cdot dP = \pi D \cdot dL \left(f\dfrac{\rho u^2}{2} \right)$$

$\therefore$ $\quad$ $dP = 2 f \rho u^2 \cdot \dfrac{dL}{D}$

Integrating between limits L_1 and L_2 in which interval pressure energy goes from P_1 and P_2 we get,

$$\int_{P_2}^{P_1} dP = 2 f \rho u^2 \int_{L_2}^{L_1} \dfrac{dL}{D}$$

$$P_1 - P_2 = 2 f \rho u^2 \dfrac{(L_1 - L_2)}{D}$$

Therefore, frictional pressure drop (ΔP_f) is given as

$$\Delta P_f = 2 f \rho u^2 \dfrac{L}{D} \quad\quad ... (7.39)$$

$$\boxed{\text{Frictional energy loss} = \dfrac{\Delta P_f}{\rho} = \dfrac{2 f u^2 L}{D}} \quad\quad ... (7.40)$$

Equation (7.40) is known as Fanning or Fanning-Darcy equation. It is used to calculate frictional pressure drop when fluid flows through pipe.

In derivation of Poiseulli's equation we have considered shear stress acting on wall and related it to velocity gradient. Here we have considered frictional force and related it to friction factor.

Shear stress per unit area (R) is related to friction factor as $f = \dfrac{R}{\rho u^2}$, then equation (7.39) becomes

$$\Delta P_f = \frac{4RL}{d}$$

Friction factor (f) in Fanning equation depends on Reynold's number.

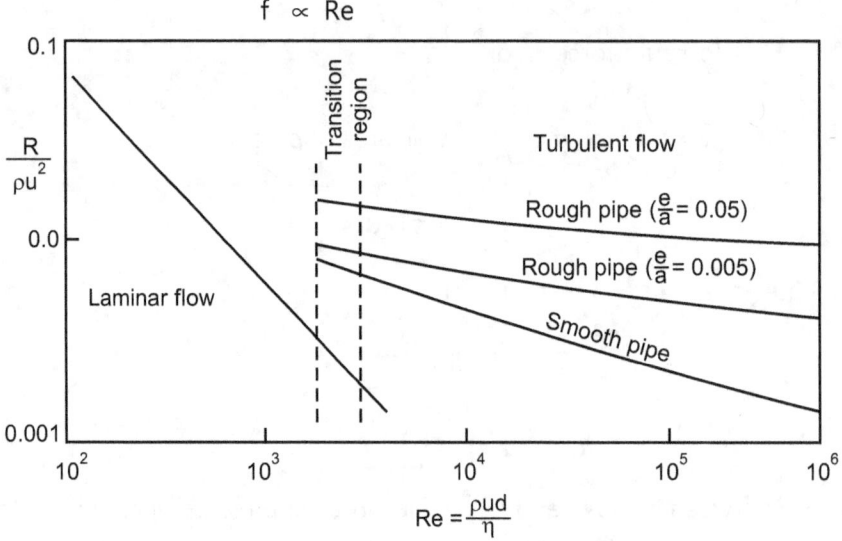

Fig. 7.20: Friction factors in pipe flow

The logarithmic plot of friction factor as a function of Reynold's number (Fig. 7.20) leads to the following conclusions:

(i) The data falls into two distinct curves separated by transition region (where $2100 < Re < 4000$).

(ii) When $Re < 2100$ i.e. flow is laminar, we get linear relationship with equation

$$f = \frac{64}{Re}$$

which shows that friction factor is dependent only on Reynold's number and is not affected by roughness of pipe. This equation is modified Poiseulli's equation. In this condition, due to boundary layer near the wall, the roughness of the wall is completely masked and it acts as a smooth surface.

(iii) At 5000 < Re < 2,00,000 when flow becomes turbulent, equation becomes:

$$f = \frac{0.184}{(Re)^{0.2}}$$

In this region, friction factor is affected by Reynold's number as well as pipe wall roughness as shown in Fig. 7.20.

(iv) At very high values of Re, friction factor is independent of surface roughness.

(Roughness of a pipe is expressed as 'Roughness ratio' which is defined as the ratio of average height of projections which make up the roughness on the wall of the pipe to the pipe diameter i.e. $\frac{e}{a}$).

Thus, once friction factor (f) is known, frictional pressure drop can be determined.

(b) Energy Losses in Pipe Fittings:

In addition to the frictional losses at the pipe wall, liquid encounters loses energy due to bends in the pipe or flow through fittings of varying cross-sections. This loss in energy is not recovered and the energy is dissipated in eddies and additional turbulence and finally lost in the form of heat. These losses occurring due to sudden change in magnitude or direction of flow induced by change in geometry are classified as:

(i) Losses due to sudden contraction or enlargement,

(ii) Losses at entrance or exit, and

(iii) Loss due to pipe curvature.

These energy losses are proportional to velocity pressure of the fluid.

General form of the equation used to calculate these energy losses is:

$$\text{Energy losses due to fitting} = k\frac{u^2}{2}$$

where k is a constant for a particular fitting.

Energy losses at sudden enlargement are given by:

$$F = \frac{(u_1 - u_2)^2}{2\alpha} \qquad \dots (7.41)$$

where, u_1 and u_2 are fluid velocities on upstream and downstream side, $\alpha = 1$ for turbulent flow and $\alpha = 0.5$ for laminar flow.

For sudden contraction, energy losses are given by

$$F = k\frac{u_2^2}{2\alpha} \qquad \dots (7.42)$$

where, $\alpha = 1$ for turbulent flow,

            $\alpha = 0.5$ for laminar flow

            $k = $ Constant

Numerical value of k depends on the ratio of pipe diameter D_1 on upstream side and D_2 on downstream side.

$\dfrac{D_1}{D_2}$	0.1	0.3	0.5	0.7	0.9
k	0.36	0.31	0.22	0.11	0.02

Energy losses in valves and fittings are calculated by Fanning equation:

$$F = \frac{2\,f\,u^2\,L}{D}$$

Numerical values of $\dfrac{L}{D}$ for different fittings and valves are given below:

Fitting/Valve	45° elbow	90° elbow	Gate valve	Globe valve
$\dfrac{L}{D}$ value	15	32	300	170

Generally, these losses are expressed in terms of equivalent length of pipe i.e. length of straight pipe offering same resistance. In other words, a fictitious length of straight pipe is added to the actual length, such that friction due to fictitious pipe is same as that which would arise from the fitting under consideration e.g. energy loss at 90° elbow is equivalent to a length of pipe equal to forty diameters. The equivalent lengths are calculated in a system for all fittings and valves and they are then added to the actual length of straight pipe, then calculate the total pressure drop using Fanning equation.

7.3.8 Fluid Past Immersed Bodies

When a solid is moving with the fluid, then the force exerted by the fluid on solid in the direction of flow is known as '*drag*'. This opposing drag force has two components viscous drag and skin drag.

In Fig. 7.21, A is a cylinder with axis perpendicular to the direction of flow. The lines are hypothetical lines drawn tangential at all points to the movement of fluid called 'streamlines'. The streamlines when past the body are split into two parts one passing over the body and below it. This causes crowding of streamlines in the zone above and below the cylinder as shown in regions D and D'. The fluid layer in contact with the solid surface is immobilised when fluid passes over the body. This induces velocity gradient around the body and in turn shear stress is on the surface. This drag or stress due to tangential force on the surface oriented parallel to the flow is '*viscous drag*'.

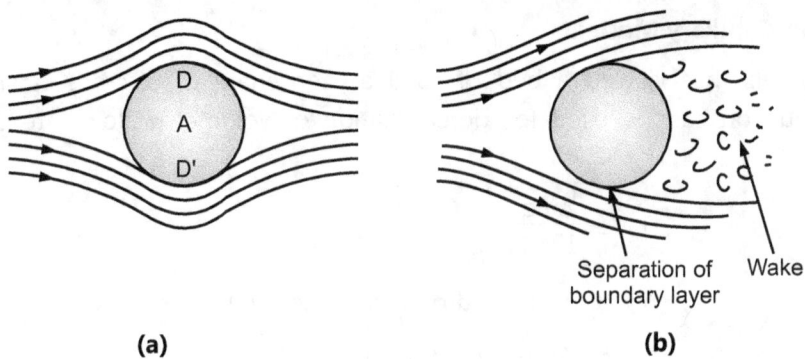

(a) **(b)**

Fig. 7.21: Flow of a fluid past a cylinder

Similarly, crowding of streamlines in regions D and D' shows increase in velocity and decrease in pressure. On downstream side, there is decrease in velocity and increase in pressure, this causes separation of boundary layer. The region between the breakaway streamlines is known as wake region, where there are eddies and vortices. This acceleration and deceleration causes dissipation of pressure energy, this drag is 'form drag'. At low fluid velocity, viscous drag predominates while at high velocities, form drag predominate.

The relation between this drag force and movement of body in fluid is given by 'Stoke's law'. Let us consider a sphere having diameter d, is moving in fluid. Where, u = velocity of fluid, η = viscosity of fluid, ρ = density of fluid and A_p is projected area of sphere. Drag force acting per unit projected area R, will be contributed by viscous drag if fluid flow is laminar.

$$\therefore \qquad R = \rho u^2 \times \frac{12}{Re'} \qquad \qquad ... (7.43)$$

where, Re' is Reynolds number employing diameter of sphere as linear dimension.

$$\therefore \qquad \text{Total drag force} = R \times \frac{\pi d^2}{4}$$

$$= \rho u^2 \left(\frac{12\,\eta}{\dfrac{d\,u\,\rho}{\eta}} \right) \times \frac{\pi d^2}{4}$$

$$\text{Total drag force} = 3\pi\,\eta\,du$$

This is basic equation of *'Stoke's law'*.

7.3.9 Fluid flow through Packed Beds

In various operations like filtration, leaching distillation using packed bed involve flow of fluids through bed of solids. This flow is analysed by two approaches:

(i) Poiseulli's approach and

(ii) Kozeny's approach.

(i) Poiseulli's Capillary Model:

This approach has viewed a bed of solid as aggregate of discrete capillaries. Then Poiseulli's equation can be used for determination of volumetric flow rate through the capillary. It will give:

$$Q = \frac{\Delta P d^4}{128 \, \eta l} \qquad \qquad \text{... (7.44)}$$

where, ΔP = Pressure drop across the capillary

       η = Viscosity of the liquid

       d = Diameter of the capillary

and l = Length of the capillary.

But in real, the length of the capillary (l), is greater than the thickness of the bed (L). But this length (l) is proportional to bed thickness (L).

Now equation will become,

$$Q = \frac{\Delta P d^4}{k \eta L}$$

Now if A is the area of bed which contains n capillaries per unit area then Q will be

$$Q = \frac{\Delta P \, d^4}{k \, \eta \, L} \times nA$$

But number of capillaries per unit area (n) and diameter of capillary are not known, so an experimental constant is used and equation now becomes:

$$Q = K A \frac{\Delta P}{\eta L}$$

where,   K = Permeability coefficient of the bed = $\dfrac{d^4 n}{k}$

This is Poiseulli's equation for volumetric flow rate through bed of solid.

This approach is contradicted as the capillaries in the bed cannot be discrete but inter-connected with each other.

(ii) Kozeny's Hydraulic Diameter Theory:

In this theory of hydraulic diameter, Kozeny considered porous bed as an assembly of channels of varying cross-section but of definite length. He has viewed the packed bed as made up of channels interconnected in a random manner and resistance to fluid flow depends on the number and dimensions of these channels.

Kozeny has defined hydraulic diameter (δ) of the pore space in a random bed as the voids volume per unit of internal surface given by:

$$\delta = \frac{\text{Void volume}}{\text{Total surface of material forming bed}} = \frac{\epsilon}{S}$$

where, ϵ = Porosity of material

$\therefore$ $(1 - \epsilon)$ = Volume of solid.

If S_o is specific surface area of material forming bed then,

$$S = S_o(1 - \epsilon)$$

$\therefore$

$$\delta = \frac{\epsilon}{S_o(1 - \epsilon)}$$

Substitute this value of Poiseulli's equation for flow through channel.

$\therefore$

$$Q = \frac{\Delta P \, \delta^4}{k \eta L}$$

From continuity equation Q = ua. Area of the channel is given by $k'\delta^2$.

$\therefore$ Mean velocity through channel $u' = \dfrac{Q}{k'\delta^2} = \dfrac{\Delta P \delta^2}{k k' \eta L}$

If we consider $k'' = kk'$

$\therefore$ $u' = \dfrac{\Delta P \, \delta^2}{k'' \, \eta \, L}$

where, L is thickness of bed.

The velocity when averaged over the entire area of bed, it gives lower value of actual velocity. This velocity (u) is given by equation

$$u' = \frac{u}{\epsilon} \text{ or } u = u'\epsilon$$

Substituting this value in equation

$$u = \frac{\Delta P \, \delta^2 \, \epsilon}{k'' \, \eta \, L}$$

Substituting value of δ in the above equation

$\therefore$

$$u = \frac{\Delta P \, \epsilon}{k'' \, \eta \, L} \times \frac{\epsilon^2}{S_o^2 (1 - \epsilon)^2}$$

$\therefore$

$$u = \frac{\Delta P \, \epsilon^3}{k'' \, \eta L \, S_o^2 (1 - \epsilon)^2}$$

Constant k'' has value between 5 ± 0.5.

Since Q = uA, where, A is area of bed,

$$Q = \frac{\Delta PA}{\eta L} \frac{\epsilon^3}{5 \, S_0^2 \, (1 - \epsilon)^2}$$

or ∴

$$Q = \frac{K A \, \Delta P}{\eta L}$$

where

$$K = \frac{\epsilon^3}{5 \, S_0^2 (1 - \epsilon)^2} \text{ is permeability coefficient.} \qquad \text{... (7.45)}$$

Equation (7.45) is known as Kozeny's equation. It is similar to Poiseulli's equation with only difference in permeability coefficient Kozeny's equation take into consideration, porosity of bed and specific surface area of material. Therefore, it can explain the effect of size, shape and porosity of flow of fluids through packed bed which is not possible by Poiseulli's equation.

Questions

1. Define absolute pressure and gauge pressure.

2. Discuss pressure measuring devices in detail.

3. Write significance of Reynold's number.

4. Write applications of Bernoulli's theorem.

5. Calculate the power required to pump castor oil from a vessel at ground level to a vessel at 7 m above ground using a glass pipe having dia. 5 cm and length 8 m. The oil has to be delivered at the rate of 16 lit./min. and frictional head for given length of pipe is 8 m.

6. Explain orifice meter in detail with diagram.

7. Write short notes:

    (a) Material balance

    (b) Energy balance

    (c) Pressure differential flowmeter

    (d) Pitot tube

    (e) Rotameter

8. Explain fluid flow through pipe.

■■■

Distillation

8.1 Introduction

Distillation is an unit operation which involves separation of a vaporizable component from a multi-component system and subsequent condensation of vapours. It has been practised as early as 3500 B.C. for isolation of odoriferous principles from flower petals, leaves etc. In eleventh and twelfth century it was widely used in Southern Italy for isolation of alcohol from wines.

Distillation differs from evaporation mainly in three aspects:

(i)   In evaporation process, the vaporization takes place at the free surface of the liquid below its boiling point. Whereas, in distillation vaporization occurs from the bulk of the liquid at its boiling point. Although, evaporation should be carried out below boiling point generally, it is carried out at boiling point so as to increase the rate of operation.

(ii)   The vapours in evaporation process diffuse through the space above the liquid whereas, vapours in distillation has sufficient pressure to push away the molecules of air or gas present above the surface.

(iii) In evaporation, concentrated residue is a desired product, in contrast distillate is generally a desired product of distillation.

8.2 Relative Velocity

The real basis for separation of two components of distillation is the difference in their volatilities (i.e. relative volatility of the system). The volatility of a liquid is indicated by its vapour pressure. Higher is the vapour pressure of the substance more volatile it is. If a mixture of two liquids A and B is heated, the vapours in equilibrium with the liquid mixture will contain more proportion of the more volatile component A, than in the liquid. The degree of enrichment of vapours with respect to A depends on its relative volatility (α_{AB}) with respect to component B. Relative volatility can be mathematically defined as:

$$\alpha_{AB} = \frac{Y_A/X_A}{Y_B/X_B} = \frac{Y_A X_B}{Y_B X_A} \qquad \text{... (8.1)}$$

where, Y indicate the mole fraction of component in the vapour phase and X indicate the mole fraction of component in the liquid space.

Subscripts A and B denote more volatile and less volatile component respectively.

8.3 Vapour - Liquid Equilibrium

Thus, to understand the process of distillation it is necessary to have a clear concept about the vapour-liquid equilibrium conditions. The vapour liquid equilibrium relations of binary systems can be studied for three different classes of systems viz. Miscible, immiscible and partially miscible systems.

8.3.1 Miscible System

The miscible binary system may have ideal or non-ideal behaviour.

(a) Ideal Systems:

Ideal binary mixtures obey Raoult's law. According to Raoult's law "a component's vaporising tendency depends on its concentration in the mixture and its vapour pressure at that temperature." In such system, the components have no effect on each other except dilution. In these systems each component acts independently for a binary system of components A and B Roult's law can be mathematically expressed as:

$$P_A = P_A^o \, X_A \qquad \text{... (8.2)}$$

$$P_B = P_B^o \, X_B \qquad \text{... (8.3)}$$

where,   P = Partial pressure of the component

P^o = Vapour pressure of pure component at that temperature.

Subscripts A and B denotes component A and B. The total vapour pressure of the mixture is given by,

$$P_{total} = P_A + P_B \qquad \text{... (8.4)}$$

The vapour pressure composition relationship at a constant temperature for a binary system is shown in Fig. 8.1.

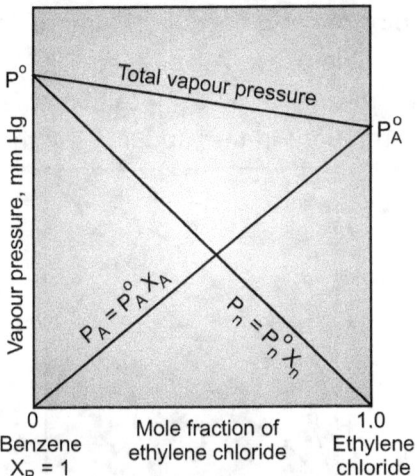

Fig. 8.1: Vapour pressure - composition curve for an ideal binary system

$$\therefore \qquad \alpha_{AB} = \frac{P_A}{P_B} \qquad\qquad\qquad ... (8.5)$$

The vapour-liquid equilibrium pattern at constant pressure can be exhibited by the equilibrium curve and boiling point diagram for a particular system.

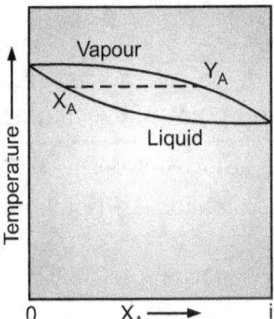

Fig. 8.2: Boiling point diagram

'Boiling point diagram' is obtained by plotting boiling points of various mixtures at atmospheric pressure against composition. A typical boiling point diagram is shown in Fig. 8.3. It shows two curves, the boiling curve which indicates the boiling points of various compositions. The second is a dew curve which gives the composition of the vapours in equilibrium with the boiling mixture. The ends of the two curves coincide at the boiling points of the pure components. Above the dew curve the mixture is completely vapour, whereas below the boiling curve the mixture is completely a liquid. The area between the two curves represents a system which consists partly of liquid and partly of vapours. As shown in Fig. 8.2, if we start heating a system containing X_A mole fraction of component A (denoted by m), it starts boiling at temperature t_A to produce vapours in equilibrium with Y_A mole fraction of A. These vapours on cooling will naturally produce a liquid phase with Y_A mole fractions of A. As A is more volatile than B, Y_A is always greater than X_A.

'Equilibrium curve ' is a plot of mole fraction of a more volatile component in vapours against its mole fraction in the liquid phase. A typical equilibrium curve is shown in Fig. 8.3. It shows that for an ideal binary mixture at all compositions the more volatile component is always present in higher concentrations in the vapour phase than the liquid phase.

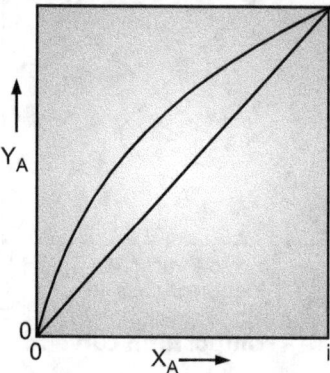

Fig. 8.3: Equilibrium curve

Although there is slight change in the relative volatility of an ideal mixture; concept of average relative volatility was introduced for theoretical construction of an equilibrium diagram. This may introduce a deviation in equilibrium concentration upto the level of 1.7% only.

The average relative volatility is calculated as the root mean square of the relative volatilities of the system at the boiling point of each component:

$$\therefore \qquad \alpha_{AB\,(avg)} = \sqrt{\alpha_{AB\,(at\,b.p.\,of\,A)} \times \alpha_{AB\,(at\,b.p.\,of\,B)}} \qquad \qquad ...(8.6)$$

By assuming average relative volatility, an equilibrium diagram can be developed as follows,

As we know

$$\alpha_{AB} = \frac{Y_A/X_A}{Y_B/X_B} \qquad \qquad ...(8.7)$$

But, $\qquad Y_B = 1 - Y_A$

and $\qquad X_B = 1 - X_A$

By substituting these values in equation 8.7, we get

$$\alpha_{AB} = \frac{Y_A/X_A}{(1 - Y_A) \cdot (1 - X_A)} \qquad \qquad ...(8.8)$$

By solving this,

$$Y_A = \frac{\alpha_{AB}\,X_A}{1 + \left(\alpha_{AB} - 1\right) X_A} \qquad \qquad ...(8.9)$$

By assuming various values for X_A in equation 8.9, corresponding values of Y_A are calculated and an equilibrium diagram is plotted.

Example 1: Construct an equilibrium diagram for binary system of benzene – toluene.

(a) Calculation of average relative volatility.

Data	V.P. of Benzene (P_A)	V.P. of Toluene (P_B)	$\alpha_{AB} = \dfrac{P_A}{P_B}$
Boiling point of C_6H_6 80.1°C	760 mm	270 mm	2.81
Boiling point of Tolulene 110.6	1,780 mm	760 mm	2.34

∴ $\alpha_{AB\,(avg.)} = \sqrt{2.81 \times 2.34} = 2.52$

(b) Calculation of Y_A

  For increment of 0.1 X_A we will calculate Y_A

$$Y_A = \frac{\alpha_{AB}\,X_A}{1 + (\alpha_{AB} - 1)\,X_A}$$

∴ $$Y_A = \frac{2.52\,X_A}{1 + 1.52\,X_A}$$

X_A	$2.52\,X_A$	$1 + 1.52\,X_A$	Y_A
0.1	0.252	1.152	0.201
0.2	0.504	1.304	0.386
0.3	0.756	1.456	0.519
0.4	1.008	1.608	0.637
0.5	1.260	1.760	0.717
0.6	1.512	1.912	0.791
0.7	1.764	2.064	0.855
0.8	2.016	2.216	0.911
0.9	2.268	2.368	0.957

Now Y_A is plotted against X_A as shown in Fig. 8.4.

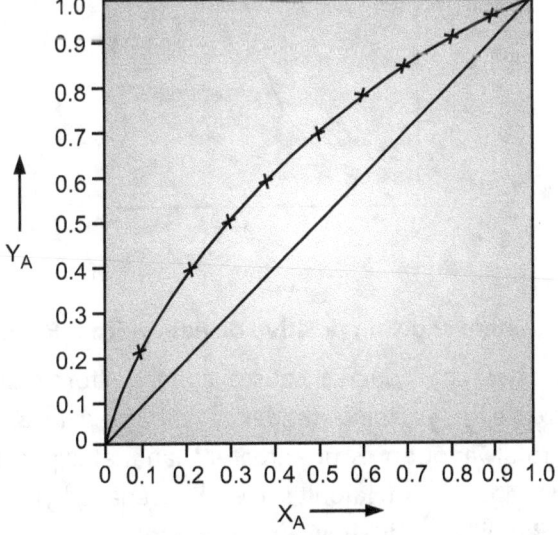

Fig. 8.4: Equilibrium curve

(b) Non-Ideal Systems:

In non-ideal binary system, there is an interaction of one component upon the other. It may be attraction or repulsion of molecules. The increase in adhesive interaction between the two components over the cohesive interaction of each component leads to decrease in escaping tendency and in turn partial vapour pressure of each component and the total vapour pressure of the system than expected by Raoult's law. This is negative deviation from Raoult's law as shown in Fig. 8.5 (a). Acetone-chloroform system exhibits negative deviation from Raoult's law.

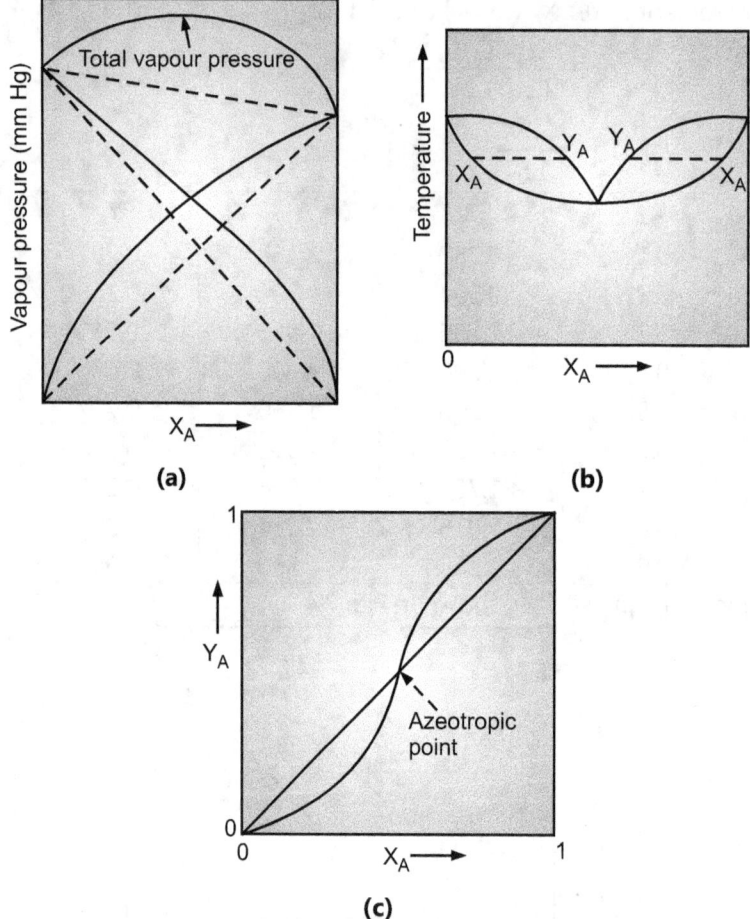

Fig. 8.5: System showing positive deviation from Raoult's law

Repulsion between two components causes cohesive force to exceed the adhesive force. This causes increase in escaping tendency and partial vapour pressure of each component along with total vapour pressure greater than that expected by Raoult's law. This is called as positive deviation from Raoult's law. Benzene ethyl alcohol system exhibits positive deviation from Raoult's law as shown in Fig. 8.6 (a).

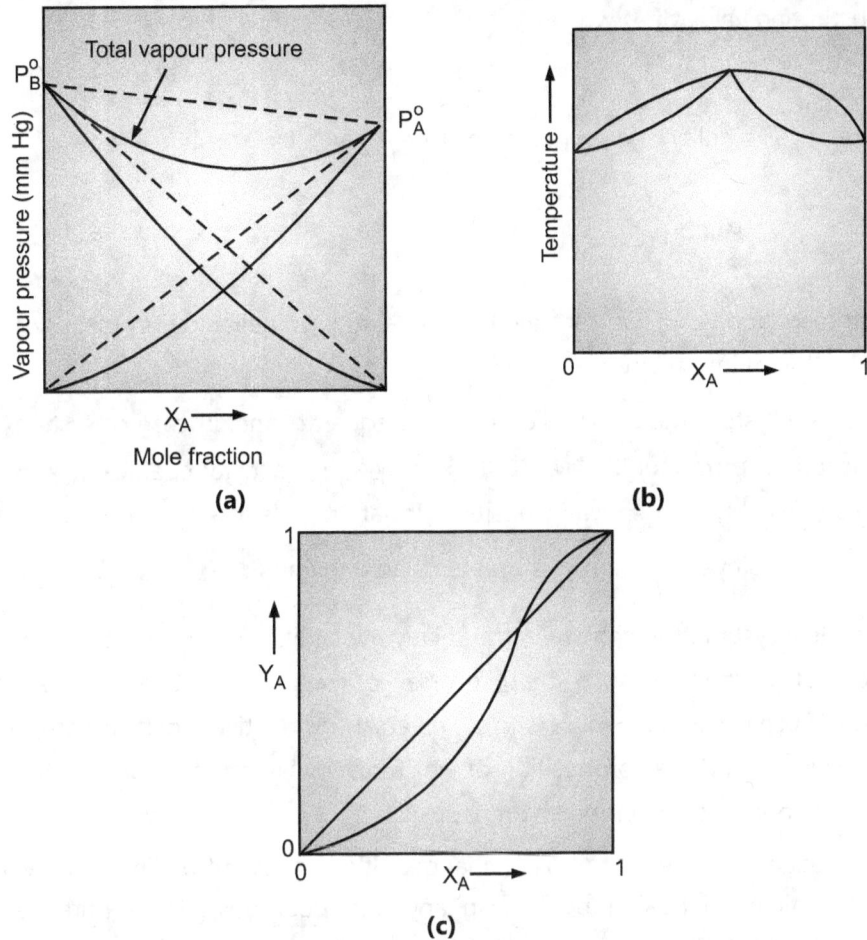

Fig. 8.6: System showing negative deviation from Raoult's law

In case of an ideal binary mixture the escaping tendency of any component is a function of its concentration (X) in the system. But in case of non-ideal mixtures deviations from ideality is shown due to the molecular interactions. Thus in non-ideal system, the effective concentration or activity (a) of the component is a real function instead of actual concentration (X).

From non-ideal mixture Raoult's law will be modified as:

$$P_A = P_A^o \; a_A \qquad \qquad \dots (8.10)$$

where, $\qquad a_A$ = Effective concentration or activity of component A.

The ratio of activity to the actual concentration of a component is known as activity coefficient.

$\therefore \qquad$ Activity coefficient of A; $\gamma_A = \dfrac{a_A}{X_A} \qquad \qquad \dots (8.11)$

By substituting value of a_A we get

$$P_A = P_A^o \, \gamma_A \, X_A \qquad \text{... (8.12)}$$

Thus, relative volatility of a non-ideal mixture is given by

$$\alpha_{AB} = \frac{\gamma_A \, P_A^o}{\gamma_B \, P_B^o} \qquad \text{... (8.13)}$$

From the equation 8.13, we can say that the relative volatility in non-ideal system differs from introduction of an activity coefficient.

For an ideal system the activity coefficient is equal to one. In case of systems showing negative deviation from Raoult's law $P_A^o \, X_A > P_A^o \, \gamma_A X_A$ i.e. activity coefficient γ_A is less than one. Whereas, for a system showing positive deviation γ_A is less than one. Whereas, for a system showing positive deviation γ_A is greater than one and $P_A^o \, X_A < P_A^o \, \gamma_A X_A$.

In non-ideal system, the change in the relative volatilities of both components with the composition of mixture is such that reversal of relative volatility occurs at certain composition. Such mixtures which shows reversal in relative volatility are termed as azeotropic mixtures and the composition of which reversal in relative volatility takes place is known as azeotrope or constant boiling mixture.

In Greek azeotrope means to boil unchanged. It is a constant boiling mixture which has maximum or minimum boiling point than any other composition or pure components [Fig. 8.5 (b) and 8.6 (b)]. An azeotropic mixture behaves like a pure component i.e. when distilled we get the distillate of the same composition. At some composition intermediate between the two pure components reversal of relative volatility takes place. Over one portion of the composition range one component is more volatile, while over the remaining of the range the other component is more volatile. Fig. 8.5 (c) and 8.6 (c) shows the equilibrium diagrams of azeotropic mixtures. The condition of the azeotropic composition can be given by,

$$\frac{\gamma_A \, P_A^o}{\gamma_B \, P_B^o} = \alpha_{AB} = 1 \qquad \text{... (8.14)}$$

At this composition the difference in the inherent volatility of two components is overcome by the deviations from ideal behaviour. Therefore, such mixture cannot be separated completely by simple distillation procedures and a modified method has to be adopted.

8.3.2 Immiscible Systems

In the mixture of two immiscible liquids, each component will tend to vaporize independently hence their vapour pressures are additive. Thus, the system starts boiling at temperature when the summation of two vapour pressures is equal to the atmospheric pressure i.e. at boiling point of a mixture,

$$P_A + P_B = 760 \text{ mm. Hg}$$

Vapour pressure - temperature relationship for an immiscible system is shown in Fig. 8.7.

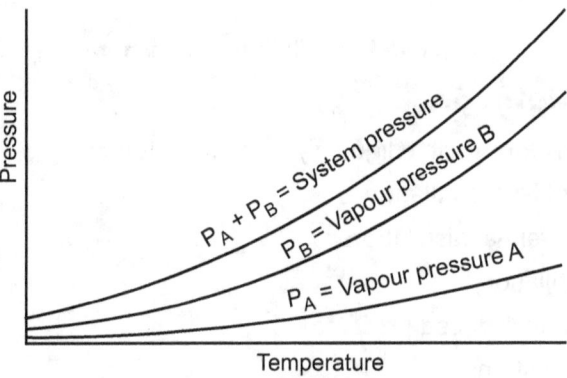

Fig. 8.7: Vapour pressure-temperature relationships for an immiscible system

Naturally, this temperature is below the boiling points of either of the individual components.

During distillation of such a system the composition of vapours produced will be in proportion of the relative vapour pressures of the two components. Therefore in vapour phase,

$$\frac{\text{Moles of A}}{\text{Moles of B}} = \frac{P_A}{P_B} \qquad \qquad \text{... (8.15)}$$

$$\therefore \quad \frac{\text{Weight of A in vapour phase}}{\text{Weight of B in vapour phase}} = \frac{P_A \, M_A}{P_B \, M_B} \qquad \qquad \text{... (8.16)}$$

This forms the basis of distillation of an immiscible system.

8.3.3 Partially Miscible System

Partial miscibility is exhibited by some mixtures like water and n-butanol. Such partially miscible system is a special case of minimum boiling azeotrope. In this type of system over a range of liquid composition, the vapour composition and boiling point are constant as shown in Fig. 8.8 (a) and (b). Over the liquid composition range Z, there are two immiscible liquid phases of compositions C and D, each having equilibrium vapour composition E.

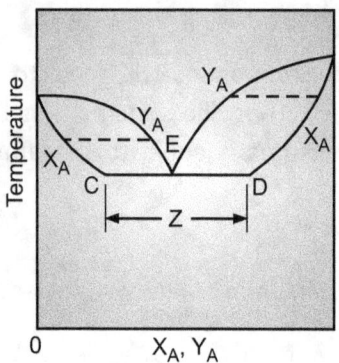 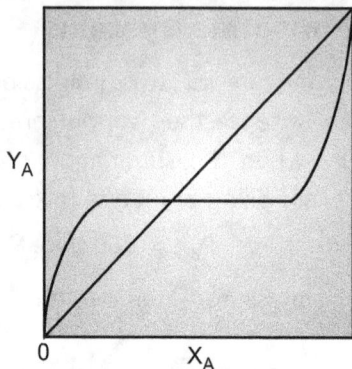

Fig. 8.8: Partially miscible system

8.4 Distillation Methods

Distillation methods for miscible liquid system are as follows:

1. Equilibrium or Flash distillation.
2. Simple or Differential distillation.
3. Fractional Distillation.
4. Distillation under reduced pressure.
    Molecular Distillation.
5. Special Distillation Methods for non-ideal mixtures
    (a) Azeotropic Distillation
    (b) Extractive Distillation

8.4.1 Equilibrium or Flash Distillation

It is a single stage operation where a liquid is partially vaporized, the vapours are allowed to come in equilibrium with the residual liquid and the resulting vapours and liquid are separated. This is used only when the difference between the volatilities of the components is very large.

Material Balance for flash distillation will be as follows:

Consider the equilibrium distillation of a mixture containing components A and B. Component A is more volatile. If we consider:

$$W_o = \text{Total moles in distillation pot at the starting stage}$$
$$X_o = \text{Mole fraction of component A at start}$$
$$V = \text{Moles of vapours produced}$$
$$X \text{ and } Y = \text{Mole fraction of A in liquid and vapours respectively.}$$

As, Moles of A at start = Moles of A in vapour phase + Moles of A in liquid phase

∴ $$W_o x_o = V_y + (W_o - V) x \qquad \text{... (8.17)}$$

The values of x and y are such that they satisfy both equilibrium curve and equation 8.17.

8.4.2 Simple or Differential Distillation

In simple distillation, vapours from the boiling liquid is removed from the system as soon as it is formed. This method is commonly used on laboratory scale, but in industry, it is used only for systems with high relative volatilities. The assembly for distillation consists of a boiler, condenser and a receiver as shown in Fig. 8.9.

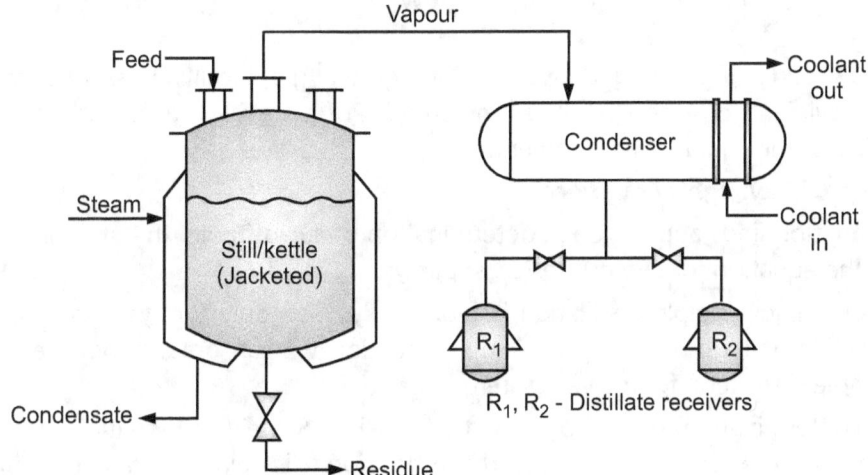

Fig. 8.9: Simple distillation unit

In simple distillation there is continuous change in the distillate composition. It is necessary to know the composition of distillate at every instant during operation so as to control it.

In 1902, Rayleigh analysed the simple batch distillation mathematically. Consider that simple distillation was started with total W_o moles of system containing components A and B. If at any given instant W moles of liquid are present in the still which contains X mole fraction of component A.

∴ $\quad\quad\quad\quad$ XW = Moles of component A present in the pot at given instant

Now, if a small amount dW is vaporized then total moles change from W to (W – dW); and suppose its mole fraction changes from X to (X – dX). The vapours produced by vaporization of dW moles contain Y mole fraction of component A.

Therefore material balance will be

∴ $\quad\quad\quad\quad$ XW = (W – dW) (X – dX) + Y dW $\quad\quad\quad\quad$ ... (8.18)

$\quad\quad\quad\quad\quad\quad\quad$ XW = XW – dX W + dX dW – X dW + Y dW $\quad\quad\quad$ ... (8.19)

dX dW is a second order differential which will be over Y small, hence if neglected we get

$\quad\quad\quad\quad\quad$ dX W = (Y – X) dW $\quad\quad\quad\quad\quad\quad\quad$ ... (8.20)

∴ $\quad\quad\quad\quad\quad$ $\dfrac{dX}{Y - X} = \dfrac{dW}{W}$ $\quad\quad\quad\quad\quad\quad\quad\quad$ ... (8.21)

As simple distillation is a continuous operation, integration function is used. Equation 8.21 is thus integrated between initial and final conditions of total moles as well as mole fractions of more volatile component in the liquid.

$$\therefore \quad \int_{X_1}^{X_o} \frac{dX}{Y-X} = \int_{W_1}^{W_o} \frac{dW}{W} = \ln\frac{W_o}{W_1} \quad \text{... (8.22)}$$

Left hand side of the equation can be integrated graphically. This equation (8.22) is known as Rayleigh's equation. It relates the amount of material distilled with instantaneous composition of the liquid at that moment.

Application of Rayleigh's Equation:

This equation finds application in determination of cut-off point in batch distillation. We will apply the equation for two purposes as follows:

1. As we know simple distillation is industrially used only for systems where relative volatility is high. By using Rayleigh's equation we can predict the effectiveness of simple distillation for a given system.

2. In determination of cut-off point; by using Rayleigh's equation we can stop operation as soon as the overhead composition falls below the required purity of the product.

The applications are illustrated below:

Let us consider that we started simple distillation of two ideal systems. M and N both containing 70 mole % of a more volatile component. if,

Average Relative volatility of system M = 1.5

Average Relative volatility of system N = 6.

Let us now analyse the systems for increments of x = 0.1.

For each value of x, corresponding value of y is calculated using equation (8.9).

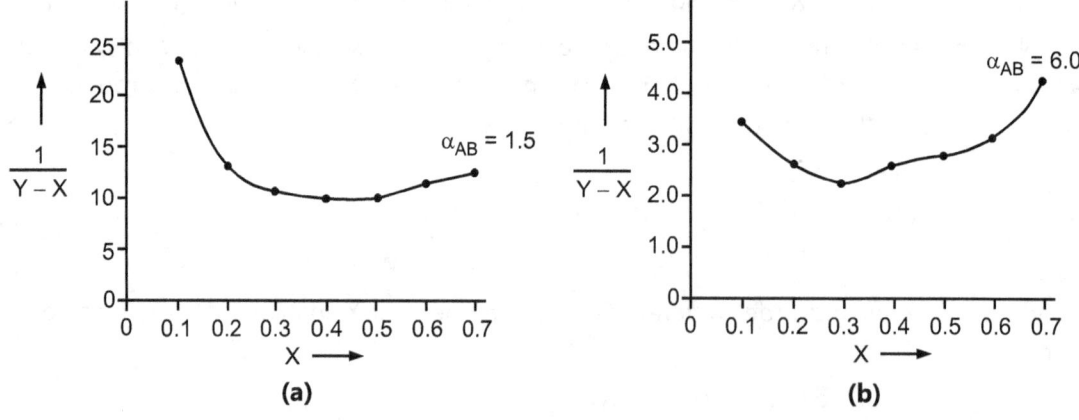

Fig. 8.10: $\dfrac{1}{y-x}$ **versus X plots**

The $\dfrac{1}{y-x}$ was plotted against X. The area under curve was calculated by integration by graph as shown in Fig. 8.10 (a) and (b). This integrated area is nothing but represents left hand side of Rayleigh's equation. i.e. $\ln \dfrac{W_o}{W}$.

Now, Antilog $\left(\dfrac{\ln W_o/W}{2.303} \right) = \dfrac{W_o}{W}$ ... (8.23)

Suppose , $\dfrac{W_o}{W}$ = a, then percent distilled is given by

per cent distilled $= \left(\dfrac{W_o - W}{W_o} \right) \times 100 = \left(1 - \dfrac{1}{a} \right) \times 100$ ... (8.24)

After following above discussed method, Tables 8.1 and 8.2 are prepared for α_{AB} = 1.5 and α_{AB} = 6 respectively.

Table 8.1

System M (α_{AB} = 1.5)

X	Y	$\dfrac{1}{Y-X}$	Integral area	$\dfrac{W_o}{W}$	$\dfrac{W_o - W}{W_o} \times 100$
0.1	0.143	23.256	7.30	1448.00	00.930
0.2	0.273	13.699	5.50	244.30	99.590
0.3	0.391	10.989	4.30	73.64	98.640
0.4	0.500	10.000	3.25	25.77	96.120
0.5	0.600	10.000	2.25	9.482	89.450
0.6	0.692	10.869	1.20	3.319	67.870
0.7	0.773	12.821	0.00	1.000	00.000

Table 8.2

System N (α_{AB} = 6.0)

X	Y	$\dfrac{1}{Y-X}$	Integral area	$\dfrac{W_o}{W}$	$\dfrac{W_o - W}{W_o} \times 100$
0.1	0.400	3.33	1.720	5.582	82.08
0.2	0.600	2.50	1.430	4.178	76.07
0.3	0.720	2.38	1.185	3.270	69.42
0.4	0.800	2.50	0.940	2.560	60.94
0.5	0.860	2.78	0.675	1.963	49.57
0.6	0.900	3.33	0.370	1.447	30.89
0.7	0.933	4.29	0.00	1.000	00.00

Now distillate composition (y) in terms of more volatile component is plotted against percent distilled as shown in Fig. 8.11.

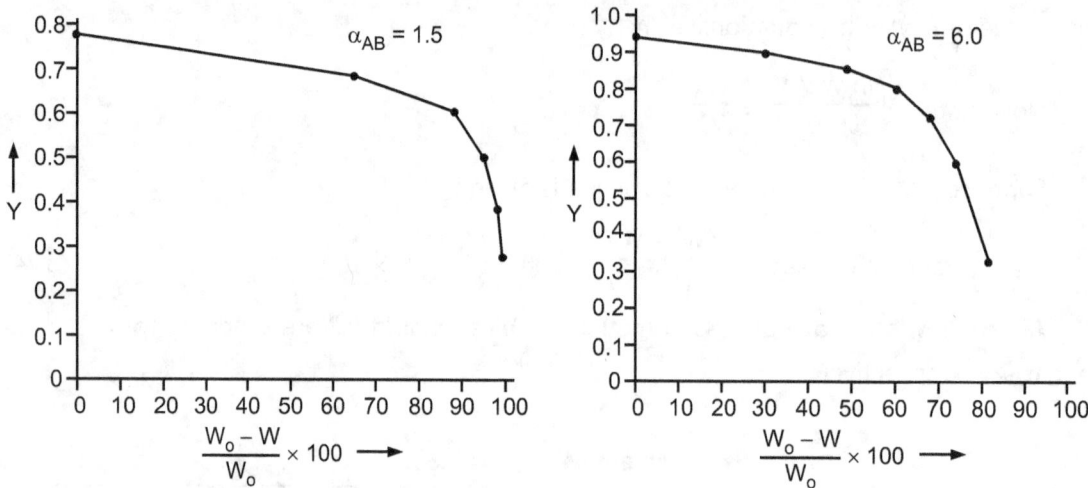

Fig. 8.11: Distillate composition as a function of percent distilled

From Fig. 8.11, we can conclude the following:

(a) If we start simple distillation with 70 mole % of a volatile component in a pot and if relative volatility of system is 6 (system N) we can get a distillate containing above 90 mole % also. But in case relative volatility be 1.5 (system M) we will never get distillate composition above 80 mole %. Therefore, in the later case we will not suggest simple distillation as it cannot enrich the component significantly.

(b) In case of system N i.e. α_{AB} = 6, if we want the strength of the distillate to be minimum 80 moles %; then stop the operation when 60% of the original system is distilled.

Aromatic spirit of Ammonia I.P. is prepared by simple distillation process. Nutmeg oil and other aromatic principles are introduced to the required degree in the final preparation when 2/3 of the original solution is distilled.

8.4.3 Fractional Distillation (Rectification)

In fractional distillation, the vapours rising from the still come into contact with a condensed but not further cooled portion of vapours. The part of the condensate which is returned to the system is known as reflux. This is used for systematic separation of a mixture into relatively pure fractions.

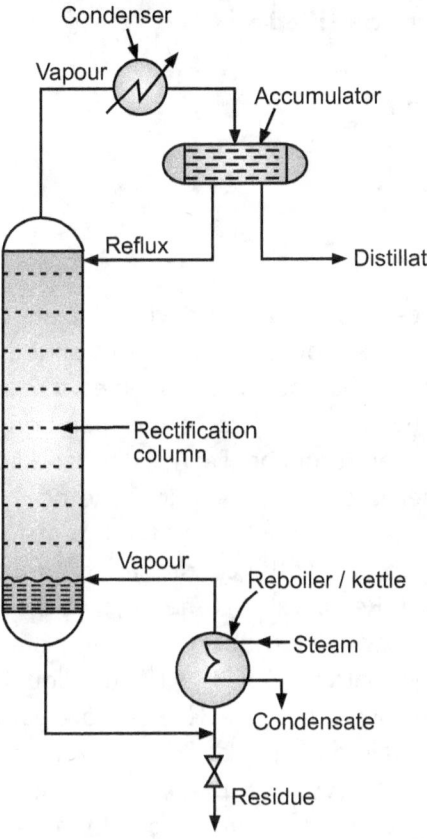

Fig. 8.12: Fractional distillation unit

The fractionation equipment as shown in Fig. 8.12, consists of:

(a) A still for generation of vapours.

(b) A fractionating or rectifying column for vapour liquid contact.

(c) A condenser for condensing overhead vapours.

The vapours are generated in the boiler or still. These vapours pass through the fractionating column, where they come in contact with the descending stream of liquid which is reflux from the condenser. Thus, counter-current contact takes place between vapours and liquid. During this contact mass transfer and heat transfer takes place. The more volatile component from the liquid phase passes into the vapour phase and the less volatile component from the vapour phase condenses and passes into the liquid phase. Thus, the vapours rising from top to bottom get enriched in a more volatile component (MVC), whereas, the descending liquid stream becomes richer in a lower volatile component (LVC). Thus, fractionating column assists heat transfer and mass transfer by bringing two phases in intimate contact. As MVC is larger at the top and LVC increases towards bottom, the top of the column is relatively cooler than the bottom of the column.

Fractionating columns are classified as:

(A) Plate columns:

    (a) Sieve plate column

    (b) Bubble cap column

    (c) Valve - plate column

(B) Packed column.

(A) Plate Columns:

A plate column is a stage-wise contacting device. A plate column consists of plates or trays on which the liquid is retained for certain length of period when it is moving down the column. The vapours rising from the bottom are bubbled through this liquid when intimate contact is achieved between two phases. Thus, contact between vapour and liquid occurs on the plate. Heat and mass transfer occurs between vapour and liquid phase. The liquid phase passing below becomes richer in LVC and vapour phase richer in the MVC from the plate above it. This occurs in all parts of column except the top plate where the concentration of MVC is maintained by returning part of the condensate from the last stage to the top plate. This is known as reflux return. Reflux ratio is the ratio of the condensate returned to the column and the amount withdrawn as product. Liquid flow patterns over a plate differ with the requirements. In crossflow pattern, Fig. 8.13 (a), the liquid flows across the plate and passes over a weir into the downcomer. In Reverse flow pattern Fig. 8.13 (b), the liquid passes across the plate and again direction of flow is reversed, thus liquid stays on a plate for longer period of time. In split flow, Fig. 8.13 (c), liquid passes on one plate from center to the sides, whereas on next plate the flow is from side of the plate to the centre. A cross-flow may be modified to a cascade cross flow Fig. 8.13 (d) where plate is again divided in stages on which liquid flows in cross-flow pattern.

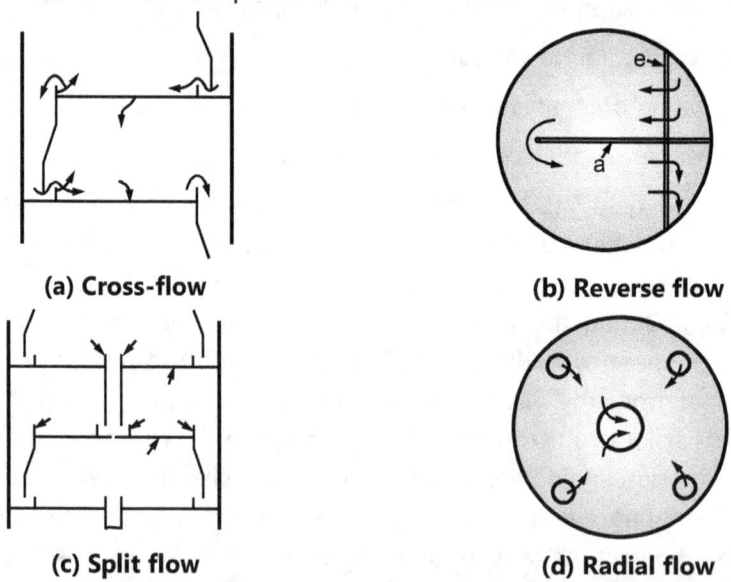

(a) Cross-flow   (b) Reverse flow

(c) Split flow   (d) Radial flow

Fig. 8.13: Flow patterns in rectification column

Very low liquids levels on plate will be unable to cover the holes, whereas excess liquid heights will increase the pressure drop. Therefore, optimum liquid heights should be maintained over the plates. The liquid height is governed by liquid flow rate and weir height.

Entrainment i.e. carryover of liquid droplets with the vapours from the plate above; is undesirable as it reduces the efficiency of the column. This may occur at high gas flow rates in such cases entrainment may be reduced by increasing diameter of the column. Thus, higher is the gas flow rate larger is the diameter of the column. Thus, higher is the gas flow rate larger is the diameter of the column. When gas at high velocity passes through the liquid over the plate there is formation of froth which increases gas-liquid surface area and increases rate of mass transfer but excessive foaming or frothing may increase entrainment. Excessive entrainment or if excessive gas or liquid is passed through the column results in *flooding*. Thus column diameter and spacing of trays of column should be carefully chosen to avoid entrainment. A smaller tray spacing increases entrainment whereas, larger tray spacing decreases entrainment but increases column height and cost.

The vapour-liquid contacting devices of plate type are:

(a) Perforated or sieve plate.

(b) Bubble cap plate and

(c) Valve plate.

Bubble cap and sieve plate are the old and commonly used devices.

(i) Bubble Cap Plate:

Typical bubble cap plate is illustrated in Fig. 8.14. Here the vapour passed through short vertical pipes called riser; on the top of which a cap is mounted. The caps force the vapour to bubble through the liquid; for this purpose the edges of cap are perforated with slots which break the vapours into bubbles. The liquid flows across the plate and then downward from plate to plate through downcomers. The level of liquid on the plate is maintained in such a way that the slots of the cap remain submerged in the liquid. The caps are spaced evenly over the entire plate with the distance between two caps at about 1 to 3 inch. The gas bubbles coming out from the slots are projected around 1 inch from the cap. The caps have diameter of around 6 inches and riser has diameter of 4 inches.

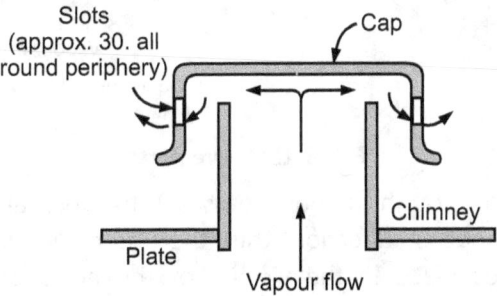

Fig. 8.14: Bubble cap plate

Thus, vapours pass from one plate to the riser then trough the bubble cap slots in the liquid and then leave the plate.

During this flow, the pressure of the gas decreases due to:

(i)   Contraction of gas as it enters the riser,

(ii)   Friction in the annualar space of a bubble cap,

(iii)   Friction due to change in direction of gas flow,

(iv)   During passage through slots,

(v)   Liquid head above the slots.

When a liquid is flowing over a bubble cap plate column due to the resistance to flow by the caps and risers, there is decrease in liquid depth as the liquid passes across the plate, thus liquid height gradient is produced on the plate. Due to this gradient, vapour is not uniformly distributed among the caps.

(ii) Sieve Plate:

It consists of a flat plate perforated with small holes having size 1/8 to 1/2 inch in diameters. The liquid flows across the plate. The upward flow of vapour keeps the liquid from flowing through the holes. The size of holes is optimum: As large holes give low pressure drop but low gas velocities and at low gas velocities some or all the liquid may drain down through the holes so that weeping takes place, causing some of the contacting areas to be by passed. The common hole size on a sieve plate is $\frac{3}{16}$. The liquid head on a sieve plate is around 2 to 4 inch. The downcomer velocity of liquid is around 0.4 ft./sec.

In a sieve plate column, the pressure drop is significantly reduced. The major pressure drop in a sieve plate is due to contraction of gas at sieve opening, liquid head over the opening and friction at the sieve opening. But liquid head in a sieve plate is significantly less.

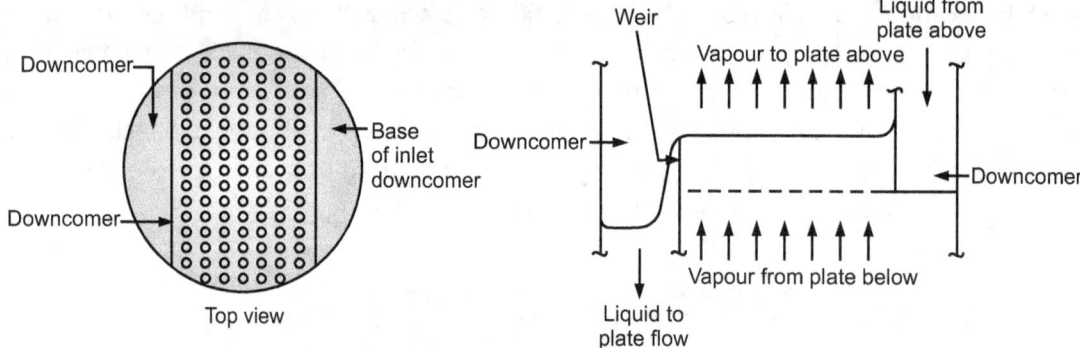

Fig. 8.15: Sieve plate

The gas when passing through the holes passes in the vertical direction forming a spray or froth, there is no change in direction, thus there is no lateral movement of the gas. Thus, mass transfer takes place in the vicinity of the holes but as there is no lateral movement i.e. less mixing or agitation concentration gradient will be developed over the plate.

A modification of sieve plate is a *turbogrid plate*. It is a plate on which there are slots instead of holes, it has a flat grid with parallel slots. It gives counter flow without downcomers.

(iii) Valve Plate Column:

In a valve plate, the hole is covered with a disk type valve which acts as a cap. As the velocity of vapour rises the cap is slowly lifted up and provides an increasing opening; and finally reaches the maximum. The vapours flow in a lateral direction. This type has an advantage of lateral flow of vapour with very low pressure drop, as larger area is available for it and contraction losses in a bubble cap are also reduced. (Fig. 8.16).

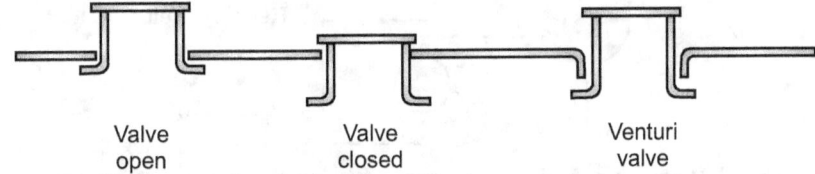

| Valve open | Valve closed | Venturi valve |

Fig. 8.16: Common types of valves

A fractionating column plate is expected to carry out equilibrium achievement between the gas and liquid phases. A plate where the vapour leaving the plate is in equilibrium with liquid leaving the plate when the plate is called as theoretical plate. There are many approaches for determination of number of theoretical plates.

Many Scientists analysed the process of fractionation for predicting the number of theoretical plates required for fractionation process. The various methods can be classified on two approaches:

   1.   McCabe – Thiele Approach

      (a) McCabe Thiele method

      (b) Smoker's method

      (c) Gilliland correlation

   2.   Ponchon - Savarit Approach

8.4.3.1 Mc Cabe-Thiele Approach

   (a) **McCabe – Thiele Method:** This method is based on the following assumptions:

      (i)   Both components have *equal molal* heats.

      (ii) There is no heat of solution and

      (iii) The operation is adiabatic.

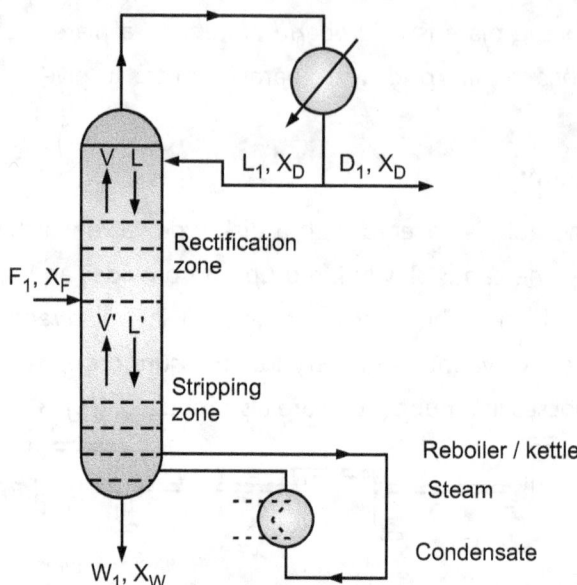

Fig. 8.17: Material balance diagram for continuous fractionation

Thus, according to these assumptions of equimolal overflow, we can say one mole of incoming vapours condense on the plate to release enough heat to vaporise a mole of material from the liquid. Therefore, the rate of *vapours rising from plate* to plate and *rate of liquid descending* from plate to plate will both be constant.

The material balance for the column can be as follows:

For this purpose the two sections are considered in the column, above the feed plate is rectification zone and below feed plate is the stripping zone. The feed having composition X_f enters the feed plate at the rate of F moles per hr.

V and L denote vapour flow rate and liquid flow rates in moles per hr. above feed plate respectively.

V' and L' are vapour flow rate and liquid flow rate respectively below the feed plate in moles per hr. D and X_D are flow rate in moles per hr. and composition of overhead product respectively.

W and X_w are flow rate in moles per hr. and composition of bottom product respectively.

Therefore, above the feed plate

$$V (Y_{n+1}) = L X_n + D X_D$$

or
$$Y_{n+1} = \frac{L}{V} X_n + \frac{D}{V} X_D \qquad \ldots (8.25)$$

And, below the feed plate we can say

$$V' (Y_{m+1}) = L' X_m - W X_w$$

$$Y_{m+1} = \frac{L'}{V'} X_m - \frac{W}{V'} X_w \qquad \ldots (8.26)$$

X and Y denotes mole fractions of the more volatile component.

Equation (8.25) represents the rectification operating line which has slope $\dfrac{L}{V}$ which is internal reflux ratio. Equation (8.26) represents stripping operating line with slope $\dfrac{L'}{V'}$.

The flow rates above and below the feed plate are related by the thermal condition of the feed as:

$$V = V' + (1 - q)\, F \qquad \qquad \dots (8.27)$$

and $\qquad \qquad L' = L + q\, F \qquad \qquad \dots (8.28)$

where, $\qquad \qquad q$ = Heat necessary to convert one mole of feed to saturated vapour divided by the molal heat of vaporization of feed.

By simultaneously solving equation (8.25), (8.26), (8.27) and (8.28) we get,

$$Y_i = \frac{q}{q-1}\, X_i - (q-1)\, X_F \qquad \qquad \dots (8.29)$$

This is the equation for q – line.

This can be analysed graphically as follows:

1. Draw equilibrium curve and on 45° line locate the points A, B and C corresponding to liquid compositions X_w, X_F and X_D respectively.

2. From point B, draw a line with slope $\dfrac{q}{(q-1)}$ (q – line) .

3. From point C, draw a line of slope $\dfrac{L}{V}$ i.e. rectification operating line, intersecting with q-line at pt. D.

4. Join AD i.e. stripping operating line $\left(\text{Slope} \dfrac{L'}{V'} \right)$

5. Step off the theoretical plates.

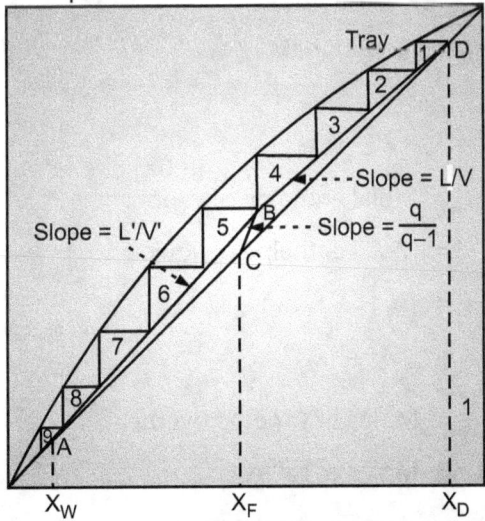

Fig. 8.18: Graphical analysis of continuous fractionation by McCabe-Thiele method

When two operating lines meet each other at 45° line; at the time the number of plates required is minimum and this occurs at the condition of total reflux.

When two operating lines intersect each other and q-line on equilibrium curve, it is the condition at minimum reflux ratio and, in such case it is difficult to determine the number of plates, as operating lines are too close to the equilibrium curve.

(b) Smoker's Method: When relative volatility of the system is low (i.e. equilibrium curve is close to 45° line) or when we require to keep reflux ratio minimum. In such cases, it is difficult to calculate number of plates by graphical method. In such situations Smoker's method is useful which can operate graphically or mathematically.

(c) Gilliland Correlation: This is useful initial approximation, where first minimum reflux ratio R_m and minimum number of trays N_m are determined. Then for any reflux ratio calculate $(R - R_m)/(R + 1)$ and from this value, graphically we get the value of $(N - N_m)/(N + 1)$ which will give us the value of N.

8.4.3.2 Ponchon – Savarit Method

The basic limitation of McCabe – Thiele method is that; some binary systems do not meet the assumptions of McCabe – Thiele Method of equimolal heats of vaporisation.

Ponchon – Savarit method does not assume equimolal overflow. It uses Enthalpy–composition diagram. It considers both material and enthalpy balance of the system. After considering both it resulted in the following equations.

Operating line equation for rectification zone is

$$Y_n = \left(\frac{M - H_n}{M - h_{n-1}}\right) X_{n-1} + \left(\frac{H_n - h_{n-1}}{M - h_{n-1}}\right) X_D \qquad \text{... (8.30)}$$

and stripping operating line equation is

$$\frac{Y_m - X_w}{H_m - M'} = \frac{X_{m-1} - X_w}{h_{m-1} - M'} \qquad \text{... (8.31)}$$

where,
$$H = \text{Molal enthalpy of vapour}$$
$$h = \text{Molal enthalpy of liquid}$$
$$M = \left(V_t H_t - L_t h_t\right) / D$$
$$M' = h_w - Q_w/W$$

where,
$$V_t = \text{Moles of vapours overhead}$$
$$L_t = \text{Moles of reflux}$$
$$Q_w = \text{Heat input to reboiler}$$

For graphical analysis by Ponchon-Savarit method.

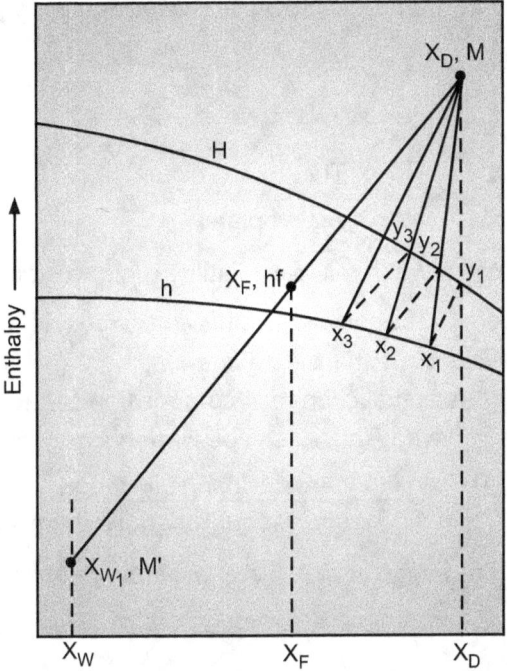

Fig. 8.19: Ponchon-Savarit method uses an enthalpy-composition diagram

1. Using enthalpy data plot enthalpy of vapour (H) and enthalpy of liquid (h) as a function of composition.

2. Locate rectification focus (X_D, M); stripping zone focus (X_W, M') and feed composition and its enthalpy (X_P, h_F). These three points lie in straight line.

3. As lines originating from M connects the conditions of composition of two adjacent trays. Join x_D to rectification zone from $(X_D\ M)$, where, it cuts H curve is the composition of vapours rising from top tray (Y_1). Now, using equilibrium curve find out composition of liquid which is in equilibrium with these vapour i.e. X_1. Locate X_1 on h–curve. Join X_1 to rectification focus which gives Y_2 on H–curve. Now, repeat the procedure same as for Y_1. Thus, we get number of theoretical plates.

4. Similarly, analyse the stripping zone using M' as the focus.

This method is used only when the molal heats of two components are considerably different. It can be used only when enthalpy data is available.

Plate Efficiency:

In case of theoretical plate, we have assumed that the liquid on a plate is completely mixed having uniform composition and the vapours reach perfect equilibrium with the liquid on each plate. But on actual plate such condition does not exist; and plate efficiency is a factor which is introduced to express the performance of an actual plate in relation to the theoretical plate.

Plate efficiency is a ratio of calculated number of theoretical plates required to the actual member of plates in the column. This is known as *Overall Efficiency* (E_o).

Overall Plate Efficiency can be written as

$$E_o = N^* / N_A$$

where, $\qquad N^* =$ No. of Theoretical plates

$\qquad\qquad\quad N_A =$ No. of Actual plates

Overall efficiency is smaller when relative volatility is higher. It is easy to use.

In contrast to the overall efficiency state efficiencies are defined for each stage. Most commonly used stage efficiency is *Murphee Plate Efficiency (MPE)*. It is the efficiency of a single plate as the ratio of the actual change in composition to the change that would occur if perfect equilibrium was achieved. Thus, it can be written as:

$$E_{MV} = \frac{\text{Actual change in vapour}}{\text{Change in vapour for equillibrium stage}}$$

The Murphee Plate Efficiency at n^{th} plate may be defined as in terms of vapour composition as:

$$E_{MV} = \frac{(Y_n)_{av} - (Y_{n-1})_{av}}{Y_n^* - (Y_{n-1})_{av}}$$

where, $(Y_n)_{av}$ and $(Y_{n-1})_{av}$ are average compositions of vapours leaving n^{th} plate and $(n-1)$ plate respectively.

$$Y_n^* = \text{Composition of vapour in equilibrium}$$

In terms of change in liquid composition MPE can be defined as:

$$E_{mL} = \frac{X_{(n+1)} - X_n}{X_{(n+1)} - X_n^*}$$

where, $\qquad X_n^* =$ Composition of the liquid in equilibrium with the vapour Y_n

The operation on actual plate can be analysed if the MPE is known. In the McCabe-Thiele diagram (Fig. 8.20), on each vertical step AB a point C is located such that,

$$E_{mv} = \frac{AC}{AB}$$

The horizontal step is drawn from C to the operating line. Each step now represents an actual plate (except the lowest step i.e. boiler which is considered as one theoretical plate). By joining points C pseudo equilibrium curve can be constructed.

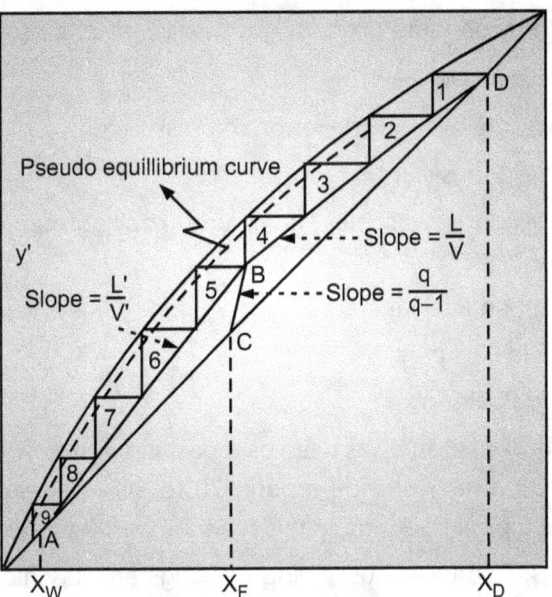

Fig. 8.20: Pseudo equilibrium curve

Murphee has assumed that due to the turbulence created by vapour bubbling there is complete mixing of liquid on the tray. But mixing is not efficient on plates of larger diameter, and there exists a concentration gradient in the direction of liquid flow across the plate. Therefore, a concept of *Point Efficiency* (E_p) was introduced, which is the efficiency at any point on a plate. It can be defined in terms of the compositions at the point of the equation:

$$E_p = \frac{Y_n - Y_{n-1}}{Y_n^* - Y_{n-1}}$$

If the liquid is completely mixed on the plates then point efficiency is equal to Murphee Plate Efficiency. Due to the general existence of concentration gradient on large plates, Murphee plate efficiency is higher than the average point efficiency.

Packed Columns:

Packed columns are also commonly used for vapour liquid contact in rectification operation. The liquid flows over the packings and where it forms a thin film exposing large surface area to the gas stream. The vapours flows in the void space inside and between the packings. The packed column thus provides intimate contact between the liquid and vapour phase, facilitating fast heat and mass transfer.

An Ideal packing material should have the following properties:

(i)   It should have a large surface area.

(ii) It should allow uniform distribution of the liquid over itself.

(iii) It should allow uniform gas flow.

(iv) It should have low pressure drop for gas flow i.e. should provide larger free space.

(v) It should be inexpensive.

(vi) It must be applicable over a wide range of pressure drop.

(vii) It must be corrosion resistant.

No ideal column packing is available. The column packing material is broadly classified as:

(a) Random or Dumped Packings.

(b) Structured or Grid Packings.

(a) Random or Dumped Packings:

Initially, quartz or broken stone was used as a packing; but now rings or saddles are the commonly used packings, which provide around 70 to 90% free space with larger surface area per unit size. Some typical packings of this type are as follows:

(a) Ring packings: Commonly used ring packings are Raschig ring, Lessing ring, Pall rings, etc. Fig. 8.21. Raschig rings [Fig. 8.21 (a)] are hollow cylinders with the height equal to the diameter. On dumping they adopt random arrangement and facilitate uniform distribution of the liquid. These rings are available in ceramics and metals. They are also manufactured in glass and carbon. When Raschig ring is partitioned diametrically with a single wall, it is referred to as a Lessing ring [Fig. 8.21 (b)].

Efficiency of these packings are difficult to predict. Similarly , due to its geometric shape this packing tends to the maldistribute the liquid if it is not properly placed. Hence, generally the packing size is less than $1/30^{th}$ the diameter of the column.

Uniform efficiency and increased capacity is obtained by modifying it as shown in Fig. 8.21 (c), it is known as Pall rings. Pall rings are available in ceramic. Its size is around 2 into 3 in.

(a) Raschig rings   **(b) Lessing ring**   **(c) Pall rings**

Fig. 8.21: Ring packings

The ring packings are relatively inexpensive but have less efficiency than saddle packings.

(b) Saddle packings: Berl and Intalox saddles are commonly used saddle packings [Fig. 8.20 (a) and (b)]. These are shaped in such a way that they can be randomly packed with no line of contact between adjacent pieces.

Berl saddles [Fig. 8.22 (a)] are negatively wrapped surface, are available in ceramics, carbon, metals and some thermosetting plastics. Similar to Raschig ring it also give wide fluctuations in efficiency but maldistribution is not to the extent that in Raschig ring.

Intalox saddle is a inner half of a 180° sector of torus. It has somewhat higher efficiency than Berl saddles. It is available in ceramics, carbon and plastics. It is a packing of choice for distillation of highly corrosive chemicals or at conditions of very high temperature.

(a) Berl saddle   **(b) Intalox saddle**

Fig. 8.22: Saddle packings

Generally, random packings offer various different paths to the liquid and lateral flow takes place due to which single central field is adopted for such packings. But sometimes during lateral flow the liquid flow may follow some preferential path causing 'channelling'.

(b) Structured Packings:

Grid packing is a structured packing which consists of rows of thin slats laid on edge and held in place by spacer bars. The girds are stacked one on the another inside the column. The liquid flows as a film over the vertical sides of the slats and passes from one slat to the next at the points of contact.

Structured packing provides a continuous vertical path for the liquid thereby avoiding the lateral flow. Thus uniform distribution of the liquid should take place at the top of the packing.

Fig. 8.23: Structured packing

Height Equivalent to Theoretical Plate (H.E.T.P.)

In a packed column there is no one definite plate upon which the vapour and liquid streams approach equilibrium before passing to the succeeding plate. But the interchange between vapour and liquid takes place gradually as they flow in counter-current manner. A definite length of packing is required to produce the same fractionating effect as one theoretical plate; as measured by McCabe Thiele diagram. Thus, height equivalent to theoretical plate (H.E.T.P.) is the height of packed section required to give the change in composition that would be provided by a theoretical plate. It is given by the equation.

$$\text{H.E.T.P.} = \frac{\text{Height of column}}{\text{Number of theoretical plates}}$$

But the major limitation of this method is the calculation of number of theoretical plates in the Mc-Cabe Thiele diagram is a stepwise procedure, whereas the process in a packed column is continuous. Due to this, concept of Height of Transfer Units (H.T.U.) was developed; which is based on an overall gas phase driving force. Its calculation is based on differential treatment of the column and defined by the following equation:

$$\text{H.T.U.} = \frac{\text{Height of column}}{\text{Number of Transfer Units (N.T.U.)}}$$

$$\text{N.T.U.} = \int_{Y_2}^{Y_1} \frac{dY}{Y^* - Y}$$

where, Y = Composition of vapour

Y^* = Vapour which is in equilibrium with the liquid at the point in column for which Y is taken.

Number of transfer units can be calculated by plotting $\frac{1}{(Y^* - Y)}$ versus Y and graphically integrating the area under curve. (Fig. 8.24).

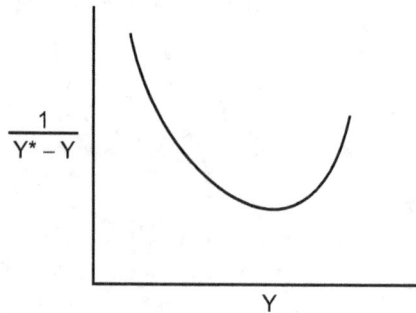

Fig. 8.24: Number of transfer units

H.E.T.P. is proportional to the *packing diameter*. It varies with the nature of the liquid and it increases with increase in molecular weight of liquid. As packed height increases H.E.T.P. increases. It is proportional to the cube root of the packed height. Larger is the size of packing more is H.E.T.P.

H.E.T.P. varies from 0.5 inches to several feet. In normal industrial equipments the H.E.T.P. is between 1 ft to 4 ft. The smaller the H.E.T.P., the shorter the column and the more efficient the packing.

Thus, Material Balances for Distillation

Equilibrium Distillation:

$$W_o\, X_o \;=\; V_Y + (W_o - V)\, X$$

Simple or Differential Distillation:

$$\int_{\lambda}^{X_o} \frac{dX}{Y-X} \;=\; \int_{W}^{W_o} \frac{dw}{w}$$

Fractional Distillation:

(i)   Above the feed plate

$$Y_{n+1} \;=\; \frac{L}{V}\, X_n + \frac{D}{V}\, X_D$$

(ii)   Below the feed plate

$$Y_{m+1} \;=\; \frac{L'}{V'}\, X_{m} - \frac{W}{V'}\, X_w$$

8.5 Distillation under Reduced Pressure

As we know, liquid boils at temperature when its vapour pressure reaches the atmospheric pressure. Thus, lowering of the external pressure will cause decrease in boiling point of a liquid. This is the principle on which process of distillation under reduced pressure is based.

Distillation under reduced pressure has many applications in separation of heat sensitive materials or when solvent recovery is desired. The simple applications include:

(i)   to minimise chemical changes due to heat and

(ii)   to change physical form of the material whereas, special application is molecular distillation.

8.5.1 To Avoid Chemical Changes

It is used to prevent destruction of enzymes in the preparation of extracts e.g. extract of Malt, or Pancreatin etc. where temperature has to be controlled below 70°C.

Extracts of Solanaceous drugs like belladona, hyosyamus contain hyosyamine which on exposure to temperatures above 60°C may get converted to its isomer atropine which is less active therefore concentrated or dry extracts of such drugs are subjected to distillation under reduced pressure. Such extracts are Dry extract of Belladona, Dry extract of Hyosyamus, etc.

Glycosides like sennosides in Senna extract, many alkaloids undergo hydrolysis at high temperatures therefore extracts containing such drugs should be subjected to distillation under reduced pressure during their concentration.

8.5.2 To Change Physical Form

Distillation under atmospheric pressure will provide a compact dry residue but if the same operation is carried out under vacuum then highly porous and friable mass will be obtained. e.g. Dry extract of Cascara sagarada a purgative if prepared under vacuum and passed through sieve will provide granular powder which can be easily compressed as tablet.

8.6 Molecular Distillation

If a high vacuum distillation operation, where the material distills from an evaporating surface to a relatively cool condensing surface. The conditions are such that, the mean free path of the distillating molecules is greater than the distance between the evaporating and condensing surface.

8.6.1 Principles and Features of the Molecular Distillation

Principles and features of the molecular distillation are as follows:

(a)   The vacuum applied during this operation is about 1 micron or less.

As we know, mean free path is the average distance travelled by the molecule in a straight line without any collision. It can be calculated by Clausius' equation as:

$$\lambda = \frac{1}{\sqrt{2\pi\,\sigma^2\,N}}$$

where,

λ = Mean free path in cm

σ = Diameter of molecules in cm

N = Number of molecules in 1 cc

It is clear from the above equation that mean free path can be increased by reducing the number of molecules per cc. At the vacuum of 1 micron the number of molecules in 1 mole of a gas have been reduced from 23×10^{24} at atmospheric pressure to around 23×10^{18}. Therefore, now the substance if heated under these conditions of pressure, the molecules evaporate from the surface and travel few cm. without colloiding with the molecules of the residual gas in the space above. If now the condensing surface is placed within this distance, a major fraction of the molecules will condense and not return to the distilland. Thus, each molecule distills by itself and hence called "Molecular Distillation".

(b)   The molecular distillation is used or distillation of compounds with molecular weight between 300 – 1100. The compounds with molecular weight above 250 to 300 have sufficiently low vapour pressure at the conditions on the condenser surface (around 50°C) and therefore, the chances of re-evaporation from the condenser are avoided. The upper limit of molecular weight is on the basis of sufficient vapour pressure at 300 – 350°C (evaporating surface condition to which the material can be subjected without decomposition)

(c)   The molecules of a distillation should get chance to reach the surface and evaporate. The molecules at the bottom of the distilland have to overcome the pressure of the layer above, to come to the surface. Hence, the layer should be thin and be in the state of turbulent movement so as to provide best chance to the molecules to reach to the surface.

(d)   The material to be distilled by this method should be effectively degased before entering the still. As the volume of the dissolved gases at the very high temperature in the still increases many folds.

8.6.2 Falling Film

In this still the distilland is made to spread over and fall down a vertically placed cylinder which is heated internally. The water cooled condenser is placed concentrically around this evaporator with the gap of few cm.

8.6.3 Centrifugal Still

It has a spinning rotor as an evaporator. The distilland is fed to the centre of the rotor, and the centrifugal force spreads it out in a thin film which travels over the rotor in a very short time, generally fractions of a second. The condenser may be placed either opposite to the rotor or within the rotor.

1. It spreads the distilland in a thin layer over large area, therefore rate of evaporation is considerably increased.
2. The distilland is given a turbulent flow. Thus, it passes the heated zone in a very short time. Therefore, exposure to high temperature for very short time.

Applications of Molecular Distillation:

1.   Vitamin Concentrates:

Vitamin A, D, E, K and tocopherols are obtained from vegetable and fish oils.

The vitamin A concentrate produced by molecular distillation are very pure and have good stability. As no chemical is used in this method which could split the ester linkage, the vitamins are retained in the natural ester form, which is the most stable form of Vitamin A. The stability of the concentrates is further enhanced by natural antioxidants distilling over from the original oil.

During distillation, oxidation products and traces of metals are non-distillable, remain in the residue.

The fractionation of oils into various components is carried out by molecular distillation.

Component	Molecular weight	Temperature
(a) Fatty acids, unsaponifiable matter of low molecular weight.	150 – 300	50 – 140°C
(b) Unsaponifiable matter like steroles, vitamins, dyes, wax alcohols, monoglycerides	300 – 600	140 – 190°C
(c) Triglycerides, sterol esters, vitamin esters, resins, waxes.	600 – 900	Above 190°C

Thus, molecular distillation can be used for analysis of fat.

2. It can be used to investigate the degree of polymerization during drying of various drying oil. Similarly core oil obtained by molecular distillation of fish oils has drying oil properties comparable to linseed oil.

3. It is used for purification and fractionation of Lanolin into various fractions like, cetyl alcohol, cholesterol, ceryl alcohol, lanoplamitic acid, isocholesterol etc.

4. On laboratory scale, it is also used for separation of PEG according to the degree of polymerization.

8.7 Distillation of Non-ideal Liquid Systems

8.7.1 Azeotropic Distillation

As we have seen, in azeotropic mixtures one component is more volatile over one portion of composition range and the other component is more volatile in the remaining range. At the composition where reversal of volatility occurs, relative volatility is one, hence separation of azeotrope becomes difficult. Azeotropic distillation is a special class of multi-component distillation, where a new substance is added to alter the relative volatilities of the components of the mixtures. The added substance is called an 'entrainer'.

Azeotropic distillation is commonly employed:

(i) To separate a pair of closely boiling liquids.

For example: Butyl acetate is used as an entrainer to separate a closely boiling pair acetic acid-water.

(ii)   To separate an azeotropic mixture.

For example: Ethyl alcohol forms a minimum boiling azeotrope with water therefore, it is not possible to obtain absolute alcohol by rectification. Benzene is used as a entrainer. Benzene forms a minimum boiling azeotrope with ethanol and water, which boils at lower temperature (64.8°C) then ethanol water binary azeotrope (78.15°C) and also contains higher proportion of water to ethanol.

Benzene is added to the feed stream. The ternary azeotrope is collected as overhead product, while pure alcohol is withdrawn from the bottom. The overhead vapour forms two layers, upper benzene rich layer is returned to the column via reflux. The lower water rich layer is fed to a second column; which also forms ternary azeotrope as the overhead product. The bottom product of a second column is a mixture of alcohol and water which split in the third column into a product of pure water and an overhead product is the ethanol water azeotrope. The overhead stream is recycled to the feed in the first column. Trichloroethylene can be used as an entrainer instead of benzene.

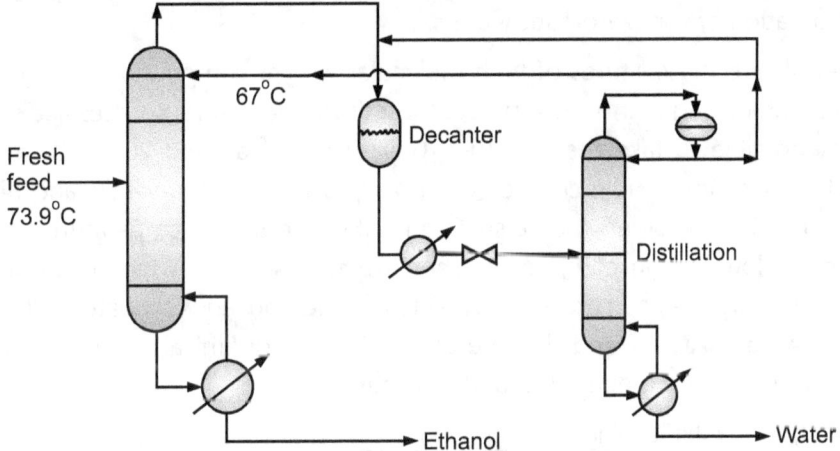

Fig. 8.25: Azeotropic distillation

8.7.2 Extractive Distillation

As in case of azeotropic distillation, a third substance is also added to a closely boiling pair or an azeotrope. The third substance added in extractive distillation is called as solvent. A solvent added in extractive distillation is a high boiling liquid and alters the relative volatilities of the components of boiling mixture. The solvent is introduced in extractive distillation column above the feed plate. The solvent used in extractive distillation has two features that, it is less volatile than the component of binary mixture and it is polar. e.g. propylene glycol can be used in extractive distillation of water-ethanol mixture and we will obtain alcohol as a top product and a mixture of water with propylene glycol as a bottom product.

8.8 Distillation of Immiscible Liquids

We have seen in the vapour-liquid equilibrium relationship of immiscible systems that the vapour pressure exerted by the components is additive i.e. when sum of the vapour pressures of two component reaches atmospheric pressure the system will start boiling which will naturally be less than the boiling point of any of the components e.g. at 80°C component A exerts V.P. 500 and component B exerts V.P. 260 then mixture will boil at 60°C (500 + 260 = 760) if A and B are immiscible. Boiling point of individual A and B is greater than 60°C. Similarly, moles of A and B collected as distillate is proportional to the ratio of their V.P. i.e. Moles of A/Moles of B = 500/260 as explained by equations (8.15), (8.16). Vacuum may also be applied in the process of steam distillation, so as to reduce further the temperature.

Applications: Based on the principle of distillation of two immiscible liquids; important application developed is *'steam distillation'*. Steam distillation is a method widely used for

(i)   Separation of volatile oil and

(ii) Preparation of some aromatic waters.

Volatile oils are the mixtures of high molecular weight compounds having low vapour pressure (i.e. high boiling point). To separate these from the natural sources like petals, barks etc. it is not possible to take them to their boiling points around 200°C. If these oils are distilled out with an immiscible component having low molecular weight and high vapour pressure (i.e. low boiling point) then distillation will occur at low temperature i.e. below the boiling point of low boiling component. Thus, water is selected which has low molecular weight of 18 and high vapour pressure. Volatile oil when boiled with water will distilled out at temperature below 100°C and the operation will be economical as molecular weight of volatile oil is very high as compared to that of water.

$$\text{As} \quad \frac{\text{Weight of volatile oil in distillate}}{\text{Weight of water in distillate}} = \frac{M_v \, P_v}{M_w \, P_w}$$

Where, M_w and M_v are molecular weight of water and volatile oil respectively and P_w, P_v are V.P. of water and volatile oil at distillation temperature respectively.

The aqueous phase which is collected as distillate is not only water but water saturated with volatile oil i.e. Aromatic water.

Thus, steam distillation is used as a method for separation of volatile oils like eucalyptus oil, rose oil, clove oil etc. It is used as a method for preparation of Concentrated Rose Water. Steam is used for its better penetration power and high energy content. Water may be used for distillation of fresh materials, then it is called as 'hydrodistillation'.

The assembly for steam distillation consists of a distillation still having a mesh near bottom as shown in Fig. 8.26. The steam is generated by boiling water below the mesh; the steam passes through the material to be extracted over the mesh. The vapour containing volatile oil is then passed to the condenser. The distillate is collected in a special type of collecting device i.e. florentine receiver which separates the oil and water depending on their densities. The aqueous phase may be recirculated so as to avoid loss of volatile oil in water.

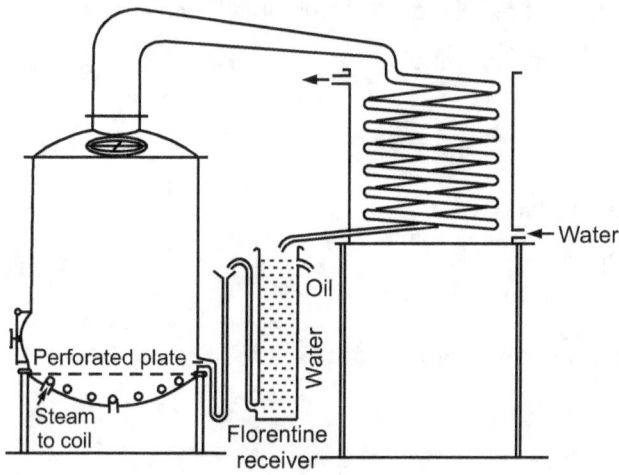

Fig. 8.26: Steam distillation

On large scale the same operation may be carried out with centralised steam generation. In this method, a separate boiler provide steam to different distillation tubes containing material to be extracted instead of generation of steam in distillation still itself. Centralised distillation units are commonly used in India in extraction of mentha oil and show better yields than decentralised method.

Steam distillation is also used in quality control of pharmaceuticals. The vegetable drugs like digitalis leaves require the leaves containing not more than 5% moisture. Thus, if these leaves containing water are distilled with toluene then distillate will contain water and toluene. Thus percentage of water can be determined.

Questions

1. Define distillation and distinguish between distillation and evaporation.

2. Explain miscible binary system have ideal or non-ideal behaviour with suitable diagram.

3. Discuss distillation methods in detail.

4. Write applications of Rayleigh's equation.

5. Give the classification of fractionating columns.

6. Write in detail McCabe-Thiele approach.

7. Explain packed columns.

8. Explain distillation under reduced pressure.

9. Write applications of molecular distillation.

10. Discuss distillation of non-ideal liquid systems.

11. Write applications of distillation of immiscible liquids.

12. Write short notes on following:

    (a) Immiscible systems.

    (b) Molecular distillation

    (c) Fractional distillation

    (d) Bubble cap plate

    (e) Sieve plate

    (f) Ponchon-Savarit method

    (g) Centrifugal still.

■■■

CHAPTER

Corrosion

9.1 Introduction

In nature metals are present in the form of their oxides, sulphides, hydroxides etc. By different processes, metals are extracted from the ores. Process of extraction increases energy of the metal. This high energy state has tendency to get transformed into a low energy form, such as oxides of the metals. This causes corrosion of the metal. Therefore, corrosion may be defined as *unintentional destruction in part or completely of a metal due to chemical or electrochemical reactions with the environment.*

Depending on the environment with which the metal reacts, the corrosion is termed as 'dry corrosion' and 'wet corrosion'.

9.2 Dry Corrosion

Dry corrosion occurs in the absence of aqueous medium. It occurs due to reactions with gases and vapours. Reaction between metal and gaseous state reactants leads to formation of an oxide film on the surface of the metal. The properties of this oxide film formed, play an important role in controlling further rate of corrosion. For example, if density of the film is low, the gases may easily pass through film and corrode the metal surface. Thus, higher is the density of film, lower is the rate of corrosion. If the film formed is highly reactive, rate corrosion will be high. The low reactivity film protect the metal hence termed as protective films. Adhesivity of film to the metal surface is also important. Dense and highly adhesive films can protect the metal better.

9.3 Wet Corrosion

Wet corrosion is the corrosion due to purely electrochemical reaction, which occurs when the metal is exposed to an aqueous solution of acid or alkali. The electrochemical reaction transforms the metal into its ionic state. For example, piece of zinc when comes in contact with dilute hydrochloric acid, the electrochemical reaction will be as follows:

$$Zn + 2\,HCl \rightarrow ZnCl_2 + H_2 \uparrow$$

This reaction involves formation of zinc ions i.e. oxidation, which occurs at anode and liberation of hydrogen by accepting electrons at cathode.

The Zn–HCl reaction can be analysed as follows:

At anode: $Zn \rightarrow Zn^{++} + 2e^{--}$

At cathode: $2 H^{+} + 2 e^{--} \rightarrow H_2 \uparrow$

Thus, for any metal such electrochemical reaction causes wet corrosion.

Different mechanisms have been proposed for wet corrosion explaining different cathodic reactions. These reactions at cathode include:

1. Hydrogen evolution.

2. Oxygen absorption.

3. Metal ion reduction.

4. Metal deposition.

9.3.1 Hydrogen Evolution

This reaction is displacement of hydrogen ions from the solution. Zn–HCl reaction discussed above, is of this category (Fig. 9.1).

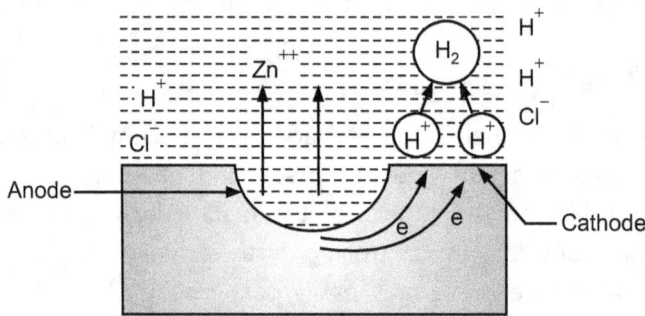

Fig. 9.1: Hydrogen evolution mechanism in corrosion

9.3.2 Oxygen Absorption

This reaction generally occurs when the electrolyte solution contains dissolved oxygen. The oxygen absorption reaction which occurs in neutral or alkaline medium are given below:

(a) **In neutral medium:** Iron in contact with water will show rusting due to oxygen absorption. An oxide film is formed on the surface of iron. If the cracked oxide film comes in contact with a drop of water, then water is neutral electrolyte, cracked film becomes anode and oxide covered is cathode (Fig. 9.2).

The reaction takes place as follows:

At anode: $Fe \rightarrow Fe^{++} + 2e^{-}$

At cathode: $2 H_2O + O_2 + 4 e^{-} \rightarrow 4 OH^{-}$

$$Fe^{++} + 2 OH^{-} \rightarrow Fe (OH)_2$$

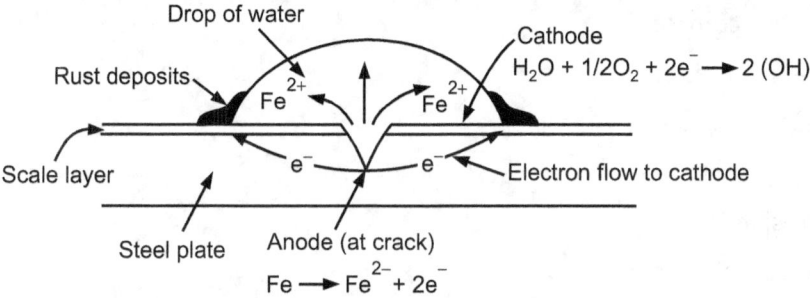

Fig. 9.2: Oxygen absorption

(b) **In basic medium:** Consider that iron piece is exposed to sodium chloride solution. Then the cracked oxide film becomes anode, oxide film as cathode and solution of sodium chloride as an alkaline electrolyte. The reactions will be as below:

$$NaCl \rightarrow Na^+ + Cl^-$$

At anode: $Fe \rightarrow Fe^{++} + 2e^-$

$$Fe^{++} + 2\,Cl^- \rightarrow FeCl_2$$

At cathode: $4e^- + O_2 + 2\,H_2O \rightarrow 4\,OH^-$

$$OH^- + Na^+ \rightarrow Na\,OH$$

9.3.3 Metal Ion Reduction

It is a step prior to metal deposition. It is a cathodic reaction, where trivalent metal ion gets reduced to divalent metal.

$$M^{+++} + e^- \rightarrow M^{++}$$

9.3.4 Metal Deposition

Metal ions from the electrolyte get reduced and deposit on the cathode surface. The rate of cathodic deposition depends on rate of anodic dissolution.

9.4 Types of Corrosion

Different types of corrosions are as follows:

1. Uniform corrosion

2. Galvanic corrosion

3. Crevice corrosion

4. Pitting corrosion

5. Intergranular corrosion

6.   Selective corrosion

7.   Erosion corrosion

8.   Stress corrosion

9.   Fretting corrosion

10.   Corrosion fatigue

11.   Caustic embrittlement

12.   Cavitation corrosion.

Of these types; crevice, pitting, intergranular and stress corrosion can cause process failure.

Types of corrosion are explained below in brief:

9.4.1 Uniform Corrosion

It is also termed as general corrosion or chemical attack. It is a superficial, unlocalized attack on the entire exposed metal surface. This corrosion never causes unexpected or premature failure of the metal components. The rates of corrosion are high at higher temperatures.

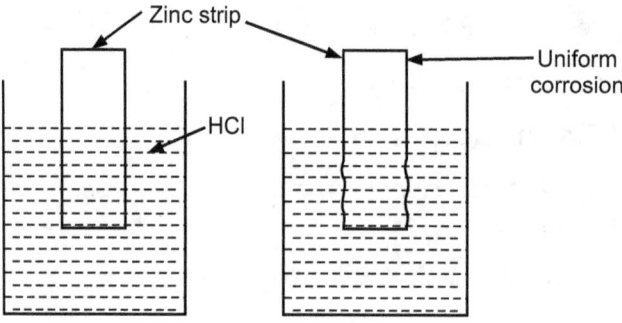

Fig. 9.3: Uniform corrosion

9.4.2 Galvanic Corrosion

This type of corrosion occurs between two coupled dissimilar metals in the presence of an electrolyte. In such a couple, one of the metal acts as an anode; the other as a cathode. The tendencies of the metals to act as anode or cathode is derived from their relative positions in a galvanic series (Table 9.1). A potential difference exists between two metals depending on their distance in the electrochemical series. The less corrosion resistant metal becomes anodic and the more resistant metal cathodic. The intensity of corrosion depends on relative positions of the two metals in the series. The corrosion is accelerated if the anodic material exposes smaller surface area to the electrolyte than the cathodic material. The possibility of galvanic corrosion is less if the metal is coupled with its alloy, as the potential will be very low.

Table 9.1: Standard electrode potential of metals (Electrochemical series) at 25°C

Metal	Potential (Volts)	
Potassium	– 2.92	
Calcium	– 2.86	
Sodium	– 2.72	
Magnesium	– 2.35	
Aluminium	– 1.68	Active or
Manganese	– 1.01	Anodic end
Zinc	– 0.76	
Iron	– 0.45	
Cadmium	– 0.41	
Cobalt	– 0.26	
Nickel	– 0.26	
Tin	– 0.14	
Lead	– 0.12	
Hydrogen	0.00	
Copper (++)	+ 0.35	
Copper (+)	+ 0.55	Noble or
Silver	+ 0.81	cathodic
Mercury	+ 0.85	end
Platinum	+ 1.20	
Gold (+++)	+ 1.40	
Gold (+)	+ 1.70	

9.4.3 Crevice Corrosion

The crevices and other shielded areas of the material retain solutions and takes longer period to dry out. A galvanic couple can occur in such areas of the same metal at localized areas of widely divergent aeration or oxygen. The metal surface having more concentration of oxygen becomes cathode and the one with less oxygen becomes anode. It progresses at a very fast rate as compared to uniform corrosion. Crevice corrosion can also occur when a metal is in contact with different concentrations of the same environment.

Crevice corrosion is observed when the rivetted and bolted joints do not get exposed to atmosphere and the area with low oxygen becomes anode and gets corroded. Therefore, gaskets are recommended. It can be observed at contact area of 316 stainless steel bubble caps with 316 stainless steel plates. In an agitated vessel, splashing of chemical occurs on inside of the vessel. Some of the surface of the vessel gets covered with chemical while other is exposed to atmosphere. This condition creates difference in oxygen concentration.

9.4.4 Pitting Corrosion

It is a non-uniform corrosion resulting due to inhomogenities in the metal. It is a localized attack which results in holes or pits. It is generally caused by chloride or chlorine containing ions. In the pit the metal dissolves at an increasing rate and creates excessive positive charge that results in migration of chloride ions to maintain electro-neutrality. The chances of pitting are higher under stagnant conditions. Austenitic stainless steel T 316 and T 317 are resistant to pitting corrosion.

9.4.5 Intergranular Corrosion

During heat treatment or welding, some of the components get precipitated at the grain boundaries of the metal. Due to this precipitation, concentration of elements in the area near the grain boundaries decreases and grain boundary becomes anodic to the remaining area. For example, precipitation of chromium carbide at boundaries during heating of austenitic stainless steel between 800 to 1400 °F causes depletion of chromium in the grains. This initiates intergranular corrosion, it is called as weld decay.

9.4.6 Selective Corrosion

It is a process where one element is selectively removed from the alloy by the corrosive environment. It is also called as *selective leaching*. For example, when brass comes in contact with sea water, or water containing high content of oxygen and carbon dioxide, zinc is selectively leached out from brass. This dezincification of brass occurring in the localized area leads to loss of strength of the alloy. Tin is added to brass to prevent this.

9.4.7 Erosion Corrosion

It is the increase in the corrosion rate due to relative movement between a corrosive fluid and metal. The material gets corroded in the direction of fluid flow, it is due to removal of metal ions due to abrasion action of the fluid. Higher is the turbulence, more are the chances of erosion corrosion.

9.4.8 Stress Corrosion

A certain area of metal may be subjected to thermal, mechanical or chemical stress. The areas which are stressed become sensitive to corrosive environment and act as anode. During stress corrosion, very fine cracks are observed in the initial stages. Hence, it is termed as stress corrosion cracking.

9.4.9 Fretting Corrosion

This type of corrosion occurs at contact areas between materials under load, subjected to vibrations. Pits form at the contact points, as a result of the continuous breakdown of the protective film. It is responsible for destruction of bearings. Therefore, equipments showing high vibrations such as sieve shaker, vibratory feeders are prone to such corrosion. Use of rubber gaskets and rigid foundation may aid in reducing fretting corrosion.

9.4.10 Corrosion Fatigue

This is a form of stress corrosion in which the stress is applied in a cyclic manner and is within the elastic range. The cyclic stress breaks the protective film which normally retards corrosion. Oxygen content, temperature, pH and solution composition affect corrosion fatigue. Highly reactive gases such as hydrogen sulphide cause loss of resistance of metal to corrosion fatigue. Chromium steels have higher corrosion fatigue resistance than carbon steels.

9.4.11 Caustic Embrittlement

It is intergranular stress corrosion. It is observed in carbon steels when they are exposed to concentrated alkaline solutions at the temperature of 200 to 250°C. It is also termed as *caustic cracking*. It can be reduced by reduction in stress, avoiding crevices and controlling stress conditions.

9.4.12 Cavitation Corrosion

Cavitation is a *process of formation and rapid collapse of air bubbles in the liquid, at the surface which is in contact with the metal*. The collapse of bubbles during cavitation produces high impact and removes the particles of metal surface forming deep pits or depressions.

This type of corrosion is common with high speed impellers, where cavitation occurs due to vaporization of liquid in the low pressure zone created in the viscinity of an impeller. Therefore, hydrodynamic pressure difference should be maintained low so as to minimize cavitation.

9.5 Prevention of Corrosion

Following methods should be adopted for prevention or combating corrosion:

9.5.1 Material Selection

Alongwith the working conditions and application, the following points should be considered while selecting the material for equipment fabrication:

(a) Pure materials have less tendency towards pitting, but they are expensive and soft. Therefore, only metals like aluminium can be used in its pure form.

(b) Improved corrosion resistance can be obtained by addition of corrosion resistant element. For example, intergranular corrosion occurs in stainless steel. This tendency can be reduced by addition of small quantities of titanium, and tantalum. These elements preferentially combine with carbon and prevent chromium depletion responsible for intergranular corrosion.

(c) Use nickel, copper and their alloys for non-oxidizing environment, whereas chromium containing alloys for oxidizing environment.

(d) Materials which are close in electrochemical series should be used for fabrication.

(e) Particular material should be selected taking into consideration the corrosive environment as shown in Table 9.2.

Table 9.2

Corrosive Material	Suitable Material
Nitric acid	Stainless steel
Hydrofluoric acid	Monel
Distilled water	Tin
Dilute sulphuric acid	Lead
Caustic	Nickel

9.5.2 Proper Design and Fabrication of Component

(a) To minimize galvanic corrosion, use rubber and plastic gaskets, insulate the materials, and keep the anodic area larger than the cathodic area.

(b) During fabrication avoid sharp corner, rivetted joints and minimize vibrations.

(c) Tanks and containers should be designed for easy draining and cleaning.

9.5.3 Alteration of Environment

(a) Keep the moisture content and temperature of working low.

(b) Liquids should be deaerated.

(c) Alkali neutralizer should be used to reduce effect of acidic environment.

(d) Concentration of corrosive environment should be reduced.

For example, tap water contains high chloride ions concentrations which corrodes stainless steel.

9.5.4 Cathodic and Anodic Protection

(a) Cathodic Protection: The metal which is to be protected is made cathode i.e. electrons are supplied to this metal. Addition of electrons to the metal suppresses its dissolution. Two methods used for cathodic protection are impressed current method and sacrificial anode method.

In impressed current method (Fig. 9.4), the negative terminal of power supply is connected to the material to be protected and positive to an inert anode e.g. graphite. Therefore, current passes to the metal to the protected and corrosion is suppressed.

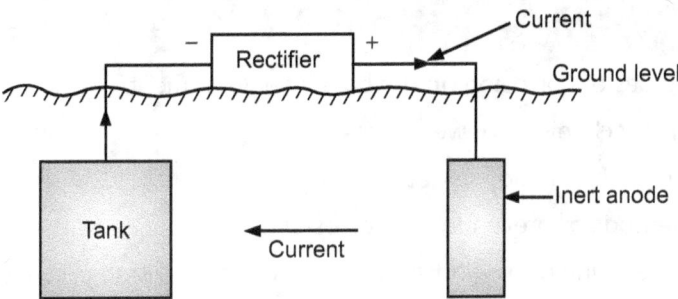

Fig. 9.4: Impressed current cathodic protection

In sacrificial anode method, the metal to be protected is coupled with a more anodic material. For example, magnesium is more anodic as compared to steel, and can be used as sacrificial anode for steel.

(b) Anodic Protection: In this method, the metal to the protected is made more anodic due to which it forms a passive film which decreases corrosion rate. But all metals can not form passive film. Anodic protection is carried out using a potentiostat, which maintains a metal at a constant potential with respect to reference electrode.

9.5.5 Use of Inhibitors

Corrosion inhibitors are the chemical agents, which when added to the corrosive atmosphere (gas or liquid), causes decrease in corrosion rate. Inhibitors generally form a protective film. There are different types of inhibitors. Adsorption type inhibitors get adsorbed on the metal surface. Scavengers are used to remove corrosive agents from electrolytes.

For example: Sodium sulphate removes dissolved oxygen from electrolyte. Vapour phase inhibitors are agents with high vapour pressure and therefore sublime and condense on metal surface. These are useful for protection of metal surfaces in closed spaces.

9.5.6 Uses of surface Coatings

Metal surface is coated using corrosion resistant materials. Coating of metal using a corrosion resistant material improves corrosion resistance, at the same time it prevents direct contact between the metal and the corrosive environment.

Various methods used for coating include electroplating, cladding, vapour deposition, organic coating etc. In electroplating or electrodeposition, the metal to be protected is made cathode while the coating metal is made anode or its aqueous solution as electrolyte. Current density, time, temperature and concentration of electrolyte are the factors affecting electroplating.

Cladding involves mechanical bonding of a sheet of corrosion resistant material with the material to be protected; e.g. nickel sheet is hot rolled with steel to impart corrosion resistance to steel. Vapour deposition is a process where the metal to be deposited is vaporized under high vacuum and deposited on the surface to be protected.

Organic coatings like paints, varnishes and lacquers are also commonly used. Coating with various polymers is also common.

Questions

1. Describe types of corrosion on the base of environment.

2. Explain the mechanisms of wet corrosion.

3. Explain types of corrosion in detail.

4. Explain methods of prevention of corrosion.

5. Describe use of inhibitors and surface coating in corrosion prevention.

6. Write short notes on:

   (a) Galvanic corrosion

   (b) Intergranular corrosion

   (c) Erosion corrosion

   (d) Fretting corrosion

   (e) Cavitation corrosion

   (f) Wet corrosion

■■■

www.ingramcontent.com/pod-product-compliance
Lightning Source LLC
Chambersburg PA
CBHW080905020726
47502CB00008B/2356